the
TORY

T.J. London

The Tory

by T.J. London

Copyright © 2018 T.J. London
All rights reserved
ISBN: 978-0-692-06128-2

First Edition

This book is a work of fiction and does not represent any individual, living or dead. Names, characters, places, and incidents either are products of the author's imagination or are used fictionally.

Edited by Kathe Robin
Cover design by Steve Miller of Look at my Designs
Copy Editing and Proofreading by Jo Michaels
Interior formatting by Gaynor Smith
Both of Indie Books Gone Wild

Published in the United States of America

*...for Dad, your doe-eyed little girl will forever
be waiting for you to come home.*

Foreword

The Tory is a historical fiction, so while the story is a creation of the author, and there are some liberties taken with time and location, my goal was to be as accurate with my historic detail and dialogue as possible. Some of the language in the story may be harsh and politically incorrect, but it is reflective of the times that we were living in, and for accuracy's sake I have tried to stay true to that. Details about the Oneida Nation and the Iroquois Confederacy is extensive and vast, however some of it is still missing as theirs was not a written history, nor was there a true tally of their numbers and losses during the Revolutionary War. I did the best I could with the history, drawing on many resources, and what I couldn't find, I tried to create as accurately as possible.

Fort Stanwix was renamed Fort Schuyler in 1776, however, to avoid confusion, I continued to call it Fort Stanwix throughout the series.

The exact location of Major John Butler's office at Fort Niagara is unknown, so I chose the Machicolated House (the French Castle), as the location for it, based on the idea that this was the officer's quarters.

Table of Contents

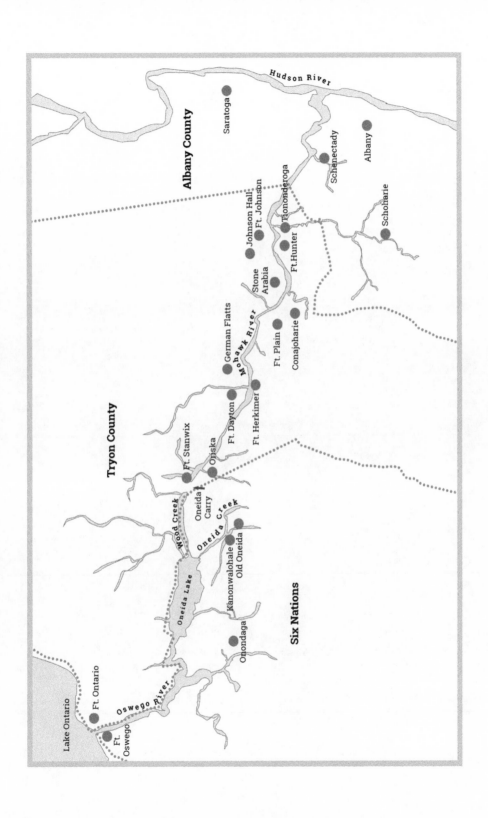

Chapter One

October 1776, Manhattan

Karma… the whore that always gets paid, but what is the price when there is so much blood on your hands?

John Carlisle already gave up his commission and his reputation, what was left?

My body? My soul?

Reaching for the bottle of rum, John Carlisle poured himself another drink, swirling it in the glass then downing it quickly. The sweet, spicy liquid burned a trail down his throat, making him wince. Too many shots to count, yet still, they stung just like the failure that ruined his once brilliant career. Looking around at the filthy walls of his office, he chuckled to himself, finding humor in his self-deprecation. Two years! Two years since he'd been banished by the court-martial, doomed to spend his days in purgatory, overseeing a damned, stinking military gaol, first in Boston, now in New York. For what? Had he not done the right thing? Yet still, he was being punished.

As the autumn breeze swept through the window, John could hear the faint sound of female voices calling his name, their breathy refrains taunting him, haunting him. Closing his eyes, he tried to shut them out, but they persisted, their sad lament crescendoing with each gust of wind. He knew what they wanted—they wanted him; they called for him every night, apparitions relentlessly haunting his dreams. *Justice… John… Justice.*

"Stop!" he yelled, grabbing the paperweight from his desk and hurling it against the wall, listening as it bounced off the stone and clanked on the wooden floor planks. "Stop, please."

Have mercy.

John fisted his hair, trying to tear the memories from his brain like ripping an unwanted page from a book. But it was all for naught. They wouldn't stop, they never did.

Desperation turned to insanity, and John reached for the bottle again—sweet solace in a glass—but it was empty. *Damn.* Opening the top drawer of his desk, he pulled out a small leather pouch and unfastened it, the contents all the money he had left in the world save what was already spoken for by taverns, women, and everyone else he owed. Pouring it out on the desk, he counted: one… two… three pence. It was his lucky day; a three-penny bit, just enough to buy another bottle, but not enough to buy company for the night and drink his fill. So what would it be? Which master would he serve tonight? Venus or Bacchus? The decision was made in a split second—he had yet to find comfort in a woman's embrace that lasted beyond one blissful moment of release, so the bottle it would be. Anything to help him forget.

"Guard!" he yelled impatiently.

John grabbed one of the coins and bounced it on the table, watching as it landed in his glass with a resonating clink. He repeated the same process again. *Clink. Clink. Clink.* How had he managed to fall so far? Not three years prior he'd been promoted to a captain in the King's Regiment, a commission he had earned on merit, something very few men were able to do. Military commissions were traditionally reserved for the wealthy upper class, those with connections and the ability to pay the exorbitant amount of money required to purchase one. Now he had nothing—disgraced, demoted, his reputation in ruins. But who cared about the truth? No one wanted to hear his side of the story, it was dirty and messy, so they hid him as far away as they could, like a bastard child they wanted to forget. At the time, he was grateful he hadn't been decommissioned, but looking around the dirty stone walls of his office, with the smell of damned stinking prisoners permeating through the floor from the hell below, he wasn't so sure this was a better option.

Bouncing the last one of his coins on the desk, John watched as it rolled onto the floor and fell between the cracks in the floorboards. Getting down on his hands and knees, he fingered the wood, pulling at the panels, trying to pry them loose, but to no avail; the coin was gone. Damn, now he was short the money to buy a bottle of scotch. Leaning against the stone wall, he put his head in his hands, smoothing his hair out of his face, the left-over tallow sticking to his palms helping to further slick it back. Looking at his left hand, he pulled off his gold pinky ring, rolling it between his fingers. He had no need for his family signet, they'd long since disowned him, but it would fetch a reasonable price.

Putting the ring in the pouch, he yelled again, "Lieutenant!"

His subordinate appeared at the door, his crimson coat and navy blue facings so perfectly arranged one would have thought he was serving for General Howe himself, and not in a military gaol. And why not? That's how it should be no matter where one served, gaol or battlefield. John did his duty to the best of his ability. Had he not always done his duty for King and country? King and country. He chuckled to himself again, so much hubris in those words, touted by proud soldiers who used them as an excuse for diabolical actions. But in truth, King George cared nothing about the cost of the war, only that the colonies remained obedient and firmly in his grasp. And John's conscience, well, that was his cross to bear. Yes, he craved honor and glory just like any soldier, yet for some reason, he lacked the ability to reconcile the atrocities inflicted on his fellow man in the name of the crown. It was his duty to serve his King and England, but could a man answer to his conscience *and* be a good soldier at a time of war?

Handing over the pouch, John nodded as the lieutenant took it. "Please get me the largest bottle of scotch or rum this will purchase. Go now, and bring back what's left over."

John walked over to the window, the moonlight shining in, casting silvery shadows on the floor. In the trees, he swore he saw the woman pointing at him, her jet-black hair blowing in the breeze while she chanted her breathy refrains, her song as familiar to him as *God Save the King*.

"I know what you want," he whispered to her. "But there is no justice to be had for either of us." Unlike the tenacious Karma, Justice was an elusive mistress, blind to his plight and forever just beyond his reach.

A sudden knock on the door woke John from a drunken, dreamless sleep. He opened his eyes to the dry, sticky feel of too much rest and a drum corps cadence beating in his head. *Knock. Knock. The door, John, get the door.* Grabbing a sheet and wrapping it around his waist, he climbed out of bed, stumbling over glasses and plates littering the floor. When he opened the door, a courier from headquarters handed him a letter—one requesting he appear immediately. *Immediately?* He let out a sigh, running his hand through his hair. It must be important, but what did they want with him, he was just a gaoler? Shutting the door, John looked around his room, unable to remember how he got back there the night before. Lying in his bed, decadently tangled in each other's arms, were two women he didn't recognize, their clothes in a pile next to his, stays and petticoats littering the floor. Suddenly, his stomach pitched. *Oh, God.* John grabbed a basin and hurled the contents of his stomach into it, retching several times before he was finally able to lift his head up without the spasms starting anew. This was bad. For the life of him, he couldn't remember anything after the bottle of rum he drank at the gaol the night before. After rinsing his mouth and washing his face, he reached for his uniform, realizing it was torn in several places. Fortunately, he had an extra one, though it gave off a fetid odor from not being laundered in weeks, and the elbows and cuffs were threadbare and worn. When he looked in the mirror, there were dark circles under his eyes, but at least he didn't need a shave, the fair hair on his cheeks barely breaking the skin.

The long ride to Fiftieth Street and First Avenue was grueling, each rhythmic stomp of Viceroy's hooves on the ground exacerbating the incessant pounding in his head and the pitching of his stomach. *Undoubtedly, it was the brightest sun known to man.* He grasped the reins of his horse with one hand, using the other to shade his eyes from the decidedly obnoxious sunlight. Unable to continue navigating the rough terrain one handed, he settled for cocking his hat sideways and pulling the brim down. He had no one to blame for his condition but himself, but the rum had certainly helped, and the scotch he drank before that, and possibly the spiced cider he started with?

It took him an hour to get to General Howe's official headquarters, long enough for the brisk morning air to reinvigorate John to the point of functionality, but nothing beyond that. Beekman House sat on a rise overlooking the East River, an elegant, large, white, two-story mansion made of wood and brick with a traditional Dutch-style roof. The mansion had been abandoned after Washington's retreat to Harlem, leaving it free to be confiscated by the British like many of the wealthy colonists' homes. The foyer was sumptuously decorated with plaster molding on the ceiling, a crimson and blue oriental rug covering the shiny wood floor, and a great Murano glass chandelier hanging from above; a reflection of the power and wealth of its former owner, James Beekman, a local dry goods merchant. John wiped off his feet at the front door and was escorted up a winding staircase, elegantly decorated with a carved mahogany banister. Taking a seat in the hall outside Major Andrews' office, John adjusted his coat and rearranged his hat, trying to further right himself for proper inspection. Being recently demoted, and not exactly one of His Majesty's finest, John found the whole summons to headquarters rather vexing. What could Major Andrews want? For all John knew, it was because of something he'd done in a drunken stupor the night before. Had he lost documents somewhere on the road, or perhaps there was a prison break? Best to just admit his fault and take his punishment. *Fall on your sword, Carlisle, well done.*

Reaching into his coat pocket, he realized his money pouch was missing along with his gold signet ring. *Damn! Did I drop the pouch?* And his ring, it was all he had left of his family. *Where could I have lost it?* The damn thing was gold and worth at least one hundred pounds. He tried to focus on all the places he had gone the night before but to no avail. The lack of sleep and a menacing hangover prevented him from forming any coherent thoughts, his brain in a perpetual state of fog. When the door opened to the Major's office, John stood up straight, trying to put on a good show.

Major Andrews motioned. "Please, come in, Lieutenant Carlisle."

John walked in slowly, delaying the inevitable reprimand that was doomed to follow. The first thing he noticed was the room's elegant décor, but that was quickly supplanted by a rush of heat so potent it was like a fist to the face. *Wow!* John resisted the urge to loosen his stock and collar, beads of sweat forming beneath the layers of woolen fabric. He cursed the giant, Dutch-tiled fireplace, blazing brilliantly, taunting him, as if it knew the intense heat would further add to his sorry state of affairs. Wiping the sweat from his forehead, he noticed that even the windows were perspiring. For October, it was already unseasonably chilly. Admittedly superstitious, John couldn't help but wonder if this was a foreboding for the war effort. A long, cold winter could mean trouble for the British, preventing Howe's men from advancing and giving Washington's army the ample time they needed to recoup their losses and prepare for the spring.

As the major shut the door, the door opposite simultaneously opened with a click and hard shove that threatened to loosen the hinges. Much to John's surprise, he found himself standing face-to-face with Major-General William Howe, the commander-in-chief of the British military in the American colonies.

"General Howe, sir!" John said, with astonishment.

"Lieutenant Carlisle," the General replied brusquely, giving John the once-over that brought with it grimace and a hand to the nose.

He suddenly felt embarrassed, noticing the look of displeasure on the General's face at his underling's slovenly appearance. When Howe's nose wrinkled, John knew the combination of spirits, sex, and his unlaundered uniform had managed to waft in the General's direction. "Yes, sir."

"You may sit, Lieutenant."

Following the General's direction, John sat down in a sizeable winged-backed chair next to the desk, his fingers nervously drumming on the wooden arm. Major Andrews excused himself, leaving John alone, waiting in awkward silence, as General Howe paced back and forth. One lap, two laps, but still, Howe said nothing. The quiet was grating on John's nerves, the suffocating warmth of the room compounding the ill effects of the night before. He swallowed hard, trying to control the nausea that refused to abate.

Then suddenly, Howe stopped his incessant pacing and turned with a surprisingly quizzical look. "You're a relation of Carlisle Shipping, is that correct, Lieutenant?"

"Yes, sir, I am. Gavin Carlisle is my older brother," John replied, still dumbfounded that he was meeting with the most superior officer of the British military. He drummed his fingers even faster in anticipation.

"I knew your father. He was a well-respected businessman and an accomplished sailor. He and my brother, Richard, were good friends. I wonder what he thought of his son joining the infantry and not the navy."

"My father had already passed by the time I joined the infantry, though I don't believe he would've been fond of my decision. Unlike him, I don't particularly care for the sea."

"From what I understand, you don't care for following orders either." The General countered.

John remained quiet, his gaze meeting Howe's in acknowledgment. What could be said? Howe, like everyone else, knew of John's transgressions over the past two years. And yes, he was guilty, but it wasn't that simple. In times of war, nothing was simple. Lesson learned. Time to move on now.

The General watched for a moment, waiting to see if his comment would spark some Rebellion in him. Satisfied with the lack of response and reticent demeanor, Howe continued. "I understand you did some intelligence work before your current post? Not only did you provide us with incredibly accurate maps, but also, you managed to obtain vital information concerning the movement of Washington's men here in Manhattan?"

"Yes, sir, that's correct." John nodded, grateful for the change in topic. It was true, he happened upon a vital piece of intelligence in the arms of his favorite paramour, which had helped the British make a decisive move during the Battle of Brooklyn. A bit of good luck for once in his twenty-seven years.

Howe started pacing again, his eyes fixed on the floor, his plaited, dark hair pulled back, drawing attention to his high forehead and strong jaw—a profile one would expect of a great general. The forty-seven-year-old looked impressive in his crimson uniform, the gold epaulets on his shoulders and detailing on his cuffs sparkling in the firelight. He was perfectly put together, not one wrinkle or stray thread to be found on his tunic, and his buff waistcoat and breeches were perfectly pressed. John still couldn't believe he was meeting with the head of the British Army in the Colonies. He looked up at the man in awe. He had the ability to advance or destroy John's career with a single command. The thought made him straighten up a bit more in his chair, hold his head higher, though little good it would do for his appearance.

"Intelligence is a rather dirty business, but necessary; do you agree, Lieutenant?"

A loaded question. John paused before answering, choosing his words strategically. This whole meeting was premeditated. Howe wanted something very specific from John and everything he said or did was being evaluated, measured, and mentally noted. *Tread carefully, Carlisle.* "Sir, I think it has much to do with the man and not the method. Not everyone who engages in intelligence has to be the unsavory type."

"Washington also has his spies—we know this from our recent capture of Nathan Hale. He was executed in Manhattan not a month ago. I spoke with Hale before he died. Surprisingly, he was intelligent and dedicated to his cause, though misguided. That being said, it's time we step up our own intelligence if we are to be successful in this war. Having already played your part, I don't believe I have to explain to you the skill it requires, nor the value of accurate and timely intelligence. You are assigned to one of our prisons in Manhattan. Prior to your role here in New York, I understand you served under the command of Major DeLancie in the Eighth Regiment at Fort Niagara?"

"That is correct, sir. I was a captain in the King's Regiment Light Infantry." John purposely made note of his specific position in Light Infantry as Howe had, personally, developed the new training for their companies not two years before.

Taking a seat, the General reached into the desk drawer and pulled out a stack of papers, depositing them on his desktop. John kept his eyes focused on the General, resisting the urge to peek while Howe leafed through the pages. "I knew Major DeLancie. He served under me during the war with France. We fought at Quebec City together. You obviously know what became of him, having played your part in his downfall—a fine repayment for the man who did so much to ensure your success."

John could sense more than a tinge of disgust in Howe's reproach. But with all due respect, he had no idea what it was like serving under Roger DeLancie. Biting back insubordinate words, John opted, once again, for reticence. "I know you're aware of what transpired with the Eighth in the Mohawk Valley. The situation was complicated. I'm not sure what else there is to say."

"Complicated? That's putting it lightly." Howe clipped with a shake of his head. "It was a damned embarrassment to the flag you both represented—a blight on this army."

"Major DeLancie and I greatly differed in our beliefs on what was appropriate behavior for officers and gentlemen. And yes, it was reprehensible what happened, and I accept responsibility for my part, but in the end, I did what I thought was right." John countered, unapologetically.

Howe sat back in his chair, stone-faced and silent.

Now I'm in trouble.

But instead of a stern reprimand with a swift reproach, he continued calmly. "You were his first officer, and knowing the Major, I have no doubt he trained you to survive in the frontier wilderness. I'm under the impression you understand the dynamic relations we have with the Six Nations of the Iroquois, or at least you used to..."

Once again, the General trailed off when referring to John's past. He mentally rolled his eyes. "Yes, sir, I worked directly with our allies in the Mohawk community as well as the neighboring tribes. Though I do have to admit, there are men better acquainted with the natives than I. It's been two years since I had contact with anyone in the territory, and I haven't spoken the languages since then. My resources are limited at best."

"I am aware of this, Lieutenant. Since Sir Johnson, our superintendent of Northern Indian Affairs, died, and his family are no longer exerting their authority in the area, our resources for gaining information aren't what they use to be. Yes, we have native spies, but their information is unreliable to say the least. What I'm looking for is someone with knowledge of the territory, but with a bit less notoriety, so to speak."

"What is it you would like me to do, sir?" John asked, his curiosity piqued. *Could Howe be offering me a position?* His heart thundered in his chest so loud he was sure the General could hear it. John took a deep breath, trying to calm himself, closing his fists tight to keep from further drumming on the chair arms.

Again, leafing through the stack of papers on the desk, Howe found what he was looking for, regarding it intently for a moment. "I believe you recognize these, do you not?" the General asked, handing the papers to John. On the top was a map of Manhattan he'd made during a short stint in intelligence. The others were maps of Tryon County, including the Six Nations Confederacy lands, and all the known settlements within the territory, based on the 1768 Treaty of Fort Stanwix.

"Yes, sir, I drew these." John swelled a bit with pride looking at the *JC* inscribed on the corner of the paper—at least one kernel of his past had not been tainted by his reputation. His skill at cartography was one of the exceptional abilities that had gotten him noticed and promoted through the ranks, along with his deadly accuracy with a firearm, both skills currently being wasted in a military gaol, much to his chagrin.

"You are rather proficient at map making. Not a talent easily obtained. How do you come by such a skill?"

John handed the maps back to the General. "I used to make maps of the waterways and seaports for Carlisle Shipping. My father found it a rather advantageous skill to have in a son, especially because he didn't have to pay for it."

"Interesting." Howe paused, his eyes scanning the maps, then leveling on John. "Any day now, General Carleton will be moving his fleet south from St. John to take Ticonderoga. With the port of New York City under our control, and our lands north and west of the St. Lawrence, all we need now is to control the Mohawk and the Hudson River, and we will sever the colonies in two, separating the North from the South. The Rebels would never recover from such a blow. This war would be over."

"I'm sure Washington and Arnold are anticipating that strategy. As we both know, Washington can be rather resourceful when challenged."

The General nodded. "They might be, but they're on the run now. Washington doesn't have enough men to handle a battle in the North and continues to hold what little ground he has left in New York. The Rebels lack the supplies and the resources to follow through. They are an unorganized army of militias, a ragtag group of rabble that could be easily dealt with if we strike swiftly and precisely."

"Like Brooklyn?" John countered, referring to Washington's ability to disappear in the middle of the night, even after being defeated and cornered against the East River.

With a shake of the head, Howe replied confidently, "We won't make that mistake again. Carleton will crush them on Lake Champlain, and his men will take Ticonderoga, then Albany. The next focal point for our efforts will be the Mohawk and the lower Hudson Valley."

John tried to focus as he looked over the map, his brain still foggy from his late-night escapades. The strategy was logical *if* they could make it work, but there were many more factors to consider. "Sir, that area is known to be loyal to the colonists, and these farms are vital for feeding their army. If we take the Mohawk and the Hudson, it will put an even bigger wrench in their supply chain. Along with the blockade, this could cripple Washington's army for good. If Carleton takes Ticonderoga then Albany, the only place left is Fort Stanwix and the smaller forts along the Mohawk. You think this is where they will try to stop us?"

Howe nodded in agreement. "Possibly."

"Fort Stanwix is in ruins, and in the middle of Oneida territory. Anything the Rebels do would be under careful watch, and the Oneidas are friendly with…" John stopped, the fog suddenly abating, Howe's plan became clear as daylight. "You think the Oneidas may already be working with the Rebels?"

Howe nodded again. "I do. Though they claim to be neutral as a nation, the cracks are beginning to show in the Iroquois Confederacy. The Oneidas specifically have been rather hesitant to discuss a treaty, and we've had word that some of them have already sided with the colonists. I'm sure you know who Joseph Brant is?"

Brant, the illustrious Mohawk war chief, was known for his cultured education and his close relations with the British army, so of course John knew of the man. The outspoken Brant had recently traveled to England to meet with His Majesty King George III to address the Mohawks' grievances concerning their land in exchange for their alliance against the Rebels.

"Brant is currently trying to rally the natives to our side, and though he is imposing, I have little faith they will follow him. I think it will require something more than words and a wampum belt to leverage their fealty. They want money, weapons, and land, and we're in the position to give it to them. Washington, however, is not."

Having been stationed at Fort Niagara, John understood the dynamics of the Haudenosaunee Confederacy, or the Iroquois, as they were known, better than most. The powerful native nation of the Northeast territory was made up of five major tribes and one lesser one: the Seneca, Cayuga, Onondaga, Oneida, Mohawk and Tuscarora. Known for being fierce, brutal warriors, adept at ambush warfare, the Iroquois could be a devastating and intimidating fighting force if their strength was wielded correctly. The colonists feared the natives, and relations were strained because of the westward expansion of colonial territories into the sacred native lands. The Mohawk, in particular, resented the expansion, because their land bordering the Hudson River and Albany was slowly being stripped away by the colonists. Bordering on Lake Ontario and Niagara, the Seneca, the largest tribe of the Confederacy, kept friendly relations with the crown due to their proximity to Canada and their ability to trade with the local British Forts. The Cayuga and Onondaga fiercely held on to their neutrality and were relatively isolated, being protected on both borders by the Oneida and the Seneca. The Oneida, much like the Mohawk, were known to be holding a grudge, but it was against the crown for building Fort Stanwix in the middle of sacred lands during the French War. Now that the colonists occupied Stanwix, the Oneida were ripe for an alliance with the Rebels. The Tuscarora, the smallest tribe of the Six Nations, shared the land with the Oneida, and were sure to side with them and the colonists.

Shifting in the seat, John looked up at his superior. "Sir, if the Oneida are helping the Rebels, and the Mohawk are with us, then it's only a matter of time before the rest are forced to declare sides. This could turn into, not only a war between us and the Rebels, but within the Confederacy itself and the neighboring tribes. It would be a brutal bloodbath of astronomical proportions. Besides, you and I both know the challenges of the frontier; the logistics of a battle there would be near impossible, to say the least."

"That is correct, Lieutenant, and our manpower is limited. But this is our best option, and taking control of the frontier will require assistance from our old allies in the Six Nations. They, as a whole, influence all the neighboring tribes from the Lakes up into Canada. Our goal is not to split the Confederacy, if possible, but to get them on our side and to bring their allies with them. That's where you come in."

"Sir?" Surprised, John looked at the General, whose expression was still unreadable.

"You know this area, likely better than most." Howe gestured towards the maps lying on his desk. "You speak their languages, I suspect very few people will recognize you, and you're an excellent map maker."

"Yes." John agreed.

The General spoke concisely, almost brusquely. "I need you to find out exactly what the situation is at Fort Stanwix. I want to know the layout, fortification, and how many men they have. What are the trade routes? How are they supplying it, and where is it coming from? Are any of the other forts active? Also, who is leading the Oneida, and what it would take to get them on our side or to remain neutral?"

Taking a deep breath, John considered the gravity of the task put before him. Not only would it be difficult, but it would also be incredibly dangerous. Tyron County was a Rebel stronghold, and they were notoriously aggressive towards Loyalists when caught; not to mention the natives, who were dangerous and suspicious of strangers. He would have to infiltrate the area and develop a relationship with the locals and the natives. But if he succeeded, this intelligence had the potential to turn the war in their favor, a momentous feat, indeed.

"I can do this, sir. It will be difficult, but I can do it," John replied, sounding more confident than he felt. Actually, he wasn't sure the mission was possible but damned if he wasn't going to try.

Howe sat back in his chair, pressing his palms together, the tips of his fingers drumming against each other as he looked over the map on his desk. "As an added incentive, I am returning you to your former rank of captain, and you will be allowed a small group of men to assist you. If you succeed, I will return you to your regiment with the potential for another promotion. A fresh start, shall we say?"

John's mind reeled at the thought. Yes, it wasn't his regiment, but still, it was an opportunity. Finally, he would be free from his purgatory, his record expunged; the professional doors that were now closed to him would be thrown open. A promotion by General Howe himself!

"Consider it done, sir."

"This must remain under the strictest of secrecy, only you and I are privy to this plan. No one, not even the new superintendent, or General Carleton, is to know what you are doing until I tell you different. I will see to filling your current post, as you won't be returning to it."

Thank God. If John never saw the gaol again, it would be too soon. "May I ask why the secrecy, sir?"

Howe finally betrayed some emotion, the scowl on his face affording a glimpse into his inner frustrations. "There are many political agendas involved and too many people who want to see their fortunes rise, sadly, even at a time of war. I have to make some decisions where to focus our efforts and allocate resources. Your information would help me do that."

John nodded. He, better than anyone, understood the complexities of war and politics. A drama being played out on a grand stage where alliances changed like the direction of the wind, even when on the same side.

"You have two days to make a plan and report back to me."

"That quickly, sir? It will take me more than two days to do this. There are arrangements to be made, supplies to be obtained."

"Captain, General Carleton is ready to meet Arnold and his men on Lake Champlain as we speak. If the weather holds out, we could be advancing on the Albany within the month. War is costly, Captain, and not only in monetary ways. We all pay the price. No one wants this war. The sooner we end this rebellion between brothers, the sooner we all get back to our lives. Your information must not only be accurate, but expeditious. Even His Majesty's army has its limitations."

Howe stood up, John followed, his mind already racing to make plans. If he had only two days to get ready, there wasn't a moment to lose.

The General walked around the desk, his shoulders back, head held high, standing before John, their eyes meeting.

"I'm giving you this chance because I see promise in you. You're intelligent and clearly honorable. But you're a mess Captain; you drink too much, and your morals are appalling. I suggest you apply the same discipline you utilize in being a soldier to your personal affairs. After all, if you claim to be an officer and a gentleman, then behave as both. You must hold yourself to a higher standard, set the example for your men. Now is your chance to prove yourself, and it won't come again. Is that understood?"

John nodded, heeding the General's warning.

"You aren't the first man to face a serious moral dilemma in the face of duty. When I consider the situation you were in, I don't know that I may not have done the same. Major DeLancie's behavior was reprehensible. Fighting alongside those savages during the French war corrupted even the best of soldiers, including him. That being said, and many would question the wisdom in my words, to go against one's superior is duplicitous. Don't make me regret my decision, and don't cock this up. Godspeed, Captain."

Taking a deep breath, John met the intense gaze, giving a promise in a moment as if written in his life's blood. "I won't let you down."

Chapter Two

"John, I heard you came looking for me while I was in Philadelphia." Celeste leaned forward, placing a lingering kiss on his lips, resting her soft, curvaceous body against his. She tasted of sweet wine and chocolate, their last indulgence before they made love. "I hope you found a way to amuse yourself?"

"I did," John replied, though he had no idea what exactly that entailed. Time had yet to elucidate the sordid details of his escapades, nor had it dropped hints as to what became of his money and his family signet. But little did it matter now; it would never happen again—no more making a drunken fool of himself. He had a mission and a promotion from Howe and the promise John would be returned to his regiment if he succeeded. His sun was finally rising; the wheel of fate turned in his favor.

Celeste shook her head, glossy chestnut curls falling over her shoulder. "You don't remember a thing do you?"

He leaned in and planted a kiss on one of her tress-gilded shoulders. "Not in the least."

"Oh, John, such a beautiful mess." Celeste wrapped her silky arms around his neck, her legs following suit, encircling his hips as she gently pulled him against her, the bed squeaking beneath them. "You were here, overindulging. I would make you pay me for the ladies, but we'll call ourselves even after your performance last night. And now that you're investing in my little venture, that makes you my partner. I suppose you're welcome to taste the vintage once in a while. Though not too much, I hope? I've been known to get jealous on occasion."

John breathed an inaudible sigh of relief. Thank goodness the ladies he'd spent the night with were some of hers. He'd hate to think he'd neglected to pay the women for services rendered, much less shorted them. Having narrowly escaped debtor's prison once in his life, he had no intention of being enlightened as to what he missed.

"By the way, John, you do owe me for the opium." Celeste grinned devilishly. "You smoked all I had left. It must have been quite a night indeed."

No wonder he couldn't remember anything—herbs and spirits, a dangerous combination. Whenever he mixed the two, someone got shot or bloodied, and he woke up with a drum corps playing in his head and no recollection of the events that preceded. "I will see that you get your money."

"Good." Celeste nuzzled her face into his neck, her hands making their way down his back, cupping his buttocks, evoking a fresh surge of desire. "Are you really leaving me?"

"Yes, I am." John loved the exaggerated sadness in her voice. Celeste was a master at manipulating her tone, a consummate actress, with impeccable timing and faultless delivery. Not a few moments before, she'd been calling his name, her voice husky with want, and now she sounded melancholy, as if she were going to shed big beautiful tears over his leaving. It was an expert vocal performance if he'd ever heard one. He had to force himself not to clap on her behalf.

"Where are you going?"

"North."

Celeste pulled away, her hazel eyes examining his face with a bit of humor. "That's not an answer, John. Tell me, where are they sending you? As you are an investor in my business, I deserve to know. What if something happened to you?"

"You're resourceful, Celeste, and I'm quite confident you can find someone to replace me, should it become a need. Your business has become the talk of the town," he said with a grin, giving her a chaste peck on the lips. In only a matter of months, Celeste's little house of decadence became the favorite of all the high-level officers and local Loyalists, turning more profit than an officer's yearly pay in a week. An advantageous opportunity for the both of them, they'd partnered together out of mutual need. She required capital to expand her business, and he wanted to buy back his captain's commission. And pillow talk always provided the most titillating and useful information, which in intelligence was fortuitous. When her original establishment burned down with the rest of the Holy Ground, earlier in the year, as her investor and most valued customer, John was more than willing to provide the additional capital she needed for profit and services rendered. It was none of King George's business how John made money, and since his wages had been garnished by the court marital, untraceable funds were ideal.

"John." She whined, with a contradictory sparkle in her eyes and a cocked brow. "Tell me where you're going."

Adjusting himself so that he lay on his side, John ran his index finger down the curve of her naked hip, following the dips and hollows of her decadent body. He loved how smooth and soft her olive skin was and how she shivered every time he touched her. She looked like a temptress, lying there, dark and irresistible, her long, silky locks resting on her graceful shoulders. He leaned down and kissed them, looking up at her with a grin. "Tryon County, my dear, that's all I can say."

"Why are they sending you there? I thought after your luck here they would promote you, or at least appoint you to something better than that poor excuse for a gaol you oversee? Tyron County; that's punishment, nothing but savages and colonists and bad weather."

John couldn't help but laugh. Celeste's description was disturbingly accurate, and the way she said it sounded genuinely desolate. But she wasn't entirely wrong. He dreaded the idea of returning to the cold, forbidding frontier. Howe's opportunity was a double-edged sword: While it was a promotion and second chance for John's career, it was also sending him back to the place where it all began—to the source of his disgrace. To the ghosts.

"Celeste, it *is* a very important mission."

She smiled, pulling a stray lock of his dark blond hair from his face, toying with it for a moment, then smoothing it behind his ear. "Does that mean I can call you Captain now?"

"It does, and I got my commission back because of what we did together." Leaning up, he touched his lips to hers, tasting their sweetness again. God, she was beautiful and so tempting. "Much thanks to you."

"What will I do without you?" She pouted, her tapered fingernail tracing the curve of his jaw, then his lips. "You've spoiled me."

Letting her finger rest between his teeth, John gave it a playful bite then pulled her hand away so he could nuzzle her palm. "Not to worry. I have complete confidence someone will take up where I left off. You're quite resourceful in a pinch."

"I disagree, John. I'm just a poor widow mourning her husband." She gave him a wide-eyed, innocent look, though the corners of her sensuous lips turned up with humor.

He laughed. Celeste was far from the poor, innocent widow she played in public. She was ambitious and ruthless when she wanted something, which served him just fine, because when she got what she wanted, so in turn, did he. They were in this business together, both determined and both enterprising—a perfect match.

Slowly, John made a trail of kisses down her neck, then between her breasts. It would be a while before he knew the pleasure of touching her again, much less any woman, so he wasn't going to waste this opportunity. Stopping for a moment, resting his chin in the valley between her breasts, he watched as she closed her eyes, indulging in his touch. "You know this is my favorite place on a woman's body." John traced his fingertip from the notch between her collarbones all the way down between her breasts, stopping at the base of her breastbone, placing a kiss there. "This beautiful valley."

"Really, Captain? I had no idea." Celeste smiled, cocking a brow. He liked the sound of *Captain* rolling off her tongue. *Captain Carlisle, that sounds good.*

"Now, while I'm gone, I need you to keep your eyes and ears open for any details of importance," he whispered, between well-placed kisses on her décolletage.

She let out a heady little gasp, goosebumps bubbling up on her arms, his cue to keep going. "I know you'll have grand parties, and you'll entertain lots of guests; just keep me informed of any important details."

Reaching over the side of the bed for his tunic, he pulled a piece of paper from the inside pocket and handed it to her. "I sent my men ahead to secure a location. This is where I will be; you can get word to me there. Any letters should be addressed to John Anderson. We'll use our usual cipher."

She yanked his queue, forcing him to look up. "You forget, John, I don't whore for you. Remember, you need me more than I need you." Celeste never hesitated to press her advantage when it suited her. Best to let her have her way, or to let her think you were doing so.

"Forgive me. I would never suggest you behave in an unladylike way. I was merely referring to our previous arrangements that were mutually beneficial, or would you rather this be purely business between us? I can play the role of an investor if that's what you wish?" he asked, reaching under her, taking the soft mounds of her bottom in his hands, using the scruff on his chin to gently graze the nub at the apex of her thighs. When he touched her with his tongue, she let out a heady gasp, her hips rising to receive more of his gentle treatment. Good, she was pliable, and wanting. Now it was time to turn the tables. John pulled away abruptly and got out of bed, reaching for his shirt and breeches.

This was the game they played, like cat and mouse. It was the chase Celeste loved most, and then the reward, but only after a long, drawn-out struggle.

"I hate how it's always business before pleasure with you, John. It's truly not fair." She groaned, rolling over on her side, watching him dress. "Is that all I am to you, a financial arrangement and information source?"

A good tup too? She forgot the most important part of their arrangement. Smiling, John leaned forward and kissed her, then continued getting dressed. But in truth, it *was* just business between them, and one he would exploit to get what he wanted, just as she did. Celeste was a smart woman; she knew the rules of the game, and to her credit, she was more than willing to play.

There were no illusions about love between the two of them. He didn't believe in true love—not in the least—it was a messy, complicated emotion that always ended up with someone getting hurt, and it was usually not him. And Celeste seemed to be in control of that tender, inconvenient part of her feminine heart, never allowing it to preclude business, nor prevent her from indulging in pleasurable pursuits.

So, it worked out perfectly between the two of them. Celeste liked being a widow with the means to control her destiny, and he liked the ability to come and go as he pleased, taking advantage of the many delights that presented themselves along the way. A wife was an impediment he couldn't afford, nor desired.

"Fine, John, if that's the way you want it to be. I can play by your rules." She smiled, rolled over, and reached for something in her bureau, then closed the drawer. As her hand trailed down her breast to her stomach, he recognized something gold sparkling on her index finger. It was his family signet ring. "I think you lost something last night."

John, with one leg in his breeches, stopped, his eyes trained to where her fingers now dexterously teased the slick, sensitive bit of flesh between her supple thighs. His gold ring winked in the candlelight with each movement of her finger, drawing his attention to it. Apparently, he'd hocked his family signet for a night with Celeste's ladies. *Things really had gotten bad.*

"If you want this back, you're going to have to come and get it." Celeste looked up at him, a smile tugging at her lips, and then gave a gasp of pleasure as she spread her legs farther, indulging in the sensation.

Climbing back into bed, assuming his former position, John kissed her inner thigh, pulling her hand away and removing the ring from her finger. "Thank you for returning this to me. And you're right, I do need you."

"Of course you do, John." She countered, running her hands through his hair, tugging at it. He knew what she wanted, but he had a few things he needed from her before he relented.

"Remember those suits you offered to have made for me?" Slowly, he trailed his lips down her inner thigh, his thumb gently stroking her heated flesh, drawing a moan from her lips. Music to his ears. "I'm going to be in need of them. Also, I could use a little money for my travels."

"John." She gasped, pulling at his hair. "Whatever you want, but don't stop."

Chapter Three

October 1776, German Flats, New York

The morning frost had melted away, but was its gentle kiss so early in the season a subtle warning of what was yet to come? Dellis carried a basket full of corn as she walked the gravel-covered road back to her family's tavern. Looking up, she embraced the sun's warmth on her skin while the cool autumn breeze blew the leaves about her in little, whirling tornadoes. She loved the fall. It was the most beautiful time of year, warm sun, cool breezes, and a symphony of colors smattered on the canvas of the forest like a perfect painting.

Flipping over the sign on The Thistle Tavern, she walked around to the back door, wiping her shoes off as she made her way into the kitchen. Turning her beloved family home into a tavern was not her life's aspiration, but it paid the bills, at least, most of the time. And as a single woman, it was about the only profession she could have and remain somewhat respectable in the eyes of the townspeople. Well, as respectable as a woman with her reputation could be.

Dellis looked around the kitchen, her heart aching with memories of better days. Once upon a time, she and her mother had worked side by side with their cook, learning to make Dellis's father's favorite Scottish meals.

Stephen McKesson would come in from a day of caring for the sick and recount his journeys to them while he secretly snatched a hot bread roll from the counter. She loved listening to his stories. Her mother, a medicine woman of the Oneida tribe, always had a bit of unique wisdom to impart to her formally trained husband. Dellis remembered the love in her parent's eyes as they went back and forth, debating the best way to clean wounds and care for patients. How she missed their playful banter. The kitchen was their happy place. Heaven on Earth. And though the paint peeled now, and the cupboards were worn and sagging, when she closed her eyes, she could still see it as it was when they were alive.

The Thistle, his glorious house, was her father's prized possession and one of the few things she had left of him. If running a tavern was the only way she could hold on to this last piece of him, then there was nothing else to be done.

"Dellis, I had a dream that you were married, and we were finally able to sell this old house," her Aunt Helena said in her thick Russian accent while she bustled about the kitchen getting ready for the day. Dellis stifled a groan as she looked at her aunt's spritely face and faked a smile—better to say nothing than start an argument.

"A woman's job is to get married and give her husband sons, not spend her life waiting on drunkards." She added.

She and her spouse were always trying to find Dellis a husband, though she would have preferred they didn't. After all, she was twenty, and most women her age were married with children. It wasn't that she didn't want to get married, actually quite the opposite, but her situation was complicated. And they weren't doing it out of a deep sense of affection for her but more a strategic move to dispose of an unwanted burden that had been placed on them when her parents died two years ago. Still, she owed them the respect of being the only close relations she had from her father's side of the family, save an uncle who lived in England.

"I don't want to talk about this, Auntie."

Dellis could feel her aunt's large, blue eyes regarding her niece with discontent, a common state of affairs between the two of them. Regardless of how contentious their relationship could be, she needed her aunt's help to continue running the tavern. The job was too much for any one person to handle, and Dellis could barely afford to pay her bartender's wages, much less someone to replace her aunt in the kitchen.

"Is that Alexei I hear in the dining room?" Dellis asked, grateful for her cousin's timely entrance.

Her aunt scowled. "My son's breakfast can wait, Dellis. We're not finished with this discussion. Eventually, something has to be done about you and your brother's current state of affairs. Your uncle and I can't continue to spend frivolously to keep this tavern open, much less maintain this house."

Dellis spoke briskly, tamping down her ire. "I was under the impression The Thistle maintained itself. I haven't asked you for money, nor would I." She turned her back to her aunt as Dellis prepared her tray. "I can take care of Stuart and myself if need be."

Stuart, her younger brother, was sixteen and sadly afflicted with her father's family illness. When the boy turned fourteen, the telltale signs appeared: seeing things that didn't exist and hearing random voices in his head. Since her parents were murdered, his condition progressed, his behavior more erratic, made worse by a tendency to drink and overindulge. Though he did little to help her run the tavern, he was her only brother, and she would always take care of him, no matter what. That's what her father would want.

"My dear, this inn hasn't made a profit in months, and with the winter coming, I've no doubt it will make even less." Her aunt stepped in front of Dellis, blocking her path. "Your uncle has been looking at the ledger, trying to figure out where to save money, but to no avail. He intends on speaking with you about this. You should prepare yourself."

She was in no mood for this conversation; worrying would only slow her down, and there was still linen to wash, candles to make, and food to be served to the dinner crowd. "Fine, Auntie, but I'd like to see that ledger for myself first."

"Dellis, you need to be reasonable."

She pushed past her aunt, trying not to think about what she was suggesting. They would have to drag Dellis out, kicking and screaming, before she would sell her father's house. It was inconceivable.

Walking into the dining room, she stopped abruptly at first sight of her former betrothed. He was sitting with Alexei, both of them head down, looking at newspapers, chatting quietly. It had been two years since Patrick had rescinded his offer of marriage, yet seeing him still pulled at her heartstrings. Would there ever come a time when she didn't ache at the sight of him? Thankfully, it didn't often happen, as he spent much of his time away from town on business.

Throwing her shoulders back, Dellis took a deep breath, preparing herself. Yes, she'd been rejected, but she still had her pride, and there was life after love, or so they say. There *was* life after love. She repeated it to herself over and over as she walked to the table, trying to convince herself it was true, but when Patrick looked up at her with his beautiful, olive-green eyes, her mantra lost its potency.

No, there was only loneliness after love.

"Good morning, Dellis," Patrick said in his familiar, warm baritone.

She froze, her aching heart preventing her from speaking, much less forming a thought. On weak knees, she served up their plates and poured the coffee, unable to look him in the eyes. Would she ever get over this feeling?

Dellis was grateful when the two men started to chat again, anything to draw her attention away from the festering wound in her heart. "There's a council with the Mohawk today," Alexei said between bites. "I'm going to travel up to Schenectady with Joseph."

"Did something happen?" Dellis interrupted, spilling a few drops of coffee on the table. Quickly, she mopped it up with her apron, her hands shaking nervously.

"Good morning, cousin." Alexei looked up from his paper, giving her a pleasant smile that lit up his handsome face and bright, blue eyes.

Alexei McKesson was the oldest son of her Aunt Helena and Dellis's father's oldest brother, James McKesson. Though looking at Alexei, one would second-guess his Russian and Scottish lineage; he looked more like a native with his long, dark-brown hair hanging loose past his shoulders and the buckskin tunic and leggings he wore. At a towering, six-foot-five inches, it was hard to believe such a robust man was once the sickly young boy that grew up in her father's care. For most of Alexei's youth, he lived with her family, amongst her tribe, and as he grew older and stronger, he was eventually made a member and trained as a warrior. Now, he served as the right-hand man to her grandfather, Chief Great Oak, much to James McKesson's chagrin. He hated all natives, especially the Oneida.

"The Mohawk village west of Schenectady was attacked a couple of days ago. Joseph is planning a meeting with the chief and the sachems." Alexei added, looking back at his paper.

"Whoever did this must be very brave or damn foolish," Dellis said, looking at both of them. Mohawks were notoriously fierce, and retribution would undoubtedly be swift and sure to whomever dared to aggress them.

"Cursing, Dellis?" Patrick said with a grin. "That's not like you."

"It is now," she clipped, tartly. Who was he to say such a thing? She could curse whenever she wanted. She had no husband to reprimand her. Wasn't he the one that broke their betrothal?

"It suits you." Patrick added. "You were always feisty. And so lovely."

Dellis blushed, her ire tamped down under his praise. He was so handsome and unique with his curly, reddish-brown hair and fair skin dotted lightly with freckles. She remembered the feel of his gentle lips against hers when they had kissed. It was magical and so very long ago.

"I agree with you, Dellis, whoever did this was foolish—and lucky. Their warriors were out hunting. The village was defenseless save a few guards."

"They were Redcoats, weren't they?" she asked, the scenario disturbingly familiar.

Alexei shook his head, though his eyes stayed fixed on his paper. "Dellis, I know where you are going with this, and you're wrong. They weren't Regulars; it's too far for the English to travel and go unnoticed. Why would they do that, anyway? The Mohawks are working with the British."

"Then who do you think did this? Could it be colonists?"

When Alexei didn't answer, she pulled his bowl of oats away, holding it high above his head.

"Honestly, Dellis, I don't know. We'll find out more information at the council, and after, we'll ride to the village and offer our assistance." Alexei's blue eyes focused on the bowl in her hands. Dellis shook her head. Men really were single-minded when it came to their stomachs. Handing the food back to him, she sat down and watched as he went at his oatmeal with the gusto of a starving man.

"Let me go with you, Alexei. I am a matron of the bear clan, now that mother and grandmother are gone. I have a right to be present at the meeting, and after, I'll follow you to the village. There might be someone who needs tending."

When he rolled his eyes, she knew she'd won. Alexei respected her ability as a healer, and it often worked to their tribe's advantage when it came to negotiating. "Fine, but stay out of trouble. You have a knack for putting your nose where it doesn't belong." He pointed to her nose, and then lightly tapped the tip of it.

"I promise." Dellis crossed her fingers under the table and gave him the most innocent, wide-eyed look she could muster up.

This was one meeting she had no intention of missing. Since the beginning of the war, relations with the Mohawk and the rest of the Confederacy were tenuous at best. The political wrangling between the colonists and the British had taken its toll on the almost three-hundred-year-old peace between the tribes. As she'd done in the past, she could leverage her medical skills and act as a buffer between the tribes if things escalated—and where the Mohawk were concerned, that was imminent.

There was so much anger and hate in the air, a perpetual miasma that precluded any chance at peace talks. At first, it was just the British against the colonists in the war, but now, it was tribe against tribe and brother against brother. The whole world seemed on the verge of catastrophe, like a powder keg ready to blow.

Her aunt chimed in from behind Dellis's position. "Dellis, you shouldn't go, it isn't right for a lady to see such things. Besides, it could be dangerous."

Looking over her shoulder, she countered. "Auntie, there might be someone that needs my help. Not to worry, I have Alexei with me. Could you watch the tavern so I can go? You won't be working alone for very long, Thomas will be here in an hour to help." Drumming her fingers on the table, she waited for a response, already planning what to take with her for the ride.

"All right, but be careful. I worry about you." Helena placed her hand on Dellis's shoulder, giving it a light squeeze.

Dellis, taken aback by the unusual show of affection from her aunt, glanced up at her and smiled. She looked like a pixie, her little face framed by soft, dark curls, and her deep-set, blue eyes turning up slightly in the corners. Petite and pretty, she reminded Dellis of the delightful little characters from her father's stories who lived in the woods working their magic on vagabonds and travelers. How she wished they were closer; her aunt was the nearest thing to a mother Dellis had. She knew her aunt cared and occasionally saw glimpses of it in a little smile or a kind word. Helena McKesson was a wealthy lady; she didn't need to work in a tavern, but she did it anyway. Deep down, Dellis wanted to believe her aunt did it out of love, though she never spoke the words.

"Thank you, Auntie," Dellis murmured, squeezing her aunt's hand.

Getting up, Dellis darted around, looking for her medical supplies and packing enough food for the day. Grabbing her basket, she filled it with a pair of scissors, some needles, thread, a bottle of whiskey, and all the linen she could find. Just as she put on her cape and tied it in place, her aunt stopped appeared. "Oh, I almost forgot, Dellis, we have new lodgers coming tonight, a merchant and three of his men. Since you need the money, and we have the rooms available upstairs, I thought you wouldn't mind. They should be here sometime this evening."

"Did they say how long they were staying?"

"No, but they paid us for two weeks." Her aunt held up a small leather satchel, allowing Dellis to admire it from afar. Too excited to wait, Dellis snatched it from her aunt's hands and opened it.

The little bag was full of coins, and English pounds to boot, not Continental currency, the almost worthless printed-paper the Continental Congress tried to pass off as money. Shaking the bag and hearing the coins clink together was like music to Dellis's ears, an answer to her plight. Now, if she could only make more money. "Do we know anything else about our guests?"

Helena shook her head, taking the bag of money back and depositing it in her pocket. "No, but Captain Anderson will discuss the specifics with you when he arrives."

Chapter Four

During their ride to the village, Alexei led the way while Dellis quietly racked her brain, trying to come up with some way to make more profit. She'd already sold most of her father's expensive furniture to pay off previous debts, and she couldn't charge for the small medical services she often provided some of the locals. After all, she wasn't a trained physician like her father; her skills were more akin to a medicine woman's. And God forbid Dellis call herself a "medicine woman." Then everyone would associate her with being native, and she would be chased out of town. Maybe if she got her hands on The Thistle's ledger, then she could figure out where to cut some corners. Next time she saw her uncle, she would make sure to ask for it. There had to be some way to make ends meet and stay afloat. Well, at least she had lodgers coming to stay; that would bring in some much-needed income and quickly.

When they finally reached a clearing in the forest, Dellis sighed in relief, ready for a break. Her back was aching, and her thighs were sore, a groove worn in the bottom of her feet from pushing into the stirrups for so long she was sure she'd never walk flat-footed again. Alexei notoriously never stopped to rest, akin to a demon when he was focused on one task, just as he was now. Thankfully, they weren't far from their destination. The council meeting was taking place at a village between the lower Mohawk castle, Canajoharie, and the town of Schenectady. As with most Iroquois settlements, the forest around it had been cleared for several yards, allowing for an unobstructed view of incoming visitors and potential threats. Surrounding the little village was a stockade of large, sturdy logs planted into the ground, with bark and branches woven between them forming a protective wall, the first line of defense against intruders.

At the entrance to the village, a fierce-looking Mohawk warrior stepped in front of them, his fists planted on his hips defiantly while he looked them up and down. Dellis waited patiently as her cousin addressed the guard in perfect *Kanien☒kéha*, Mohawk dialect. "*Shé:kon*. I'm Alexei, and this is Dellis. We represent Chief Great Oak, offering friendship to the Brothers of the Flint from your Brothers of the Standing Stone. We've come to attend the council."

As an Oneida, she was accustomed to warriors in face paint with their characteristic shaved heads and scalp locks. Mohawk warriors, in particular, were fierce fighters and notorious for their strength and prowess in battle. This one appeared to be no exception with his intimidating size and commanding presence.

The Mohawk stared them down for a moment, his dark, hawk-like eyes full of suspicion. "The council will meet outside." He pointed towards the woods. "Over there."

From behind the guard, Dellis could see a whirlwind of activity: chickens running loose as the village women gave chase, the ground littered with pots and pans and gardening tools. Above the ruckus, she could hear the sounds of a woman sobbing, a painful, desolate cry of loss carrying on the breeze.

"Did something happen?" Dellis asked the guard while watching one of the women cleaning a wound on a young girl's forehead.

"We were attacked earlier in the day, several of our women were injured, and some were killed."

As expected, the guard offered up little detail, both suspicion and reticence expected after such a devastating event took place, but it only served to further provoke her anxiety. "Alexei?" She looked up at her cousin, her heart racing nervously. "Another village attacked?"

"Do you know who did this?" Alexei asked calmly, though Dellis could read fear in his traditionally stoic countenance.

The Mohawk shook his head. "No, now both of you, leave."

Before Alexei could respond, Dellis stepped in front of him, her womanly instincts suggesting an emotional plea instead of continued inquiry—they were getting nowhere fast. If the guard would tell her nothing, at least she could do her own investigating once inside the village. "Please, I would like to help." Holding up her basket of supplies for his scrutiny, she added, "I'm a medicine woman. We were planning to go after the council to help the other village that was attacked a few days ago." She paused for a moment, looking into his eyes. "I can help, if you let me."

The guard looked her over for a moment, then nodded, allowing her and Alexei to pass.

The village was small, with only three traditional longhouses, flanking each other, and five small cabins neatly situated around them, the whole perimeter surrounded by the stockade. As she saw earlier, the ground was littered with items that were extracted from the houses during the raid. The pens and fences that kept the chickens and livestock were destroyed, and now, the animals were running loose around the village, creating a commotion.

"I'm going to find out more about what happened. You work your magic, but stay out of trouble," Alexei said, walking past her toward one of the cabins. "I'll be back."

Dellis rolled her eyes at Alexei then walked over to the lady tending the child and stopped. "Can I help you?" she asked, in *Kanien'kéha.*

The woman looked at Dellis for a moment, then nodded. She put her basket down on the ground and kneeled in front of the little girl. "My name is Dellis. I'm going to clean this up, and you'll be all better."

With a quiver in her little lip and tears in her eyes, she replied, "Thank you."

Gingerly, Dellis used a linen cloth doused with whiskey to clean and inspect the little wound. It was long but not deep, and with pressure, the bleeding eventually stopped. After she finished, she stood up and wiped the dust off her skirt, taking another look around the village. This was all too familiar to her; women beaten and murdered, livestock and supplies stolen, and the perpetrators disappearing without a trace.

Suddenly, the gut-wrenching cries started again, tugging at Dellis's heart strings, evoking memories too painful to recollect. She turned to the woman sitting next to the child and said, "I would like to help. Where is she?"

The woman pointed to the longhouse closest to them. "In there, but you're too late."

With a nod, Dellis opted to investigate before her cousin returned to say otherwise. Alexei would be furious with her for snooping around, but so be it. After all, as clan matron, it was her duty to provide counsel. How could she do that if she didn't have all the facts and not the abridged version her cousin notoriously offered?

Dellis lifted the deerskin flap door to the longhouse and walked inside. She waited for a moment, giving her vision a chance to adjust to the darkness, the only source of light coming from small skylights in the woven bark ceiling. When she could see better, she started down the center hallway, sidestepping several fire pits, almost tripping over one along the way. The longhouse smelled of frying fish and burning wood, the smoke wafting into her face making her eyes water. On each side of the hall, there were small, individual living spaces, family quarters, with cots made of straw and wood, and various personal belongings adorning the walls, giving it a homey feel.

She marveled at the size of the longhouse; from her rough estimation, it was large enough to accommodate at least fifteen to twenty families. It was no longer common for her people to live in communal housing, the tradition long since abandoned for more private, European-style quarters. Her village had converted to cabins many years before when Presbyterian missionaries came through the area and introduced her people to the new style of housing, but she appreciated the common heritage, and this village's fervent desire to maintain it.

When the woman's sobs grew louder, Dellis picked up her pace, searching diligently for the source. Suddenly, her path was blocked by something heavy; cloaked in darkness, Dellis kicked it several times trying to discern what it was, but to no avail. Reaching up, she uncovered one of the skylights, allowing a bright, ethereal beam to illuminate the ground with its heavenly light. At her feet lay the unclothed bodies of three Mohawk women, all of them scalped, their faces unrecognizable from the swollen, discolored tissues.

"Oh my God." She gasped, putting a hand to her mouth. When Dellis looked over her shoulder, Alexei was standing in the doorway to the longhouse speaking with one of the women. "Alexei, come quickly." With shaking hands, she waved him over. "It wasn't the first time she'd seen scalped corpses, it was part of her culture and all too common, but the gruesomeness still managed to take her breath away.

"What is it?" Alexei ran up behind her, then stopped abruptly, his eyes fixed on the corpses.

"Who would do this?" Dellis asked, a tremble in her voice.

"I don't know," Alexei replied, looking around.

Dellis got down on her knees and examined the bodies quickly, looking for other tell-tale wounds, anything to help identify their attackers. Gently, she closed the eyes of one of the women, the dark empty gaze sending chills down Dellis's spine.

"Alexei, why did they leave them like this? Why aren't they buried?" she asked, looking up at her cousin.

Alexei hesitated, rubbing his neck and looking around, trying to appear inconspicuous, though it was a wasted effort—he was hiding something.

"Alexei, tell me." Dellis persisted, refusing to let him circumvent the truth.

Her cousin took a deep breath, huffing it out loudly with annoyance. Alexei didn't like being questioned or told what to do, but that was his problem, she wanted answers. "The village was attacked while all the men were gone. There were only women and children here when the raid took place."

Her heart skipped a beat, then started again with a rapid, abnormal rhythm that mimicked her fear and anticipation. "Alexei, this isn't a coincidence. Don't deny it. I'm no fool."

"Dellis…" Before he could say another word, the sobbing she heard earlier started anew. Getting up, Dellis walked all the way to the end of the house, where she found the source: an elderly woman clutching the body of a dead woman. Crouching down, Dellis gently touched the elderly woman on the shoulder, trying to get her attention. "I'm a healer. May I look at her?"

The woman released the body, though her cries continued. Dellis rolled the corpse over, inspecting the wounds. This one was also scalped, with a knife wound in her breast, and her clothing torn, exposing her upper torso.

"I'm very sorry for your loss," she said, taking the woman's hand and giving it a gentle squeeze. Dellis understood the depths of the woman's grief. Not two years before, Dellis had held the body of her father, a bullet wound in his back, as his murderers rode away, their red coats and gold adornments flashing in the sunlight. She would never forget that feeling—not ever.

"Alexei, we need to find out who did this," Dellis said, looking over her shoulder at her cousin. "This is twice now in a matter of days that someone has targeted Mohawks. It too much like what happened to our village."

"Dellis, you're jumping to conclusions based on your own fears. There are no signs that Redcoats did this, none at all. It looks like a tribal attack, probably retribution. The Mohawk have been rather provocative lately; especially Joseph Brant with his British rhetoric trying to stoke up discontent." He gave her a look of warning then walked to the door. "I need to find Joseph, he and the men should be here by now."

Racing to her feet, Dellis stopped Alexei before he could get away. "It's too much of a coincidence; don't you see that? This is a setup. Someone wants us to believe it's nothing more than another inner tribal fight." But he ignored her just as everyone else did when she asked the difficult questions. "Fine, disregard me, but I'm going to do my own investigating." Dellis pushed past him through the door, determined to get to the bottom of the mystery. Her cousin could deny the similarities, but she refused to be a party to his calculated ignorance.

She rushed through the village, back to the stockade, where the guard stood on post as he did earlier. Addressing him again, she asked, "Did anyone see who did this?"

He shook his head. "I was scouting the area, and when I returned, I heard screaming coming from the village, our guards that stayed behind were all dead. The thieves took our gunpowder and some of our livestock, and four of our women were gone."

"Hostages?"

He nodded again, his dark eyes betraying no emotion.

"Was it another tribe? A mourning ritual?" Dellis asked, referring to the Iroquois practice of taking enemies or members of other tribes to replace lost loved ones.

"No, they were white men. That's what the women said."

Her heart fluttered in her chest, like a bird trapped in a cage. "Did they belong to the Great Father, King George?" Alexei was right, there hadn't been a Royal regiment or militia in the area since the colonists had chased Guy Johnson, the new superintendent of Northern Indian Affairs, and John Butler, a local Loyalist, to Canada. It would be difficult for Redcoats to travel the area unnoticed but it wouldn't for a private militia. It had to be the British. This was exactly their style. She knew it all too well.

"They were not the Great Father's men. They were colonists; some of the women recognized their coats."

"You must be mistaken." It wasn't possible. No, he had to be wrong.

The guard shook his head. "I'm not. They were colonists."

It didn't make any sense. Dellis had heard of colonists killing natives but only after a skirmish or some provoked act. This was premeditated.

Scalping women and stealing supplies was too specific, and whoever did this waited for the perfect time to take on a Mohawk village—while the men were away hunting. They knew exactly what they were doing.

"Dellis?"

Recognizing the sweet-sounding female voice, Dellis turned around quickly and greeted her cousin. "*Shekoli* Skenandoa, what are you doing here?"

The two women embraced lovingly, then pulled back at arm's length. She was so pretty; she reminded Dellis of her grandmother. They both had the same wide, deep-set eyes, high cheekbones, and a stubborn chin. Skenandoa styled her long, jet-black hair in two large, silky braids that hung on both sides of her face. She wore a doe-skin dress with leggings and a brightly-colored blanket wrapped around her shoulders to protect against the autumn wind. They'd grown up close; Shenandoa's father was Dellis's mother's brother. When the girl's parents died of smallpox, Dellis's mother took care of Skenandoa, and they grew up as close as any two sisters could be.

"I came with Grandfather for the council," Skenandoa replied.

In the distance, Dellis could see her grandfather's unmistakable figure and their village sachem, Rail Splitter, walking together. A crowd was forming around them; the council was about to begin.

"Come with me; I want to show you something." Skenandoa tugged Dellis's arm, leading her towards the woods.

"I need to listen to the council."

Dellis tried to direct her cousin back toward the village, but she persisted. "This is more interesting, I promise. That's just old men blustering like the wind and puffing up like big clouds."

Dellis snickered at her cousin's accurate, though impolite, description of the council meeting. "What did you find?"

"I found tracks in the woods. From what I can tell, there were at least five men, all of them on horseback. They rode off towards the river, but they stopped there." Skenandoa pointed at the forest, towards the eastern bank of the Schoharie River. "They crossed and there and then continued north. I didn't follow them any farther. I couldn't find any tracks showing their approach."

She was a notoriously good tracker. If she couldn't determine where the men went, then no one could. Someone had to have seen them; maybe the women of the village knew something. Dellis excused herself and went back into the longhouse where the woman she had met earlier was still holding the corpse. "I'd like to help figure out who did this, but I need to ask you a few questions. Do you remember what any of the men looked like? Even the smallest bit of information would be helpful."

The woman sniffed a few times then nodded. "He was tall, dark hair, wearing a blue cloak."

"Were they the Great Father's men?" Dellis asked. They had to be King's men. She could feel it in her gut. The fact that they weren't wearing redcoats was irrelevant. This was all a ruse, a cover up to hide their misdeeds.

The woman shook her head. "No, they had braves with them."

"Do you know who they were?"

"They were our brothers, Oneidas."

Dellis's heart skipped a beat. It was impossible; there hadn't been inner-confederacy fighting of this type in years. No, it couldn't be right.

"Are you sure?" she asked, praying it wasn't true.

The woman nodded again. Getting up quickly, Dellis dusted her hands off on her skirt and ran outside to find her cousin. He needed to hear this now, before the council started.

But she was too late, the tribal chiefs already commencing the meeting. Alexei stood back, watching her grandfather speak with the Mohawk chief, while Rail Splitter waited nearby, ready to provide counsel. Anytime there were negotiations between warrior chiefs it was a delicate matter. She was too far away to hear what they were saying, but from their hand gestures and the look on her grandfather's face, she could tell it wasn't going well. So, her people had been implicated in the event; no wonder the guard was so hostile. They were under suspicion.

Dellis walked up to Alexei and elbowed him. "I can't hear what they're saying. I'm getting closer."

Alexei stopped her mid-stride. "Dellis, stay here. I'll go."

She watched as Alexei walked through the crowd, taking his place next to her grandfather, his distinguishing height making him easily visible. It was frustrating to have to stand back and wait while her grandfather and cousin negotiated. She was, after all, a clan matron now that her mother and grandmother were dead, and this gave her the right to be involved in negotiations and advise the chiefs of her clan. But because of her age and lack of experience, her grandfather forbade her to take part, wanting her to listen and learn. She hated how everyone wanted her to wait until she was older and had more experience. How did one get more experience without experience?

When the meeting was over, Dellis raced to Alexei, anxious to hear the details. "What did the Mohawks say?"

"They told us to leave. Their chief said if our Oneida brothers are going to side with the colonists, then the Confederacy is as good as finished."

"But it's not possible, we're not siding with the colonists. We would never go against the Confederacy. This is all a misunderstanding. It has to be."

Alexei walked past her, his strides so quick she had to run to keep pace with him.

"What about the hostages, Alexei?"

"Joseph pledged to find them, as an act of goodwill, to prove we are innocent. We need to get started as soon as possible."

"Alexei, would you calm down?" Dellis grabbed his arm, forcing him to stop. From the look on his face, he was wound up and ready for a fight, just like a provoked rattler. "Think about this whole situation for a minute. It. Doesn't. Make. Sense. There is more to this story. Someone is playing us false, and we're walking right into their hands."

"Well, there's one way to figure it out, and that's by finding the men that did this, and that's what I intend to do." Her cousin towered over her, his icy blue eyes fierce, his jaw set.

"Fine." Dellis stepped out of his way, letting him pass.

"I have no doubt there's a Tory militia behind this. They're trying to make us look guilty," Alexei muttered under his breath as he walked back to his horse and mounted up.

"*Us?* What do you mean *us?*" Dellis asked, looking up at him. "Are you referring to our tribe or the Rebels?"

She knew her cousin had colonist sympathies; lately, he and Patrick had been meeting with the colonel at Fort Stanwix separate from her tribe. On several occasions, she'd heard him spouting off at her grandfather, encouraging him to comply with the Rebel leaders and form a treaty.

"Dellis, mind your own," he said, turning his horse away from her and riding towards her grandfather and the rest of the warriors.

Alexei could be so thickheaded, and there was no reasoning with him when he acted like this. At least her grandfather would go with him; his cool head prevailed when Alexei blustered like a hot summer wind. The rest of the Oneida warriors gathered around on horseback, her grandfather among them.

Dellis walked over to him and patted his horse, then gently tugged on his legging. "*Lakso'tha'*, Grandfather?"

"Dellis, what are you doing here?" Joseph asked, looking down at her.

She could see lines of concern creased in his ancient brow, his long, salt-and-pepper hair hanging in his face adorned with brightly colored feathers and beads. "I came with Alexei. We were supposed to ride on to the other village after the council."

"You should go home. There's nothing left to be done. Our brothers told us that our help is not wanted."

The edge in his voice was indicative of how deeply concerned he was by the whole event. It would be devastating for their tribe if they couldn't prove their innocence. "Grandfather, you don't believe any of our people did this, do you?"

"No, I don't, but our brothers do, and that's what matters. We must prove our innocence." His black eyes were serious, the lines of age etched in his ruddy, leathery skin growing deeper with worry. He wore his finest attire: His light beige, buckskin tunic, decorated with rows of purple and white beads sewn in an alternating pattern. Around his neck, he wore the metal gorget given to him by the British Military for service during the Seven Years War, and on each of his wrists, he wore beautiful silver bracelets, gifts from neighboring tribes.

She could feel the smooth fabric of his buckskin leggings under her fingertips as she touched his leg again. "Do you think the colonists at the fort had anything to do with this?"

"No." He shook his head, looking away. She followed his gaze toward the horizon where the sun had just dipped below, bringing with it the familiar purples and blues of autumn's twilight. "We've been scouting their activities for a long time. Something this serious wouldn't have gone unnoticed by our men."

"You think this will give the Mohawk more reasons to side with the British, don't you?"

He didn't respond, his silence confirming what she feared. "I won't keep you any longer, Grandfather. You have much to do."

If anyone could get to the bottom of the mystery, it was her grandfather. Dellis prayed the women were found alive, but in her heart, she knew it wouldn't be so. This kind of barbarity knew no boundaries or chivalry towards women. She'd been a victim of it before.

Chapter Five

"Beautiful."

So beautiful. Like a curse or enchantment, her hauntingly dark eyes and luxurious black hair, a temptation he couldn't resist—a power so adept it held him in its thrall for a lifetime. Taking her long, silky tresses in hand, he held them to his nose, feeling his body respond. She smelled of lilacs mixed with sunshine on a spring morning, evoking a memory so pleasant he trembled with recollection.

Beautiful. Lily.

"Don't cry." He grazed the woman's cheek with the backs of his fingers, wiping her tears away with one gentle swipe. "This is not your fault, my dear. You are innocent, so perfectly innocent."

She looked up at him, her black eyes wide like a frightened doe facing its adversary before the kill.

"I'm sure they will come for you. One so lovely will be missed. But, it will be too late if you don't do as I say." Grabbing the front of her buckskin tunic with both of his hands, he rendered the fabric in two with one hard tug, exposing her bare skin to the elements. A ripple of goosebumps traveled down her dark, flawless skin, making his hands ache to reach out and touch her softness. She screamed frantically, shrinking away when he reached for her.

"Do you want to end up like the others?" he yelled, pointing towards the woods. "Do you?"

Her eyes followed the direction of his finger to the pile of fresh corpses, naked, scalped, and discarded haphazardly in the grass. "No, please." She shook her head, tears streaming down her cheeks, leaving behind fresh tracks.

He leaned in, nuzzling her neck, rubbing her scent all over his face. Again, he could smell sunlight and her own heady, musky scent, making him want her all the more. Greedily, he lapped up a tear that trailed down to her chin, swirling it in his mouth. *Fear tastes good.* It was tangible, visceral; he could feel it deep in his gut, making him anxious, aroused, and eager to possess her.

"Lily," he whispered into her ear, then lapped at her tiny, perfect lobe.

Yes, Lily. He closed his eyes, imagining dark eyes and long, jet-black tresses piled on top of her head exposing that elegant, swan-like neck—the one he loved to kiss. For too long he had forbidden himself the indulgence of remembering her. Much too long.

Opening his eyes, he looked down at his captive, taking in her unique, natural beauty. "I don't want to hurt you. I didn't want to hurt them, but they wouldn't do as they were told. But you will to save your friends, won't you?"

She nodded.

He followed her gaze to the three women tied to the tree as they looked on in terror.

The fear in his captive's eyes was more than he could bear. He was close, on the verge, but restraint was such sweet torture. Forcing the woman to her knees, he ran his hand down her cheek, tipping her chin up so she could see his erect manhood through the fabric of his breeches. He waited, his body aching for her to please him, and he motioned with his hand for her to begin.

Looking up, she hesitated, the anticipation like a slow death. Tracing her lips, he parted them, slowly inserting his finger into her mouth, groaning when her wet warmth closed around it.

"Yes." He gasped, closing his eyes, her lips and tongue gently toying with him. "I like that."

The haze of pleasure suddenly transformed into gut-wrenching pain. The woman bit down on his finger, her eyes focused on him, a smile turning up the corners of her lips. With a crack of bone a howl tore from his lips, he tried to pull his hand away, but she clamped down harder, blood running down her lips and chin in crimson streaks. He slapped her cheek with enough force to send her head whipping to the side, freeing his tortured finger. Removing his neckerchief, he wrapped his hand, blood pumping from the wound, the tip of his finger dangling by a small bit of flesh. She spat on him with a satisfied grin, leaving a bloody stain on his snowy white shirt, then sat back on her haunches, watching him.

"Whore!" he yelled, slapping her again, sending her sprawling in the dirt.

When she tried to get up, he grabbed her ankle, dragging her back towards him. The woman fought to get away, her hands clawing at the ground, her fingers leaving long, deep tracks in the dirt. When she was beneath him, he pinned her down with his body weight, straddling her hips.

Grabbing a large tuft of her hair, he jerked her head back and leaned in, bringing his lips close to her ear. "You should not have done that. She wouldn't have." He hissed, feeling his inner-beast unleash. "Now, I no longer have a use for you." He gestured towards his flaccid manhood, his passion for her quelled.

She swallowed then met his gaze, obstinately showing no fear.

"I know you're trying to be brave. You're a good squaw of the Flint, the need for you to fight back is innate. These forests belonged to your forefathers, and their spirits are always near." He pointed to the trees, then the sky, her eyes following. "You think they'll protect you, but they won't. Nothing will save you now, and I get to claim your spirit and your scalp for my wall."

Reaching into his pocket, he pulled out his dagger, holding it in her face so she could see it. "What do you think of this? You'll do as you're told now, won't you? This is all you understand, isn't it? The blade? The gun? War? That's the only language you savages speak, isn't it?"

He ran the metal blade across her forehead then down her cheek, letting her feel the cold steel against her flesh. He wanted her to know the method of her death intimately, feel its strength. When she screamed and tried to pull away, he yanked her hair, forcing her head back. *One must look their kill in the eyes.*

"Please, let me go." She begged, a solitary tear rolling from the corner of her eye into her hairline, disappearing in a mass of silky, black locks. "I'll do as you say."

She looked beautiful and submissive beneath him, his doe smothered and ready for the kill—now to finish her off. With questing hands, he caressed her back, feeling its smoothness, relishing every curve of her lithe frame. Her struggles brought on a fresh surge of lust, the feel of her buttocks moving between his thighs, sweet torture. Leaning forward, he whispered in her ear, "It's too late for you."

Gently, he placed one last kiss on her earlobe, tasting the salty tear that rolled there.

"Goodbye, my Lily."

The woman shrieked as he pulled back her hair, exposing her high forehead, and with expert precision, he brought the blade down, cutting a circle at the crown of her head, blood trickling from the wound. The color crimson brought with it a rush of excitement, his heart thundering in his chest wildly, while a symphony played in his ears, drowning out her frantic screams. Then quick as a flash, he tugged her hair, ripping the scalp away from the layers of connective tissue beneath, exposing the bone. Fixing his stance, he brought the blade down to the base of her skull, severing what flesh was still connected with one easy slice. She shrieked, writhing in pain, her arms and legs flailing as she landed, face down, in the dirt.

"Shall we try this again?" he yelled, holding up his prize, blood and gore dripping from the bit of flesh.

Throwing the scalp down on the ground, he walked past the screaming, discarded woman towards the other three. He motioned to one of his men. "Bring me another."

He was high from it, light-headed and powerful and so incredibly aroused his cock ached and pulsed against the confines of his breeches, release painfully on the brink.

The soldier untied one of the women and threw her at the feet of his superior. "What do you want me to do with the bodies, Major DeLancie?"

"Not to worry, I have a plan for them when I'm finished."

Gently, he touched the woman's chin, lifting it so he could look into her ebony eyes. Yes, she would do nicely. "You will do what I say, won't you?"

She nodded, her eyes cast down submissively.

"Ahh… the greatest victory is one that requires no battle."

Chapter Six

Damn! Even with a waistcoat, overcoat, and cloak, he was still freezing! *Why couldn't I be assigned this mission in the summer?* He would rather sweat it out in the heat and humidity than face another notoriously long winter on the frontier. During his five years of serving at Fort Niagara, he'd seen his share of blackened fingers and toes from frostbite and men freezing to death in their sleep. Not two years before, he almost died from falling into a river while on patrol. Afterward, he suffered through weeks of a lung infection that nearly finished off what Mother Nature started with a vengeance. Since then, he had an almost phobic aversion to being cold.

Now, after three days of travel, John was tired, saddle sore, and he could go for a honey pot, a cup of tea, and a shot of whiskey. Simple wants. Yes, the prospect of a cozy bed and someone in it with him evoked warm thoughts, though the chance of it happening was highly unlikely. When in doubt, a good bottle of scotch would do the trick, and hopefully, The Thistle Tavern would have some on hand. He could drink himself into a good night's sleep and get up early in the morning to head out to Fort Stanwix for some reconnaissance.

The woods were ominously quiet, save the sounds of Viceroy's hooves rhythmically beating on the dirt. John knew this forest all too well. Its mystical beauty in the daytime turned into a dangerous and forbidding labyrinth in the dark. If one managed not to get lost, then they faced an even greater adversary in the native tribes that called the forest their home. Travelers were known to disappear into the woods, some of them captured, never to return again, and others murdered for trespassing on native, sacred lands. Giving his horse a gentle kick, he sped up, trying not to tempt the fates or awaken the spirits that lurked in the trees.

John passed through the town of German Flats and continued west until he reached the very edge of the little hamlet. The town was dark, not even a street lantern still lit, only the moon, brilliant and full in the sky, to help him find his way. When he reached The Thistle Tavern, it, too, was dark, but he could see that it was a large, white, Dutch-style house, two-stories high and three-windows wide. It looked to be a bit run-down and mundane, but still rather grand for such an isolated, rustic area.

Just a few feet behind the tavern was a stable, and next to it, a small storage building. The stable was immaculate inside with eight stalls, four already occupied, one of them inhabited by an angry stallion that was already fussing from their presence. John dismounted and led Viceroy to one of the empty stalls, grateful that they had a secure place to leave his precious mount. Quickly, he unpacked his belongings and removed Viceroy's saddle, hanging it on a metal hook. Removing his gloves, he rubbed his hands together to warm them while he looked around for a brush and some food for his horse.

The rhythmic pounding of hooves beating on the ground drew his attention as a horse and rider sped into the barn as fast as lightning. John's soldier's instincts taking over, he backed into the stall and pulled out his pistol. Who would be coming in this late in the evening? Another traveler? Highly unlikely; it was surely after midnight. But to his surprise, it was a woman, her tall, lithe form outlined by the moon's light. Concealed in shadows, he put his gun back in its holster, moving a little closer to investigate.

She nimbly jumped down from her horse and led it to the first stall. With a sweet feminine sigh, the woman removed her bonnet and great cloak, depositing them on the ground. Hypnotized, he watched as she pulled the pins from her hair, a silken cascade of dark tresses falling down her back in waves. When she started to untie the laces of her bodice he stiffened, the prospect of seeing this unknown woman undress in her barn like some glorious fantasy. *Is she real or am I dreaming? Did I fall asleep on my horse during the long journey?*

John mentally scolded himself for playing the voyeur. As a gentleman, he should make his presence known, yet he was too intrigued, his curiosity piqued. Who was she and what would possess her to disrobe in a barn? Like Actaeon glimpsing Artemis bathing in the woods, he watched as she removed her bodice and skirt. She let out another sigh as she ran her hands over her ribs, rubbing them slowly, soothing herself. Nimbly, she reached around and unlaced her stays, then removed her petticoat, letting them both fall to the ground in a pile of fabric. Stretching her arms high above her head, he could see the outline of her long, slender figure and the curve of her full breasts through the gauzy fabric of her shift.

How he would've loved to let the fantasy play out to completion, but if he remembered the myth correctly, Actaeon found himself turned into a stag once discovered. Not the outcome he anticipated, but she was destined to be upset with him once he made his presence known. No matter what he did now, he was doomed to look like a blackguard who came to ravish her in the night.

An officer and a gentleman, John. Such were the words of Howe, repetitively playing in his mind, reminding him of his duty.

Facing his fate, John coughed gently, then stepped out of the stall. The woman froze abruptly, her eyes focused in his direction, searching the darkness. The next thing he knew, he was staring down the barrel of her pistol, the click of the hammer being pulled to full cock, a warning of her intent.

Grabbing the bodice of her dress from the ground, the woman held it to her chest, trying to shield herself. "Show yourself," she yelled, waving the pistol, directing him towards the moonlight.

"Don't shoot." John held up his hands so she could see them, hoping to diminish her fears, but instead she aimed the pistol at his face and fingered the trigger. "Please, put the gun down, I didn't mean to startle you."

Her chest heaved under the fabric of her bodice, her body visibly trembling, yet her hand on the pistol didn't waver in the slightest. She was terrified, but still in control. *Intriguing.*

"I didn't intend to frighten you." He added, taking a step closer so he could get a better look at his would-be assailant. "I mean you no harm."

"Really? My experience with King's men has taught me different." She countered. He noticed the tinge of haughtiness in her voice, another indication of a willful spirit. "Are you a Regular?"

"I'm not a soldier." The lie rolled off his tongue with expert precision—a good start to his mission. "But I'm English." He added, stepping towards her. Clearly, his more proper accent had not gone unnoticed. *Headstrong and observant, too?*

"Then what are you doing sneaking around my stables? If you're not a Redcoat, then what are you? A thief, or just a randy fellow looking for someone to warm your bed? I do have a stallion. He could take you for a row, though I'm sure you wouldn't be walking quite so well after that, English."

Stifling a laugh, John replied, "Truly, I'm not a Redcoat, my name is Captain John Anderson, I'm a merchant and new this area. My ship is in port at Oswego. I believe the owners of The Thistle are expecting me."

Still aiming the pistol at him, she stepped forward, their eyes meeting for the first time in the moonlight. "Do you make it a habit of sneaking up on solitary women in the dark without announcing yourself, Captain?"

This time he couldn't hold back a laugh. "Not usually. Although I have to admit, I don't often find women undressing in a stable this late in the evening on such a bloody cold night."

As he moved closer, John could see the woman had lovely, high cheekbones. Her large, dark eyes were regarding him with distrust, her strong jaw set in defiance. The low neckline of her shift accentuated her elegant, long neck and broad shoulders. Noticing the path of his gaze, she pulled the fabric of her bodice against her breasts, once again trying to shield herself.

"Put the gun down, I won't hurt you," he said, with command.

She snorted, aiming the pistol at his heart, only a few feet separating him from the barrel. "I have one shot here that says you won't, that's for sure."

The woman was being downright unreasonable. Her folly had gone on long enough to try the patience of a saint, his own long since reached its limits. "Put the gun down, Miss."

When he stretched out his hand to her, motioning for the pistol, she shook her head in silent warning.

Frustration set in, giving an edge to his voice. "Shoot me then. But if you're bloody well going to do it, at least hold the pistol with both hands— the kickback is liable to throw your aim off. You'll shoot the horse and not me, and he isn't the one you're angry with."

To his surprise, the woman dropped her bodice and grasped the pistol with both hands. His anger waned, supplanted by humor. John chuckled to himself. Wow, she was tenacious and not in the least intimidated by him. With both her hands holding the weapon, her large breasts pressed together at the top of her chemise, begging for him to cast a glance. What a delicious vision she made in the moonlight, her long tresses hanging down to her shoulders, the outline of her body fully exposed through the thin, diaphanous fabric. Yes, he was most definitely living out a fantasy, but with conviction, he knew wasn't going to end the way he desired.

The woman smiled, cognizant of his gaze, yet she made no move to cover herself. Surprisingly, she wasn't provoked by his ungentlemanly behavior. *Yes, she is intriguing indeed.* "What are you doing hiding in my barn?"

"Truly, I didn't mean to startle you. I am who I claim to be. My men should already have arrived. Please, put the gun down."

John held his hands up again, trying to put her mind at ease. She hesitated for a moment, eyeing him suspiciously, then un-cocked the pistol and lowered it. Though he hated to admit it to himself, he breathed a sigh of relief watching her put it back in the holster. *Bloody coward.*

Feeling it was the only chivalrous thing to do, John leaned down and picked up her bodice, handing it to her. "I'm very sorry."

The woman snatched it back, but made no attempt to shield herself—the damage already done. "You should be. I'd send you and your men packing if I hadn't already accepted the money you paid. Now, if you will excuse me, I'll meet you inside, and we'll discuss your living arrangements while staying at my tavern."

Attempting to relieve the tension of the last few moments, he removed his hat and bowed. "Your servant."

She snorted, walking past him, aloof to his gallant gesture. Putting his hat back on, John suddenly felt like ill-mannered reprobate for his behavior. Ashamed, he uncharacteristically stumbled over his words, trying to find a way to make amends, "Madam, I ahh… well… Truly, there's no need for us to address this tonight. I can discuss the arrangements with your husband tomorrow morning when I formally apologize for showing up so late and frightening his wife."

Turning her back to him, she picked up her cloak from the ground and wrapped it around herself, then carried her clothes to the little storage shed next to the barn. He watched as she stomped up the back stairs and opened the back door to the tavern.

"For your information, I am the owner, I don't have a husband, and we will discuss this tonight. Now care for *our* horses, and meet me in the dining room when you finish." With that, she slammed the door shut, the whole house shaking from the force of her anger.

Chapter Seven

What kind of man would sneak up on her and watch while she undressed? Clearly, not a gentleman. *Impudent brute!* He could stay the night, but that was it; he and his men would have to find another place to bed and board. Yes, she needed the money, but not at the expense of her person. *What a cad.* She'd changed in her barn hundreds of times, and never had someone snuck up on her and watched. He'd obviously been standing there for several minutes, and then he had the audacity to leer at her once caught.

Dellis's hands shook as she tied the laces of her bodice. The dress she wore earlier was absolutely filthy and covered in blood; not to mention it rained during part of her journey. When she arrived home, she was soaked all the way down to her stays and refused to traipse mud through her clean kitchen. And her soiled clothing was sure to leave a mess on her linen, so she'd opted to change outside, which she'd done hundreds of times. *Damn.* She should have been more careful and brought an apron with her. It would take her hours to clean the blood and stains out of her dress, and sadly, it was one of only three she owned.

Looking herself over in the mirror, Dellis took a couple of deep breaths, trying to steady her nerves. Quickly, she pinned her hair up at the nape and tucked a white kerchief in the bodice of her muted, blue, wool dress, hoping to deter his eyes from further ogling her person.

When she walked into the kitchen, it was dark with only two small tallow candles lit, the kitchen fire reduced to smoldering embers. Her bartender, Thomas, was asleep, peacefully snoring with his head resting on the table. Dellis grabbed a tray and some mugs from the cupboard, slamming the door shut.

What was she paying him for?

"I'm awake," he yelled, his head flying up from the table like a startled cat. Still half asleep, Thomas looked around, his eyes glazed over from a night of sharing rounds with the customers.

Smothering a laugh, Dellis placed the mugs on the table next to him. Thomas was her father's best friend and as dear to her as any family member could be. When her father died, it was Thomas's idea to turn The Thistle into a tavern, and since then they'd worked together, sharing responsibilities to keep it running smoothly. It was his duty to close the tavern down for the night, which meant he often used it as an excuse to drink himself to sleep, her table his makeshift bed.

"Thomas, do we have any cider?"

"Aye, we do. I'll get you some." Rubbing his eyes, Thomas got up, walked through the archway that connected the kitchen to the bar, and searched under the counter. "Why are you still awake?"

Excellent question. She was tired and weary, but better to get this done now than let it wait. She would give her lodger his money back and send him and his men on their way. "My lodger is supposed to meet me in the dining room. I'm just waiting for him."

"He's sitting near the fireplace." Thomas pointed to the corner next to the large, stone fireplace, where the man sat with his back to them. "Your eyes aren't too good are they?"

"It's been a rather long evening." An understatement if she'd ever made one.

Grabbing the jug, Dellis walked through the bar into the dining room, her ire rising with each step. The man deserved a potent earful for his behavior earlier, and she was more than ready to oblige. As she approached the table, he stood up, rather abruptly, removed his black cocked hat, and bowed to her again. Taken aback, she stopped dead in her tracks. Rarely, if ever, did a man bow to her, and certainly not twice in one night. Still, his sudden rash of politeness wasn't going to circumvent the well-deserved tongue lashing she was about to deliver.

"Captain John Anderson at your service, Miss."

When he looked up, there was a sparkle in his sapphire blue eyes and an irresistible dimple in his right cheek. In the soft glow of candlelight, she could see he was incredibly handsome. There was something boyish and youthful about his face, with his large, close-set, almond-shaped eyes and high cheekbones. A day's worth of stubble graced his strong jaw, giving his full lips a sensuous quality. He was a head taller than her and muscular in build, his lean frame and broad shoulders accentuated by the expert cut of his finely worsted navy suit.

The polite thing to do would be to offer her hand, but she had no intention of playing society's games. She didn't like to be touched and certainly not by a stranger who just watched her undress, courtly ways be damned.

The captain stood up, holding his hat in his hands. "Is there something amiss?" he asked, grinning at her, little lines forming at the corners of his eyes. The smooth baritone of his voice sent shivers down her spine. Yes, even his voice was handsome.

"Nothing is wrong." Dellis snapped, trying to ignore the butterflies that danced in her stomach. She was no stranger to attraction, but there was an allure about him, like a magnet drawing everything in the room towards him, including her.

Avoiding his gaze, Dellis sidestepped him, placing the tray on the table. "I hope you don't mind cider?"

"That will be fine, though I have to admit, I do prefer tea." He winked at her playfully.

Dellis resisted the urge to roll her eyes; it would take more than a wink and a smile to charm her. "Of course you do, Captain." She countered. "How very British of you."

With his elegant clothing and courtly ways, he was obviously cultured, with a predilection for English habits. *A Redcoat, no, but a Tory, perhaps?*

"As you so astutely pointed out earlier, I'm English. But technically, so are you." Their eyes met briefly, an arrogant cock in his brow as if he was waiting for her to take the bait. He didn't wait for her to answer but threw down a challenge instead. "Is it a crime to drink tea?"

The man was fishing around for her loyalties, and she had no problem setting him straight, no matter how handsome he was. She wasn't that easily smitten. "I'm pretty sure the events in Boston settled both of those issues for good. His Majesty and the East India Trading Company can keep their tea caddies to themselves or find them in the bottom of the harbor. And just a word of advice, I wouldn't go around referring to the locals as British. You're likely to get yourself in a bit of trouble... maybe even shot."

He laughed, loud and hearty. "Point taken. Though I fear there may be no hope for me, at least, where the tea is concerned. You won't hold that against me, will you?" He winked at her again, this time, making her heart race.

When he pulled the chair out for her, Dellis ignored his polite gesture and sat down across the table from him, passively asserting her control. She needed to put some distance between the two of them, once again feeling herself falling victim to his charming thrall. *No one ever pulled out chairs for her.* "Please sit, Captain, and we can discuss the terms of your lodging."

Placing his hat on the table, he took a seat, crossing one of his long legs over the other. She couldn't help but notice how fine his clothing was, from his black felt hat to his snowy white, linen shirt and shiny leather boots. No detail missed, he was apparently a man of means and took pride in showing it.

"I'm afraid you have me at a disadvantage, Miss. I didn't hear your name."

"It's Dellis McKesson," she replied, pouring cider into two pewter tankards, then handing one to him.

"Your name is McKesson?" he repeated, sounding a bit confused.

"Yes, is there a problem?"

He hesitated for a moment, then shook his head, as if he was trying to wake himself up, a yawn escaping his lips. "No, forgive me, please. It's been a long journey."

Dellis noticed how his gaze remained surprisingly above her décolletage, almost too focused on her face. Apparently, behaving like a gentleman was required only when there was candlelight.

"Miss McKesson, I still feel the need to apologize for earlier."

She blushed at the mention of their clandestine meeting in the dark. So, it was just as awkward for him as it was for her. Hiding her red face in the rim of her cup, she countered. "Well, it was definitely not the way to make a first impression with a lady."

"Agreed, though, I was caught off guard. As I said earlier, I've never encountered a lady undressing in her stable before. You must admit, it's rather odd."

Reining in her temper, she replied, "Still, a gentleman would have turned his back and waited till the lady finished, or at least averted his gaze when confronted—you did neither."

He nodded his head in agreement. "You are correct, and I should've done so. I apologize. Forgive me."

She looked up at him in surprise. Never had she heard a man apologize with such ease and candor—she almost felt sorry for calling him out. *Almost*. "Why don't we start over from here, Captain, and let what's in the past remain there? I'm afraid the events of the evening don't reflect well on either of us."

"Perfect." He smiled, taking her hand in his own, and kissed the top of it. At first contact of his lips on her skin, she blinked, little fractals of light exploding through her body, emanating warmth all the way to her core.

"I'm Captain John Anderson, and the pleasure is all mine."

"It's very nice to meet you." She nodded, trying to pull her hand away, but he held fast, his grip strong but gentle. Her hand noticeably trembled in his. He looked up at her, one of his eyebrows cocking in question. "Now that the pleasantries are finished, Captain, shall we get down to business?"

"Absolutely," he replied, releasing her hand.

Breathing an audible sigh of relief, she pulled her hand away, holding it protectively against her chest. She didn't like to be touched, especially by men. "Do you know how long you will require rooms?"

Thankfully, he disregarded her *faux pas* and continued on with their conversation. "I would say a month, for now. It all depends on how quickly I can sell what I have. My boat is currently docked in Oswego, and my next shipment is due in port sometime next month. When I get word of its arrival, I'll be moving on. As you can imagine, the winter does present problems in my business. I have to move quickly while the weather permits."

"That will be fine, and to put your mind at ease, you'll be able to sell your goods without trouble. It's hard to get supplies so far from the city, especially at this time of year. And I'm more than willing to assist you with that."

"Thank you, that would be most helpful. And for your information, I'll sell to anyone who has the means to pay. I have no affiliations or prejudices that prevent me from doing business," the Captain added, crossing his arms over his chest, the seams of his jacket threatening to burst from the taut muscles flexing underneath.

Dellis couldn't help but smile, the man was a true merchant, concerned only with his pocketbook and not who filled it. She could use that to her advantage. "I assume you and your men need to eat. If you have access to food, I would be grateful if you would be willing to sell to me first. We could deduct it from your rent. As I said, supplies are difficult to get this time of year. But I fear if you choose not to help, then you may be eating shoe leather by lunchtime tomorrow, as I'll have to start rationing. This tavern is all I have by way of supporting myself above poverty, and my funds are limited at the moment."

Dellis knew she was being bold, but she was also being honest about her sorry state of affairs. If he and his men were going to be staying in her tavern for long, it would affect them, too. Better to be upfront and circumvent any misunderstandings.

Suddenly, that irresistible dimple appeared in his left cheek, slowly evolving into a lazy, lopsided grin. "I could arrange that, provided that you allow me my tea."

"So now we're negotiating? This is my tavern," she replied, feigning outrage.

"Forgive me this one indulgence. I'll supply the tea, and only enough for myself—or can't your Rebel sentiments tolerate such a blatantly British habit?"

He was teasing, she could see it in his eyes, but once again he was fishing for her loyalties. "I'm half Oneida; my father and my uncles were both in the Royal Navy; Thomas, my bartender, is a Rebel; and my aunt is Russian. All are welcome at The Thistle, even your tea. To that point, I actually would like some—it's been awhile."

"Thank you for making this one concession on my behalf," he replied with mock gratitude.

A long, curly lock of his hair fell into his eyes, Dellis watched as he smoothed it back behind his ear. Now that they were easily conversing, there was something pleasant and familiar about him—his blond hair and proper British ways were so like her father's. Perhaps that's why he had such an immediate effect on her.

"Captain, I'll expect your rent at the beginning of every week. I assume that won't be an issue since you already paid for the first two."

"That will be fine, anything else?"

Dellis nodded. *Time to lay down the rules.* "I expect that all of your men, including yourself, will behave like gentlemen in this establishment to both my customers and staff. You will not sneak up on them when they are disrobing, nor will you come anywhere near my private quarters unless accompanied by myself." She paused, noticing his little smile when she referred to their earlier meeting. Yes, she was once again being bold, but this was her inn, and she wouldn't allow more disreputable behavior under her roof. "Am I clear?"

Before he could answer, the front door flew open, bringing with it an arctic blast and a loud thud. Her brother landed on the floor in a giant heap of dirty clothing and matted hair, her cousin Alexei following, slamming the door behind them.

Oh, no. Smothering a gasp, Dellis watched as Stuart crawled on his hands and knees, trying to stand. "Excuse me for a moment, Captain." Getting up from her chair, she walked over to her brother and offered him a hand. "Stuart, where have you been?"

Slapping her hand away, Stuart stood up, wobbled on his feet for a few seconds, and then fell back against Alexei.

"What happened to him?" Dellis looked over her brother's shoulder at her cousin.

"I found him drunk, sitting outside The Crossing." Alexei covered his nose and shook his head. "I don't think he's changed clothes in days."

Lifting Stuart's chin, Dellis cringed at the sight of dark, sunken eyes and hollowed cheeks. He was covered in dirt, his tattered clothing hanging off his tall, emaciated frame. A pungent, sour aroma, mixed with the spicy scent of whiskey, permeated the air, from days of binge drinking and not washing. He looked absolutely pitiful. So many times she had tried to help her brother, but it was no use, he was content to bury himself in a bottle, his inner demons too much for him to withstand. It was painful to see him this way, the sweet little boy she knew from her youth now trapped inside this drunken, demented man.

"Stuart, why do you do this to me?" she said quietly, so only he and Alexei could hear.

"Do what to you? I'm the one who's drunk." He pointed to himself, his breath so strong it would ignite with the slightest spark. "Besides, the spirits told me I needed to have another, so I obliged. Don't you hear them?"

Dellis shook her head—there was no point in trying to reason with him when he was like this. "Alexei, please take him into the kitchen and get him some coffee and bread. I'll join you when I finish my meeting."

"Is there enough food for me? I'm starving."

"Of course, and now that I have a merchant staying here, I may be able to keep up with you and Stuart. You're both eating my cupboards empty, and that's before I feed my customers."

"Your new lodger is a merchant?" Alexei asked, giving her new guest a sidelong glance. "What goods is he selling?"

That was Alexei, always concerned with his stomach and his own personal wants. "I'm not quite sure. I'll introduce you later. Please, take Stuart in the back."

As Stuart slithered towards the floor, Alexei grabbed the young man by the seat of his pants, standing him up. Frustrated and embarrassed by his sorry state, Dellis reached under his arms and yanked him upright.

"Don't touch me!" Stuart yelled, shoving her so hard she fell back, landing on the ground at the Captain's feet.

With wide eyes, he leaned down and offered her a hand. "Are you all right?"

"I'm fine, thank you." Wiping her dirty palms on her skirt, Dellis ignored him and stood up, her face red with embarrassment. This was just what she needed, her brother's drunken antics when she was trying to appear businesslike.

Alexei smacked Stuart on the back of the head. "What in the hell do you think you're doing? Apologize to your sister and her guest."

"NO." Stuart shook his head petulantly, and then with a wry grin, he staggered towards the Captain, sniffing the air around him. "I know why you're here. You've come for the innocents." He paused for a moment, casting a questioning glance at his sister, then at Alexei. "He's come for the innocents, don't you hear them calling?"

Alexei tried to drag Stuart towards the kitchen, but he pulled away. Stumbling towards the Captain, Stuart hissed. "You hear them screaming, don't you?" When her guest didn't respond, Stuart pointed at the man, gesturing to his clothing. "Where is your red and gold?"

God, give me strength. The whole encounter had gone from bad to worse in a matter of minutes; it was time she intervened, for everyone's benefit. "Alexei, take him in the back before he scares my lodger away."

Grabbing Stuart by the sleeve and the scruff of his neck, Alexei dragged her brother towards the kitchen while he kicked and screamed all the way. "He's come for the innocents! Don't you hear them calling?"

Dellis turned toward her guest, embarrassment making her blush again. "Forgive my brother, Captain. He's not right in his mind. I promise I'll keep him away from you and your men."

"No need to apologize. I understand, Miss McKesson. Now, where were we?" he asked calmly, his eyes following Stuart as he fought Alexei all the way to the kitchen. "I believe you were giving me a tongue-lashing on how my men and I should behave."

She laughed, appreciating that he was trying to lighten the conversation for her betterment. "I don't believe I need to say more, do I?"

He shook his head. "I'll keep my men in check, as promised. There should be no need for you to worry about us."

Dellis barely heard his reply, the noise from Alexei and Stuart fighting in the kitchen drawing her attention. She winced at the sound of plates shattering, a pot flying through the archway into the bar area, landing on the floor with a hollow clunk. It was time for her to mediate before they destroyed what few dishes she had left and set fire to the house.

"Miss McKesson, is everything all right? I can stay and help." He flinched and jumped back when a tankard flew over top of the bar and landed on the floor at his feet. "This might be a bit too dangerous for a lady, even one as capable as yourself."

Dellis stifled a laugh at his jest. "No, but I appreciate the gesture." She handed him his key. "Your room is upstairs, the first one on the left. I'm assuming your men have already arrived. My aunt should have set them up in the other two rooms at the end of the hall."

"Then, I believe I've taken up enough of your time." He plucked his hat from the table, bowed, and then put the cap back on his head. She couldn't help but notice how he turned the point of his cocked hat slightly to the right and tipped it down towards his eye. It gave his whole polished look a bit of élan.

"Goodnight, Miss McKesson." When he tried to take her hand, Dellis pulled away, holding it against her chest. Again, he noticed her reaction, but this time he questioned her. "Is everything all right?"

"Excuse me, Stuart was filthy." Dellis wiped her hands on her apron, then pushed past him, grabbing the cups off the table. "Oh, for future reference, I'm an excellent shot."

"I find myself duly warned. Especially if you keep a pistol hidden in your petticoats." The Captain gave her the once over and a devilish grin that made her heart flutter.

Dellis blushed again, looking up at him through her eyelashes. "Good night, Captain."

Chapter Eight

John had to admit, there was something rather fascinating about his innkeeper and also strangely familiar. She was uncommonly beautiful, with a casual elegance unstifled by powdered wigs, face paint, and all the other frivolities of society women—it was fresh and natural and unassuming. And the combination of her European and Native lineage was not only striking but exotic. Her skin was as fair and smooth as Chinese porcelain, contrasting against thick, jet-black hair that hung in luxurious waves at her shoulders. She had the largest dark-brown eyes he'd ever seen, deep and fathomless, like windows into her thoughts, with tapered eyebrows that arched and moved with her slightest change in mood. His hand ached to caress those high, sculpted cheekbones, like the chiseled marble of the Venus de Milo. She was spirited and haughty, too. In one evening, she had pulled a gun on him, called him out on his ungentlemanly behavior, and aggressively negotiated the terms of their business arrangement. But what he found most intriguing was her vacillation between fear and willfulness. At one minute she aimed a gun at him and legitimately threatened to shoot, yet later, she pulled her hand away as if repulsed by his touch. Yes, she was intriguing, beautiful, and tempestuous—and she looked incredible in only a shift.

Opening the door to his room, John was pleasantly surprised to find it was in immaculate shape. The pale yellow paint on the walls was fresh, and the oriental rugs on the shiny wood floor looked brand new. The fireplace, with a thick, wooden mantle, dominated the outer wall, flanked by two large windows. Closer to the door was a finely crafted mahogany desk with an equally handsome chair behind it. The curtains were drawn back on the four-poster bed, which was covered in dark blue-and-white blankets, turned down in anticipation of his visit. On the wall adjacent to the window was an exceptionally large mirror above an aged mahogany chest of drawers.

John lit the two beeswax candles on the mantle and the one next to his bed, their warm glow and sweet smell bringing a pleasant ambiance to the room. He walked over to the mirror, taking a moment to admire its ornate wooden frame and the console underneath it; both were Chippendale, designed in the French Rocco style, based off the Louis XV design. The rest of the bedroom set also matched the same pattern. The furniture must have cost a fortune. The last time he'd seen its likeness was at his family estate in England, and only in his father's personal rooms. It didn't make sense; the tavern and the rest of the house seemed somewhat neglected and wanting, but this room was fit for nobility.

Dropping a few belongings on the bed, John removed his hat and coat and unpacked his haversack. The only thing he focused on now were the welcoming linen sheets and pleasant dreams. His stomach growled loudly, reminding him of its presence, but it could wait until morning, his need for sleep superseding all other wants. Leaning down to remove his boots, he heard the door swing open and the clicking of heels on the wood floor.

"Captain, Lieutenant Clark here."

Standing in the doorway, back straight, head held high, was his stalwart junior officer, looking fit and read for duty.

"Simon, it's good to see you." John walked over to Clark and offered a hand.

"Difficulties be damned," the shorter man said, his Scottish brogue over-enunciating the words.

"Difficulties be damned," John repeated. They shook hands then embraced, slapping backs robustly. It had been a long time since he had seen his friend, much less been greeted with his regimental motto. "When did I last see you? It seems forever and a day."

"Almost two years, and you better believe I never thought I would see your sorry arse again."

John laughed. "I would have to agree with you on that account."

"It's good to see you, John. Now, are you going to tell me what we're doing in this God-forsaken place? I was fat and happy in Manhattan, working guard duty, when I got word that I had been requested for a special assignment. No one could tell me any details, only that I would be working for you."

John knew that wasn't all that was said, the mere mention of his name always brought with it a barrage of jests and lewd comments. Simon was just being kind, keeping the specifics to himself. "Are Hayes and Smith with you?"

"Yes, sir, both of them are passed out down the hall," Clark replied, flashing a toothy, infectious grin.

"We're going to need them." John was grateful to have his best men on such an important mission, all three of them loyal to a fault and trustworthy—necessities in espionage. When he had requested their reassignment, he knew his former subordinates wouldn't hesitate to work under him again; the three of them were comrades in arms.

"John, they're never going to readjust to barrack life after having their own rooms and good food in their belly. Being assigned to this mission might actually be advantageous if one can ignore the snow and the bloody cold." Clark laughed loud and hardy.

Remembering the Spartan living conditions of regimental life at Fort Niagara, John, too, would have been grateful for such small favors. It seemed forever since he'd lived in the fort with his men, being so far removed from that life in Manhattan. What he wouldn't pay to get back to it, the idea of communal living and daily drills preferable to the gaol he oversaw.

"Now, are you going to tell me why we're here? After the court-martial, I never thought I would see you in a command position again."

John put a finger to his lips, then closed the door. "We're here to investigate the Oneida involvement with the Rebels and the refortification of Fort Stanwix."

"I take it the merchant business is our cover?"

He nodded. "Yes, it was the best way I knew to interact with the locals and the fort and not be under suspicion. Howe only gave me two days to come up with a plan. The profiteer cover seemed the best option."

"Fair enough," Clark replied, taking a seat behind the desk, throwing his feet on top of it. "So, the goods we brought with us, they're from Carlisle Shipping?"

"Yes..." John knew what question was coming next.

"Your brother agreed to this?"

"Not exactly. Captain Denny was willing to help us in the interim. Hopefully, we won't have to get Gavin involved." There was no way his brother would help, not even for the war effort; their relationship had long since soured past repair. Luckily, one of his brother's captains was an old gambling friend and fellow carouser. They had made a deal, and Denny was able to procure the supplies John needed to make the mission happen.

Clark shook his head. John sensed Clark's disapproval, but he wasn't the one who had to come up with a plan in two days with limited funds. John did the best he could.

"I'm curious, John. Why did Howe come to you for this mission? There are already reconnaissance missions around Fort Stanwix, as we speak. No offense, but you're not exactly His Majesty's finest."

"I don't know," he lied, dismissing the unflattering remark, his friend being the one person John brooked such impertinence. "We don't have much time. Carleton is going after Ticonderoga, and if he succeeds, we could see battle before winter sets in. I plan to meet with some of the locals tomorrow. Smith is going to travel for us. I need him to be in Oswego to receive the shipment and procure a couple more boats for transport. Did you find a place to store our supplies safely?"

"We rented a small section of a barn from one of the local shopkeepers. He doesn't use it anymore, and he gave a fair price for it. Are you worried there might be thieves about?" Clark grinned from ear to ear, insinuating exactly what was on John's mind.

"Would you fault me if I did?" He countered tersely. "I've learned my lessons. Now we have a mission, and that's my focus moving forward. I have no intention of repeating old mistakes."

"John, don't be getting angry with me, the village is not far from here. How could either of us forget, it ruined both of our careers?"

He refrained from comment, though Clark was right, how could they forget?

"I'm just worried about my scalp with them thieving savages all around us. I would rather keep it, receding hairline and all."

"I agree," John said.

They'd both seen plenty of men and women scalped by natives and fellow soldiers. The whole practice disgusted him, and most of the higher-ranking officers frowned upon it, Howe included. But there were some officers, particularly those in the northern army, who were willing to pay up to eight pounds sterling for Rebel scalps, making them a valuable prize for the natives. Rumor had it that General Burgoyne supported the practice.

"I'm not interested in having my scalp hanging on anyone's wall." Clark ran his hands through his auburn hair, checking for its presence. "I often wonder why anyone would want to live in this God-forsaken place. How did we ever make it through these horrible winters?"

"You know the answer to that," John replied.

Major Roger DeLancie. While they owed their superior officer for his tutelage, his methods left much to question. Their training under him was brutal. He was a strict disciplinarian, and even the slightest hint of insubordination would get you fifty lashes with the cat-o-nine tails. On several occasions, John witnessed fellow junior officers marry the adjutant's daughter for questioning even the smallest of orders.

"Clark, see that Miss McKesson gets her share of supplies delivered tomorrow— enough to feed the four of us, plus four more. I want Smith and Hayes on the road at first light. We need to be quick about this. I don't have to explain to you the value of the information we are gathering."

"This is significant, Howe trusting you."

That fact wasn't lost on John; this was his last chance to salvage his career. "Yes, and I have no intention of messing this up," he added with conviction. "I'm going to bed before I fall over. I have to be up early to do inventory and see what we have to trade. Our innkeeper is going to take me to town and introduce me to some of the locals. Good night, Simon."

After Clark left, John undressed quickly, then blew out the candles and climbed under the sheets, his exhausted body unwilling to relax even in the warmth and comfort of the room. He chuckled to himself, reminiscing about his first encounter with the loving and willful Miss McKesson. It was unusual, to say the least. And there had been something strangely familiar about her brother, his voice and the eerie look in his eyes, but John couldn't place the young man. The longer John mulled it over, the wearier he became.

As if on cue, the moment he started to drift off to sleep, the singing started again with a voice so soft, and a song so sweet, it rivaled a lullaby. He could almost have drifted off to it, but suddenly, the old woman was standing at the foot of his bed, her lament getting louder as she pointed to him, a bloody scrap of fabric clutched in her fist. The nude bodies of the slaughtered women were lying all around him, and their bloodcurdling wails were incomprehensible save one word… *justice.*

No! Waking abruptly, John sat up and threw the blankets off, sweat plastering his fine linen shirt to his chest, little beads forming at his brow. He wrapped his arms around himself, his body trembling, the memories so vivid he could almost still see them. The women. All Dead.

"…*sadly, you will all die.*" Then, a gunshot went off in his head. He jumped reflexively. *God, please, make it stop.* John fisted his hair, pulling and tugging at it, trying to wrench the memory out of his brain. He looked around the room, but there was nothing to drink, nothing to help him calm the demons that invaded his sleep, holding sweet repose hostage.

He hated the night. He could never hide from them, their forever captive in the dark.

Lying back against the pillows, he took several deep breaths. *It was just a dream, pull it together, Carlisle.* Yes, he could convince himself of that. It was a dream. But John knew, when he closed his eyes, the ghosts would be waiting for him, and they were determined to never let him forget.

Chapter Nine

John had seen many skilled horsewomen, but Dellis McKesson was beyond exceptional. Without a look back, she took off at breakneck speed, leaves flying into the air, her mare expertly navigating the wooded trail at her master's command. Giving Viceroy a gentle kick, he followed close behind her, enjoying the opportunity for a lively sprint.

"We're going to take the northwest trail towards my grandfather's village," she yelled over her shoulder, tendrils of her dark hair loosely flying into her face. "I hope you aren't afraid of savages? Not to worry, they won't shoot if you're with me."

"I don't scare so easily, Miss McKesson," John replied, speeding up so he was next to her. "You're trying to bait me."

"Perhaps. Now, Captain, do try to keep up." She gave him a sidelong glance, her lips curling into a smile, as she sped up, passing him. So, she was feisty, willful, *and* competitive, an utterly delightful trifecta of qualities in a woman. He couldn't help but wonder what she would be like as a lover. Surely just as spirited. It would take a patient man to tame her wild horses, but what a dalliance it would be.

"Are you challenging me?" he questioned. Her mare was no match for a combat trained horse like Viceroy, but he was enjoying the game she was playing. "Shall we make a wager?"

"Perhaps." She countered, her eyes alight with mirth. "Now, follow me, Captain." With that she took off, her mare disappearing into the woods, leaving him to cough in her wake.

Shaking his head, he gave Viceroy another kick, pushing his mount to catch up with her. There was no way he was going to let that haughty little tart win.

As they raced deeper into the forest, an ominous feeling came over him, slowing his pace. The bare tree branches, like spindly fingers, grabbed at his clothing, their wooded claws scratching his face, drawing little trickles of blood. The natives believed the spirits of their dead lived in the woods, a haunting presence that welcomed some and forbade others. It was as if they knew he'd returned and were reaching out to reclaim him; but he had no way of knowing if they would remain benevolent or seek to punish him. Just like the gods of Olympus, they could bend the will and fates of man to their slightest whim, and now, he was at their mercy.

When John finally caught up with her, Dellis stopped abruptly and dismounted. "We're not far from the village, Captain, we should rest our mounts." He followed her lead, pulling Viceroy by the reins.

"I want to thank you, Captain, for having the supplies delivered today. I'm truly grateful," she said, smoothing some stray hairs back from her face. She looked lovely, her fair skin flushed and dewy from their ride.

"You made such an impression on me; I didn't think it could wait a day. Personally, I don't prefer eating shoe leather."

"Yes, well, my boots are safe for another month." She laughed, pulling her mare behind her. "I did say that, didn't I?"

"I'm afraid you did."

She shook her head incredulously, though her lips curled into a smile. "Yes, well, I *have* been known to be a bit spirited when I'm tired."

"A bit?" He laughed, unable to hide his amusement. "Spirited, that's what you call it?" She ignored his comment, though another smile turned up the corner of her lips.

As they got closer to the village, Dellis stopped abruptly, turning to him. She looked as if she was contemplating something dire, the tedium of putting words together vexing her. After a moment of silence, she finally blurted it out. "Captain, before I take you to meet my grandfather, I just need to be sure that you are... How do I say it and not offend you?"

"Please, be frank with me, Miss McKesson. You haven't hesitated thus far."

"I need to be sure that you are in earnest."

Following her meaning, he asked, "You want to know if I'm a profiteer or, perhaps, a thief?"

She nodded, sheepishly. "It's not often we have merchants who are willing to trade with us. My grandfather and the villagers are desperate, and they can little afford much as it is. I would hate for them to count on you and nothing come of it."

Her concerns were not unsubstantiated. With the difficulty of moving supplies up the Mohawk or down the St. Lawrence, trade was costly and rarely came to fruition. Only ten boats had permits under the Provincial Marine to travel up and down the St. Lawrence, and it was near impossible to obtain one. Then, there was also the matter of the British Blockade and the runners who inflated the prices so high they were beyond what her people could afford. She had good reason to be skeptical. Trying to put her mind at ease, John replied, "Could I not be a profiteer and still be legitimate?"

"I suppose," she stammered, her eyes darting to and fro then looking back at him.

"Then it shouldn't matter how or where I obtain the supplies, only that I have them and I'm willing to trade. Or does that go against your feminine sensibilities?" he asked.

"You're right, Captain, it doesn't matter." She smiled, her lips parting, exposing her even, white teeth. "And you've followed through on your promises thus far, so I'm willing to trust you again."

He'd anticipated a frank answer. There was nothing pretentious about Dellis, just pure honesty—a trait he found refreshing in a woman, though he was unaccustomed to it.

"Follow me, we are almost there."

As they neared her village, John's stomach started to churn, an onslaught of memories flooding his mind. A reminiscent foreboding. It had been two years, but he would never forget this place—they wouldn't let him.

"Captain, shall we continue?" Dellis asked over her shoulder.

John looked at her but couldn't answer, too stunned by his revelation. His feet, like two stones, holding him fixed in space.

Suddenly, a young Oneida brave jumped down from the trees, a fierce look in his eyes, as he aimed his musket at them. Reflexively, John held up his hands in surrender.

"Wait here." She nodded to him, then ran up to the guard.

Surfacing from his reverie, John listened in as Dellis and the guard exchanged pleasantries in Oneida. It'd been a while since John had heard the language spoken, but he could still make out most of their conversation. When she waved him over, he walked slowly, waiting for the young brave to put his musket down. What if someone recognized John? Looking up in the trees, he saw the guards watching the interaction with curiosity and a hint of trepidation.

"Captain, please let me introduce you; this is Ho-sa-gowwa, one of the village guards, and a good friend of mine. Ho-sa-gowwa, this is Captain Anderson. He has goods to trade with Grandfather."

The young brave couldn't have been more than sixteen-years-old, but he was already an accomplished warrior if he was trusted to guard the village. Wearing a buckskin tunic and leggings, and armed with a tomahawk and musket, he looked every bit the fierce warrior. His hair was shaved off except for a small section at the crown that hung down to his shoulders, adorned with bright red and blue feathers. His black eyes leveled at John with an untrusting gaze.

"*Shekoli*, Ho-sa-gowwa." John nodded, showing his respect.

The young brave was silent, fists on hips, as he gave John the once-over, sizing him up.

"Ho-sa-gowwa, the Captain is my friend, and he is your friend, too. I promise," Dellis said, sweetly, touching the young man's arm. "Trust me."

The guard nodded, then put his hand on his tomahawk, a warning that their truce was on her behalf alone.

Dellis pointed towards the village, drawing attention away from the young brave, who was eyeing John with the voracity of a hungry falcon. "Don't mind him, please, he's just protective. One of the nearby Mohawk settlements was attacked yesterday by some militiamen. Our village was attacked two years ago; his mother was killed, and he wasn't here to protect her."

"Where was he?" John asked, keeping eyes on the guard. Every one of his soldier's instincts were on alert, anticipating a strike from any direction.

"My friend here was with the rest of the men at the Confederacy Council in Onondaga. Guy Johnson and Samuel Kirkland called a meeting to discuss the colonists' aggression towards the Crown. There were only women and children in the village when the Regulars came."

"What happened?"

Dellis looked up, the wind blowing a long, curly strand of hair into her face. John clenched his fists at his side, resisting the urge to brush it away. "They burned it, and then they did what soldiers do when they encounter unprotected women." He noticed how she shivered, her gaze focused on the village, but there was pain in those fathomless dark eyes, he didn't need to see them to know it was true.

"By the time they left, they had murdered all but ten of the women in this village, and several of them bore bastard children. One of the girls was only thirteen."

John closed his eyes, remembering the young girl, screaming and fighting as she was dragged from her home, one of his men tearing off her clothing. Was there no end to this nightmare?

"Women are very important and powerful in our tribe. Our clan matrons have the authority to appoint and depose chiefs. There are three clans in the Oneida tribe: bear, wolf, and turtle. My grandmother was the bear clan matron. She and the other two matrons died that day, leaving us without their spiritual guidance. It devastated our village."

"Why did that happen? I thought there was a truce between the Six Nations and the King." John had no doubt what her people were told in the aftermath of such a devastating breach of treaty: a combination of denials and political niceties to cover up the soldiers' failure to behave with the decorum of King's men.

"I've heard many explanations, but none of them make sense. Funny, isn't it? They call us savages, but what do you call men who rape and murder unarmed women and children?" Another look of pain crossed her lovely features as she turned away, her body visibly trembling like a leaf on the breeze. "I'll never understand it."

He nodded, unable to find words through his guilt.

As they walked through the stockade into the village, John was surprised to see that everything had been rebuilt. Instead of the older, cruder cabins he remembered, there were several well-made log cabins with brick chimneys. The land had since been cultivated for farming and livestock; corn planted in long, straight rows, cows grazing in the field, and the pigs in pens were looking fat and well fed. All around him, the village bustled with life; women sewing and grinding corn while some of the men were laying fish out to dry in the warm autumn sun. It was more like a little hamlet than a native village.

Dellis turned to him and smiled. "You look surprised."

He nodded. "I am. This isn't what I expected."

"We're used to that." She added, pride in her voice. "We don't live like savages, though we are often accused of it."

"Touché," he said, her point received and well delivered.

As they passed through the entrance in the stockade, John could sense the natives watching him, their gazes inquisitive yet not unfriendly. They were accustomed to white travelers, but not alone, and certainly not accompanying one of their women. Every face that looked in his direction was a haunting reminder of that bloody day. But did they recognize him? Could they see into his guilty heart?

Looking over her shoulder at him, Dellia said, "Captain, my grandfather is the chief, and we must meet with him first, out of respect. After, we can talk with some of my friends and see if there's anything else they need."

"I understand," he replied, following her.

There was no mistaking the war chief of the village. The elderly man was in excellent physical shape, his graying hair and the lines in his face the only proof of his age. Everything he wore was richly detailed, from his tunic and leggings to the belt around his waist, a representation of his status in the tribe. His long, salt-and-pepper hair was pulled off his face, much of it braided and intertwined with colorful feathers and beads. Around his neck, the chief wore a gleaming gorget, tied in place by a black kerchief. As they got closer, John noticed it bore the seal of the Eighth Regiment. His Regiment.

"*Shekoli, Lakso´tha´*." Dellis nodded to her grandfather. "This is Captain Anderson, a merchant I've brought here to trade with you." Pausing a moment, she turned to John and smiled. "Captain, this is my grandfather, Great Oak, but you may call him Joseph."

Great Oak of the Oneida was renowned throughout the valley for being both a skilled fighter and a diligent peacemaker. During the highly contested negotiations of the 1768 Treaty of Fort Stanwix that redrew the borderlines between the colonies and the native territories, Great Oak had worked hard to secure peace between Britain and the Six Nations, earning him respect on both sides.

"*Shekoli*, Captain," Joseph said, eyeing John suspiciously.

"It's an honor to meet you, Joseph." He nodded, showing his genuine regard for such an illustrious man. "Thank you for allowing me to visit."

"You are welcome here if my granddaughter says so. She is very wise for her years." As expected, his English was good, though accented. "Please, give us a moment, Captain."

John stepped away, his ears tuned in to their dialogue. Though they were speaking softly, he heard the strain in Dellis's voice as she pleaded with her grandfather to prepare for the winter.

He conceded, his voice firm but tender, too. "All right, Granddaughter, but you must be more careful when bringing strangers to the village. The attack on our neighbors should remind us of our own past—no one is completely trustworthy."

"I promise you, Grandfather, you can trust him. Please, don't turn your back on help out of pride."

Her words pricked John's conscience. Yes, he was there under false pretenses, and yes, he was a spy, but he did intend on trading with them, that much was true. If the Oneidas played along and made the treaty, wouldn't they all benefit from his deception in the end?

"What do you have to trade, Captain?" Joseph walked up to him, Dellis close behind.

The two men bartered back and forth for several minutes until they settled on a modest fee and a trade of some beaver furs and buckskin. It was hardly what the goods were worth, but it was invaluable if John could get the Oneida to trust him. Besides, his business ventures with Celeste could more than cover the additional cost of the shipment. Now that the well of beaver pelts had dried up, he was sure to fetch an exceptional price for them. Celeste would salivate over the prospect of having such a luxurious fur, and so would many traders.

As they finished up their conversation, John noticed a woman hovering near him like a curious bird looking for food. She was pretty, with a round face and large, black eyes that were regarding him with curiosity. He turned to her, recognizing her instantly. *Get away, now.*

Her eyes widened, and she raced up to him. "It's you! You've come back." But before he could turn and walk away, she grabbed his hands, pulling him in closer. "I knew I would see you again."

Dellis looked at both of them, her brow furrowed in confusion. "Have you met before?"

"I don't believe so." He lied. Oh, they had met.

"Kateri, you're mistaken, this is Captain Anderson. I promise you, he's never been here before."

"No, it *is* you," She insisted, gesturing to his hair and his face. "I would know my fair-haired angel anywhere. You saved my life." The woman's hand was so close to his face, it almost skimmed his cheek. His stomach lurched, his breakfast churning in an uneasy pit of guilt and trepidation.

"I could never forget this face." Kateri persisted, much to his dismay. "He shot the man who was trying to hurt me, and then he let me go free."

"No, Kateri, Captain Anderson wasn't here." Looking back at him, Dellis shrugged her shoulders. "She must have you confused with someone else. She thinks you saved her when our village was attacked."

Trying to make light of the situation, John replied, "It must be my blond hair and the accent. Now, I am the victim of cliché, Miss McKesson."

Dellis rolled her eyes, though a grin tugged at the edge of her lips. "So it would seem, Captain."

Kateri grabbed his hand again, her eyes pleading with him. "I know it's you. You've come again to protect us, haven't you?" Desperation pained her voice.

Protect them? John shuddered at the thought. That was far from his goal. He, like Ares, was a bringing the war to them, a battle not of their making, but one they would soon have to fight. He could take no more. *Get out, John, now.* Time was running out, someone would eventually catch on to their meeting and recognize him. When he tried to pull back again, Kateri held his hand firmly, preventing his retreat.

"I know you're afraid, so I will ask no more of you. But before you go…" Quickly, she removed something from around her neck and put it in his palm. "God sent you to protect me, my angel. Take this and wear it; he will protect you when the time comes."

"Thank you, Kateri," he replied, holding the trinket in his fist. Better to go along with the charade than further add to suspicion.

Just as John started to walk away, Kateri reached up and took his face in her hands. He froze, his heart sprinting in his chest. "God be with you," she whispered, her gentle fingers caressing his cheeks. He remembered the look in her eyes as he led her into the woods and told her to run.

"...go, now, before they catch you." John pulled his knife from his boot and handed it to her. "Use this to protect yourself."

"Thank you, my angel of mercy."

It was the same look she was giving him now, the look of someone whose life had just been saved from certain death. There were no words to describe it.

"God be with you, my angel." Releasing him, Kateri took a step back.

When John opened his hand, a bit of metal glinted in the sunlight. It was a silver cross, tied to a long piece of leather. Humbled by her gesture, he replied, "Thank you, I'll treasure it."

Putting the necklace in his pocket, he spied Dellis watching him curiously.

"I tried to tell Kateri she was mistaken about you, but she refused to listen," Dellis said. "Thank you for accepting the gift; it will give her comfort believing it's with its intended."

He nodded, his nerves still on edge. "If taking this will give her peace of mind, then the lie is well served. It's the least I can do."

Dellis reached out her hand, gesturing to him. "May I see it?"

Handing it to her, he watched as she unwound the leather bands, running her fingers over the small metal cross. "Silver is very expensive—this was likely passed down through her family. It's an honor that she gave this to you. Whoever it was intended for must have made quite an impression on her."

Dellis handed it back to him. Carefully, he knotted the leather bands around his neck, slipping it under his collar, the metal cold against his skin. Another encounter like this, and his true identity was sure to be discovered.

"Captain, before we leave for town, I need to make one last stop. Measles has been going through the village, and I need to check that some of the children are on the mend."

When John glanced over his shoulder, Kateri was still watching him, her dark eyes like a ghost from the past—a past he seemed unable to outrun.

"All right, lead on, Miss McKesson," John replied, turning his back to Kateri, trying to shut her and the memories out. But could he?

Chapter Ten

As the two of them trudged up the leaf-covered trail, John eyed the trees, and just as he anticipated, several Oneida braves were standing guard, watching with muskets in hand and tomahawks at their hips. Suspicious eyes followed his every turn, and with the slightest misstep, they would shoot first then descend on him like hungry vultures to pick apart his remains. Their unspoken truce with him was on behalf of his kind but naïve guide. Yet, Dellis had no sense of what was going on around her, content to just yammer on as if nothing was wrong and he weren't on verge of being ambushed.

At the top of the hill was the large, wooden barn, and about thirty feet across from it, a little log cabin with smoke billowing up from the brick chimney.

"By the way, have you had the measles?" Dellis asked..

"I have," he replied, turning his attention back to her, trying to ignore the prying eyes that followed him.

As they neared the barn, John stopped dead in his tracks. It was as if he'd been transported through time, back two years to when the nightmare began. High-pitched wails carried over the forest, gun shots popped rhythmically, one after another, as the village went up in flames. He'd seen the missing powder and weapons go inside the barn, and within a matter of hours, when he returned with his men, they found nothing. Absolutely nothing.

Suddenly, Dellis's hand touched his shoulder, her quiet voice bringing him back to the present. "Captain, come with me. This was my father's cabin, where he took care of patients. We use it now to isolate the sick from the rest of the village."

He followed her into the little log cabin, shutting out the past with the turn of his back and a close of the door. The cabin was crude inside with an earthen floor, a large fireplace on the rear wall, and three little straw cots. Two women sat on rocking chairs next to the fire, one quietly nursing a baby and the other sewing. They both looked up when he entered.

"Anna, and Skenandoa, this is Captain Anderson, he's a merchant here to trade with us. Is there anything you need?"

"We could use linen and something to clean wounds," Skenandoa said, standing up and walking over to them. "We have very little left."

Dellis turned her attention to him. "Is this something you can help us with?"

"I have plenty of whisky, but I'll have to get linen with my next shipment. Can it wait that long?"

"That would be fine. And just so you know, we use it for cleaning wounds—we don't drink spirits in this village." Dellis added.

"You don't have to explain, Miss McKesson, I would not question your wisdom or motivation. I'll get you what you need."

John understood all too well what alcohol had done to her people. It was like a disease from the moment they took their very first drink, and it was also the weapon of choice for the English when they wanted to manipulate the natives. Sadly, he, too, had used it to cheat the local tribes when he was stationed at Fort Niagara. Thank goodness her village had been spared this one atrocity.

"One last thing before we leave." She led him back towards the village, stopping at one of the smaller log houses. "This is my family home. I just need to get my cloak, I left it here accidentally."

Her house was small, like the ones he remembered from years before, with one large common room. There was a wooden table in the center with drying flowers hanging over it from the ceiling above. On one side of the cabin was a large stone fireplace and hearth that served as the kitchen area, and on the other was the sleeping quarters with three wood and straw cots. He watched as she rifled around for a few minutes then got on her hands and knees looking under one of the cots.

"I'm going to need this now that the weather has turned so cold," she said, standing up and putting a large, gray cloak around her shoulders.

"Where did you get that?" he asked, unmistakable awe in his voice, and of course, she didn't miss it.

"Is there something amiss, Captain?"

John walked over to her, touching the wool fabric, carefully examining it. When he flipped one of the corners over, he could still see his initials, *JC,* sewn into the fabric. "This is military issue."

"It was my father's. It's the only piece of clothing I have left of his, so I treasure it." Lifting her arms, she laughed, the giant cloak dwarfing her small, lithe frame. "I admit, it's a bit big for me, but it's warm and it serves its purpose. I vaguely remember him covering me with it when I was sick."

He looked up at her and shuddered. The memory was so vivid, as if he could still see the boy sitting on the floor screaming, a dead woman in his arms. Lying next to him, unmoving, was the body of a younger woman. She had a large, black-and-blue bruise on her forehead, her face swollen beyond recognition from being severely beaten, and her dress had been torn to shreds, exposing handprint bruises all over her neck and shoulders. He'd picked her up and carried her to the cot, removing his great cloak and covering her nakedness with it. Gently, he caressed her cheek, noticing how soft her skin was and how unusually fair for a native woman. When he looked up at Dellis, there was no mistaking her; the two women were one in the same. Though her face had been indistinguishable at the time, her luminous skin and high cheekbones were unforgettable.

"Captain, is something wrong?" she asked.

"Not at all," John replied, trying to shrug off the memory. If he was to succeed at his mission, he was going to have to come face to face with his past many times—better to accept that now and find a way to deal with it.

"Shall we go? We still have much to do."

No one else seemed to recognize him as they left the village, though the same threatening eyes followed them all the way out to the stockade. Kateri stood at the entrance of the camp, her hands nervously wringing at a piece of fabric while she watched him go. John looked over his shoulder and nodded to her, and she responded in kind, a silent understanding between the two of them.

Grabbing the reins of her horse, Dellis pointed to Kateri. "I think she fancies you, Captain, if you're looking for a wife. Though, I'm afraid you might find an Oneida squaw entirely too free spirited for your civilized Tory blood."

"I'm not so sure about that." John rubbed his chin as he mulled over the delightful prospect of having a feisty woman in his bed. *Oh, the mind wanders.* "I wouldn't mind a merry chase now and then to keep things interesting."

"Wouldn't you, now?" Dellis said with a grin, mounting up, then turning her horse so she faced him. "Well, then, let's see if you can catch me."

John laughed, her jest further taking the edge off his nerves. There wasn't a chance she could outrun him on horseback, but he was going to love watching her try. He gave her a moment's head start, and then took off after her, glad to leave the demons of the past behind.

Chapter Eleven

"I bet you're pretty proud of yourself. Aren't you supposed to let a lady win?" Dellis laughed as she dismounted her horse. "So much for being a gentleman."

Captain Anderson leaned against the stall, grinning like a fool, his arms crossed over his chest. "I'm sorry, but you made it entirely too easy for me to win."

Resisting the urge to kick him, Dellis threw her shoulders back and stomped away, making a show of her haughtiness. The man had given her a head start, and then suddenly, he sped by her like Hermes with a message for Zeus. The next time she saw him, he was leaning against the stall with that ridiculous look on his face.

"Here, let me help you with this." He grabbed the reins from her and tied up the horse. "You're so angry you might injure yourself, or the horse. It seems to be quite a common state of affairs with you."

When the Captain started to laugh, Dellis rolled her eyes skyward. Apparently, he was the only one who found his witticisms amusing. "Be glad I don't have my pistol with me. You never know what I might do."

"Don't be angry; I won fairly." He teased, his blue eyes sparkling like gems. "My horse is faster, it's very simple, and I'm a more skilled rider."

Dellis let out a little, "Huh?" then walked out of the barn, her ego smarting from her loss. The man wasn't going to charm his way out of this situation. She already gave him a pass for the incident in the barn the night before, but it would take more than fine eyes and a grin to win her over.

She could hear him race up behind her, his heels clicking on the stone path that led from the stable to the little street.

"You're a poor loser, Miss McKesson." He persisted against her purposeful snub.

Dellis stifled a laugh then opted to play along, relishing their playful banter. "Follow me, Captain. Do try to keep up. Hopefully, you're as good on foot as you are in the saddle."

Her hometown of German Flats was far from the bluster and activity of New York City. The sleepy little hamlet was nestled on the south side of the Mohawk River, fifty miles west of Albany. It was so small that everyone in the town knew each other from the blacksmith to the miller and all the local tavern owners. Most of the townspeople were farmers, with a smattering of businessmen and wealthy landowners, her Uncle James included.

Dellis introduced the Captain to the local merchants and shop owners, and with little difficulty, and minimal haggling, he sold what remained of his supplies. There was something innately likable about him, his demeanor both warm and captivating—an asset when one was a salesman. But what amazed her most was how easily he conversed, treating everyone with the same respect from a woman walking into the store, of which he held the door for, to the local drunk that tried to pilfer coin from them on the street. She envied that about John. Most people found her personality aggressive and somewhat headstrong, qualities that were considered an asset in men but an inconvenience in a woman. But at least she wasn't the only one he'd managed to charm with his elegant manners and pleasant disposition; everyone he met seemed to fall under his spell.

When they finally finished, she was anxious to get back to The Thistle, having once again neglected her duties for the day. As they walked back towards the stable, the Captain stopped in front of one of the local watering holes and pointed to the door. "Miss McKesson, I would like to buy you a drink. You have been so generous, taking time away from your work. Let me at least thank you in this small way."

Dellis looked up at the sign and cringed. *Why here?* The Silver Kettle wasn't known for being particularly friendly to natives, and that included those of mixed descent. But he was trying to be kind, for her benefit, and it would be rude to refuse. Dellis relented with a nod. "If you like." Perhaps they could sneak in and out without drawing too much attention. She could only hope.

The Kettle was the busiest tavern in German Flats and her toughest competition. It was in the perfect location for success; right in the center of the town and next to the church—one could drink their fill and confess in the morning. As expected, it was packed wall-to-wall with townspeople and local drunks. The pungent smell of burnt food and too many unkempt bodies permeated the air in a musty cloud that hung over the dining room. The tavern was much smaller than The Thistle with room enough for only for two long tables and a couple of smaller ones that flanked the soot-covered stone fireplace. It was filthy inside and crudely decorated; the once-white walls now an aged cream from years of burning candles, and the wood floor was badly in need of a polish.

"This is quite a place," he said, sidestepping her and taking a seat.

"Not like the parlors and salons you're used to in the city, Captain?" she asked, continuing their earlier banter.

When the Captain didn't volley back a jest, she thought he didn't hear her, but then the corner of his mouth turned up in a smirk. *Oh, he definitely heard her.* But was she right about him? He was obviously cultured in the ways of society, yet there was something about him that was strangely at ease in their provincial environment, almost as if he belonged.

"If I had half the clientele that The Kettle has, I would never have to worry about going out of business." She looked around, eyeing the customers coming in and out. It was confounding to her that such a disreputable place managed to stay in business. *What am I doing wrong?*

"Is The Thistle in trouble?" He was serious, no longer in the mood to verbally spar with her.

She hesitated to respond to his question, the answer steeped in a reality she had long been avoiding. But he persisted, much to her chagrin.

"Miss McKesson?"

Dellis took a deep breath and let it out slowly, there was no point in running from the truth any longer. "It will be in trouble if I don't start turning a profit." The prospect of losing her father's house was devastating, and suddenly, all too real.

His fingers drummed on the tabletop for a moment before he looked up. "Is there something I can do to help?" There was no mock sincerity in his voice, only genuine concern for her welfare.

Before Dellis could answer, a buxom waitress walked up and put a pewter mug down in front of him. "Good evening, sir. This is the house cider unless there's something else you would prefer?" Before the captain had a chance to reply, she leaned forward and wiped the table, giving both guests a view of her ample female assets.

"Excuse me," the waitress said curtly.

Dellis lifted her arms off the table just in time to avoid being rammed by the woman's cleaning cloth.

"Cider will be fine, thank you," he replied, smiling at her, laugh lines bracketing his full lips, giving his face a boyish look.

The waitress giggled, twirling a long, blond curl that hung down from her cap. "Would you care for some whiskey?"

"No, this will do."

She nodded, turning her back to Dellis, blocking her view of the Captain. "Well, you just let me know if there's any little thing I can do for you. My name is Jussie."

My goodness. Dellis coughed loudly, appalled at what the waitress was implying. Never had she heard such a brazen offer. And to a man Jussie didn't even know?

The Captain gazed around the woman's hip at Dellis, a sparkle in his blue eyes. Looking up at the waitress, he asked, "Perhaps something for my guest?"

"We don't serve her kind in here—Miss McKesson knows that. She needs to leave." The waitress sneered, throwing a nasty look over her shoulder.

Dellis cocked a brow in challenge. She knew Jussie wouldn't dare throw someone out; she wasn't that bold.

The Captain glanced at Dellis then back at the waitress. "Surely, Miss McKesson is welcome here. Is she not also a local tavern owner? Is there not such a thing as professional courtesy?"

"We don't serve her kind, tavern owner or not." Jussie hissed, looking down her nose at Dellis.

The woman was being downright impertinent. Outraged, Dellis grabbed the edge of the table and stood up. "And just what exactly do you mean by…"

Jussie interjected, leaning in as if she were posturing for a fight. "Shall I tell the gentleman what the townspeople say about you? Shall I? How would you like that?"

"Go ahead… you…" Dellis started, but the captain stood up, putting himself between them.

"Enough!" He threw both of his arms out, directing both women to their respective corners. "Miss, if you are unwilling to serve the lady, then we will be leaving."

When he started for the door, Jussie put her hand on his sleeve, her blue eyes lighting up, a dimple forming in her fleshy cheek. "For you, I'll make an exception." Her voice sounded so overly sweet it made Dellis want to heave.

"Thank you," he replied, flashing one of his charming grins. "Jussie." He said her name with such intensity it made the waitress giggle and blush like a young girl.

"Excuse me for a moment. I'll get that drink." Jussie glared at Dellis then picked up the rag and walked away.

The minute that Jussie was out of earshot, Dellis turned to him, her temper on the verge of boiling over. *Insufferable woman, how dare she?* "If my staff behaved in such a manner, I would have them thrown out on their ear. The nerve of that woman."

"I just about had a bar fight on my hands. Wouldn't that have been amusing?" He winked at her over the top of his mug then suddenly put it down. He was politely waiting for her drink to come.

"Captain, I can brook no one's defense of me. I'm perfectly capable of taking care of myself."

He nodded. "Of that, I've no doubt, but it would be less than chivalrous of me to let her continue."

"I've noticed you have a charisma that is rather advantageous when it comes to getting your way, Captain. Once again, if you're looking for a wife, I believe Jussie might be happy to oblige."

Instead of further jesting with her, he turned serious. "Forgive my flirtation with the waitress—I don't make a habit of it. I just wanted to avoid a scene, for your benefit. She was in the wrong."

Somehow, Dellis doubted that he didn't make a habit of charming waitresses to get his way; the man clearly knew he was handsome. His smiles and winks were always perfectly timed for maximum effect; even now she felt herself falling prey to it. They sat quietly for a few moments, the waitress finally bringing the drink to the table, again leaning over and affording the Captain a view of her assets. Dellis reached over the table and switched tankards with him.

He grinned, watching as she took a sip. "So, you're going to let me have the drink she spat in?"

Dellis smiled over the lid of her tankard, then winked at him—two could play his game. "Touché," she said, tartly, using his own quip against him.

"Miss McKesson, I'm beginning to think you don't like me. Not only did you just give me your potentially contaminated drink, but you've twice tried to rid yourself of my company, once to Kateri, and now with the waitress."

Dellis countered with wide, innocent eyes, but inside she was laughing loud and hearty. "I'll leave you to guess. A lady never gives away her secrets. What say you now?"

"All right." He nodded curtly. "A man knows when he's been put in his place."

After a few moments of uncomfortable silence and her eyes doing laps around the bar, Dellis realized that she might have been a bit sharp with him. Had she really hurt his feelings? It was only a jest. When she looked over at him, he was quietly watching the patrons while he sipped his drink. After several moments, their eyes met across the table in a silent stare down, the corner of his lips turned up in a wry grin that slowly spread all the way across. *Insufferable rogue.* He was playing a game with her. Dellis rolled her eyes.

Say something.

And as if on cue, he said, with all seriousness, "If you don't mind me asking, how do you come to live in German Flats if your family is Oneida?"

Dellis took a sip of her cider, wincing at the sour, pungent taste—the apples were too early in season. "My Uncle James was already living in German Flats when my father traveled here with his younger brother, Dane. There was an outbreak of smallpox in our village and my father, being a doctor, went to help. That's how he met my mother. She was the tribal medicine woman. After they were married, my Uncle Dane built The Thistle for them as a wedding gift. We lived between both places, the village and here in town. My father and mother were known for their medical skills, they used it to try and rebuild relations between the locals and our village."

"So, you're half Oneida and half Scottish?" he asked, putting the pieces together.

"Yes, my father was from Scotland. But my mother was Oneida, so I am Oneida," she replied, proudly. "That's the rule in our culture."

The Captain nodded. "I'm familiar with the tradition. But what I don't understand is why the issue with getting supplies? This town looks to be able to care for itself and capable of trading with your village."

"There's a long history between the locals and the tribes of this area. During the war, the French and their Mohawk allies attacked German Flats. Since then, relations between our tribe and the town have been nonexistent. And there are some things we can't make on our own, like bullets and other metalwork. My grandfather has only recently managed to start trading with the local blacksmith. But there's still no trust between the town and my village, so we keep our distance. It's a fragile peace, if that's what you call it."

"What was the trouble you mentioned earlier?"

"Four Mohawk women were kidnapped from a village not two days ago. Whoever did it was traveling with a Rebel militia, and they spoke Oneida. My grandfather tried to make peace with our brothers by promising to find out what happened."

"So, what now?" the Captain asked, putting his tankard down on the table.

That was an excellent question, if only she had an incantation or some magical spell so she could use it to see the future. "Rumor has it the Mohawk are already siding with the British. If that happens, it could be bad for the whole Confederacy."

"When we were riding into town, I saw construction on the north side of the river…"

She interrupted him, her ire rising. "Damn the Rebels. They are rebuilding one of the old forts here in town and another across the river. That's probably what you saw. It's the worst thing that could happen to us. I wish they would just go away."

"Why?" he asked, his eyes scanning the room.

"Because it's only a matter of time before they approach my tribe wanting support for their cause. The Confederacy lost so much after the French war; we don't need to be involved in another one. It would tear us apart." Looking up, she spotted Alexei standing near the bar. "Will you excuse me for a moment, Captain?"

Getting up quickly, she walked over to her cousin and tapped his shoulder. "Alexei?"

"Dellis, what are doing here?" He turned and gave her one of his usual scowls. "You left my mother running the inn by herself?"

Patrick came up from behind him, a tankard in hand and a cheeky, suggestive grin on his lips. Apparently, the two of them had been at The Kettle for a while. "Dellis, how are you?"

"I'm fine." She nodded, noticing how his eyes uncharacteristically dropped below her chin. Yes, he'd been drinking *way* too much. "I'm helping my lodger sell some of his goods. We just stopped in for a drink."

"So, you're helping the Tory sell his wares, are you?" Alexei smirked, looking over at John, the two men nodding to each other.

"He's a Tory?" Patrick asked, nudging Alexei in the back, some of the ale spilling from his cup all over his arm, staining the fabric.

"Please, don't allow my cousin to put foolish ideas in your head." Dellis afforded Alexei a tap on the arm and then one to the side of his head, messing up his long, straight hair. He was always quick to draw conclusions but never apologized when proven wrong. "You have no basis for your comments, cousin. Besides, that man gave me enough food to feed all of us for the next two months. You should be grateful to him."

"He looks like a Loyalist to me," Alexei muttered, smoothing his hair back into place. "And keep your slaps to yourself, cousin."

She shook her head—Alexei was behaving like a complete idiot. "We're being very rude. Allow me to introduce you to him, and you'll see he is quite pleasant." She led them both back to her table, making quick introductions.

"I understand you're a merchant?" Alexei asked, crossing his arms over his chest, fixing his stance. "Or would it be more appropriate of me to call you what you are, a profiteer?"

Captain Anderson nodded, cocking a brow. "You're not wrong. I'm just one of many."

"I'm curious as to how you come by your supplies—blockade running is rather difficult these days. And if you do have goods to sell, why would you bring them here of all places? Surely business is more lucrative in New York harbor than a little town like this."

"Is that relevant?" the Captain asked, his gaze unflinching. "I have no doubt you do business with plenty of my sort, or do you just steal what you need?"

Dellis couldn't help but notice how calm Captain Anderson was, his feathers completely unruffled by Alexei's taunts. Her cousin, on the other hand, was ready for a fight, his stance fixed, and his hackles raised. It was nice to see him match wits with a worthy adversary. Alexei had asked for it, and the captain was more than capable of delivering.

"You should be more careful, Captain, a Tory could get himself in trouble around these parts." Alexei added, the timbre of his voice dropping an octave.

She waited for the captain to respond, but he just shrugged off Alexei's threat with one of his boyish smiles.

"Did you hear the British attacked the flotilla on Lake Champlain?" Patrick asked, purposely interrupting the face-off between the two men.

"What does that mean?" Dellis looked at her cousin, then at Patrick, her stomach doing a nose dive all the way to her feet.

"If they get through, they'll go after Fort Ticonderoga and then Albany," Alexei answered. She noticed how her cousin and Captain Anderson stared each other down, almost posturing for a fight.

"My God." She gasped. Their isolated little town had been relatively protected from the war until now. The thought of the British so close to home brought back terrifying memories. Part of her wanted to hole up in her room with the door locked and never come out.

Sensing her distress, the Captain touched her arm gently then patted it. At the corners of his eyes, little wrinkles formed, softening his features. "It'll be all right. Arnold and his men will stop them."

She knew he was saying this for her betterment, but it didn't work, not one bit. It was all happening too fast; the war, their disagreement with the

Mohawk. She just wished the world would stop spinning for one day. Why was peace so hard to attain? "Do you mind if we go? It's been a long day, and I still have work to do at home."

He nodded, his brow creased with concern. "Of course. Gentlemen, will you excuse us? I'll see the lady home."

As the Captain led her to the door, Jussie linked her arm through his and pulled him aside. Glancing at Dellis, Jussie spoke just loud enough to be heard above the crowd. "You be careful with her; rumor has it everyone's had a ride on that mare."

Jussie's words were like a knife in the gut, but Dellis refused to let anyone see how they wounded her. What did Jussie know of the truth anyway? And if Captain Anderson was the type of man to indulge in rumors, so be it. Dellis held her head high and stomped out the door, ignoring the exchange.

"Miss McKesson," the Captain called from behind, racing to catch up to her.

Dellis stopped but didn't turn around, her eyes suddenly stinging with unshed tears.

Thankfully, he didn't touch her or try to turn her around. She would have lashed out if he did, and that would have given further credence to all the rumors floating around about her. "I don't listen to gossip. Please, believe me."

Taking a deep breath, Dellis composed herself quickly, then faced him. "Thank you, Captain." Those were all the words she could muster without bursting into tears.

He followed with a curt, "You're welcome."

As they quietly walked towards their horses, Dellis glanced over her shoulder, sensing an unfriendly presence. Someone was watching them. Standing near the barn was the most impressive Mohawk brave she'd ever seen. He was gigantic, almost as tall as Alexei, but the brave's chest was three feet deep and rock solid with muscle. He wore buckskin leggings and a linen shirt, his hair in the traditional warrior's scalp lock. His dark eyes followed the pair intently, unwavering even when she stopped and faced him.

Grabbing her arm, the Captain pulled her towards the horses, his voice suddenly edgy. "We should go."

"He's a Mohawk," she said, mounting her horse, turning it so she could get another look. But he was gone. "They don't come into town, not after what happened years ago. I should tell my grandfather. He needs to know."

Captain Anderson didn't reply. He mounted his horse and rode off quickly. There was something strange and unsettling about the way the Mohawk looked at them, as if he knew the Captain, but he'd never been to German Flats before. *Or has he?*

Chapter Twelve

Roger DeLancie could hear the sounds of hooves beating on the ground, their pace slowing as the horse and rider neared the camp. Rising to his feet, he deposited the pistol he was cleaning on the table and walked outside to investigate. It was Eagle Eyes. The native spurred his horse faster, vaulting across the rolling terrain, bridging the distance with expert precision. Dismounting quickly, Eagle Eyes handed the reins of his horse to a young native boy, giving him terse orders how to care for the mount. The boy nodded vigorously, rushing off to do Eagle Eyes's bidding.

Intimidation was so useful when wielded correctly. DeLancie smiled. The sight of the giant Mohawk in native attire would send even the bravest of men running in the opposite direction.

"Major, we need to speak in private," Eagle Eyes said, walking past into the large canvas tent.

It was unlike the stoic Mohawk to be in a rush; he was traditionally reticent and tight-lipped—something had disturbed him.

"What do you have for me, Eagle Eyes?" DeLancie's gaze shot to the nude bodies of the four Mohawk women lying outside of his tent and smiled. It had been an excellent night.

"Something unexpected."

He waved off his servant, waiting for him to leave the tent. When they were finally alone, DeLancie turned his attention to his friend. "Tell me your news."

"I saw John Carlisle today."

"Now that *is* unexpected—where was this?" The mere sound of DeLancie's former second-in-command's name evoked excitement and a myriad of possibilities. John Carlisle. How DeLancie had missed his old friend.

"He was in town with an Oneida woman."

Interesting. What would John be doing in German Flats meeting with an Oneida woman? Last DeLancie had heard, his former subordinate was rotting away in Manhattan, working in a military prison and keeping company with a local whore. "Did you recognize her?"

"Yes, she is from a local village. He was pretending to be a merchant. She was helping him sell his wares."

Motioning to the chair, DeLancie said, "Please, sit."

The giant Mohawk sat, his hulking size dwarfing the chair, the wooden legs and wicker seat creaking loudly, threatening to break under his impressive stature.

DeLancie picked up the pistol he'd been cleaning earlier and started to buff it with a swatch of linen. It was a meticulous process, cleaning every inch of it, from the barrel to the pan, and then the grip. He relished the feel of steel in his palm; it was powerful and dominant, almost phallic. "Tell me more about John. I have waited so long for news of him."

Something particular must have brought Carlisle back to Tryon County, and undercover to boot. Checking that every nook and cranny was adequately wiped and cleaned, DeLancie placed the pistol in its velvet-lined case and closed the lid.

"They stole the supplies from his storage shed," Eagle Eyes replied. "I saw them do it last night."

DeLancie grinned, knowing exactly to whom Eagle Eyes was referring. "Oh, Johnny, history does love to repeat itself." *Yes, it certainly did.*

"What do you want to do, Major?" the Mohawk asked, reverting to his usual stolid self. A man of few words—DeLancie liked that about his friend. Besides, action, not words, was what got results. And the less DeLancie's orders were questioned the better; he would brook no more discord from his men. He'd already paid the price of an insubordinate second-in-command going rogue once before.

"Do you like chess, Eagle Eyes?" he asked, giving the native a sidelong glance.

"White men's games are tedious."

DeLancie chuckled. Just the response he would expect from his native friend. If there was no abject violence or ambush, then there was no pleasure to be had. An admirable perspective, but not entirely accurate; anticipation and preparation made the reward so much sweeter.

"You're wrong, my friend. You see, it's not just about the win. The thrill of outsmarting your enemy is what makes chess so satisfying." DeLancie got up and walked over to the table where his chess board was set up as if a game were already being played. "It's about picking your move slowly and methodically so that your opponent doesn't see you coming—knowing his weaknesses better than he does."

He picked up one of the white pawns and held it up for Eagle Eyes to see. "The pawn is the most basic piece on the chess board." DeLancie placed the piece on the board, sliding it forward on an angle to take the black pawn diagonal to it. "It can only move forward or capture on an angle, like a solider when he holds the line in battle. It is a strong position but incredibly vulnerable at all times. The most expendable player."

With that, he slid his black rook across the board in a straight line and captured the white pawn with ease. "It's all about knowing where your opponent is going to go next before they get there."

Turning back to his friend, DeLancie smiled. "If you know your enemy as you know thyself, you need not fear the result of a hundred battles. Like the pawn, John is strong but vulnerable. He can only move forward; he can't see what's coming from behind. He has forgotten his Art of War."

"Carlisle was always soft," Eagle Eyes said with disgust.

"But going after an easy prey lacks imagination and sport; we need to give him time to get used to his surroundings again. Let him toughen up a bit." DeLancie stopped for a minute, a plan forming in the recesses of his mind. "Let him be for now. I have other things that are more important at the moment. We leave tomorrow for Niagara, at first light."

He pointed to the bodies of the four dead women lying just outside the tent. "See that they get deposited in the right location."

Picking up the cherrywood case, DeLancie carried it over to his trunk and gently placed it inside. Running his hands over the lid, he glanced at the engraving on top: *For years of devoted service to His Majesty's Infantry, 8th Regiment, Major Roger DeLancie.* As Eagle Eyes picked up one of the bodies, Roger walked outside, the cold wind whipping through the bare trees. He remembered the last time he saw John—the look on Carlisle's face was so smug as he plunged the proverbial dagger into his superior's back and twisted it deep.

"You would betray the man who made you? Traitor! Judas! There's a place in hell for you. I'll see you get there!" DeLancie yelled, his eyes locking with John's.

Oh, yes, DeLancie would see that John got there. It was time. *Finally.*

The wheel of fate had turned in DeLancie's favor; the traitor had returned. With the winter coming, soon the rivers would freeze, and they would be trapped together, just the two of them—the teacher and the student, man against man.

Turning back to Eagle Eyes, DeLancie said, "While you're out, my friend, see that you bring back some company for the two of us. I feel like celebrating. Only this time, bring me one like my Lily."

Chapter Thirteen

"Dellis, you shouldn't go out there by yourself. I forbid you. It's dangerous," her aunt yelled, following Dellis to the door. "Let Alexei and your grandfather handle this."

"Auntie, I'm going, and there's nothing else to say. Besides, everything is prepared for the day: There is dough rising for bread, the soup is already bubbling in its pot, and I even got everything cut up for the evening stew. Thomas will be in any minute, and he stays until close." She looked over her shoulder and smiled. "I *even* made candles and set the linen to soak. Everything is done. No need to worry. I'll be back in the morning before you even get here."

Grabbing her gray cloak, she pulled the hood up, tying it in place. Determined to get away before her aunt could object, Dellis bolted through the door and walked right into the Captain as he came up the steps. "Excuse me, Captain," she said, side-stepping to the right to avoid going face-first into his chest. "I need to take care of something. My aunt will see to your tea."

Somehow, he managed to latch onto her arm before she could get past him. "What happened?"

Dellis glanced at his hand on her wrist, her heart racing. His touch always brought with it quivers that started in her stomach and traveled all the way down to her toes. It wasn't unpleasant, far from it, but it was unsettling. "Please, let me go." She begged, quietly, under her breath. "This is urgent."

Her aunt walked up behind them, wiping her hands on her apron. Great, now Dellis would never get away. "Dellis, I forbid you to go. If someone is kidnapping women from the local villages, it's best you stay here, where it's safe."

"Did they find the missing Mohawk women?" he asked, his hand tightening on her wrist. When she looked up, his blue eyes were focused and penetrating, boring deep into hers.

"Yes, Captain, the bodies were found near Fort Stanwix, about thirty miles from here. I'm going to see if there are any clues as to who is trying to frame our people. Now, if you'll please let me go, I can make it while there's still daylight and spend the night in my village." Pulling her arm from his grasp, she readjusted her cloak and hood and continued down the steps at lightning speed.

"Captain, please, don't let her go by herself," she could hear her aunt beg from the doorway. "It's too dangerous for her to go alone."

"I'll go after her," Dellis heard him say from behind her.

As she neared the stable, her Uncle James rode in, and just like Alexei, James was wearing one of their inherent, resting scowls. "Dellis, I need to have words with you," he said, dismounting and chasing her down before she could get away.

"Sorry, Uncle, I'm going to help Alexei." She lied, knowing the truth would only infuriate him. He hated anything that had to do with her tribe, his personal prejudice always causing an argument between the two of them. "I'll be back tomorrow."

As Dellis tried to mount her horse, her uncle seized the reins, stopping her. "Don't you dare defy me."

She knew he wanted to talk about The Thistle's finances—her aunt had said so—but it was the farthest thing from Dellis's mind at the moment. Besides, she wasn't ready to face the inevitable yet, content to bury her head in the sand for a few weeks more, or at least until she could make heads or tails of the ledger. She needed to have a plan, an idea how to cut corners or make more capital, before she pleaded her case to her uncle. He was far too good at intimidation, always talking around the subject, leaving her dumbfounded and yielding to his control. The Thistle was too important to her to give in so easily.

"Uncle, I'm a counselor in my tribe. There are sure to be negotiations taking place." She pleaded. Again, with the lie. "I need to go."

"Those women are dead; there's nothing for you to do now. Besides, you're a woman, and negotiating is men's work. You would do well to remember that." Her uncle sneered, his nostrils flaring.

From behind him, she could see the Captain standing just outside the stable doors, his back turned to them. Grateful for his presence, she decided to use it to her advantage. "Captain Anderson, please, come in. This is my uncle, James McKesson."

Her uncle gave her a warning look, then turned to the Captain, the two men shaking hands. She knew her uncle would never argue with her in front of a guest; he was too concerned about his reputation and keeping up appearances. "The Captain is a merchant, and he and his men are staying at The Thistle," she said.

"And we are grateful for Miss McKesson's hospitality," the Captain said, giving her a knowing look. "She was also kind enough to help me procure buyers for all of my goods."

Her uncle nodded, his expression calmer, more composed than earlier, but she knew he was slow-brewing. "That's good to hear. Tell me more about yourself. Where do you put in port, Captain Anderson?"

Her ears perked up. She couldn't help but be curious—the man never disclosed even the slightest bit about himself, not even in passing conversation.

"New York Harbor, most of the time, and I have a boat in Oswego," the Captain answered, offering nothing more on the topic. Once again, he was vague about his origins. Maybe Alexei was right. Perhaps he *was* a

Tory and just trying to keep up pretenses long enough to do business and get out of town safely. It made sense. "Sir, you need not worry about Miss McKesson's safety, I'll travel with her."

Dellis noticed how her uncle looked the man over suspiciously. James, too, was intrigued by her mysterious lodger. "It's a pleasure to meet you, Captain. Dellis, I'll speak with you later, when you return." James pointed a finger at her in warning. "Don't try to avoid me again."

Once he was in the house, the Captain turned to her, a grim look on his face. "My apologies, I didn't mean to interrupt your conversation, but you looked like you could use some help."

She shook her head. "I'd rather not talk about it. If you're going to join me, then let's go now, before he changes his mind."

There was no use in trying to stop the Captain from coming along, so she relented, accepting the situation while he quickly saddled and mounted his horse. She had to admit, the prospect of having company made the long ride seem less tedious. After all, he was pleasant, and their playful banter always lightened the mood. Especially with what she was about to face; she could use a little friendly diversion.

It took them several hours to reach Fort Stanwix, stopping a couple of times to rest, feed their horses, and have some of the cheese and cider she stuffed in her bag for refreshment. Both times, they easily conversed about the history of her village and the relations between the tribes. He seemed genuinely interested in what she had to say, and she found him remarkably knowledgeable about the history of the Confederacy and the territory. It wasn't often she encountered someone who gave a wit about what was happening to the local natives. Perhaps it was due to his line of work that he was so worldly and personable. Still, she couldn't help but be curious about him. *What sort of world did he come from? Where is home? Does he have a wife or children?* Truly, it was none of her business, but she couldn't help herself; she wanted to know more about this handsome, interesting stranger.

The sun was already high in the midday sky as they neared the fort, the chilly autumn breeze and bare trees reminding her that winter was on the brink. From a distance, she could see the clearing as they neared the outer ramparts of the fort, the wooden walls rising up from the earth. Slowing down, she turned her horse around so she could face him.

"Captain, you really didn't need to come with me, I'm capable of caring for myself. I'm sure you have plenty of your own work to do."

He nodded in agreement. "I have no doubt you can take care of yourself." She could tell he was fighting back a grin, but instead of delivering a witty comment, he spoke candidly. "But I also agree with your aunt; it's not safe out here. I couldn't possibly let you travel here alone."

Accepting his answer, she turned her horse around, walking it around the grassy field so she could investigate. "Why would they leave bodies here? It has to be a setup," she whispered to herself.

"Of course it is." He interrupted her private conversation. "Anyone else would've buried or burned the bodies to hide the evidence. The question is who, and why would someone do this?"

Excellent question.

He dismounted quickly, and then walked over to her and offered his hand. His snowy white cuff, trimmed with lace, showed from under his forest green coat, his outstretched hand waiting for her to accept. She ignored it, dismounting by herself.

"I plan on getting to the bottom of this situation, Captain," she said curtly, lifting her skirts so they didn't drag in the wet grass, and starting to walk.

The star-shaped fort was situated on the southeast banks of the Mohawk River, on the portage known as the Oneida Carry, a strategic location that linked the Mohawk River to Wood Creek and then to the St. Lawrence. From a distance, the wooden structure looked impressive; the earth built up so that it gently sloped towards the wooden fence that surrounded it. The parapet was visible atop the rampart, with large stakes jutting out from the walls. Wooden sentry boxes were visible on top of the parapet of each of the four bastions. The main entrance faced south, protected by a drawbridge that crossed over a ditch leading to the main gate.

The fort was surprisingly active. Last she'd heard, it was all but abandoned. Dellis looked up at the wooden towers of the gate, the sounds of hammering and soldiers chatting rising over the walls. Her heart pounded as the truth became disturbingly evident. They were preparing for war, the proof right before her eyes.

"Wait here," she yelled over her shoulder to the Captain, and then jogged up to the drawbridge where a sentry stood watch. After asking him several rounds of questions, he finally relented and pointed to the little wooded area near the northwest bastion.

Together, she and John scouted the area, but there was nothing; no tracks or signs of any struggle, not that she expected to find anything. Whoever did this at the Mohawk village had been rather tidy with the cleanup. Still, she needed to look for herself, if only to placate her nerves.

Dellis waited as the Captain walked the perimeter of the fort, his eyes scanning the area meticulously. "You didn't find anything, did you?"

"No," he replied, his back turned to her. "I think this was pretty much a waste of time."

"I couldn't find anything either, though tracking isn't my strong suit."

"Really, what is?" he asked, giving her a wry grin from over his shoulder.

"Shooting," she answered, climbing into her saddle and taking off down the dirt road. She could hear him chuckle from behind as he mounted his horse and caught up to her. "Let's go to Oriska—being so close to the fort, they might know something we don't."

The Oneida castle of Oriska was twelve miles from Fort Stanwix, situated on high ground between the Oriskany Creek and the Mohawk River. It was a larger village than hers, made up of rough-looking log cabins and a few Dutch-style houses with barn-shaped gambrel roofs and brick chimneys. Oriska had flourished from years of trading with the British and the colonists at Fort Stanwix, allowing the city to become rich and prosperous. Because of its location and proximity to the river system, it remained one of the more progressive Oneida villages, continuing to interact with traders along the Oneida Carry.

It took the pair several hours to get Oriska, the sun just dipping below the horizon as they neared. Even from this distance, Dellis could see a meeting was already taking place. She recognized several of the warriors in the group: Han Yerry, the chief of Oriska; Two Kettles, the chief's wife; her grandfather, Great Oak; and the rest of the warriors. And like a great tree towering over the group, Alexei stood back with his fists on his hips, watching and listening intently.

Dellis could sense the tension amongst the group. Something was amiss. Better to investigate first, and then bring the captain into a volatile situation. "Stay here," she whispered. "I won't be long."

He gave her a nod then dismounted.

Dellis ran up to the village guard and addressed him. "*Shekoli*, I'm the granddaughter of Great Oak. Will you allow me to pass?" She pointed to the Captain, who was waiting patiently with his back to them, trying to be nonchalant. "He is with me."

The warrior cocked a brow in question but waved her on. While the Oneida of Oriska were no strangers to white travelers in the region, allowing one to attend their private council was uncommon. As they passed through the stockade, she could hear the men talking loudly, the inflection in their voices spoke of an argument. A fire blazed in the middle of the congregation, emanating such warmth she could feel it from several feet away.

Before they went any farther, Dellis stopped and turned to him. "I'll be right back. Things could get tense; I wouldn't want anyone to be suspicious of you." Dellis stepped closer to him, bridging the distance that separated them. "I'm not trying to exclude you."

She meant what she said, and he understood. "Not at all," he replied, nodding his head.

Dellis walked around the group, passing through a bunch of paint-covered bodies, smudging some on her sleeve as she went for her cousin. When she was behind him, Dellis tugged on the back of Alexei's tunic to get his attention. "What's going on?" she asked, barely able to see around all the warriors.

"Han Yerry and Joseph are meeting with a representative from Fort Stanwix."

"Who is he?" She pointed to a man in a navy blue jacket with a myriad of gold trim that sparkled in the firelight.

Alexei whispered from the side of his mouth, "He's one of Colonel Elmore's men."

Dellis stepped in front of her cousin so she could get a better view of the meeting. Her grandfather was easy to find amongst the crowd. He was wearing an ornately adorned Gustoweh on his head, large eagle feathers springing forth from the top, specifically, two pointed up and one down, signifying the Oneida nation. Next to him was the infamous Han Yerry, the half-Mohawk-half-German chief of Oriska.

"We have received a formal letter from the British and our brothers to the north. If we don't join forces with them, they will assume that we have broken with the Confederacy, and they will attack," Han Yerry said to the Lieutenant, the deep tone of his voice resonating over the group. "We have actively scouted for you, going against the neutrality of the Confederacy, but now, we are in danger. We find ourselves slowly being divided. Many of our Mohawk brothers are working with Joseph Brant and Colonel Butler. This incident could make things worse."

The officer shook his head, his hands resting on his hips. "We had nothing to do with this, I promise you. You must believe me."

"Our Mohawk brothers claimed the bodies, but they were not satisfied with our explanation. Since detaining the British in Kanonwalohale, they suspect us of scouting for you. We must protect ourselves, and we want to stay true to our word to General Schuyler, but we are desperately in need of supplies. There are no longer traders passing through the Carry, and the colonists are hesitant to meet with us. The Great King's men offer us anything we want if we agree to work with them. You will lose our brothers Seneca and Onondaga if you don't find a way to trade with them," Joseph said, his voice grim.

The Lieutenant looked at Joseph and Han Yerry with a reticent expression, betraying nothing, and offering even less. "I will speak with the

General and see what we can do. For now, please, be patient. I'll get word to both of you after I have spoken with him."

Han Yerry nodded. "Our people will continue to scout the area, but that's all for now. We must protect ourselves and appeal to our brothers to remain together."

Once the meeting officially ended, Dellis moved through the crowd, pushing her way towards her grandfather. "What did you learn?"

The lines of his face grew more pronounced when he caught sight of her. She'd never seen him so worried. "The bodies of the Mohawk women were found close to the fort by Han Yerry's men. He sent word to Canajoharie offering our sympathies and our support, but it wasn't received well."

"Wasn't received well—what does that mean?" She stepped in front of him. Her grandfather was purposely being nebulous, but she was determined to get the truth from him. "Do they know you're scouting for the Rebels? Is that why they don't believe us? We are brother tribes; is there no trust between us any longer?"

The look on his face spoke volumes. She was right. Her grandfather walked past her, his long stride forcing her to run to keep up. "I'm right, aren't I? That's why you—"

"Dellis, you must stay out of this," he said, turning back to her.

But she persisted, determined to say her piece. "You don't need the Rebels to trade with—Captain Anderson will get you all the supplies you need. Don't you see they're both trying to blackmail you? British or Rebel, it doesn't matter. Grandfather, they are using us for their own gain."

"Then we must take control of our fate and decide on where our fortunes lie." He finished, his expression as impassive as stone.

She rubbed her forehead, an ache developing behind her eyes as she considered the consequences of their actions. Why was she the only one who could see what was happening? They were being dragged into this war by both sides, British and American. Neither party was innocent, nor did they care what they were doing to the Confederacy.

"Is there anything I can do for you, Miss McKesson?"

When she looked up, the Captain was standing next to her, his blue eyes full of concern. Unable to think past the issues of the moment, she shook her head. "No, just get the supplies that you promised to my grandfather as soon as possible." But would trading goods make any difference on their plight now?

He nodded. "Of course. Shall we go back?"

Before she could reply, her cousin walked past her, grim-faced. "Dellis, you need to stay out of this. You'll only get in the way."

"What did you say?" Whirling around, she looked her cousin in the eye, daring him to spit out more of his vitriol.

"I told you to stay out of this. It's dangerous."

Clenching her fists, she let it go, unable to hold back her frustration. "Alexei, what are you doing? I know you're the one encouraging this alliance with General Schuyler. Don't you see? If we choose sides and go against the Confederacy, we'll lose everything. You're a fool if you think the colonists will help us, a naïve fool."

"Better to take a side and defend what's ours than to hand it over," Alexei replied, his blue eyes like a hawk's, piercing and focused on her like prey. "And believe me, if we don't choose, the British will take what they want. Better to fight and die on the side of right."

"The only cause you care about is your own, Alexei." She shook her head in disgust. "United as a confederacy we are strong, but as separate tribes we are weak. We both know there will be no going back if that happens. Then what's to stop the British or the colonists from taking everything from us?"

The Captain walked over to her, though his eyes followed Alexei's every move. "Why don't we go back? It's getting late."

"Are you afraid of the savages in the forest?" Alexei taunted, advancing on the Captain until there were only inches separating them. "Or spending a night in a native village?"

"Not in the least. Should I be?" Looking up at Alexei, John smiled, his blue eyes twinkling, but there was a bit of challenge there. "Now, if you will excuse me, the lady and I'll be leaving."

The Captain quickly shrugged off Alexei's blustering, as always, then turned back to her. "Miss McKesson, shall we?" John waved his arm in the direction of their horses, gallantly allowing her to lead the way.

"I must apologize for my cousin's behavior; twice now he's been rude to you for no reason. He fancies himself a Rebel, and he thinks everyone he doesn't know is a Tory. You have been so kind and patient…"

They both stopped walking and faced each other, the gravity of their conversation weighing between them. "Please, there's no need to be sorry." He looked at her with such intensity, her heart leaped in her chest, his hand gently resting on top of hers, sending a shiver down her spine. She pulled it away quickly, but he didn't flinch or make a move to stop her. "Tell me, how is Alexei one of your tribe? Is he not your uncle's son?"

She nodded. "Yes, but he grew up with my family. As you probably can tell from earlier, my uncle is not a kind man. When Alexei was young, he was very sick and needy, and my Uncle James had no patience for him. My mother and father took Alexei in and cared for him. He grew up more like an older brother to Stuart and me than a cousin. Eventually, he became one of the tribe, though his father isn't happy about it. My uncle hates anyone with native blood."

They walked the rest of the way to their horses, and thankfully, he didn't try to help her into her saddle. Putting her foot in the stirrup, Dellis mounted her horse. "I'm afraid Alexei's passionate belief in the Rebel cause has spread to the rest of the tribe. This land is sacred to us. The spirits of our loved ones reside in these woods, watching over us, protecting us. Since the Treaty of Fort Stanwix, things have been strained between the British and my people. So much of our land was taken away, and that bitterness isn't easily forgotten."

"And after what happened to your village, and the loss of your land, can you blame your grandfather for wanting to protect all of you?" he asked, mounting his horse.

"No, not entirely, but I don't believe the Rebels will do any more right by us than the British."

He smiled, a lock of his hair blowing into his face, softening his features, giving him that boyish look again. Initially, she didn't want his intrusion, but now she was thankful for his presence—he had a way of helping her forget the drama playing out around her. It was as if he could conjure up a private little world where the two of them could get lost together for hours. The quiet respite he brought was welcomed, even if only for a moment, before reality reared its ugly head again.

"I would race you back to town, but I think Viceroy has had a little too much riding for one day. His ego couldn't handle being beaten by your mare."

"His ego or yours, Captain?" she said, grateful for the return of their playful banter.

He let out a laugh, and then shook his head with incredulity. "Touché, Miss McKesson. A well-played hand, indeed."

It was rather a good dig, if she had to say so herself, but it also provided her an excellent opportunity. With a grin, she said, "So, I'll take it slow on you two old men if you tell me all about Manhattan. I've always wanted to go there. My father used to live there; he liked to go to the theater. Tell me, have you ever seen a play, or perhaps the opera?"

"Both and many times," he replied, and left it at that, much to her chagrin. *What is he hiding?*

Chapter Fourteen

"Captain, we're almost there. It's just past the clearing," Clark said, pointing towards a cluster of trees, and small barn, a few yards ahead of them. "What did you find out from your travels today?"

Before John would answer, he surveyed the area, the ever-present sensation of eyes watching him making him all the more cautious. A bitter chill had set in. He pulled his cloak up high around his neck, blowing on his hands, trying to warm them. "The Oneida from Oriska and one of the smaller villages are scouting for the Rebels. I was near Fort Stanwix today. It's being refortified, along with two others in town."

"Where are they getting their supplies? Schuyler is begging for men and whatever he can get to defend Lake Champlain. Washington is broke. Rumor has it that he's begging their Congress for money and supplies."

"I'm not sure where they're getting them from." He had his suspicions, but he was going to keep them to himself for now.

"What else did you find out, John?"

It was dark, the clouds, like a blanket, blocked out the moonlight, offering up no light to guide their way. As expected, the little village was quiet, the townspeople already in their beds for the night. But for him, this was just when the evening began. Had he been in York City, he would be getting ready for a night of carousing, prepping with a few tots of whiskey and a tankard of ale before he headed off to Celeste's house. A drink sounded good right about now, and a woman even more so.

"Clark, does the name McKesson sound familiar to you?"

"It's a good Scot's name. So?" Clark shrugged his shoulders. "I know of an Admiral McKesson, the one that's a duke. Why?"

It was apparent Clark had yet to put the pieces of the puzzle together, content not to look for conspiracies or coincidences. That's what made Simon such a valuable second-in-command; he was far from calculating and loyal to a fault. But after a day spent traveling with their innkeeper and a visit to her village, there was no mistaking the true identity of the lovely Miss McKesson.

"Simon, our innkeeper is from that village, and her last name is McKesson."

Clark pulled his horse to a stop and looked at him. "John, you think she is related to…"

Before Clark could finish he nodded. "Her mother was Oneida and her father was in the Royal Navy. Both of them are dead."

"You think her uncle is Admiral McKesson, the Duke of McKesson?"

"I believe so." John pulled the reins again, starting to walk his horse closer to the storage barn.

"John, this whole situation just got significantly more complicated. There are rumors that the Duke is still trying to find those responsible for his brother's death. This could be a problem if our identity is discovered."

That was an understatement if he'd ever heard one. "She told me that all the warriors and sachems had gone to Onondaga for a tribal council, both Samuel Kirkland and Guy Johnson were there. This was no small meeting. DeLancie knew about it, I would bet my life on that."

"John, we have a job to do. And you have a better chance of repairing your reputation by doing Howe's bidding than chasing after ghosts and digging up our past failures."

He wholeheartedly agreed, but for some reason, the past seemed to be resurrecting itself and not at his command. Fate's sleight of hand. "The woman I rescued saw me at the village. She recognized me. I managed to cover it up, but I know Miss McKesson was suspicious."

"You need to keep your distance from our innkeeper, and that means in every way."

He could hear condescension in his friend's voice. They'd known each other for many years and if anyone could berate John about his personal habits or his lack of decorum, Simon could. But in this case, he was grasping at straws. "Give me a bit more credit than that. I have no interest in her save gaining the information we need to complete our mission."

Simon shook his head vigorously against John's dubious insistence. "I've heard that one before."

While he found Miss McKesson incredibly alluring, he had no intentions towards her, and even less so now that he knew the truth. In spite of her outward appearance of strength, she clearly had deeply entrenched fears of men. The first time they met, she'd pulled her hand away from him abruptly, and on other occasions, she'd avoided his assistance though he was just trying to be polite. She had good reason to be afraid—what happened to her was nothing short of a nightmare. He remembered her torn dress and the handprint bruises on her thighs. She'd been used violently. It would take a patient man to help her overcome such fear, and he was definitely not the one. He couldn't be. Clark was right; John needed to keep his distance.

But still, his conscience pricked at her sorry state of affairs: her family was all gone, her brother a witless loon, and she was about to lose her home. By no fault of her own, she'd been deemed the town pariah when she was actually an innocent victim. When the waitress at The Kettle insulted Dellis, he felt hard-pressed to defend her honor; though, in truth, it was he who had inadvertently set her life on its current path. A small part of him desperately wanted to help her, though her ego would never allow her to accept. Nothing he could do would ever make amends for all that had come to pass, nevertheless, he wanted to do something for her.

As they approached the storage barn, John dismounted, already noticing something was awry, even in the darkness. The door was cracked, the lock hanging open. "I thought you had someone guarding this, Simon?"

"I did," Clark replied, a few steps behind him.

Grabbing the broken lock and handing it to Clark, John threw the doors open, already knowing what he would find. The barn was empty, stripped bare, and there was not one barrel of rum or bag of grain left behind. He chuckled at the irony of the situation while he resisted the urge to put his fist through a wall.

"Well, this presents a bit of a problem," John said sarcastically, though his anger was boiling under the surface like a stew pot ready to overflow. Knowing the skill of the local thieves, they had taken the supplies, and there wouldn't be a footstep or hoof print left behind to track. He'd seen it done before, and when he tried to catch them, they disappeared like ghosts in the forest—the same damn forest that always protected them. Suddenly, it felt like history was repeating itself.

Damn. Walking back to his horse, John mounted up, refusing to waste another moment trying to investigate and give Dolos more fodder for his amusement. Let the god of deception make a mockery of another man, John would brook no humor at his expense.

"I don't know how this is possible. I had a guard keeping eyes on the barn," Clark said. "And I was here yesterday and the day before. I swear to you, John. It must have just happened today. They must have had eyes on me."

The whole situation was so obvious; Clark was overlooking the facts, seeing the proverbial trees and not the forest. "That's exactly what happened. Don't further distress yourself, friend. Your guard either worked for the thieves or they paid him off. Either way, when you left, they came back and took what they wanted."

Slamming the door behind him, Clark let out a loud curse. "Damn it, John, I wasn't followed. I would have known it."

"Frustrating, isn't it?" Chuckling to himself, John knew exactly how his friend felt. "No matter, all the goods are marked with the symbol of

Carlisle Shipping. I anticipated something like this would happen. If they turn up, we'll be able to figure out who took them."

"What do we do now?" Clark asked, mounting his horse.

That was an excellent question. He had promised supplies to two different merchants and Joseph. Denny was due any day in Oswego, but that was dependent on his ability to slip through the British ports on the St. Lawrence and not get caught. They would have to use that shipment to fill their agreements. Now, not only was his timeline pushed back, but he owed the cost of the lost cargo, something he couldn't afford to front.

"John?" Clark rode up next to him. "Gavin doesn't know you're working with Denny. He's going to expect payment for those supplies. Are you going to write him?"

"Absolutely not. That's not even an option." Involving his brother would only make things worse and further complicate the mission. Somehow, John would figure out another way to cover the cost. "Everything happened so quickly. I was lucky Denny was docked in the harbor at the time we made the arrangements. He did me a favor helping me out with this situation. If I write to Gavin, it will expose Denny's failings. I can't repay my friend by exposing him and costing him his job."

"What now?"

"We've got time. It will take months before word gets back to Gavin. I'll have this solved before that happens."

"I have a sinking feeling I know who took those supplies," Clark said, looking back at the barn.

John rubbed his forehead, considering the entirety of his conundrum. He had tried before to go after missing supplies, little good that did him, and he needed to befriend the Oneida, not accuse them of theft. Perhaps Celeste would have the money. He would write her when he got back to his room; a nice flowery letter full of innuendos would do the trick.

"For now, we keep our eyes open. Something is sure to turn up. We need to stay focused on the mission and get word to Smith."

Clark chewed his lip, looked at the empty barn, and then looked at his companion. "This isn't good, John."

"No, it isn't." John laughed again, the irony of the situation not lost on him.

"I wish you would let me in on what you find so amusing."

He shook his head. "It's not amusing, not in the least." But lashing out at the culprits would solve nothing, nor would violence. This time, he would be smarter and handle the situation on his own terms. Thankfully, he had no DeLancie to deal with, only thieves and their native friends. There was a way to make this work to John's advantage; time would reveal the answer, he just needed to be patient. "I have to get information back to Howe soon. I'm sure he is waiting to make a decision about what to do next."

"I heard in town that Carleton and his men fought Arnold around Valcour Island. The whole battle was a bust. Arnold burned what was left of his ships and disappeared into the forest like a ghost in the night. Even if Carleton takes Ticonderoga, there's no way they'll go after Fort Stanwix with the winter so close."

"Simon, we don't know that for sure. He asked me to be expeditious with my information, and that's what I intend to do. I'll scout the fort tomorrow and see what I can find out."

"Yes, Captain."

"Tomorrow, you and Hayes ride out and meet Smith in Oswego. As soon as the supplies come in, bring what we need and store the rest there. Be quick about your mission, we're already behind schedule."

Turning his horse, John suddenly remembered something else he wanted to tell Clark. "By the way, I saw Eagle Eyes yesterday."

"Did he see you?" Clark asked.

"I have no doubt. The question is, what is he doing here?" Eagle Eyes didn't like colonists, nor did he make it a habit of frequenting local villages. If he was in town, then he was looking for something. Something particular.

"Do you think he might have gone after our storage?"

John stopped for a moment, considering the validity of the question. "I don't know, but I wouldn't put anything past him." He hadn't set eyes on the Mohawk scout since the day his superior was taken to the gallows. The look in the native's eyes had been palpable. He blamed John for what happened to DeLancie, and the warrior wasn't the type to forget.

"John, if he saw you, then you better watch your back. We both know he wants revenge."

"I'm aware," John said calmly, revealing none of his inner consternation. "Believe me, I'm aware."

Chapter Fifteen

Examining his nails carefully, DeLancie made sure there were no rough edges or specks of dirt underneath. He'd been sitting the hall for almost an hour waiting for the Major to finish his meeting. DeLancie didn't like waiting, patience not a virtue he cared to indulge, but he could make an exception for someone as important as John Butler. As the recently appointed deputy agent of the Canadian Indians at Fort Niagara, Butler reported directly to Major-General Guy Carleton, the Governor-in-Chief of Quebec. A native of Tryon County, Major Butler spoke all dialects of the Six Nations and was well connected with the illustrious and influential Johnson family, including the new superintendent.

"Major Butler will see you."

DeLancie looked up at the guard, irritated that he didn't address DeLancie as Major or salute him, as he rightly deserved. Standing up, DeLancie made a mental note of the man's face; when the time came, DeLancie would make sure this soldier never forgot to address someone properly again.

"My guide will be joining us." DeLancie gestured to the giant Mohawk standing nearby, noticing how the soldier flinched at first sight. Roger grinned, appreciating his scout's ability to intimidate at just a glance. *Oh, the fear.* DeLancie licked his lips, moistening them. *Tastes good.*

"All right." The sentry nodded then escorted DeLancie and Eagle Eyes into the office, watching the native with much trepidation.

Butler's office was exceptionally large, a sign of power and influence that he should be allotted such grand space in a tightly packed fort where living quarters were a precious commodity. A fire blazed from a stone hearth in the corner, cracking and popping with vigor, though it barely warmed the room. The stone walls and high, oak-paneled ceiling gave it a cavernous feeling, further accentuating the chill that permeated. In Niagara, one got used to being cold; the breeze coming off the lake year-round was frigid, and it blew through the drafty windows with the tempestuous fury of a wronged lover.

This should have been DeLancie's office. He looked around, fighting back fury with clenched teeth and tight fists buried in his pockets. *All in good time.*

Standing behind the desk, short and stout in build, Butler waited in his bright green tunic with red facings, the usual scowl plastered on his face. "Major DeLancie, it's a pleasure." Butler's eyes darted from Roger to Eagle Eyes, sizing up the giant Mohawk against DeLancie's six-foot-one frame. "What brings you to Niagara?"

DeLancie waited for the sentry to shut the door before speaking, wanting to brook no suspicion—this was for Butler's ears only. "I think, perhaps, it's what I can do for you."

"Please, sit."

DeLancie eyed his Mohawk friend, a silent understanding passing between the two men. Eagle Eyes crossed his arms over his chest and leaned against the door, blocking out any unnecessary intrusions. Once the door was covered, DeLancie took a seat in the sizeable winged-backed chair opposite of Butler's.

"It's been a long time, Roger. I was sorry to hear about your unfortunate situation." Sitting down, Butler drummed his fingers on the arm of his chair nervously. "You know that all of us here in the northern department still respect you and your service to the King."

"Yes, and I'm sure you did everything in your power to help." DeLancie watched Butler's face for a reaction, but he remained stoic, expertly reticent, a skill obtained after years of political intrigue that required the ability to suppress one's dismay. But Roger knew different. His sudden appearance wasn't welcome, and Butler felt no shame about what happened to DeLancie's career. This was all a rouse, a charade to keep up the pretenses of politeness. Butler would throw the man out if it was possible.

"Roger, as you well know, there was nothing more I could do—too many powerful players on the chessboard." Gesturing to him, Butler smiled. "Though, you seem to have fared well, no noose around your neck. At least I was able to manage that. I had no doubt, when enough time passed, you would be useful again."

DeLancie nodded, though disgust oozed through his veins at Butler's self-righteous indignation. But this was an alliance it was necessary to cultivate; Butler could be both powerful and useful if appropriately directed. *Tread lightly.* "Well, Major, it would seem that time may have come already."

"And what does that mean?" Butler asked, cocking a brow.

"I understand you've been made deputy agent."

Butler smiled, his toothy grin, long nose, and prominent chin making him look a bit like one of James Gillray's caricatures. "It hasn't been confirmed by the King yet, but General Carleton has appointed me. I have no reason to believe it won't come to fruition."

"Of course. Who better? I'm sure Daniel Claus agrees."

DeLancie noticed how Butler flinched when he mentioned Claus, the man he had supplanted for his current role. Political games among the ranks were something DeLancie didn't miss—he was never very good at them.

"The General felt I was the better man for the job. But, we both know this should be your position."

DeLancie refrained from comment. He *was* better suited for the position; John Butler wasn't half the soldier DeLancie was, nor did the man have as much experience with the Confederacy. The commission would've been Roger's, if not for his traitorous second-in-command.

"So, how can you help me?"

"I anticipate Howe plans to take the Mohawk Valley by going after Fort Stanwix and Ticonderoga."

The Major didn't respond, his eyes frequently darting over to Eagle Eyes, beads of sweat forming on the Major's brow that he wiped away with a linen kerchief. Cracks were beginning to show in his well-honed performance. Usually, he was better at hiding his apprehension. DeLancie smiled openly. *Fear tastes good.*

"You'll need the cooperation of the Six Nations to be successful," DeLancie said, with confidence. "And I can help you with that."

Butler nodded, running his hand over the edge of his desk then stopping to scratch his nail into the wood. "And how do you intend to do that?"

"Like you, I know the Six Nations—they want this fight, it's in their blood. I can rally them to our cause. I can—"

"No." Butler interjected, shaking his head. "We need them to stay put until the spring, and only when we are ready to engage will they be allowed to fight. Setting them loose in the valley now would only cause chaos."

Damn, the man was weak. He could never lead an army of natives—a man so passive could never earn their respect. "Ah, but you miss the point, Butler, in the midst of chaos, there is opportunity. Attack now and they will take down whoever stands in our way."

"Not all of them are with us." Butler looked up at Eagle Eyes, then back at Roger. "The Mohawk are the only tribe that has made their feelings known and the Seneca, to a degree. The rest are trying to maintain their neutrality, but we're negotiating with them as we speak. It's only a matter of time before they all take up the cause."

"Bribing them with trade goods and treaties?" DeLancie asked. The natives were notoriously fickle, and their allegiances often changed when it suited their needs. "That will only take you so far. You need to promise them more."

"What about your misanthrope Mohawk friend?" Butler gestured to Eagle Eyes, further supporting the point. "If you think he is working for you out of loyalty, you're wrong. Just like his Mohawk brother, Joseph Brant, he wants their lands back, and they're willing to do anything to get them. Eventually, he will turn on you just the same. It's a foregone conclusion."

"I have no problem with that. A man fighting for his home always has the advantage. We would do well to remember that and harness their energy to the fullest. It will only serve to our betterment." DeLancie grinned, their eyes locking. "So, Major, what do you intend to do about the Oneida?"

"The Oneida have declared themselves neutral. Besides, they're in no position to go against the Confederacy. With the Mohawk on one border and the Onondaga on the other, they'll have to follow. They can't afford to do less. Many of them in Oquaga have already joined Joseph Brant's cause. They are divided and small in numbers compared to their brothers."

"Really? I think you've been sitting in this office too long," DeLancie said, leaning forward in his chair. "It's no coincidence that the Oneida detained local Tories at Kanonwalohale. They were stopping them for questioning on Schuyler's bidding. They have already thrown in their lot with the Rebels, especially those from Oriska."

"You don't know this."

"I do, actually, firsthand. They've been patrolling the area and stealing supplies for Fort Stanwix. Samuel Kirkland might be a missionary, but he is also a Rebel, and the Oneida follow his lead."

"Go on," Butler said. His curiosity was piqued.

Finally, DeLancie was making an impression on the obstinate, overconfident Major.

"Eagle Eyes witnessed them stealing from a merchant only days ago. I have no doubt the supplies have reached their destination by now. Fort Stanwix is under the control of Colonel Samuel Elmore and is being refortified as we speak. The Rebels know we're coming, and they'll be ready for us unless we get the manpower now and take them by surprise."

"The winter has set in, and a siege on Fort Stanwix would be difficult and costly. I'll be surprised if Carleton continues on to Fort Ticonderoga."

"No, you're looking at this the wrong way. The winter is a blessing, Major. In war, the way is to avoid what is strong and strike what is weak."

Butler examined his nails for a moment, then looked up. "What do you want from me?"

"We both know diplomacy won't work with the Confederacy. It will take force to bring them to our side. Give me some additional men and weapons, and I'll unite the tribes for you. Then"—sitting back, DeLancie smiled, knowing exactly how to appeal to the man's ego—"you get all the credit."

"What about the Oneida?" Butler countered. "You tried that once before, and we both know how that turned out. Hence, your present state of affairs."

DeLancie gripped the arms of the chair, resisting the urge to jump over the desk and choke the egotistical fool. The man was a weak idiot, but one that was needed. *For now.* Taking a deep breath, DeLancie willed his temper in check. "They will never take up our cause. But once their treachery is known, the other tribes will turn on them. I've already planted the seed. Now, we watch it grow."

"Why do you hate the Oneida?" Butler asked, curiously. "They're no different than the rest."

Oh, they are very different. "The Oneida have always been traitorous and self-serving." He looked out the window. The blue waters of Lake Ontario sparkled in the sunlight, reminding him of jet-black hair blowing on the breeze and deep, soulful eyes that followed the birds flying over the beach. *Lily.* "They took something that was mine. Now, what say you?"

Butler ran his hand over his chin, contemplating DeLancie's proposition. "I have my orders from General Carleton, and I intend to follow them."

DeLancie nodded. Of course, Butler was a lap dog who lacked imagination, why expect anything different from the man? "That's fine.

Perhaps I should approach Guy Johnson. He's in Manhattan; I can get there easily."

A frosty look and a snort told DeLancie exactly what Butler thought of that idea. Both Carleton, as the governor of Quebec, and Guy Johnson, the superintendent of Indian Affairs, held prominent positions, but neither man had much respect for the other. It was a fine line Butler walked between the two, forced to placate both men to maintain his position.

"He has Joseph Brant and his men carrying Howe's belt around trying to make treaties with the tribes on Howe's behalf. Why would he want you? Pugnacious as he is, Brant is still very effective."

"Because I get results, and he knows it." DeLancie reminded Butler. "Brant will be lucky if he gets one hundred men."

"We've known each other too long, Roger, for me to believe you're doing this on behalf of King and country. What do you get out of this?"

"I want a commission and, perhaps, a militia. I find operating free from all the pageantry suits me." DeLancie smiled as he considered all the possibilities a militia could afford him: autonomy and all the manpower he needed. "Also, I get the chance to prove that I was right all along."

"Right about what?" Butler glanced up at Eagle Eyes, then back across the desk. It was apparent the man didn't trust the native listening in on their conversation.

"The Oneida—they've been working with the Rebels since the beginning. They're treacherous liars; not only to us, but to their brethren. I mean only to expose the truth."

Butler stared DeLancie down over the desk. "What do I get out of this?"

Of course, self-serving to the end, Butler was always about his own well-being first, but that was his weakness. DeLancie smiled, playing to the man's ego. "You get to say you succeeded in uniting the tribes, and when we crush the Rebels and take the Mohawk Valley, you get to lead them."

Considering those words for a moment, Butler reached into his desk, pulled out a letter, and handed it over. "This is a message from Johnson to unite the tribes of the Six Nations and set them loose on the Rebels in Tryon County. Do what you want with it."

DeLancie read the letter then handed it back to the Major, watching as Butler held it over the candle, the flame cracking and popping as it greedily consumed the paper.

"And my supplies?"

"Take what you need," Butler said, standing up and adjusting his waistcoat and tunic. "But, know this: If you fail, I had nothing to do with it, and you will deal with the repercussions on your own."

"And if I succeed?" DeLancie asked.

"We'll cross that bridge when we get to it. Now, don't ever come here again. I can't be seen with you, or it will be the end of us both."

DeLancie stood up and nodded. "Good day, Major." Putting on his hat, he walked out, Eagle Eyes following close behind. There was so much to do, and now, DeLancie had the means to do it.

"Thank you, Butler," DeLancie whispered to himself. "Thank you."

Chapter Sixteen

Celeste let out a lovely, exasperated groan. "Oh, Johnny, when are you coming back?" Out the window, she watched as powdery flakes fell from the sky, dusting her busy, cobble-stone street with a blanket of downy white snow. He'd been gone for two weeks. *Two weeks.* And still no word. For all she knew, he could be dead and rotting, his scalp dried and hanging from the belt of some savage. That would be incredibly inconvenient. Not only would she need to find a new lover, but a new business partner as well. Acquiring a new investor wasn't difficult—those were easy to find— but Johnny had a rather unique skill set in the bedroom she would sorely miss. And, oh, those blue eyes and his lips. Her mind wandered to their last meeting. Yes, she would miss his lips and all the little things she could make him do with them.

Rolling over, Celeste looked down at the dark-haired man lying next to her and suddenly wished he would just disappear. He wasn't bad, but she preferred a little more fight in her man and a lot more submission. Tapping him lightly, she tried to wake him. He twitched and pushed her hand away, falling back to sleep. *Time to go.* She touched his shoulder again, but he just continued to snore like a drunken street urchin lying in the street. Frustrated, she opted to climb over him, grabbing her robe from the chair next to the bed and putting it on.

Celeste sat down at her console, admiring herself for a moment. Thankfully, there were no wrinkles around her eyes, and her olive skin was still as bright as a young girl's at first bloom, taut and dewy and incredibly soft. Yes, she could attract another suitor, but she didn't want to. She wanted John. As she carefully brushed her long, glossy, chestnut mane, there was a knock on her door. "Come in," she yelled purposely, hoping to rouse her sleeping guest and get him on his way.

Her dark-skinned assistant stepped into the room and shut the door behind her, glancing at the man sleeping in the bed. "I'm sorry to bother you, should I come back?"

Putting the brush down, Celeste turned around and rolled her eyes. "Don't worry about him. I tired him out."

Agnes nodded, her eyes darting around the room then cast down at the floor shyly. But, like a good girl, she offered no discourse. That's why Celeste liked the girl; Agnes knew her place, slave or not, and she was easy to intimidate. At first, it had been advantageous to free the slave when Celeste's husband, Frederick Allen, died—one less mouth to feed. But much to her surprise, Agnes turned out to be rather good with numbers and taking care of various women's issues, and that was essential when running their type of business. Now, the former slave served as a bookkeeper and maintained Celeste's house for the affordable payment of food and shelter—and not a penny more.

"Mrs. Allen, there's a man downstairs waiting to speak with you."

Celeste tied her robe tightly around her waist and pulled the neck line closed. "Did he say his name?"

"No, Miss, he just said it was important. He's in uniform."

Celeste bubbled over with excitement. *Maybe it was word from John.* "Get my stays and my emerald dress."

Agnes left and returned moments later with the dress and undergarments, and dangling from her fingers, a pair of emerald green shoes. Removing the robe, Celeste admired herself in the mirror while Agnes bustled around helping with the dress. Time had been kind to

Celeste. She was trim with high, full breasts and a waist tiny enough to rival an eighteen-year-old girl's. At thirty, that was a blessing. Rather conveniently, her husband had died when she was only twenty-four, leaving her his modest fortune and his sterling reputation, allowing her to move through society unattached—exactly the way she preferred it.

While Agnes quickly arranged Celeste's hair, she opened up a coveted pot of carmine rouge and applied some to her cheeks and lips. When she was satisfied with her attire, she rushed downstairs, practically knocking one of her ladies and her escort down on the way.

Opening the door to the office, Celeste mustered up one of her most brilliant smiles as the officer stood up and removed his hat. He looked handsome in his crimson red tunic with gold trim, the color combination accented well by his swarthy skin tone and brown hair. *What woman doesn't love a man in a uniform?* Though she preferred the British redcoat to the Rebel navy, there was something dangerous and sexy about the color red. Grinning to herself, she remembered countless nights she made John keep his tunic on while he made love to her. Oh, how she missed him.

"Mrs. Allen," he said, taking her hand and kissing it, his eyes darting to her décolletage quickly then back to her face.

Celeste grinned knowingly. "Sir."

"I'm Lieutenant Dokes of His Majesty's Royal Welsh Fusiliers. I've come to speak with you about an important matter."

"Please, sit, Lieutenant." She gestured to the chair as she took a seat behind her desk, smoothing down her voluminous skirts neatly. Leaning over, she reached for her decanter of whiskey and a glass, purposely affording him a view down her bodice. "Would you care for a drink?"

"No." His reply was curt. "And my visit here isn't a social one."

She fought back a laugh. There wasn't a man alive who could visit her business and not indulge. It was impossible. They were all weak, especially when it came to the pleasures of the flesh. *Now to figure out his poison of choice, women, men, or both?*

"Then what can I do for you?" She rested her arms on her desk and leaned forward, giving the Lieutenant her undivided attention.

"Because of your affiliation with Lieutenant Carlisle, my men have frequented your establishment, almost exclusively, for the past several months."

"Yes, and I thank you for your patronage. And it's Captain Carlisle now." She gave him another of her most dazzling smiles, and he nodded gallantly in return. *So, it was women. Perfect.* The seed was planted—now to watch it grow.

"A fortnight ago, some of my men attended a social gathering here. One of them reported witnessing one of your ladies passing a sealed letter to another gentleman not long after she left his company. They attempted to follow the gentleman, but to no avail. However, last week, my men saw the same two gentlemen leaving your establishment, and when they approached your patrons, they were attacked. My men were able to subdue them, but hidden on their persons we found documents containing information about the British position in Manhattan. These men were Rebels exchanging information and utilizing your ladies and your establishment to cover up their transactions."

Damn. She told her ladies to be more careful; helping local Rebels was a new thing she was experimenting with. It was rather exhilarating to be privy to the secrets on both sides of the war, and her establishment provided the perfect cover to move intelligence. Now that she'd been caught, all she could do was try to play the whole thing as if she were innocent. Considering her options, she decided on the dramatic—that always seemed to work best with men.

"That's preposterous!" she exclaimed, clutching her chest dramatically. "Are you accusing me of helping Rebel spies? I am loyal to His Majesty."

"Do you deny that you have allowed Rebels to frequent your establishment in the past?" he asked tersely.

"No, of course not," she answered, realizing her performance didn't have the intended effect. Time to step up her game. With wide innocent eyes,

Celeste shook her head, clutching the string of pearls that hung around her neck. "If you remember, not so very long ago, I used my establishment to gain information for His Majesty's army, all of which I turned over to Captain Carlisle. He will corroborate with this. Ask him yourself."

But again, the Lieutenant was unmoved, his voice stolid. "Captain Carlisle is away on duty."

Celeste's eyes darted around the room while her mind raced to come up with a plan. *Damn John for leaving.* If he hadn't gone off on a mission to the middle-of-nowhere, this wouldn't be happening.

Lieutenant Dokes stood up, throwing his shoulders back with authority. "I'm closing your establishment, by order of His Majesty's Magistrate and Governor Tryon. You are under arrest for treason against His Majesty, King George III."

Reason took over where panic threatened. She could handle this. Men were easy; they all had the same weakness. Now, to tap into it. With a grin, Celeste stood up and walked over to him, letting her hips sway suggestively, while her eyes stared him down with the promise of decadent delights to come. She slowly ran her hands up the facings of his coat, occasionally stopping to finger the brass buttons. "Lieutenant, this is all a big mistake. I am loyal to His Majesty. I have supported your presence in New York and, as I said earlier, even provided information to General Howe himself. Captain Carlisle is a friend of mine. I was allowing those men to frequent my establishment so I could gain information for him. Can we not come to an agreement? If John were here, he would tell you so."

Reticent, Dokes extricated himself from her grasp and put his hat back on. "As of now, your business is closed. My men are waiting outside to take you into custody. As you previously stated, we are in control of Manhattan now, and you, Mrs. Allen, are a traitor. I have orders to follow."

Reaching into his coat pocket, he held up a letter bearing a royal seal. It was an arrest warrant. "You're under arrest, Mrs. Allen."

"Wait!" Celeste grabbed his sleeve, desperate to stop him before he left. Once the guards got their hands on her, she'd go to prison, or much worse, the gallows. Her fate would be sealed. "John Carlisle is on a mission for General Howe. He must be aware of our arrangement and how we gained information for him. Could you speak with him on my behalf? Please, I'm only a woman, I don't belong in prison."

When he didn't respond, she looked up at him through her lashes, batting them a little for effect. "How much would it take to make this go away? Isn't there something I can give you? I promise you; I'm no spy."

Dokes turned back to her with a look so hot it burned a trail from her lips down to her décolletage. Suddenly she felt a lush release at her core, then squeezed her thighs together against her growing need. *Men are so easy.* Sliding her hands up his chest, she reached around his neck and untied his stock, her fingers gently stroking his nape. "There must be some arrangement we can agree on?"

"Are you trying to bribe an officer in His Majesty's army, Mrs. Allen?" he asked, cocking a brow. "That wouldn't be wise."

His words were terse and firm, but the look in his eyes said something entirely different. She persisted, though dubiously. "Come now, surely there's something that you want? Something you need desperately."

Her heart threatened to leap from her chest—he was her last hope. She waited with baited breath, the seconds ticking by like hours. But he was silent, the wheels of thought turning behind his dark eyes as they scanned her face inquisitively. When he reached up and gingerly brushed a stray lock of hair from her cheek, she knew she'd won. *Now for the price, but what will it be?*

"Fifteen hundred pounds, and I'll still have to close your establishment," the Lieutenant replied, caressing her cheek with the backs of his fingers.

Celeste swallowed down the bitter pill. Without her business, she would be out of money in a matter of months, her lifestyle reduced to poverty. No, there had to be some other option. "Why must you close it?"

"To send a message to any potential Rebel sympathizers." He leaned forward and gently kissed her lips, his tongue pushing at the seam, but she was still in too shocked to respond. He pulled back and looked into her eyes. "But I'll let you go and tell General Howe the matter has been handled. I suggest you find somewhere else to do your business in the future—somewhere far from Manhattan."

The situation was downright serious. Where was she supposed to go? Leaving Manhattan was not an option.

Celeste ran her hands down the front of his shirt to his waist, the muscles of his abdomen twitching as she fingered the buttons of his breeches. "Is there nothing I can do to change your mind?"

She undid the front fall of his pants, reaching in and gently taking his cock in her palm. He was thick and turgid and ready for her. She wrapped her fingers around him, and started to stroke, watching him close his eyes with rapt pleasure. He leaned back against the door, his hips already rolling back and forth, making love to her hand.

With one last valiant effort, Celeste pleaded, "Are you sure there's nothing I can do to persuade you?"

She stopped purposely, waiting for his answer, teasing him with light grazes of her fingertips. "No, Mrs. Allen, but the alternative is a noose around your lovely neck." Grasping her hand, he used it to show her what he wanted. "Now, don't stop."

Chapter
Seventeen

Now that the supplies were missing, John was going to need Celeste's help more than ever. He hated having to depend on her; there was always an inevitable catch to her assistance. She was like the Devil with a contract; one favor afforded by her meant two more from you, and it usually involved a firstborn child or your life savings. The woman was as wily as Mephistopheles and just as cunning. Luckily, they'd turned a pretty nice profit in the six months they'd been in business together. She could front him the money; he'd just be paying her in services rendered for the next two years. *What does it matter?* He was young, and their arrangement suited his needs, both physical and financial. John quickly penned his letter to her. As planned, he used a bit of flattery to appeal to her sensual side then sealed it shut with wax and affixed his seal. Pulling on his overcoat and grabbing his hat, he rushed out the door towards the stable. He'd made a noon appointment to meet with the suttler at Fort Stanwix, and he didn't want to be late, but first, he needed to mail the letter in town.

The occasional snowflake fell, then steadily it picked up, large fluffy bits of snow sticking to his overcoat and hat. The sky was murky, the sun perpetually hiding behind the clouds as if it had forsaken the north as punishment for some unknown transgression. The road to the fort was quiet with only the sound of Viceroy's hooves beating on the ground, though occasionally, he could've sworn he heard a woman's voice on the wind calling his name. His ever-present specter of justice.

When he neared the fort, John decided to stop and do a bit of reconnaissance and take some measurements for his maps. From this vantage point, he could see the fort in its entirety; to the west, the Oneida Carry, on the east, the Mohawk River that curved around to the north and then flowed back in the opposite direction, and on the south side, where the new barracks were being built. He made a note of the trails around the fort, especially the one Miss McKesson had taken him on when they visited Oriska the week before. That road, in particular, was one of the secret trails the natives had used to communicate vital knowledge back and forth during the French war.

John's meeting with the suttler was in a large canvas tent next to the new barracks, outside the fort, on the south side. The trader gave John a list of supplies the fort was in need of, from powder and muskets to grain and linen, then negotiated a price with him. He paid minimal attention to their conversation, his eyes watching the fort, tracking the movement of soldiers in and out, trying to estimate their numbers and their post schedules. When the suttler was called away for several minutes, John spent ample time noting all the sentry boxes and the position of their cannons. It was obvious the colonists were anticipating a strike. He figured at least one hundred men were outside the fort, and based on what he knew from historical maps of Stanwix, at least two hundred more could be living inside. Undoubtedly, General Howe was unaware of how much preparation was going on. Previous intelligence inferred that Stanwix was all but abandoned. Once back to The Thistle, John would send a dispatch to Howe detailing those findings. Such information would be vital to Carleton and Burgoyne's advance, whether it took place in the winter or the summer.

As John rode back towards town, he contemplated what he would write in his missive. Sending a map wouldn't be possible for fear of interception, but he could, in code, detail what he saw down to the exact longitude and latitude. So focused on the content of his letter, he barely noticed his surroundings. Stopping to give Viceroy a rest, John took a sip from his canteen, his eyes scanning the trees, now bare, their branches reaching towards the heavens like spindly fingers. The forest was quiet save the occasional rustle of leaves across the ground and the wind whipping around him in a wintry gale that sent a shiver down his spine. An ominous feeling came over him, as if the all-seeing eyes of the forest had leveled their gaze on him. John pulled out his pistol and fingered the trigger. He waited for a moment, unmoving, his eyes tracking around him, searching for signs of movement. But there was nothing. Too long he'd lived with nightmares, his dreams haunted by memories, and now his conscience was getting the better of him. John pulled Viceroy's reigns and started again, kicking his horse into a canter, when suddenly, a bullet whizzed by him, grazing his left shoulder, tearing a hole in his cloak. Then, not a moment later, another bullet flew by him on his right side, just missing his thigh. John's war-trained horse instinctively sped up, racing off the path into the woods. He held his pace and looked over his shoulder, cocking his pistol and aiming. But as expected, his assailants had disappeared into the labyrinth of forest that protected them. He knew who they were and why they shot at him. They saw what he was doing, and they wanted him to know—a warning for him to stay away.

John continued on, racing back to town, though his nerves were on edge for the remainder of the journey. The sleepy village was quiet as the day came to a close; the sun now dipped below the horizon, just a smattering of blues and purples streaking the twilight sky. To the west, he could see dark clouds rolling in, and the temperature had dropped significantly, bringing with it a few intermittent snowflakes. It was a good thing he got back to town when he did. A storm was brewing, and he was all too familiar with the wintery weather of the north. Easily, he could find himself stuck in a blizzard of ice and snow, unable to find shelter, no food or beverage to consume. Mother Nature, she could be tempestuous and unpredictable—a tart of the worst sort. He'd felt her wrath before and wanted to avoid it.

The village of German Flats surrounded a small section of the Mohawk River on both sides with a bridge for crossing. On the highest point in the area, he could see construction on one of the old forts, and on the opposite side of the river, a stone stockade was being built around a church. The Rebels were making provisions to protect the little town should war come. With three forts being rebuilt at the same time, someone had to be providing them with raw materials. He drew a quick map of the surrounding area, drawing attention to the north side of the river where Fort Dayton sat, Schell's Bush, and on the edge of town, Pietrie Mill. On the south side, he noted Shoemaker's Tavern, The Silver Kettle, and Fort Herkimer, and at the very west edge of town, almost to the forest, The Thistle Tavern.

After he finished his map, John rode across the bridge to the south side of the river. Next to Shoemaker's Tavern, The Kettle was the liveliest place in town and with a notorious reputation to boot. Spirits had a tendency to loosen lips and lower inhibitions; what better place for him to ask a few questions without appearing suspicious. When he walked inside, the large tables were full from one end to the other. John chose a seat at the end of the long table and waved to the bartender. It was far from the type of place he liked to frequent, but the most valuable of information was often obtained in the seediest of places, and The Kettle certainly fit the bill.

Jussie walked up, putting a tankard down in front of him. "Welcome back," she said, resting her hands on her hips, grinning ear to ear. "Where's your friend?"

Her large breasts threatened to spill over the top of her bodice, drawing so much attention he was unable to avert his gaze. John smiled. "I'm alone this evening."

"Good, you can do better than that whore." Sitting down next to him, Jussie reached under the table and put her hand on his knee, making him flinch. "Now, what can I do for you, Captain?"

"I could go for something to eat. After that…" His voice trailed off as her hand moved up the inside of his thigh, his cock stiffening in response. Again, he jumped reflexively. She was certainly forward. *Focus, Carlisle, focus.*

"We have beef stew if that will suit." She stroked a trail up the seam of his breeches, her hand stopping when it reached the top of his thigh.

"That will be fine." He removed her hand from his leg before it reached its destination and held it for a moment, squeezing it gently.

When Jussie got up, John adjusted himself, looking around to see if anyone noticed their exchange. He wasn't in the least bit attracted to her, though his body seemed to be saying something entirely different. Since sobering up, he found the company of such women uninspiring, though they were often privy to the most interesting information. Still, three weeks without a woman, and things were starting to look a bit desperate. Surely, even in a rustic, isolated village, he could find a woman willing to indulge in a quick dalliance other than Jussie.

When the waitress returned, she had a large tray in her hands, the edge resting on her shoulder. "Do you mind if I join you? I haven't eaten either," she asked, placing two bowls of stew on the table with a loaf of bread.

"Please." John stood up and pulled the chair out for her.

They chatted until he finished his dinner, the exchange providing very little significant information. He spent most of the time intercepting Jussie's hand, preventing her from servicing him under the table in full view of the bar. Looking for a reason to get up, he noticed the storm that was threatening earlier had commenced, large, fat flakes coming down like feathers from a ripped down pillow. "Please, excuse me, Jussie. I need to be getting back before the weather progresses. I have things to attend to."

She grabbed his thigh just as he tried to stand, her fingernails biting into his flesh. He stifled a groan and sat back down abruptly. "You could stay here, Captain. We have rooms upstairs. I could keep you company."

"Forgive me. But, I have a contract with Miss McKesson. It wouldn't reflect well on me to break it."

Jussie shook her head, one of her bouncy, blonde curls falling from her cap into her eyes. "Who cares if you break a promise to her? She'll be out of business soon. No one in their right mind would stay there, present company excluded. You didn't know about her reputation."

Finally, something John wanted to hear. He released her hand, letting it rest on his leg. He could handle a bit of groping if she actually provided him with some useful information, and the weather was sure to cool him off when he went outside in the blizzard. "Miss McKesson seems like a pleasant lady. Should I be concerned?"

"Oh, she's nice if you're a Redcoat," Jussie said under her breath. Leaning close to him, she lowered her voice. "Rumor has it that her fiancé dumped her for sleeping with some Regulars a couple of years ago."

"Really?" he replied, feigning surprise.

"She was engaged to Patrick Armstrong-Jones, the magistrate's son, when word got out that she was deflowered. Her uncle apparently paid the magistrate to keep everything quiet, but you can see how well that worked. Since then, she's been running that tavern. Honestly, I don't know how she stays in business. No one will stay there. Not to mention her brother is a lunatic drunk who talks nonsense."

John watched her twirl the golden lock around her finger nonchalantly, as if the information she was disclosing wasn't about a real person. He suddenly found himself feeling very protective of his innkeeper, knowing the sad truth of her predicament. She'd been the butt of Jussie's lewd comments the last time they visited, but Dellis bravely stood up to the insults, brooking no amusement at her expense. But how embarrassing and painful it must be for her to live with such a reputation, having all the townspeople know of her disgrace. For a woman, it was a deal breaker—she was tainted goods—and no man of means would be associated with her, even if it wasn't her fault.

"I should feel bad for Dellis, but I don't. She has the nerve to carry on like it never happened, as if she isn't the laughing stock of our town. This is all her fault. That's what she gets for whoring around. She did it to herself."

Jussie shook her head and rolled her eyes primly as if she were some society virgin and not the waitress that just propositioned him under the table.

Women are evil to each other. Instead of countering with an ungentlemanly remark, he changed the subject. "If her uncle could afford to pay off the magistrate, maybe that's how she keeps The Thistle open?"

Grabbing his tankard, Jussie sipped his ale, smiling at him over the rim. With a wink, she continued. "That whole situation is interesting, too. Rumor has it that her Uncle James was dirt poor when he came to town, but now he owns a farmhouse large enough to rival Johnson Hall. He and his wife are the pillars of polite society, though everyone knows they used to be Loyalists."

Confident that there was no more information to be had from Jussie, he took her hand and kissed it. "Thank you for the conversation; it was enlightening. But I do need to get going. Until next time."

Flashing him a cheeky grin, she waved goodbye to him. "I look forward to it, Captain."

Get out quickly, Carlisle, before she follows you.

As he rushed out the door, John bumped into a group of drunks on their way inside. Grabbing one of them by the arm, he waved for him to come closer. "If I can give you a bit of advice, I wouldn't eat here. The food is shite. I just spent the last few minutes pissing through my teeth behind the building."

"Thanks for the warning, sir," the man said, with a nod. "We'll go somewhere else."

Reaching into a pocket, John pulled out a bag of coins and handed it over. "If I can make a recommendation, try The Thistle tavern—the hash is tasty, and the waitress is easy on the eyes."

"Will do, sir. We'll go right now."

Perhaps Jussie deserved a bit of her own medicine, and he was all too happy to oblige. At least this was one thing he could do for his unfortunate innkeeper. If he could help her save her precious house, keep the poor woman and her brother off the streets, then the lie was well served. John smiled to himself and walked back to where he boarded his horse and mounted up. It had been a very successful day.

Chapter Eighteen

It was dark by the time John returned to The Thistle. He'd been away the whole day doing reconnaissance and drawing maps of the territory. Tucking the papers inside his coat pocket, he crept in the front door, trying not to make a sound. All the candles were out, the fire in the dining room extinguished, with the sitting area already clean and ready for the morning.

Walking into the kitchen, John stoked the fire and lit one of the candles on the table. Removing his hat and cloak, he hung them up near the door then patted the snowflakes from his hair and jacket, little droplets of water flying into the air. On the kitchen counter was a bottle of whiskey; he poured himself a tot, downed it, and then poured one more for good measure. From his pocket, he pulled out three pence and dropped it on the counter. Payment for the drinks. Leaning against the countertop, he looked around, noticing how immaculate the kitchen was: the counters clean, hearth swept, the cupboards neatly arranged, all the dishes stacked and ready for the breakfast patrons. Even the embers were fresh from late in the day, the little metal pail empty and turned over. It took hard work and a deep inner pride to keep a house this size so clean, traits he admired in a solider and in a woman. This house was her whole world.

On the other side of the kitchen, the little hallway that led to Dellis's private quarters and the parlor was dark. Initially, he'd been surprised at the

146

size of the house. With such a large kitchen, four upstairs bedrooms, and a spacious dining area, it was not what one expected in such a rustic area, but it was all beginning to make sense to him now that he knew she was the niece of Admiral McKesson. *But, if she has such an illustrious uncle, one with the means to buy and sell her house ten times over, why is she scrounging for every penny? Why have both of her wealthy uncles forsaken her?*

Finishing his shot, John put the glass down and blew out the candle. As he leaned down to pick up his sack, he felt the sensation of cold steel at his neck and strong fingers holding his jaw. Instinctively, he grabbed the wrist of his assailant as the edge of the blade sunk into his flesh, cutting him with a clean swipe.

Years of training took over, and with a quick shot of adrenaline, John elbowed his assailant in the abdomen, the dagger falling on the floor, clanking against the wood. In one swift motion, he grabbed his attacker's wrists, whipped the person around, and threw him down on the ground, straddling his hips.

"Who are you?" John yelled, slamming the attacker against the floor with a resounding thud. "Who are you?"

Thud!

"Stop, you're hurting me!"

John recognized that voice. It was high pitched and feminine—and familiar. It was Dellis. Stunned, John leaned back, his eyes adjusting to the darkness. The moon cast rays through the window, illumining the shape of her face and highlighting her distinct, strong features. "Miss McKesson, are you all right?"

"Let me go, please," she screamed, a high-pitched wail reminiscent of an injured animal. She pounded her fists into his thighs, left, then right, over and over, trying to free herself.

He tried again to reach her. "Dellis, it's John." But she didn't hear him, frantically fighting back, punishing his thighs with her fists.

Finally, he grabbed her wrists, pinning her to the floor. "Stop, Dellis, it's me. Look at me." He leaned in so she could see his face, but she was unreachable in her terror.

"Please," she begged, her eyes tearing up, her legs kicking and flailing underneath his weight.

She was hysterical, fighting him as if her life depended on it. Taking her face in his hands, John looked into her eyes, appealing to the saner part of her brain. "It's me, Dellis. You're safe. I didn't mean to frighten you." When he leaned back on his haunches, she planted her knee in his groin, with the accuracy of a proficient warrior.

Groaning in pain, John rolled off her, his balls feeling like they were lodged in his throat and ready to explode. Dellis rolled onto her side, grabbed the discarded knife and scooted away from him into the corner where the wall met the cupboard. Her long hair had fallen from the chignon at her neck, hanging in tendrils about her shoulders. The bodice of her dress was torn from their tussle, exposing her stays and the top of her breasts. With one hand she held the knife out, ready to defend herself if need be, the other pushed a stray lock of hair behind her ear.

John took several deep breaths, his stomach pitching furiously from the pain. *Have mercy.* He wouldn't be able to walk for a week, much less relieve himself. "I'm sorry. I didn't mean to scare you. When you pull a knife on sol"— he paused, remembering his cover—"on a man, it's second nature to fight back."

He reached out to touch her, but she inched further into the corner, holding the knife so he could see it. She was an interesting dichotomy of emotion, one minute, brave enough to pull a knife on an unknown assailant, and the next, she was hiding in the corner like a frightened cat.

Women. He groaned out his pain and frustration.

"Miss McKesson, I'm very sorry. I came in late and got a drink. I didn't mean to frighten you." The words came out through clenched teeth, the pain not abating in the least. The woman was apparently dangerous with a knife and her knee. God forbid she actually had fired the pistol when they first met, his mission would've been over before it even started.

After several moments, Dellis looked up at him, her breathing more relaxed, her eyes no longer darting around like a wild cat in the woods. "I thought you were an intruder."

"So you pull a knife on me? Why didn't you call for help?" he asked, completely flabbergasted. "For all you know, I could've been your Uncle James or Alexei. You could've killed me."

"I can take care of myself," she said, sounding a bit more like her usual, haughty self. Though he disagreed with her overconfidence, having easily subdued her, she did manage to sneak up on him and nearly deliver a fatal blow. A small part of him refused to believe he got lucky.

"Besides, my uncle or Alexei would have knocked. They wouldn't have been lurking around in my kitchen in the dark," she said with an accusing glare.

"Are you all right?"

She nodded, standing up, still holding his dagger in her fist. "I'm fine. You knocked the wind out of me, that's all."

John sat for another moment, his balls still feeling like they were going to burst, the linen of his breeches feeling suddenly restrictive. When he finally managed to get up, he snatched a towel from the bar top and held it to the wound on his neck, applying pressure. Instead of helping or offering up any sympathy, Dellis just watched him, her eyes as wide as a doe's. She was obviously still in shock.

"Well, I think you've cut me good." He pulled the blood-soaked linen from his neck, folded it over on itself then reapplied pressure to it. The damn thing stung like the devil—and so did his ego.

Slowly recovering, she handed him a fresh piece of linen from the counter then gestured to the chair. "Sit down, Captain, I'll take a look at it."

Frustrated, John sat down, untied his neckerchief, and opened the collar of his shirt. How she sneaked up on him and took his dagger from his hip without him noticing was baffling. Too much time out of the field was making him weak, his senses not as honed as they used to be. It was a disgrace to a light infantry soldier, an officer nonetheless, to be caught so easily unaware. Snatch and grab was his specialty. He was the best in his company—hence his promotion to Captain. How some foolish, untrained woman with a dagger and an overinflated ego bested him was beyond thinkable.

Women. His Achilles heel, they always had been.

Carefully, Dellis removed the towel, her eyes narrowing as she examined the cut, making him more concerned. "Huh?" She let out a little sound, leaning in closer.

This situation was getting more embarrassing by the minute. "How bad is it?"

To his surprise, she smiled, a twinkle in her dark eyes when she looked down at him. "My aim was a bit off today, lucky for you. It's not very deep, but it's long, and they tend to bleed a lot if you don't close them. Keep holding pressure on it while I get some supplies."

John was not in the least amused. The blood saturated the linen and started running down his hand, staining the cuff of his brand-new shirt. He quickly removed his overcoat and rolled up his sleeves, trying to prevent staining another piece of clothing he couldn't afford to replace. When Dellis returned, she had pinned up her bodice and replaced her kerchief. In her hands, she was carrying a small wicker basket full of supplies, plus two bottles of spirits and a glass.

"Thank you. I could use a drink."

She shooed his hand away when he reached for the bottle and started to pour for himself. "This is for my nerves, and now, thanks to you, my sore back. The whiskey is to clean the wound."

He snorted, watching her pour herself a tot and throw it back with the gusto of an experienced drunk. "What about me? I'm the one who's injured."

"You poor thing," she teased, though he could detect a tremor in her voice. Pouring the dark liquid into the glass, she downed another shot, and then refilled it and handed it to him.

It was scotch, his drink of choice. And it was very high quality, peaty, yet smooth and aromatic. Not what he expected from a little tavern in the middle of nowhere, but precisely what he needed.

Heaven in a glass.

"Would you care for another?" She took the tot from him and started to pour again.

"No, thank you." Having a particular weakness for scotch, he figured it was better to quit while he was ahead. With his luck, and her accuracy with a weapon, he'd wake up in her bed next to her missing body parts.

"Too strong for your English palate?" she said with a wink.

"Actually, I'm rather fond of scotch." He inclined his head towards the bottle. "Perhaps too fond of it, and that's quite good."

"In a Scottish family, it's a necessity. I keep a stash for special occasions."

"I wouldn't exactly consider *this* such an occasion." He chuckled, watching as she tried to thread her needle unsuccessfully. Her hands shook so much she cursed and dropped it on the table.

"Why don't you have another, just to steady your hands?" When in doubt, it always worked for him, especially before a duel. And if she were going to sew up his neck, he'd rather she was calm before she started. "If not for you, then have one for me. It will help your aim and save my skin."

She obliged, then tried again with her needle, only this time, she was successful. "You're not squeamish?" she asked, giving him a rather serious look. "I can get a chunder bucket."

"Not in the least," he said tersely, rolling his eyes. "Get on with it."

Leaning back in his chair, John opened his collar and tilted his head to the side, giving her better access. She doused the linen with whiskey then ran it over the cut, the liquid burning on contact with the wound.

"Damn!" He winced and cursed simultaneously.

Gently, she held his chin, tipping his head to the left, positioning him. "Try not to move too much."

Again, he winced in pain the first time he felt the needle pierce his skin. She paused for a moment, resting her hand on his shoulder, her eyes focused on the wound. "I told you not to move, Captain. It will make this much harder if you don't do as I say."

Their scuffle had loosened her hair, a few of the silky strands grazing his cheek as she leaned into him. Acutely aware of her bosom, only inches from his face, he glanced down, appreciating the milky smoothness of her skin and the roundness of her breasts brimming the edge of her bodice, just under her kerchief.

"Lean back a little, and tilt your head to the side." She grabbed his chin and repositioned him how she wanted him. "Stay just like this. Don't move.'

He complied, finding it rather arousing to be ordered about by a woman, specifically, this woman. She felt no shame and brooked no hesitation when she dictated her wants. A jolt of pleasure shot through his loins, imagining her telling him what she wanted him to do in that lovely crevasse between her perfect twin peaks.

As she took a step closer to get a better look, Dellis bumped the chair and almost fell into his arms. He grabbed her wrists, steadying her. She stopped for a moment, their eyes locking, her chest heaving at the edge of his gaze as a lovely flush stained her neck and cheeks pink. "Sorry, still a little unsteady. You can let go now." Her eyes followed his hands as he rested them on his thighs.

Damned if he wasn't thoroughly enjoying himself. Closing his eyes, he clenched his fists, resisting the urge to pull her down on his lap and show her how a man treats a woman. *Focus, Carlisle, focus.* He tried to think about his mission, a dip in an icy lake, anything to help him forget the sensation of her lithe body between his thighs and her exquisite breasts in his face.

Stepping back, she scrunched her nose, examining her work. "You're going to need one more. Sorry."

"By all means," he replied with a grin.

She gave him a curious look then went back to her work. "You're taking this rather well."

You have no idea.

John watched her turn around and pick up her needle, admiring the view of her from behind. She was long, and lean, and graceful as a swan. Her broad shoulders and long torso tapered perfectly into her tiny waist. The curve of her backside could just barely be seen through her layers of skirts. He imagined her legs and bottom were just as lovely as the rest of her. When she lifted her arm, he got the slightest peep of the side of her full breast, sending another jolt of pleasure to his core.

Turing towards him again, Dellis wiped the wound one last time, and then, to his surprise, she stopped. Gently, she touched his forehead, smoothing a lock of his hair back, tucking it behind his ear. He closed his eyes, imagining her hands running through his hair, tugging at it, while he explored every inch of her lovely mouth with his own. He could almost hear her ordering him about in her saucy way, telling him how she wanted to be touched then demanding it. God, he wanted it. Too long he'd been without the gentle caress of a woman. When he opened his eyes, she was watching him intently; her lips parted, her fingers light as butterfly wings as she ran them down his cheek then along his jaw. He wanted to reach out and touch her so badly, but he knew it would only frighten her away. She was like a doe in the woods and he the hunter.

She pulled back abruptly—seemingly unfazed—finished the last stitch, and then started cleaning up her supplies. John re-tied his neckerchief and smoothed his hair back, mentally pulling himself together. His blood roared through his veins, hot and lusty. A cold dip in the lake would have been welcomed, or perhaps just immersing himself in the brisk night air; anything to help him dampen the passion she so easily evoked in him. It was just an innocent flirtation, nothing more than a stolen caress here or there, yet his body reacted as if she seduced him with the skill of a seasoned temptress.

When she finally turned around, he noticed how she flushed from her cheeks to the top of her breasts. "That's it, Captain, you're done." Rubbing her hands on the front of her dress, she backed away and grabbed her basket.

"Mind if I have another drink?"

"Don't tell me I made you squeamish?" she asked, pouring one and handing it to him.

Throwing it back, he shook his head. "Not in the least." On the contrary, it was to soothe the exceptional case of blue balls and unanswered passion he was taking to bed with him. He pulled the front of his waistcoat down, hiding the proof his predicament from her. She'd been frightened enough by him for one night.

Ready to put an end to his long day, John grabbed his overcoat and shoved his right arm into it, causing the maps in his pocket to fall on the floor. Dellis bent over and picked them up, her eyes quickly examining them before she handed them back. When he went for his dagger on the table, she snatched it away before he could reach it.

"That's mine now, Captain. A weapon lost in battle is no longer your own." She said it so seriously, he had to laugh.

"Is that so?" he asked, crossing his arms over his chest.

"That's correct. You lost it to me. May I have the cover?" Smiling, she held out her hand, gesturing to the small case at his hip.

"But, I won," he said. Her logic made no sense.

"That might be so, but I took it from you, so now it's mine," she said.

"That's not a native tradition." What sort of game was she playing at?

"No, you're right, it isn't. My cousin Alexei taught it to me. And if you're fool enough to lose your blade in battle, then you deserve to get cut with it. I've learned my lesson several times, and now it's time for you to learn yours. Admit it, Captain, I bested you."

"This is all because I'm a better rider than you, isn't it?" He couldn't help himself, throwing a playful jibe in her direction. This game of hers was utter nonsense.

She smiled and tipped her head to the side, a twinkle in her brown eyes. Again, she stretched out her arm, her hand opening and closing playfully while she waited for him to surrender his case.

Admiring her boldness, John removed the case from his belt and handed it to her. He knew that natives trained their women to protect themselves, but apparently, her cousin had taken it a step further. She was skillful, having pulled the blade from his hip without him knowing and cutting him swiftly. And even in the face of her fear, she had fought back. Yes, putting his ego aside, he had to admit that she earned the blade as well as his admiration.

"Thank you," she replied, putting the dagger in its case and placing it in her basket of supplies. "Good night, Captain. Make sure you clean that daily."

Thoroughly amused, he watched as she walked out of the room, completely calm, as if nothing had happened. Yes, the woman was an enigma, one incredible, beautiful, delightful enigma. *Wow.*

Chapter Nineteen

"**M**other, please, wake up," Dellis cried, frantically. Her mother was lying on the floor, her body limp, unmoving, a knife buried deep in her chest. Just as Dellis scooted out from under the bed, she felt a strong hand grab her neck and the back of her dress, pulling her to her feet. She kicked the man several times then planted her heel to his instep.

"Whore," the soldier yelled, slapping her so hard she fell back against the table, the sting of it going all the way to her toes. From behind, she heard her brother's loud screeches as one of the other soldiers wrestled him to the ground, pinning him down.

"Help, please, help," she pleaded, reaching out to her brother. "Stuart!"

When her brother was finally compliant and subdue, the solider yanked the boy to his feet, a long, ugly knife at his neck.

"Is this your sister?" the man who held her captive yelled, looking over his right shoulder at Stuart while the man undid the buttons of his front flap.

Stuart nodded, his eyes darting back and forth from her to the man holding her captive. The solider that held the boy in place dug the knife into his neck, blood trickling from the wound. Stuart yelped, and then a fresh stream of tears began to fall from his eyes.

"Good. Then you'll enjoy watching each one of us take turns fucking her." The man's grip tightened on Dellis's hair as he turned her about and *threw her against the table, her chest hitting the wood, knocking the wind out of her. She coughed painfully, trying to catch her breath while still fighting back.*

"Stop fighting, whore!" he yelled, fisting her hair, pulling her upright then slamming her against the table again.

The pain of hitting the table with her chest and the side of her face took what little breath she had left away—but she would not relent. Dellis kicked and flailed with all her might, but he held her down using his hips to pin hers against the tabletop.

"Please, don't do this, please!" she screamed between labored breaths, his hands grabbing the back of her skirts and pulling them up. A powerful gust of wind whipped through her house, cold and punishing against her exposed flesh. She screamed, "No! No! Stuart, help me!" Her brother fought against the hands holding him, his eyes locking with hers, a stream of blood running down his neck, staining the collar of his buckskin tunic.

Suddenly, she felt the barrel of a pistol at the back of her head—cold, hard steel against warm skin. "Stop fighting or I'll put a bullet in your head, whore." The solider followed her gaze and turned, aiming at Stuart. "Or better yet, I put one in his."

"No!" she shrieked, shaking her head, tears streaming down her cheeks. "Don't hurt him, please. Do what you want with me, just don't hurt him."

The man's hips thrust against hers, slamming her thighs against the table. She was pinned; there was nowhere for her to go, nothing she could do.

"Don't do this, please..." She begged. "Please."

"I'll do what I want." He grabbed her hips, and then suddenly she felt a searing pain, deep inside, as if she would render in two.

"No! Don't do this!" she screamed, flailing and kicking wildly. "Father, please help us."

"Dellis, wake up. It's all right."

A familiar voice broke through the haze, the dream ceasing immediately with the first glance of her cousin's handsome face. "Alexei?"

"Aye, it's me." He wrapped his arms around her, drawing her into his tight, cocoon-like embrace. "Are you all right?"

Never. She would never be all right. *Not ever.* Dellis held on to him for several minutes, his arms like steel bands enveloping her tight against the warm wall of his chest. His were the only arms she trusted, her only safe haven from the world and her memories. Thank God for Alexei. At one point, her cousin was all she had for comfort; her parents both dead, Stuart's feeble mind twisted and consumed with rage, and her Uncle James unsympathetic to her plight. Alexei was always there for her, no matter what. Pulling away, she wiped the tears from her eyes with the heels of her hands. "It was a bad dream, that's all."

"It was about the men that attacked you, wasn't it?"

She closed her eyes, unable to block out the memory of what came next in her nightmare. Her whole body shook with fear and reminiscent pain so visceral she ached from it. "Yes."

"How often do you have them?" Alexei tilted his head to look at her, his hand gently brushing some of her tears away.

"It's been a while. I don't know what set it off." Again, she lied, knowing exactly what caused it. Captain Anderson.

He had gotten too close. Between the shock of their tussle and the heady feelings he evoked when he touched her, it was overwhelming. Her heart raced, remembering the feel of his silky hair and his soft skin against her fingertips. Whether it was too much spirits weakening her resolve, or just a moment of loneliness, she had wanted him to touch her, yet part of her was terrified of what would happen if he did.

Changing the subject, she asked, "Have you seen Stuart? He's missing again."

Alexei nodded, backing away from her. "He and my brother have taken up with the local militia. They were at drills yesterday. Both of them slept in the barn last night."

She smiled. Her cousin Ruslan, Alexei's younger brother, was the only person who could still reason with Stuart. They'd been childhood playmates and were still bosom friends in spite of all his issues.

"Has there been any news about the war?" She was almost afraid to hear the answer.

"There were some rumors that Butler and Brant were going to launch an attack on the county with tribes from the north. Grasshopper has gone to Niagara to find out more. No one knows what to believe."

"Grasshopper? Well, if anyone can get to the truth of the matter, it's him," she said. The famous Oneida sachem was known throughout the region for his wisdom and his far-reaching connections. "What about Grandfather? Are you still encouraging him to do more than assist the Rebels? Alexei, I know you want us to join the fight."

"Enough of this, Dellis," he clipped, getting up and walking out of the room.

Dellis got up slowly and dressed, pulling on her light brown bodice and skirt, and then tying up her hair in a small cotton cap. She pinned an apron to the front of her bodice, and then tied it around her waist, over the top of her skirts. Lifting her arms above her head, she stretched slowly, her neck and back smarting from being slammed into the floor several times the night before. When she walked into the kitchen, Alexei and Patrick were standing at the table, already drinking coffee and eating leftover bread they'd stolen from the cupboard.

"Come on, you two, out of here. Go sit down and let me get something proper for you to eat." Dellis shooed them both out of the kitchen and started breakfast for the morning. Quickly, she hung the kettle over the fire for tea, fried some eggs and ham, and then pulled the biscuits out from the bread oven. When everything was ready and piping hot, she prepared the plates, finishing off with a neat little daub of strawberry preserves on top of each biscuit.

Dellis stepped back, looked at the plates full of food, and smiled. And her aunt thought this was too much work for one person. *Nonsense.* Dellis could do it by herself if need be. It only took her a few minutes of good, hard work to finish, and she even had a tea service prepared to go upstairs to the Captain. Satisfied with herself, she started filling the trays, readying them to go out to her customers.

As she walked through the bar, Dellis could hear Alexei and Patrick yammering on in the dining room, and then suddenly, they stopped as if they had spotted a deer in the woods and were ready to shoot. Curious, she put down her tray and walked into the bar, ready to put a stop to whatever nonsense was taking place in her dining room. But to her surprise, sitting at the table nearest the door was a woman in a pink dress, pretending she didn't notice Alexei and Patrick gaping at her like besotted fools. The woman smiled brilliantly, her eyes occasionally glancing to their table while she made a show of smoothing her hair and checking her face in the mirror she pulled from her little velvet purse.

Dellis wiped her hands on her apron and walked over to the table.

"Can I help you, Miss?" she asked, noticing how the woman looked Dellis up and down disapprovingly. Feeling self-conscious, she tucked a stray lock of hair behind her ear and mustered up a smile. "We have coffee or tea, and there's some eggs and ham for breakfast. The biscuits and preserves are nice, too."

"No food." The woman shook her head, her upper lip curling with disgust. "I'm looking for Captain Anderson. I understand he lodges here. Is that correct?"

"Yes, he's here."

She was exquisitely dressed, her lovely gray wool cloak open in the front, revealing her pale pink dress with delicate, white lace trim around the top of the bodice. Her glossy, chestnut hair was elegantly piled on top of her head in a style fit for court. Around her neck was the most beautiful, double-strand pearl choker, tied at her nape with a pale pink ribbon. The woman slowly removed her gloves, her eyes focused on her task as if she couldn't bear to look up at Dellis.

"Would you please tell the Captain that Mrs. Allen is here to see him?" The woman examined her tapered fingernails, briefly glancing up as she said her name.

"I will tell him. Can I get you something to eat while you wait?" Dellis asked.

Mrs. Allen wrinkled her pretty, pert nose and shook her head. "No, thank you, but if you could manage some tea, that will do."

"Of course."

Dellis rushed back to the kitchen and prepared a tea service for her guest, using her father's best china and some of the Captain's leaves. He wouldn't mind her using a bit of his tea; after all, Mrs. Allen was an acquaintance of his. After taking the woman her tea, Dellis quickly walked upstairs, stopping for a moment to wipe the flour off her face and straighten her dress.

"Captain?" she said quietly, knocking on his door.

"Come in, please."

He was standing behind the desk reading a letter when she peeked around the door. When he saw her, he flashed one of his boyish smiles, making her heart leap and do a jig in her chest. "Good morning, I hope you suffered no ill effects from last evening's events?"

Feeling herself blush from head to toe, she replied, "I'm well, and you?"

Touching his collar, he smiled, the little lines forming at the corners of his eyes, softening them. "Fine. What can I do for you?"

"There's a Mrs. Allen here to see you. She's waiting in the dining room."

His brow furrowed, the pleasant lines at his eyes disappearing instantaneously. He put down his letter and pulled on his overcoat. "Have her come up, please."

"Would you not rather meet her downstairs? You could use my father's parlor, it's still very private," she asked. "I could serve your morning tea there." Though her tavern was run down and often attracted those far from polite society, she still liked to uphold the pretense of propriety. It was untoward for a man to entertain a woman in his private quarters without a chaperone.

"No, here will be fine," he said, nonchalantly, as if he thought nothing of it. "Send her up."

"All right." She nodded then shut the door behind her.

Dellis made her way downstairs, glaring at Alexei and Patrick, who were now sitting at the same table with Mrs. Allen, chatting. The woman let out an exaggerated laugh and touched one of her delicate hands to her breast, drawing both men's attention to her décolletage. Dellis rolled her eyes, knowing an act when she saw one, but of course, her cousin and Patrick were drinking it up. *Men—so predictable.*

Dellis cleared her throat loudly, getting their attention. "Captain Anderson said you could meet him in his quarters. It's up the stairs. Follow me, I'll show you the way."

Mrs. Allen stood up, offering her hand to both the men, bidding them goodbye with a demure smile. Dellis watched as Patrick kissed the woman's hand, his eyes meeting hers with a half-lidded, seductive glance. If Dellis hadn't felt invisible earlier, she surely did now. Mrs. Allen ascended the stairs as haughty as a queen entering court, and Dellis was the lady-in-waiting, trailing behind.

Dellis's stomach bottomed out at her knees when she saw how the Captain's eyes lit up at first sight of Mrs. Allen. Those twin blue jewels widened as a grin spread from one side of his mouth to the other, bracketed by his indelible laugh lines. She apparently was someone very special to him. *His lady.* Dellis glanced at the woman again, with her expensive clothing and elegant manners; of course he would associate himself with such a woman.

"Mrs. Allen, it's always a pleasure," he said in his usual, mellifluous way.

"Hello, John," Mrs. Allen purred. She smiled when he kissed her hand, touching his cheek gently before he pulled away.

Dellis couldn't help but notice how Mrs. Allen batted her eyelashes at him and then glanced over at Dellis in challenge. Did this woman envision Dellis as a rival for the Captain's affections? Preposterous. Why, he'd never taken a second glance at her.

Feeling emboldened, Dellis said, "Captain, are you sure you wouldn't prefer to use my private parlor for your meeting? I wouldn't want the lady's reputation to be tarnished by being alone in a room with a gentleman unaccompanied."

He shook his head, flashing her a look of confusion. "No, thank you. Here is fine."

"Well, as long as you're not concerned about her reputation, then neither am I," Dellis said curtly with a mustered-up smile.

Their gazes locked, a smirk crossing Mrs. Allen's lovely mouth, acknowledging Dellis's well-placed gibe. "Oh, Miss McKesson, could you please bring the tea up here for myself and the Captain? I think we're going to be busy for quite some time and will require refreshment."

"Of course." Dellis nodded, turning her back and walking out before she said something tart and made a fool of herself.

Walking through the dining room, she picked up her tea service from Mrs. Allen's discarded table and carried it into the kitchen. Reaching into the cupboard, she pulled out the tin of the Captain's favorite tea and a jar of sugar and put them on the counter. Slamming the door closed, she leaned her back against the counter and shut her eyes, trying to block out the vision of the Captain kissing Mrs. Allen's hand. A slight pang developed in Dellis's chest, thinking about the two of them alone in his room and the familiar way the woman had touched his cheek. What he did in his private quarters was none of Dellis's concern, she reminded herself.

She prepared the tea quickly, setting up the tray with her finest cloth and her best cups and saucers, no chips or breaks on any of them. Once everything was just so, she carried the tray back through the dining room, giving both Alexei and Patrick knowing looks on the way. "Eat your breakfast and get out of here before I dump those eggs over your heads."

"Jealous?" Patrick teased with a sidelong glance.

Putting the tray down on the nearest table, Dellis rushed back to her room and shut the door behind her. When she looked into the mirror, what she saw made her want to cry. *What a mess.* Both of her cheeks still had traces of flour on them, her brown calico dress was faded and worn, with patches everywhere from repairing the skirt several times over. Brushing a lock of inky black hair out of her face, she compared her dark eyes to Mrs. Allen's beautiful hazel ones that sparkled brilliantly, and Dellis's almost too thin figure was nothing to the curves that were hugged by the satin of that pale pink dress. She wondered what it was like to wear such lovely clothes and have the Captain admire her with those incredible eyes. Letting out a deep breath, she accepted the truth: Patrick was right—she was jealous, and the monster had hazel-green eyes.

Chapter Twenty

"What can I do for you, Celeste?" John leaned against the front of the desk, watching as she daintily lifted her skirts and sat down. She looked lovely, and as usual, she had everything on display. Celeste had always been all about attention, and in such a little town, she was sure to draw her share in her high-fashion, courtly attire.

She looked him up and down with hazel, hooded eyes full of desire. "I missed you, Johnny. It's been weeks, and you promised to send word."

Not the opening act he anticipated. She was up to something. "There must be something else that brought you this far north. You hate traveling. And though I would love to flatter myself that you missed my specific talents, I find it rather hard to believe. You have plenty of suitors willing to take up right where I left off."

With a pout, she reached out and traced a line from his knee up to the top of his thigh, stopping when she reached his hip. "Couldn't it wait? Surely, you've missed me as much as I've missed you."

His body responded to her touch immediately, the unanswered ache in his loins from the night before still smoldered like an ember—and she just stoked it to a blaze. Her eyes were alight with suggestion, trying to provoke him while she allowed her fingers to continue their assent. No matter how badly he wanted it, he wanted to know the motivation for her appearance that much more.

Gripping her arms, John pulled her to her feet. "Celeste, why are you here?"

She cocked a brow and gave him one of her devilish grins. "We have business ventures that need to be discussed."

Gently, she traced her finger down his cheek then along his chin, conjuring the memory of Dellis touching him, her fathomless dark eyes searching his with wonder. He stiffened, painfully, just thinking about it.

"Tell me you missed me." With that, she ran her hands down his chest, over his abdomen, and then between his legs, starting to work the buttons of his front fall.

"No, Celeste." He jerked her hand away, more forcefully than intended. "My innkeeper will be here any minute with your tea. This is hardly the place for an intrigue."

"Are you not allowed to entertain ladies in your quarters?" She looked around the room, wrinkling her nose in disapproval. "This room is as good as any, though a bit lacking in style." With a grin, she said, "At least there's a bed. I remember times when we had much less."

John rolled his eyes. Her attempts at seduction were paltry and lacking taste, even for Celeste. Before he could offer up a stern rebuke, there was a knock on the door.

Dellis pushed the door open with her backside, in her arms was a tray with their tea service on it, a pile of delicious looking biscuits in the center, drawing his attention. "Captain, I have your—" She stopped abruptly, her eyes widening when she saw the two of them. "My goodness, I didn't mean to interrupt."

"Thank you, Miss McKesson." Pulling away from Celeste, he walked over to Dellis and took the tray, placing it on his desk. He noticed her wince when she bent forward to pour their tea. She was hurt, most likely from their scuffle the night before. "Please, I can pour. Don't worry yourself."

Dellis backed away, keeping her gaze averted, then raced to the door. "Let me know if you need anything else," she said over her shoulder.

He didn't like the way she avoided looking at him. It was unlike her to be so skittish. He resisted the urge to go after her and find out. First, he would deal with Celeste.

"Well, John, only you could find a place in the middle of nowhere with a female innkeeper. Now tell me, do you actually pay your rent, or do you just service her directly? From the look on her face, I would say it was the latter of the two." Celeste snorted then rolled her eyes. "Really, John, you could do better."

Considering the totality of the situation, he almost laughed at Celeste's ridiculous insinuation. Sitting down, he poured them both a cup of tea and started to drink. "Celeste, she is my innkeeper, that's all," he said between sips. "You're imagining things."

Walking around the desk, Celeste placed her ample bottom on the edge of it and tipped his face up for inspection. She looked lovely and furious with her right eyebrow cocked in suggestion. "If you believe that, then you're a fool. I saw the way that woman looked at you. She's smitten. But that doesn't bother me; lots of women look at you, John. You're beautiful." She paused, the expression on her face turning cold, her hazel eyes narrowing. "What I find more interesting is the way you looked at her. She's quite attractive if you prefer that sort of woman."

He didn't like what she was insinuating, not in the least. And while he sensed Miss McKesson's attraction to him, the idea that she was "smitten" was a stretch. Pushing Celeste's hand away, he replied, "Jealously doesn't become you, Celeste. You sound a bit like a wife. Now, tell me what really brought you here."

"Fine," she said, crossing her arms over her chest. "We have a problem. Are you familiar with a Lieutenant Dokes, from the Twenty-third Welsh Fusiliers?"

"I'm acquainted with him, why?"

Taking a seat, Celeste poured herself a cup of tea and slowly added milk; her eyes focused on the task as if she were sewing delicate lace. She was purposely taking her time, one of the techniques she used to assert control. John knew it well. "He came to visit me several days ago. A few of his men got into a tussle with some local vermin on the streets outside of my establishment. Apparently, they were Rebel spies passing information concerning the fortification of Manhattan. He assumed they were using my establishment as a meeting place. I told him I didn't know what he was talking about, and then he accused me of being a spy."

Knowing very well this was a ruse, John opted to play along just to see how far she would take it. "So, what was the final result?"

"He closed me down and was going to arrest me for treason. I gave him all the money I had. It was the only thing I could do. He was going to send me to the gallows." The look of innocence on her face was so masterfully executed, he almost believed her, save the fact he knew she was a consummate actress and a convincing liar. "Someone framed me, John. I would never spy for those nasty Rebels. If you came back, you could tell them I didn't do it."

"How much did you pay him?" he asked, dreading the answer.

"Fifteen hundred pounds."

John closed his eyes, the astounding sum like a fist to his gut. He knew the Lieutenant to be a respectable man. If this was true, the only reason to demand such a sum was to buy a promotion, or else Dokes was deeply in debt, much like John himself.

"John, it was the only way he would let me go." Putting her cup and saucer down, she stood, a little pout forming on her lovely lips. "He told me he would handle the situation with the authorities, but he suggested I leave town. I came here because I knew you'd help me. I had nowhere else to go."

When she put her hand on his jacket, he knew what was coming next, he'd seen this rendition before; first the seduction, then a night of passion and indulgence and then she sunk her claws into you. "You will help me, won't you, John?"

Speechless, he just stood back, enjoying her calculated performance.

Gently, she ran her finger over his lips, leaning up and kissing him. She nibbled and sucked on his bottom lip for a second before she pulled away.

"You know you want to help me," Celeste purred, looking into his eyes. "You can't resist me."

He would've laughed if he weren't so damned infuriated. The woman was utterly predictable and so cliché. "I can't help you. I don't have any money."

"You must be joking."

"I'm not." He said flatly, pulling her hands away, and taking strategic steps back. Some distance between the two of them was a good idea, for his hands ached to wring her lovely little neck. "My shipment disappeared without a trace several days ago. I have nothing. I'm in debt as it is. If you remember, at least a third of the capital in your business was mine, and now, it too, is gone. So, I'm unfortunately unable to help you, or even myself, at the moment."

"Then take me to Philadelphia. With your help, I'll start a new business there."

The sheer absurdity of her statement forced a laugh from him. "I'm not taking you anywhere. I'm on a mission. Besides, I have no money, nor do you."

"Yes, you do. Isn't General Howe bankrolling this little venture of yours?" Pausing for a moment, she smiled. He could almost see the wheels turning in her lovely, devious head. "No, he isn't, is he? Of course, why would he, when he has a disgraced officer willing to do anything to salvage his damaged reputation?"

She'd gone too far; he was done playing her childish games. Grabbing her by the wrist, he twisted her arm around her back, pulling her body against his own. "Enough of the performance, Celeste, it's wasted on me. Tell me the truth."

She let out a groan that evolved into a sweet, feminine sigh of pleasure, her eyes closing, her teeth biting her lower lip amorously. "I love it when you're rough with me. I've missed you." Laughing, she leaned forward bringing her lips an inch from his, her eyes searching his own. "You and I both know you won't hurt me, but you're welcome to try. You know I'll

like it. Although, if I remember correctly, it's you who prefers the pain…
Too bad I forgot my crop. Ouch!" She whispered playfully, faking a wince.

Their eyes locked in challenge, hazel-green clashing with sapphire-blue. Celeste wasn't easily intimidated, and he wasn't the kind of man to rough up a woman. Releasing her abruptly, he walked around the desk, clenching his fists against the urge to throttle her. *Damn her.* She was playing both sides of the fence, and she'd used his money to cover up when she got caught. This could cost him everything; his career, his freedom—hell, his life! It was treason.

"Do you have the arrest warrant?" he asked, reining in his fury.

She smiled, her face lighting up. "It's in my room at The Silver Kettle. Would you like to see it?"

"Actually, I would." If he could get his hands on the warrant, then he might be able to go back to Dokes and threaten to turn him over to Howe if he didn't get his money back.

"Shall we?" Celeste asked sweetly, linking her arm through his and giving him a wink. "Agnes will be glad to see you."

Chapter
Twenty-One

John rolled out of bed and dressed quickly. Initially, he had no plans of spending the night with Celeste, but he passed out, looking over her ledgers, drinking enough to forget his precarious situation temporarily. Looking at himself in the mirror, he pulled his hair back and tied it tightly, then wiped the red stain from Celeste's lip rouge from his cheeks. Suddenly a pillow hit him in the back, and when he turned around, Celeste was smiling impishly, her bare leg dangling over the side of the bed. "You can't be leaving, Johnny, you were no use to me last night."

"Sadly, it happens sometimes," he replied, turning back to the mirror, applying shaving lotion to his jaw. Usually, he wasn't so nonchalant about his lack of sexual prowess. Actually, it was rather distressing, but he found her treachery less than stimulating to his libido, and in truth, she wasn't the one he wanted in his bed. Thankfully, the alcohol gave him an excuse for his lack of performance, and he fell asleep to dreams of silky, black hair and dark, smoky eyes.

"John, you were yelling in your sleep again. Are you still having nightmares, or was that just drunken ravings?"

Ignoring her, he finished shaving, pulled his coat on, and gave himself the once-over in the mirror, smoothing a stray hair back.

"Fine, don't answer me, but it was a bit distressing, watching you thrash about in your sleep like a wild man. You kept yelling for me to stop singing. What's going on, John?"

"Nothing I wish to further discuss with you." He gave her a weak smile from over his shoulder, knowing how it infuriated her when he was tight-lipped and reticent.

She grinned. "There's a key on the dresser, make sure you take it with you. You can let yourself in tonight."

John disregarded the key and walked over to the bed, sitting down on edge next to her. She scooted over to him, wrapping her arms around his neck, allowing the blanket to slip down from her breasts. As expected, she pressed them into his chest, trying to lure him back into her arms and her thrall. "If you come back to bed, I think I might be able to make things work." She put her finger between her lips, sucking on the tip. "And if you're really good, I promise to tie you to the bedpost and make you beg for it."

She was beautiful, and so tempting, but something about her no longer sent his blood roaring through his veins. It wasn't just her betrayal—it was her. She no longer enticed him as she used to. There was nothing organic or natural about her; everything was a well-scripted act, every move calculated down to the last step.

Leaning forward, John kissed her lips, brushed a lock of her silky hair out of her face, and smiled. "My dear, it would seem we are at an impasse."

Pulling away, she drew up the covers with a look of confusion. "What is that supposed to mean? John, are you still drunk?" There was outrage in her voice and a tinge of fear.

"I'm not drunk. As a matter of fact, I'm far from it. I see things very clearly. You, my dear Celeste, no longer have a business for me to invest in, and I'm apparently no longer able to service you." He stood up and grabbed the arrest warrant off the nightstand. "Just as you said, I was no use to you last night."

"What are you talking about?" She rolled her eyes, a grin tugging at the side of her lips. "Did I insult your fragile male ego?"

"Actually, no, I can accept my failures in the bedroom, or perhaps, yours." She straightened her back, her eyes narrowing with fury at his dig. "Celeste, you are beautiful and devious, but you're not stupid, and neither am I. Lieutenant Dokes is a competent man, and this warrant states that his men witnessed one of your ladies passing letters. You were allowing Rebels to use your women to exchange detailed information about the fortification of Manhattan. They would only do such a thing on your specific orders. Don't try to deny it. When you got caught, you used your money, half of which was mine, to save yourself. This is treason, Celeste. Thank God I wasn't there, or I would have been implicated along with you."

Grabbing his hat from the dresser, he stomped to the door, then turned back to her one last time. "May I make a suggestion?"

"What's that?" she asked, climbing out of bed, putting her robe on.

"If you're looking for a new profession, I recommend you try the stage. You have the talent, and you aren't afraid to use your assets to get what you want. Though I have to say, this most recent performance of yours was sorely lacking."

"You're a drunk and a scoundrel, John Carlisle," she said, walking towards him, tying her robe around her waist. "And no matter how you try to pretend, you're no gentleman."

"You're right. I'm not." He nodded, finding no fault in her logic. "Sorry to disappoint, but your insults are wasted on me. Now, if you will excuse me, I have business to attend to."

Slamming the door, John ran down the stairs, his temper threatening to boil over with each passing second. At least he had the warrant, though little good it was going to do him with Dokes in Manhattan. Making way to the door, John heard a familiar voice calling his name from behind. Looking over his shoulder, he saw Stuart's reflection in the mirror behind the bar, his dark, piercing eyes focused on John.

"They don't serve your kind here, Tory," Stuart yelled, his voice echoing in the little tavern, rising above the noise. Suddenly, everyone in the bar turned their attention to him, and it was dead silent. "Where's your red coat?"

Stopping for a moment, John thought about Dellis and what she would have to deal with when Stuart returned home in a drunken stupor raving like an idiot. Walking up to the bartender, John leaned over and asked, "How much does he owe you?"

"Three shillings, sir, and that includes what he drank last week and the week before."

John reached into his pocket, pulled out a bag of coins and dropped them on the counter. "That should cover his bill and extra for you to send him home and not give him another drink ever again. Besides, I was under the impression you don't serve his kind at The Kettle?"

The bartender shook his head. "I don't know what you're talking about. I've got no problem with anyone as long as they can pay in coin."

John snorted. Clearly, Jussie's rule about natives extended to Dellis in particular.

The bartender reached over the counter and took the tankard away from Stuart. "Okay, son, you're done for the day. Either you go home on your own, or this nice gentleman and I will see that you get there, and I don't reckon you'll like how we do it, either."

"Did you pay him off with your Tory money? Does he know what you've done?" Stuart spat.

"You don't know what you're talking about." John grabbed Stuart's upper arm, trying to pull him towards the door.

Wrenching his arm free, he hissed. "But I do, don't I? I know who you really are."

There was no reasoning with him, his mind was addled and made worse by chronic drinking. It was sad. "You're leaving now," John insisted, pushing Stuart towards the door. "Let's go."

"Hey, everyone, he's a Tory," Stuart yelled over his shoulder, pointing at John. "And he's tupping my whore of a sister. What do you think about that?" The bar suddenly got quiet again—all eyes fixed on John. When two of the men at the counter got up from their chairs and started walking towards them, John rushed to the door, dragging Stuart along. The last thing John needed was to be tarred and feathered because of a drunken fool spouting off nonsense.

"Stuart, you're going to get both of us in trouble."

Turning around, pointing a finger at him, Stuart sneered. "I'm sure my sister would like to know about the company you keep." He looked at the staircase that led to Celeste's room, then back at John. "Moved on to another one now that you've had my sister? Or perhaps you like having both?"

Grabbing Stuart by the collar, John threw the man against the door, slamming his back into it a few times before releasing him. "Do *not* speak of her that way, Stuart. She deserves your respect. Now, go home, before I use my fists on you."

"Better your fists than your cock, Tory." He hacked and spat on John's coat sleeve, and with a smile, Stuart ran out the door.

Chapter Twenty-Two

Dellis could hear her aunt talking to someone in the dining room, their voices echoing through the house. It was Uncle James, his deep, distinctive voice always evoking an uneasy feeling in Dellis's gut. They weren't trying to be quiet or hide their topic of discussion. It was about The Thistle. Putting on her apron and pinning it in place, she walked through the bar, smoothing her hair out of her face, trying to make herself look more presentable.

The sight of her Uncle James always gave her pause. His resemblance to her father was striking, both men were tall and lanky, with the same pale-blue eyes and razor-sharp cheekbones, but unlike her father's messy blond locks, James's hair was dark brown and always perfectly arranged in a tight queue. Her uncle was never happy, a morose mood his normal state of affairs with an unpredictable temper that came on as fast as a tornado, where her father was innately sweet and jovial every day to the end of his life.

"Dellis, nice of you to finally wake up and join us," her aunt said, looking up from her breakfast.

"I didn't know you slept in a while your aunt did all the work. Does this happen often?" Uncle James looked at his wife, then at Dellis, accusation in his icy-blue gaze and anger in his voice.

"Uncle, I'm sorry. I was up late taking care of the kitchen," she replied, expecting no sympathy from him. He hated her mother's people and showed his disdain for Dellis's heritage by treating her and Stuart as unwanted mongrels that sullied the family bloodlines. "What brings you here today?"

A stack of mail was sitting on the table next to him. When he noticed her eyeing it, James shoved it into his finely tailored coat pocket then looked up at her, almost daring her to say something in defiance. "You know why I'm here; that's why you tried to evade me the other day. The Thistle is losing money, and by the end of the winter, we'll no longer be able to keep it open."

She glanced at her aunt, looking for some support, but finding none in her stony countenance. "What are you trying to say, Uncle?"

"The Thistle doesn't bring in enough profit to maintain itself. Out of respect for your father and his wishes, I've done my best to try and help you and your brother continue to live here. Your aunt has worked here for the past year without pay. This will no longer do. I'm closing The Thistle. This place has fallen into ruin, and it will cost too much to make it respectable again. It was completely impractical for your father to think you could do this." He looked her up and down, his expression unreadable. "We'll sell the house, and what little is left of the money, after I recoup my losses, will be split between you and your brother. Since your unfortunate situation has prevented you from marrying, you'll come live with us and help maintain our home. Stuart can help Alexei care for the land."

Dellis swallowed, carefully considering her words before speaking. The last thing she needed to do was provoke him into an argument. "With all due respect, Uncle, I won't give up this house. It's all I have left of my father. I'll find a way to keep The Thistle open. Besides, business has picked up lately. Hand the books over to me, and let me manage the accounts. I'm sure I can find a way to cut corners."

He shook his head impassively. "You know nothing of managing money, Dellis. I've never known a woman with a head for figures, much less balancing a ledger."

No, this couldn't be happening. "I'll write to Uncle Dane again. He promised he would help if I needed him," she said, refusing to let her uncle intimidate her into complying. "He built this house for my parents. I know he would want me to keep it. What is left of Father's Chippendale furniture will surely bring in a profit. I'll ask Captain Anderson. He will help me sell it."

"I wouldn't count on His Grace, the Admiral, helping you with anything. My youngest brother is much too busy with his affairs to worry about his poor relatives, especially you and Stuart."

"Uncle Dane loved my father. I know he will help me." Straightening her back, she willed herself to be strong, though her heart felt like it was cracking with each embittered word that passed through her uncle's lips. "I'll find a way. I will. Just give me time."

James McKesson stood up, his great height allowing him to cast a shadow on her, just as he did over her life. How she wished they could be close, but there was little chance of that. The distance that had separated him from her father extended to her and her brother as well. "You have until the end of the winter. After that, the two of you are moving in with me. Your aunt and I will do our best to find you a husband, but I'm not expecting much to come of that."

Dellis watched as her uncle gave her aunt a surprisingly loving kiss, his hand gently brushing against her tiny, perfect cheekbones before he pulled away. He put his hat on and turned to Dellis. "One last thing, Dellis, don't you ever run away from me again when I'm trying to talk to you. You owe me more respect than that, after all I've done for you and your brother. Do you understand me?"

"Yes, sir," she replied, biting her tongue.

"And if I were you, I wouldn't count on the Admiral for anything. I know you write to him, and I know he has never answered you back. He never will. He doesn't care about you or your brother."

As he walked out, an icy blast and puff of snow flew through the door before it slammed shut. A chill ran down her spine, giving her goosebumps.

"I told you we weren't finished with this conversation, Dellis. You didn't take me seriously." Her aunt got up from the table, walking past, never once looking back in Dellis's direction. "I'm sorry, my dear." She heard her aunt whisper over her shoulder.

Once alone, the unshed tears that stung Dellis's eyes burst forth in a shower of pain and hopelessness. Sitting down on one of the chairs, Dellis looked around the dining room, remembering it as it was when she was a child and all was right in the world. The once beautiful blue-and-white damask wallpaper was all gone, and the paint that now covered the walls was yellowed with age. The wood floor that used to shine so that she could see her reflection in it was scuffed and worn, with holes and an occasional missing board. Most of her father's precious Chippendale furniture had been sold; all that remained of it was in her parent's bedroom, which now served as the Captain's quarters.

Help me, Father. If only he could hear her.

The front door swung open, and with another gust of wintry air came the Captain, his nose and cheeks red from being out in the cold. Wiping her eyes, she got up from the table and walked to him, trying her best to look happy.

"Miss McKesson, good morning." He removed his hat, his blond hair loose from the wind, thick, curly strands of it hanging in his face

"It's almost afternoon, Captain," she said. "You must have been too busy to notice the time."

She turned away, and started towards the kitchen, paying no mind to if he was following her.

"Yes, well." He stammered. "I was quite busy."

She nodded. "I'm sure you were." He'd been gone all night with Mrs. Allen. "Can I get you something to eat?"

"No, thank you. Is something amiss?" he asked, stepping into her path, stopping her in mid-stride. "You look troubled."

"My back is a little sore." She lied, resisting the urge to confide in someone, anyone who cared enough to listen, but it wasn't his problem. "How is your wound? I should take a look at it."

179

"Can you do it now? I have business to attend to, and I'll be gone for the rest of the day."

Dellis showed him to her father's private parlor, just behind the kitchen, then went to her room and grabbed her basket of medical supplies.

When she entered the parlor again, the sight of John in his well-tailored, forest-green coat and breeches made her stop for a moment to admire. He was handsome with a smile so infectious it brightened up her day no matter how upset she was. He had this ability to fill every room he was in with his strength and vitality, drawing her in like a moth to a flame. She couldn't resist it. Or him.

"Do I not meet your approval?" He grinned, making a show of adjusting his overcoat and smoothing his stray hairs back. "I confess this is one of my better jackets."

After the initial excitement of seeing him wore off, she motioned for him to sit, her despondent mood resurfacing. "Shall we, Captain? I have to get back to work, as you know, my kitchen doesn't run itself."

He sat down on one of the pale-yellow couches and removed his neckerchief, opening his collar for her. Gently, she ran her fingers over the wound, his skin was warm and smooth, a faint smell of shaving lotion and spicy cologne wafting in her direction, sticking in her nose. He smelled good. Her heart fluttered when he turned his head a bit and eyed her, lines of humor bracketed his mouth as he watched her perform her examination. The sutures looked good; they were clean with no signs of infection. Noticing a small, cherry red mark on his neck, she ran her fingers over it, rubbing it gently. "What happened here? I must have bruised you and didn't realize it."

"It's fine," he muttered, as he quickly tied his neckerchief and adjusted his collar. "No need to worry about that. By the way, I saw your brother this morning at The Kettle. I'm afraid he was rather intoxicated."

"He must have charged up quite a tab. I'll go over and take care of it." She had little money as it was, but the last thing she needed was for Stuart to end up in debtor's prison, rotting away for the rest of his days. He would never survive that, and he didn't belong there.

The Captain waved her off nonchalantly. "No need, Miss McKesson, I took care of it."

When Dellis looked up, there was something akin to sympathy in his blue eyes, but she didn't want it, she could take care of herself. She was no man's charity case. "No, Captain, I can't let you do that, Stuart is my problem. I'll pay you back when I have the money. Just give me a little time."

"Deduct it from my rent," he said. "Problem solved."

He shrugged the incident off like it was nothing, but to her, it was everything. He was intentionally helping her yet allowing her to keep her pride. "You have no idea how much this means to me."

"I think I do," he replied with all seriousness, their eyes meeting. "Now, if you have finished, I'll let you get back to work. I assume I'll survive?"

"Yes, you will." As he stood up, she rested her hand on his arm, stopping him before he walked away. "I would like to apologize for my behavior the other night. I don't make it a habit of attacking my lodgers with a knife."

"I hope not," he said on a laugh. "You can count on my discretion, Miss McKesson."

Lightening up the mood, she volleyed a jibe in his direction for good measure. "I believe this makes us even. You walked in on me changing in my stable, and I attacked you in my kitchen."

"Touché," he replied, with a cock of his brow. "Touché."

"Don't give me a reason to do it again." She teased as he walked out the door. She could hear his infectious laugh coming from the hallway and the clicking of his heels as he walked up the stairs. It was truly difficult to remain sad in his presence, a thankful respite from the melancholy of the day.

Dellis packed up her supplies, their banter lightening her sullen mood enough to where she let out a chuckle. Touché. The man said that word with such arrogance and conviction it would be written on his tombstone.

"What are you doing?" Stuart hissed, interrupting her pleasant reflection.

Dellis whirled around, stunned by his unexpected appearance. "What do you mean, what am I doing?"

Grabbing her shoulders, Stuart shook her so hard her teeth jarred together with a click. "Did you forget they killed our parents? I see how he leers at you. You're whoring for him, aren't you? He's one of them!"

"Stuart, you're drunk; you don't know what you're saying," she said, trying to break free from his steely grasp but failing miserably. He was strong with rage and male potency.

"I know what I saw." He held her tight, his grip like a vice. "You want him. I see it in your eyes. You're whoring for him, just like you did for them."

Steeped in outrage, Dellis slapped him, his head whipping to the side forcefully. "How dare you say that to me? You, of all people, know what they did to me. I'm no man's whore. He was injured, so I helped him. That's all."

"I saw him with that woman last night, and I saw him leave her room early this morning," he said, his stale breath reeking of rum and rotten teeth. "She's his whore and so are you."

"It's a bit late to be concerned about my welfare." Dellis knew there was no use arguing with him, but once she started, the words ran out fluid and quick like a waterfall. "You haven't cared a lick for The Thistle or me for the past two years. Now, you're worried about my reputation? You're not my brother. You're a drunk."

Suddenly, Stuart lunged at her, his fist connecting with her cheek, knocking her back into the wall. Tears welled in her eyes as she touched her face, pain shooting into her cheek when she tried to open her mouth. "Get your things and go. You're not welcome anymore."

"You forget this is my home, too," he said, his body visibly trembling from his head all the way to his feet.

When she started to get up, he offered her a hand, but she slapped it away. He regretted what he did, but little did it matter to her anymore; he had to go.

"This may be your home, but you're not my brother, I don't know who you are anymore. Now, get out."

Stuart stumbled and ran out through the kitchen, leaving a trail of muddy footprints behind him. Dellis massaged her cheek, opening and closing her jaw, wincing with each shooting pain. Rubbing her eyes, she looked around the room, remembering how her father loved to read his journals on the couch next to the fire. His medical books and journals still filled the beautiful cherry wood shelves, row after row, still neatly in the place where he left them. It was his personal sitting room, and their little retreat, where he would teach her everything he knew about medicine. She ached for him. Her father could always control Stuart, especially when he raged uncontrollably at the voices that haunted him. Father's touch was like magic, so gentle, so soothing, and just like that, Stuart would be at peace with one simple caress. What she wouldn't do for one more moment with their father.

Dellis pushed the loose tendrils of hair behind her ears, running her palms over her eyes one more time, catching the leftover tears before they fell.

When she looked up, her aunt was standing in the doorway her hands on her hips. "What happened? I could hear yelling in the kitchen."

"Stuart." Dellis stood up and smoothed her skirt down, composing herself. "He was drunk and in one of his moods."

"Are you all right?"

Not in the least. "I'm fine, just give me a minute."

Her aunt nodded, walking out of the parlor. Dellis took a moment to steady herself, then put the room to right before joining her aunt in the kitchen.

"Dellis, here's the Captain's mail." Her aunt handed over a stack of letters. Dellis flipped them over and scrutinized them, checking the wax seals for tampering. Were these the letters she saw in her uncle's pocket? All of them were intact, so if they were the ones her uncle took, he hadn't opened them.

"Oh, Jussie Simpson came by a few moments ago, and she left this for the Captain." Her aunt reached into a pocket and pulled out another letter, handing it to Dellis.

"Thanks, I'll take these to him," she replied, grabbing the letter and making her way through the dining room. A small crowd of people was filing in through the door for the dinner menu, a welcome sight for her heavy heart. But it would take more than a few loyal patrons to save The Thistle. As she started up the stairs, something slid out of one of the envelopes and landed on the step with a loud clank. It was a brass key. She bent down and picked it up. The envelope was open, and she couldn't help but notice the feminine signature on the letter inside—it was from Mrs. Allen.

Dellis slowly walked upstairs, her stomach churning as she considered the implications of a Mrs. Allen sending the Captain such a trinket. Dellis wasn't naïve; she knew there was an intrigue going on between the two of them, but seeing the key, knowing he'd just spent the night with the woman, felt like a knife to the gut. Dellis had no right to be jealous, yet she was. She couldn't help herself.

The Captain's door was open. He stood with his back to her, looking out the window. Gently, she knocked on the door. "Captain, there's mail for you."

He turned around immediately, his gaze focused on her cheek. "Dellis, what happened?"

Crossing the room quickly, he reached up to touch her cheek, then pulled away, allowing his hand to hover a few inches from her skin, as if asking for permission. Nodding, slowly, she turned her head, letting him look his fill.

He hesitated for a moment, her heart racing in anticipation, waiting, wanting, until finally, he ran the back of his fingers over her cheekbone with a touch so light she could barely feel it. His brow furrowed as he took her chin in his hand, turning her face slowly. His thumb gently grazed her lips as he cupped her cheek in his hand, sending a jolt, like lightning, straight to her heart. She closed her eyes, her body trembling like a leaf in the breeze.

184

"I just saw you moments ago. Who did this to you?" he asked, his voice unusually rough. Again, he ran his fingers over her cheek. Her breath caught in her throat, both of them suspended together in time, the moment passing ever so slowly, yet all too fast. "Tell me, and I'll have words with them."

Avoiding his gaze, she reached up and pulled his hand away. "It doesn't matter. It's just a bruise. I'll be fine."

"It does matter, Dellis. No one should hit you." The look in his eyes was serious for a moment, but then they softened, a bit of humor in their depths. "I'd be curious to see what you did to him in return. Tell me, does he still have all his appendages?"

"It's my affair, not yours," she said tersely. Remembering why she came, Dellis reached into her pocket and pulled out his letters, handing them to him. "The courier just brought these."

He took them from her, putting them in his coat pocket, his eyes never once glancing away. "Dellis?"

"Captain, please, stop." She hated the desperation in her voice that betrayed the calm façade she was trying to maintain. "It's none of your concern, and please, call me Miss McKesson. I'm your innkeeper."

In a voice laced with anger, he said, "Tell me who did this, and I'll handle it. No one should take a hand to you."

"You're right, no one puts their hands on me," she replied, shocked at his sudden streak of possessiveness. How presumptuous of him. "I will thank you to keep out of my affairs."

Reaching into her pocket, she pulled out Celeste's key and held it up so he could see it. "You must have forgotten this. It's from Mrs. Allen. Jussie brought it over this morning."

He took it from Dellis and stuffed it in his pocket, a hint of frustration in his countenance. *Good.* She could tell he was put out by her rebuff. "Thank you, Miss McKesson."

"You're welcome, Captain."

Chapter Twenty-Three

John needed to get out and clear his head. With Celeste's sudden appearance, and his argument with Dellis, he wanted to avoid the fairer sex as much as possible. Both women were unanticipated problems that had nothing to do with his mission. A bit of work would clear his mind and disperse the amorous spell that had been cast over him and kept him from his focus. Although the snow was coming down with a vengeance, he rode into town anyway, spending several hours scouting Fort Dayton and the older fort across the river. Construction on both locations had come to a halt, the snow and blistering wind making it difficult to continue any refortification. It would seem even the Rebels had determined that further battles were going to have to wait until Mother Nature's fury had subsided, more news he could relay to Howe in the next missive. By the time John returned to The Thistle, the sun had set, the weather progressing to where it was no longer safe to travel. Several inches had fallen since he'd set out in the afternoon, leaving the little dirt roads in the town near impassable. He'd managed to stay away long enough to put some distance and perspective to his personal issues, resolute to avoid both women for the time being. Celeste, he could handle when the time came, but Dellis, well, that was a non-starter, a place he couldn't go. Better to end it now than take it a step further.

Kicking the snow off his boots, John removed his hat and made for the stairs quickly before Dellis saw him. When he reached the top of the stairs, he realized the door to his room was cracked open. *Did I forget to lock it?* Quietly, John walked inside, scanning every inch of his room, looking for signs of an intruder. He searched his desk and then the drawers, but everything seemed to be in place, his clothes and haversack also appearing to be undisturbed. Perhaps, when he was in a rush to leave, he forgot to lock the door behind him.

Sitting down at the desk, John reached into his pocket, pulled out the letters Dellis brought him earlier in the day, and dropped Celeste's key in the top drawer. The handwriting on the first one was familiar—it was from Lieutenant Clark. Turning it over, John noticed the wax had been disturbed, a small mark where the edge of the seal met the paper, as if someone ran a knife under it. He examined it carefully, but there were no other signs that it had been tampered with, the paper intact, no smudges in the ink. Perhaps it was just an error when it was sealed.

He opened it and skimmed it quickly.

Dear Captain,

The supplies you requested have arrived, and we will be in transit within a day. As long as the weather holds out, I estimate we shall arrive around the 20th of November. Captain Denny has sent word. I will happily bring his message and the excellent bottle of rum he gave me to wish us well in our business ventures. I must warn you, I have already consumed half of it.

Your servant,

Clark

The timing of his shipment was perfect. Now that the weather had progressed, the Oneidas would be desperately in need of trade goods. John threw the letter into the fire, watching it burn while he opened the next one. It was from General Howe's office.

Captain Anderson,

After your most recent departure, I remembered I forgot to wish you luck on your travels. As my business partner, it behooves both myself and my pocketbook for you to have a safe and prolific journey. Forgive my lack of decorum when we last spoke, as you know, I was dealing with matters of the most sensitive nature. Mrs. Chambers thanks you for your understanding. Please visit me upon your return to Manhattan so we can further discuss our business.

Yours,

Henry Chambers

The letter itself was meaningless—it was a cipher. The first word started with an A, for acid, a code they had agreed upon before he left. Howe used ink made of gallow-tannic acid to write the letter. John grabbed the bottle of ferrous sulfate reagent from his desk, doused a piece of linen with it, and wiped it lightly over the message. Satisfied with the application, he walked to the fireplace, bent over, and put the letter close to the flames, using the heat to speed up the drying process.

Carleton will not proceed to Ticonderoga, the expedition on hold until spring, Burgoyne has returned to England. Continue with the mission. Your timeline has been extended until late winter. Maintaining control of York City is our primary focus. I will expect a report of your progress. I have alerted Carleton of your presence. He will contact you when necessary.

John re-read the letter then threw it into the fire, watching it burn until it turned to smoldering embers. Just as he expected, the northern winter had put a stop to any chance of the British advancing, forcing Carleton to pull back his men to St. Johns and then Quebec. Arnold had managed to delay just long enough for the weather to progress, either a lucky move or a well-calculated one. It was well known that General Burgoyne didn't like winter in the colonies, and now that he was on his way back to England, there was nothing left to be done but sit and wait.

Sitting back at the desk, John rifled through the drawers, searching for his inkwell and pounce. His ink pot had tipped over in the top drawer, spattering all over the papers underneath, leaving a black, sticky mess. As he leafed through the stack of documents, trying to salvage them, he noticed a small, black fingerprint on one of the parchments. Carefully, he lifted the paper up to the candle, the light shining through the thin paper giving further detail to the print. He placed his thumb in some of the wet ink and pressed it to the page, examining both prints side by side. It was not his. Someone had tipped the pot over and accidentally touched the paper. Rubbing his finger on the print, he tried to smudge the ink, but it was dry.

Again, John rifled through the rest of his desk, though everything else seemed to be untouched, he knew that wasn't the case. Unlocking the center drawer, he pulled out his maps, shuffling through them, taking a mental inventory of each one. There were two missing. Laying them out on the desk, he scanned each one, trying to figure out which ones were gone, then it dawned on him; someone had taken his maps of the port of Oswego and Fort Stanwix.

Quickly, he leafed through the rest of his letters, and all of them seemed to be accounted for, with no marks or fingerprints on them. Pulling the drawer out, he sifted through it. The lock's integrity was functional, no scarring or signs of picking on the metal. He locked and unlocked it a few times, trying to trick it, but to no avail. Whoever stole the maps could access the drawer.

The only person he knew for sure had a key to his room was Dellis. *But could she have done it?* He'd seen her eyeing his maps, and she'd admitted looking at his letter from Celeste earlier in the day. *Could someone have taken the key from her?*

Whatever the truth, he needed a different place to hide his private papers. Getting down on his hands and knees, he felt around the floorboards for one he could pry loose and turn into a hiding place, but everything was sound. Walking over to the fireplace, he pulled on the wooden mantle, trying to loosen the trim, his fingers feeling underneath for a small space or cubby.

Suddenly, he heard a loud pounding noise coming from the dining room and the slam of a door. He raced down the stairs, just in time to greet Hayes at the front door holding up the limp form of Simon Clark. There was a large red stain on his breeches, and his head lulled forward as if he'd been knocked out and had yet to gain consciousness.

"My God, what happened?" John asked, helping Hayes the rest of the way through the door.

Dellis came out from the kitchen, rushing over to them. "Oh my, what happened?"

"Miss McKesson, please get your supplies, we'll need your assistance," John said, ducking under Clark's arm.

Together, John and Hayes carried Clark up the stairs and down the hall to John's room, depositing the man on the bed. John quickly removed Simon's great cloak and wet boots, trying to get him warm. When his eyes rolled open, John breathed a sigh of relief. *Thank God.*

"Simon, you've gained a bit of weight," John quipped, his breath still short from their trip up the stairs. "Tell me what happened."

Hayes shook his head with disbelief and looked over at John. "We were ambushed, Captain. It was a complete white-out. We could barely see more than a foot in front of us. Suddenly, they were on us, and before we knew what was happening, they took everything and disappeared. It's as if they knew the weather was coming, like a witch had cast a spell for them."

"Who?" John asked, looking at both of men.

"Savages. There had to be twenty of them to the three of us," Hayes replied.

John carefully removed the makeshift tourniquet from around Clark's thigh and rolled his breeches back to get a better look at the wound. It was big, about two inches long, and gaped open exposing meaty, pink flesh. It started to ooze a fresh stream of blood down his leg, staining the snowy white sheets beneath him. John untied his neckerchief and wrapped it around his friend's leg, using it to put pressure back on the wound. "Where were you?"

"On the Carry, near the Fort," Clark replied, through a painful wince.

Not exactly a surprise. "Where is Smith?"

"He's still on the road trying to figure out which way they went."

John took a deep breath, looking at both of his men. This whole situation had an all-too-familiar ring to it, a harkening back to two years before. "I have an idea where they went, but it's not in the direction you think."

He ran down the hall to his room, grabbed his maps, and ran back to Clark's room. Putting them down on the bed, John pointed to Mohawk River, and east towards Oriskany Creek.

"This isn't even close to where were ambushed," Hayes said, pointing towards Fort Stanwix and the Oneida Carry. "This is where we were."

"I know, but it's too far for you to go back tonight, and I have a hunch this is where they'll be exiting the river." He pointed back to the junction of the Mohawk and Oriskany Creek. "Oriska is right there, and another Oneida village is only seven miles east of that location. They could make it there in an hour. Unless... Perhaps they took it directly to the fort?"

"John, what do you think?" Clark asked with a wince, fisting the sheets underneath him.

"I think they'll take what they need first and give the rest to Elmore at the fort."

"Do you really want me to go out now? The weather's gotten worse," Hayes asked.

"Absolutely, if the weather slows you down, it will slow them, too. If we're going to learn anything about their whereabouts, now's the time."

A tap on the door interrupted the remainder of their conversation. It was Dellis. John quickly folded up the maps, stuffing them in his coat pocket just as she entered. Her eyes darted back and forth, catching him rearranging his coat, and adjusting the papers at his breast. But instead of commenting, she played it off, nonchalantly, putting a basin of water on the nightstand with a pile of linen, and then removing the basket of supplies that dangled from her forearm and depositing it on the bed.

"Is it all right if I get started?" she asked, glancing at him then at Clark.

He waved her on. "Please, Miss McKesson, work your magic."

She smiled at his comment, taking a seat next to Clark on the bed. "There's no magic here, Captain, just needle and thread and good, old-fashioned sewing." Looking up at Clark, she asked, "You're not squeamish, are you?"

"Tell her yes, and she'll give you scotch," John said, watching Clark's eyes light up. "It's very good, too."

"Well, now, lass, are you holding out on me?" Clark looked up at John then back at her, grinning from ear to ear. "I haven't had good scotch in a while. Suddenly I'm glad those savag—"

John coughed loudly, stopping Clark mid-sentence; there was so much wrong with what was about to come out of his mouth. The word savage alone was sure to raise their innkeeper's hackles, not to mention what just happened to their supplies.

"Captain, go downstairs and ask my aunt for the bottle of scotch. It's under the bar top. And have her give you the whiskey, too. There's excess linen in the cupboard at the end of the hall, bring that with you when you come back. Make haste."

She threw orders at John like a commander directing men in the lineup, but never once looked up in his direction, her eyes focused on what she was doing. Clark cocked a brow curiously, and then rolled his eyes. Apparently, he wasn't the only one who noticed how she liked to give John orders. Patting his friend on the leg, John stood up and excused himself, gesturing for Hayes to come into the hall. Shutting the door behind them, John whispered to his friend, "Find Smith, do the best that you can. Go now."

Hayes nodded as he pulled on his gloves and buttoned his cloak. "Yes, sir."

Once John had gotten the two bottles and found the linen, he stepped back into the room, only to find Clark grinning from ear to ear like a disreputable cad. John could barely contain his laughter when he realized why: His friend had a clear view down the front of their lovely innkeeper's bodice. With a shake of the head, John gave Clark a knowing look. It was hard not to admire her. She was so genteel and innocently focused on her work that she neither suspected their lewdness nor realized the view she was affording. And to her credit, she *was* beautiful.

"Thank goodness it didn't get to the vessel, and it just missed your knee joint. You are fortunate, my friend," Dellis said, looking up at Clark.

He smiled and nodded, his eyes like saucers. "Thank you, Miss, and I'm grateful for your help. How many more stitches do you think I'll need?"

She examined the wound, chewing her bottom lip in the process. "Likely another five or six, it's a pretty good size cut. Did you get hit with a tomahawk?"

It was definitely a tomahawk wound, the shape and depth of the cut a tell-tale sign. John gave Clark a look of warning before he could answer. "I didn't see what hit me, I just felt it. The snow was coming down something fierce."

"Fair enough," she replied, seemingly satisfied with his answer. But John knew better, she was inquisitive and far too curious for her own good, like a dog with a bone, tenacious when her interest was piqued. "Captain, pour him some scotch. It will help with the pain."

Once again, she ordered him about. The woman was haughty and rather bold to do so in front of his men. With a grin, he did her bidding, handing Clark a drink. John watched from over her shoulder while she cleaned and wrapped the wound, feeding Clark additional shots of the fine scotch, per his requests. "That should hold, for now. I'll check on you tomorrow morning. Is there anything else I can get you?"

Clark shook his head, his large brown eyes glazed over from all the spirits. "I'm all right, lass, and now, I'm going to close my eyes and dream sweet dreams of large, round—"

"Ahh!" John yelled, giving Clark a look of warning. "Miss McKesson, let me help you take your things downstairs."

Dellis packed up her belongings and slung her basket over her arm. "Grab that." She pointed to the basin of bloody water and eyed him. Another order. He followed her out the door, shutting it behind him, his arms full of linen, the basin in hand.

When they got to the kitchen, she put her things down on the nearest table and whirled around like a tempest, confronting him. "Captain, that is a tomahawk wound. I know one when I see one."

"There's no need to worry yourself, Miss McKesson, this is my affair," he replied, tersely. She winced, realizing he had purposely used her words from earlier against her.

But instead of backing off, she persisted. "I don't think you understand. It could've been the same group who are trying to frame my grandfather's village. You must tell me what you know."

She was flustered and angry, her face turning beet red with frustration, her body posturing towards his. He liked her boldness, it was unfettered and real. She wasn't hiding from him, no shrinking back into her protective shell.

"Miss McKesson, allow me the opportunity to look into the matter. I promise to tell you what I learn. Please, if not for your safety, then for my sanity."

She gave him a quizzical look, her eyes narrowing, almost squinting. "I didn't know your sanity was on the brink. I can suggest an herb for that."

Shaking his head at the sheer ridiculousness of her statement, it took a Spartan's effort to keep himself from throttling the woman. She was infuriating, alluring, and haughty all at the same time. "Miss McKesson, I would feel better if you would let me handle this."

194

"Fine," she said, grabbing the basin from him and setting it down on the table. "By the way, Captain, when will you have the goods you promised my grandfather? The winter has set in early, and I'm afraid they will need them as soon as possible."

Curious about her reaction, he opted to tell the truth. "Both my storage and my shipment have been stolen. My men were transferring it this afternoon when they were set upon by thieves."

"Oh, no," she said on a gasp, her dark eyes widening with genuine shock. The look on her face alone confirmed what he already suspected— she was innocent. No one could feign that reaction. "What will you do? The village is desperately in need of those supplies. They won't make it through the winter without them. Captain?"

The frantic tone of her voice further abated any residual suspicion of her. She really had been depending on him, and damned if he didn't want to follow through on his promise. "I'll look in the morning. Whoever took my supplies couldn't have gotten far. Please, this is none of your affair."

He watched her wipe down the counter then the large wooden table that was piled high with dirty dishes and leftover pots from the day's cooking. The fire burned brightly, warming the room to the point of cozy, while several pieces of linen hung in the hearth drying. A large tub full of soapy water and dirty mugs sat on the floor. He leaned over and picked it up, putting it on the counter.

"Thank you for helping Clark," he said, watching her wipe the table so vigorously he was sure she'd wear a groove in the wood.

"Of course, Captain," she said over her shoulder then continued with her work. There was a tartness in her tone—she was angry with him.

It suddenly dawned on John that they were alone. She was making a paltry show of ignoring him, starting to wash the dishes as if he wasn't standing there waiting for her to say something. As she bent over the counter, her bottom thrust out towards him, moving rhythmically while she scrubbed, her long, inky-dark hair falling loose from the pin, cascading down her nape. She looked so utterly tantalizing; his hands ached to take her into his arms and find out what sorts of lovely things could ensue in the confines of that kitchen.

When he stepped closer to her, Dellis turned around abruptly, her back to the counter. Realizing he had her cornered, she looked up at him defiantly, almost daring him to try something. She looked incredible, her full red lips swollen and parted, practically begging for him to slide his tongue between them and sample her sweetness. He could imagine it even now; she would taste like honey and vanilla, sweet and smoky at the same time and so tantalizing. He advanced a little more, looking into her eyes, their bodies so close his legs grazed her skirts, her pillowy, full breasts only inches from his chest. The heady smell of lavender wafted into his nose, like an English garden in the spring. John knew he should back away, keep his distance, but he couldn't; he lacked the fortitude to resist. In spite of everything, he wanted her, and though he didn't deserve it, he wanted her to trust him.

Gently, John ran his thumb down her cheek, and just as he remembered, her skin was as smooth and delicate as the finest Chinese porcelain. She closed her eyes, her body visibly starting to tremble when he lightly brushed the backs of his fingers over the purplish-blue bruise on her cheek. At first, he wasn't sure what to make of her response. When he went to pull his hand away, she placed her hand on top of his, her eyes leveling on him, dark and hooded, drawing him into their fathomless depths. He could get lost in those eyes, a total cessation of time and place, a prisoner to her slightest whim.

She caressed his cheek gently, letting her hand slide down his neck to his chest, then resting it on the front of his jacket, making his heart quicken underneath, a surge of lust shooting straight to his core. The sane, thinking part of him knew he should put a stop to their intrigue right then, but the rest of him was content to suffer her sweet assault on his senses, if only for a moment more. He marveled at her omnipotent power over him. So little experience, yet she held him in her thrall like a skilled temptress,

Cleopatra or even Delilah. Somehow, she'd managed to do what no other woman had ever done. It was fascinating yet wholly disarming.

Taking her hand in his own, he lifted her palm to his lips, nuzzling and worshiping it with soft little kisses. When he touched the tip of his tongue to the pad of her index finger, a breath caught in her throat, her neck and chest flushing the color of crimson rose petals on white snow. Her eyes smoldered, watching him kiss each and every one of her fingertips, making him lightheaded, almost drunk with desire. He wanted more, and she obliged. Reaching up, she lightly touched his lips with her fingertip, tracing their shape, intricately learning every curve and crevasse of them. He stifled a groan when her thumb grazed his tongue, his body betraying him to the point of pain despite the chaste intimacy of the moment.

Back away, Carlisle. It was all too much. He'd gone too far. John stepped back, releasing her hand abruptly.

"Good night, Miss McKesson," he said brusquely, mentally berating himself for giving in to his desire

"Good night, Captain," she replied, with a tremulous voice. With that, she turned her back to him, continuing with her work as if nothing had happened.

"Damn," he muttered to himself, slamming the door to his room. *Why didn't I just walk away?* Their moment in the kitchen was far from a seduction, yet he reacted as if he were an inexperienced schoolboy having his first kiss. *What are you doing, Carlisle? She's an innocent, and far from the sophisticated women I prefer.* It was pointless to ask—he knew why—because he couldn't have her. Not to mention, her spirited nature and her lack of experience that drove him to the brink. She was curious, yet she resisted him, but it wasn't a game for her, lacking the usual coquetry of the majority of her sex. Someone had violently put the fear in her eyes that he saw lurking just below the surface. And that fear extended to him, too, and rightly so; if she knew the truth about him, she would run as far as she could, only after putting a bullet in his head.

John walked over to the window, watching the snow come down in full force. He'd have to wait until morning for word on his supplies, and by then, they were sure to be long gone. In such a short period of time, his whole plan had gone to waste, and there was little he could do to remedy the situation. It was as if the Fates were playing a cruel game with him, dangling the carrot of his professional future before his eyes then snatching it away.

His room was freezing cold. The fire had burned itself to embers, little crystals of frost forming on the windows panes. He grabbed a log from the pile and threw it on the fire, stoking it gently with a poker. Looking up, he noticed a small crack in the underside of the mantle. Running his finger over it, he could feel that it was more than just surface damage; it was an actual opening, purposely hidden under layers of paint. Gently, he pulled at the wood, but it wouldn't budge. Grabbing a letter opener from his desk, he traced the lines of the panel, prying it loose.

Reaching inside the little cubby, he pulled out a small pile of papers and two small, square-framed miniatures. Turning them over, he immediately recognized the woman in one of the paintings. It was Dellis. She looked younger, her face youthful and full, with the same impish grin she'd flashed him on several occasions. He assumed the other one was her mother. She looked similar to Dellis, strikingly beautiful, but with a darker complexion and a wider face. Having painted his share of portraits in the past, he could appreciate the skill and precision of both pictures. Whoever drew them had affection for the two women because both were rendered with incredible attention to detail and an expert hand.

Leafing through the papers, he found shipping records, accounting sheets, and a stack of letters tied together with a red ribbon. Putting the pictures and the other papers down, he untied the ribbon and unfolded one of the letters. The paper was brittle and yellowed, the signature faded but still readable, all of them signed by either Admiral, His Grace, the Duke of McKesson or Stephen McKesson.

Suddenly, John heard a door slam, the echo carrying all the way up the stairs to his room. He put the letters back in their hiding place and replaced the wooden mantelpiece. Glancing out the window, he spotted a horse and rider racing off towards the woods. He opened the window to get a better look, the snow blowing into the room bringing with it a gust of wintry air. It was Dellis—he recognized her gray cloak billowing in the wind behind her.

"What is she doing now?" He groaned, slamming the window shut. Of all the ridiculous, impetuous things to do, going out in a winter storm, at night, by herself. *Damned headstrong woman.* John threw his hands up in frustration. Now he had to go after her, if only to save her from herself.

Grabbing his cloak and gloves, he sprinted out the door to the stable. She had a head start on him, but he had no doubt where she was going: the village. Luckily, Viceroy was much faster and more agile than her mare; he should be able to catch up to Dellis before she got too far. John mounted up, dug his heels into the horse's flank, and took off with a vengeance.

No stranger to winter storms, having served his whole military career at Fort Niagara, he was convinced this was the worst one he'd ever seen. The sky was dark, a mixture of snow and ice coming down in every direction, causing a perpetual whiteout. The dirt road was completely covered with snow, the piles already several inches deep, forcing him to slow down, his mighty warhorse forced to work harder than usual to keep up with his commands. Her tracks had long since disappeared, covered by a blanket of fresh, downy snow and a thin layer of ice. A vision of her lying injured in the cold flashed before his eyes. John crouched low over his mount, again, pushing the beast harder, while he scanned the area. She was an excellent horsewoman, he reminded himself, but that didn't quell the nervous feeling in his stomach.

God, please, let her be safe.

John knew when he finally reached the village, a glimpse of stockade appearing a few yards ahead of him like a tiny beacon of hope shining through the thick flakes that whipped around in powerful gales. With a glance to the ground, he spotted her tracks again, though they didn't go towards the village, but around it and up the hill towards the barn.

"Dellis!" he yelled, looking in every direction.

His heart pounded with exertion, his damp hair stuck to his forehead, and underneath his clothing was soaked with sweat in spite of the freezing cold. He knew the barn was at the top of the hill, a good place to rest before he set out again. The grade was too steep and icy to take while seated, so John jumped down from his saddle and carefully led Viceroy through the slippery terrain, breathing a sigh of relief when the barn finally came into view.

Tying his horse to the tree, he walked over to the barn, searching the perimeter quickly for any signs of Dellis or potential threats. The last thing he needed was an unanticipated visit with wildcat or a bear, for no one would be foolish enough to be out riding on a night like this. He snorted. Well, except him. When John was satisfied that the barn was safe, he opened the door with one hard shove and the last bit of effort he had stored up in his muscles. It was pitch black inside and quiet, the sweet aroma of hay emanating from within wafting into his direction, filling his nose. John pulled out his pistol and walked into the darkness. With slow, methodical steps, he took a turn around the massive structure, doing a double check. When he reached the far wall, he grabbed the door handle and pulled it open, allowing the moonlight to shine inside. Looking around, the only things he saw were a few barrels stacked near the door and a horse boarded in its stall with a blanket neatly covering its back.

It was Dellis's mare. John let out a sigh of relief. Thank goodness, she was safe somewhere in the village.

"Dellis?" he called again, his voice echoing off the walls. But still, she didn't respond.

John walked back towards the door, inspecting the barrels, turning them so he could use the moonlight to his advantage. Removing his gloves, he ran his hand over the letters burned into the surface, royal insignias on all of them. They were rum barrels, for rations. He wasn't surprised to find spirits stored in the barn, as it was commonly given as a gift by the British to the natives, although he did remember Dellis telling him the village was dry.

Breaking open one the barrels, John took a whiff of the rum. The pungent aroma brought a smile to his lips as he dipped his hands in and took a sip. It was Caribbean rum, still concentrated, sweet and strong, and so much better when it wasn't diluted for distribution. It burned a trail from his throat to his stomach, the warmth coursing through his veins, emanating all the way to his frozen toes and his fingertips.

John walked the outside perimeter of the barn once more, but still, there was no sign of Dellis or her tracks in the snow. Viceroy whinnied several times, and fussed around, drawing his attention.

"You don't like the snow either, do you, boy?"

John led his precious mount into the barn and tied him in the stall next to her mare. At least he knew Dellis was safe, the fact that her horse was unsaddled and taken care of for the night a good indication. Now he could rest until the storm let up then head back to town when it was safe. Whatever provoked her recklessness, he would address when she returned; though he had a sneaking suspicion it had something to do with his supplies disappearing. Why she felt the need to take on the problems of the world was baffling, first the war and her tribe, now his missing supplies. The woman fancied herself a one-man battalion, locked and loaded and ready to fight, or perhaps a martyr, prepared to sacrifice herself for her cause. But to what purpose?

John took another drink of the liquor and sat down on the ground, resting his back against the wall. He hated the cold, but if he had to be stuck in a snowstorm, he was thankful for the rum and a decent bit of shelter, many a time he had much less.

Looking around the barn, John remembered the last time he saw it. With his own eyes, he had watched as the natives carried their plunder inside, but when he searched it, there was nothing, not a barrel or gun to be found. Standing up, he took another sip of rum and then walked towards the center of the structure. *How is it possible this is happening to me again? More bad Karma? Carlisle, haven't you had enough?*

Dellis's mare whinnied, the horse's breath steaming in the cold air, making her look like a fire-breathing hell beast. "Where is your mistress?" he asked, the liquor and lack of food making his head swim. "I'm sure you were none too happy to come out in this weather, poor girl."

The mare whinnied again, moving her head up and down as if nodding in agreement.

John chewed his thumbnail, looking around, his mind mulling over the details his men told him earlier. If the Oneidas stole the shipment near the fort and followed the same path they used before, there was no way they would have returned yet. The weather was too treacherous for them to travel so far with his supplies in tow. The village should be empty, or at least the men would be gone still, save maybe a guard or two.

Then something dawned on him. Dellis had overheard them talking about the ambush, and she knew Clark's wound was from a tomahawk. *Had she come to warn her people that he was on to them?* She could easily have been listening in on all their previous conversations, and someone with a key had breached his desk and stole his maps. He needed to go back to the village and find her—now.

Suddenly, he heard a loud crack and then the pop of a twig underfoot. Instinctively, John reached for his pistol, but slowly, trying not to draw any attention to his movement. From behind, he heard footsteps coming from the right, their pace picking up with each passing second. He was about to be ambushed. Taking a deep breath, he drew his pistol, pulled the hammer to full cock, and aimed into the darkness. The silence was deafening, his heart raced to a sprint, threatening to burst through his rib cage. Again, to his right, he heard movement and the clanking of metal. Chains. They meant to take him prisoner. *Like hell they would.* Whipping around, John had a split second to see his assailant before he felt an intense pain at the base of his skull. He groaned and grabbed his head, the crushing pain blooming from its point of origin to his eyes, rendering him immobile. Everything faded to black, his body suddenly too heavy to stay erect, and with a Herculean effort he raised his pistol and fired, praying he took his attacker with him on the way down.

Chapter Twenty-Four

The sun peeked through the frosted windows of the little cabin, a ray shining directly into her eyes. *Please, go away.* Turning over, Dellis pulled the fur blankets over her head, trying to drown out the daylight for a few minutes more. She'd only slept about two hours, the rest of the time she lay awake berating herself for letting her anxiety get the better of her. It was stupid and dangerous of her to go out in such severe weather. Once on the road, she'd realized her error in judgment, but by then, it was too late for her to turn back.

If he'd just left her alone, she might not have run out in the night like a damned fool. She could see his blue eyes sparkling when he kissed her hand, the lock of sandy blond hair falling into his face, making her hands ache to touch it. Part of her wanted to beg him not to stop, and the other part wanted to run the other way like a caged animal finally breaking free. *Why won't he just leave me alone? And why didn't I tell him to stop?* The man left her feeling crazed, confused, and so damned frustrated. Her world had been complicated enough without all his casual smiles, gentle caresses and female companions. With war on the brink, and someone trying to frame her village, there were so many things she would have to deal with in the coming days, and then there was a looming threat on The Thistle. He was just an unwanted distraction that would come to nothing more than casual flirtation. But now, she had all these feelings…

When she had finally reached the village, the fires were extinguished, and all the houses were dark and abandoned. Thankfully, when she rode up the hill, she saw a light coming from her father's little cabin across from the barn. Inside, her cousin sat quietly mending a piece of clothing while the children slept peacefully on cots near the fireplace. She had no choice but to stay in and rest for the night, in the morning she could find her grandfather and tell him what she learned about the Captain's supplies, though little good it would do after the fact.

Throwing the blankets off, Dellis sat up and stretched, every bone in her body aching from the strenuous ride. Skenandoa was already dressed and feeding the children. Dellis smiled, watching their little faces as they gobbled up their corn mash and stuffed pieces of bread in their mouths.

"Good morning, Dellis, how did you sleep?" Skenandoa handed over a small bowl of the mixture made from boiled, mashed corn and water.

"Not the best." Dellis shoveled the food into her mouth quickly, wanting to get back home before it started to snow again. "I have to leave now. I need to get back before my aunt starts to worry. Can you saddle my horse for me while I get ready?"

She dressed quickly, stuffing her pack with some leftover cornbread and cheese for the ride, and then filled her canteen with water. Having left in such a hurry, she'd forgotten to leave a note for her aunt, and she was probably in a panic by now.

Pulling on the cloak and tying the bonnet in place, Dellis grabbed her canteen and pack and slung them over her shoulder, ready for the long ride home. Walking out of the cabin, she noticed her cousin carefully examining something in her hands.

"What is that?" Dellis asked, picking up her skirts and huffing it through the snow that was now above her ankles.

"I found a glove lying in the snow. I thought you might have dropped it."

Dellis took the glove, running her fingers over the supple, black leather, then holding it to her hand. It was too large to be hers. It looked vaguely familiar, but she couldn't figure out why.

"Well, it's definitely not mine; it's too big, and I could never afford one so nice." She hugged her cousin, handing the glove back to her. "You keep this, just in case it's one of Alexei's. He'll be looking for it. Be safe. I'll see you soon."

Dellis rode slowly through the village, surprised to see it bustling with activity, the men already working to clear a trail through the snow. She jumped down from her horse and lifted her skirts, trudging through the drifts to her grandfather's cabin. He opened the door before she had a chance to knock, his eyes widening when he saw her.

"*Kheyatléha*, come in, it's too cold for you to be out." He waved his arm, inviting her inside.

Her grandfather's cabin was Spartan-like, consisting of one small room with a stone fireplace, a large wooden table, and two little cots. The walls were adorned with furs and skins from his years of hunting and a wooden rack where he stored several of his muskets. A fire blazed brightly in the fireplace while two cast iron pots bubbled in the hearth, and the pleasant smell of venison stew permeated throughout the little room. Above his table was a large rack from which hung a variety of pots and kettles and other kitchen utensils. Since her grandmother died, his home felt empty, her feminine touch and effervescent spirit noticeably absent.

"*Shekoli*, Grandfather," Dellis said, hugging him. "How are you?"

With a flash of annoyance, he replied, "Dellis, what are you doing out in this weather?"

"I came looking for you last night, but no one was here. I assumed you left for Oriska." As the winter progressed, it was custom for her people to travel to Oriska, to conserve supplies and for protection.

"We didn't make it very far before it got icy and we had to turn back. It was too hard on some of the women."

"Thank God you're all safe." She hugged him again, indulging in his warmth. The colorful wool blanket he wore over his linen shirt was soft and comforting against her cheek. "The Captain's men were attacked on the road just off the Carry, close to the fort. All of our supplies were stolen."

Her grandfather didn't seem surprised. He quietly sat down at his table and picked up his musket. "When did this happen?"

"Last night. One of his men was hit in the thigh with a tomahawk."

"What else did they tell you?" he asked, starting to muzzle load his gun. She watched as he pushed the frizzen forward, pouring some powder into the pan. The whole process of loading a musket was like a dance, with intricate steps that one repeated over and over—all too many times.

"I wasn't able to ask questions. I overheard them talking when I was in the hall outside their room," she said, and then cringed, anticipating his response.

"Dellis, you shouldn't be listening in on other people's conversations."

She knew her grandfather would scold her for spying on the Captain's conversation, but she couldn't help herself. Besides, it was for their betterment.

Her grandfather continued loading his musket, stoically calm and silent. He was angry with her. Dellis watched as he pushed the frizzen back, clicking it into place, and rested the long, wooden stock on the floor. She was used to muskets being around; they were a necessity with the dangers of growing up in the territory. On many occasions, she and the rest of the women in the village had to sit side-by-side with the men and load while they fired on intruders.

"Grandfather, I know I shouldn't have done it, but when I heard them talking about the Carry, I had to listen." She sat down and rested her forehead in her hands, guilt setting in with each passing second of silence. "I was hoping you could track them. Maybe it was the same group that attacked the Mohawk camp trying to stir up more trouble?"

From his horn, he poured some powder down the muzzle then dropped the lead ball inside. "Dellis, there's a big difference between men who steal and those that murder innocent women and children."

She looked up at him through spread fingers. "I don't understand."

"This was the act of someone in desperate need. Trading has been difficult for all of us since the break between the King and the colonists. It could've been our Onondaga brothers; the Captain's men were passing through that territory."

Her grandfather was right; the two incidents were very different. Had they wanted to, the thieves could've killed Clark and his men, but they hadn't.

"Dellis, riding out in such weather is dangerous. You could've fallen from your horse and frozen to death before anyone found you. You must think before you do something so foolish again." Ramming the ball into place, he finished loading his musket then placed it on the rack.

"I'm sorry, Grandfather, I just wanted to help. I know things are difficult right now. I thought if you could catch whoever did this, you could try to reason with them."

"I know you want to take on your grandmother's role as a clan mother, but you're too young. You must listen before you speak; wisdom will find you with years and experience." His large hand was warm and soft as he touched her forehead, smoothing a lock of her hair behind her ear.

She looked up and smiled. "I will try, I promise."

He nodded, placing a soft kiss on her forehead.

She inhaled deeply, taking in the earthy smell of buckskin and the fragrant soap her grandfather used to wash. That scent was so familiar; it would forever remind her of him. "You're just like Lily; a wild, restless spirit always moving, like the wind. Your grandmother and I could never stop her. She was always getting involved where she shouldn't. It is she who got us involved with the Great King's men—that's how she met your father. When you were born, you had the same fire in you; that's why we named you after the valley, hoping you would grow to be peaceful and steady. My sweet, Fennishyo."

Dellis laughed in spite of the tear that rolled down her cheek. He was the only one who called her by her Oneida name. It sounded so breathy and beautiful when he said it. "I fear there's nothing peaceful or steady about me."

"You've not been given a chance to be. The world, like a great storm, has been raging all around you. But after the rain comes the sun and a peaceful spring. I have hope for you, with time and a husband."

"Thank you, Grandfather." She nodded, acknowledging the war that waged within her, just as potent and fierce as the one that was threatening her people. "I promise to try."

A bone-chilling wind picked up as she made the arduous trek through the blanketed wilderness. The snow was so deep that her horse had to fight to navigate the rough, slippery terrain. It was almost noon when she walked into The Thistle, the stifling warmth of the kitchen penetrating the layers of her clothing, making her sweat. Quickly, she removed her cloak and bonnet and hung them up next to the door.

Before Dellis even had a chance to turn around, her aunt came up behind Dellis and hugged her. "We've been looking everywhere for you." There was genuine concern in her aunt's voice. It made Dellis feel all the worse for not leaving a note.

"I'm sorry, I didn't mean to worry you."

Looking up, she saw her Uncle James's looming form walking into the kitchen. "Dellis, where were you?"

"I stayed overnight at my grandfather's. I set out before the snow started, and I couldn't leave once the weather progressed. Is everything all right?" She looked at both of them, making a mental note to pray for forgiveness for her lie. They didn't need to know the sordid details.

"Stuart is missing. He wasn't at our house this morning. Neither Alexei or Ruslan have seen him today," her aunt replied.

"Dellis, do you know where he is?" Uncle James asked, planting his fists on his hips. He was angry. Dellis knew that look—the furrowed brow, the flaring nostrils—it was the same one Alexei got when he was about to lose his temper. Like father like son. Now for the tirade.

"Honestly, I don't. I threw him out yesterday." She confessed boldly, ready for the backlash that was inevitably going to ensue. For some reason, her uncle expected her to be two places at once, acting as Stuart's keeper yet still finding time to run her tavern.

"Why would you do that, Dellis?"

She pointed to the prominent, black-and-blue bruise on her cheek. "He hit me the other day. He was drunk and out of control, and I'm tired of dealing with his erratic behavior. He's scaring my customers away."

"Well, he's missing now," her uncle said brusquely, with an exaggerated nod.

Dellis rubbed her forehead, trying to get the image of Stuart frozen to death out of her mind. "I'll go look for him."

"Fine," Uncle James replied. It seemed he only valued the men in their family; women were insignificant, and her even less so because of her heritage.

"You will do no such thing." Her aunt stopped Dellis before she could reach for her cloak and bonnet. Helena looked up at her husband, with wide, pleading eyes. "James, be reasonable."

"This is her mess. She can clean it up." He shot Dellis a condescending look and a glance down his nose. "You should be ashamed of yourself. What would your father think of you?"

"Stuart hit me," she said. "My father would never have tolerated that. He was a gentleman, and he taught Stuart to be one, too."

James snorted. "Your father would have served you better by teaching you to know your place and not talk back, Dellis."

"What do you want me to do?" she asked, clenching her fists at her sides. "I have no idea where he goes. Shall I close The Thistle and spend my days watching over him? That's what you want to do anyway. Now you have an excuse. Close The Thistle and take all that is left of my father from me. But answer me one question, Uncle: why do you hate me so? Is it because I remind you of my mother or my father? I know you hated her

210

and thought she was a savage and beneath my father. I also know that you were quarreling with him before he died. Is it your anger you take out on me or your guilt?"

As he pulled back his hand to strike her, Helena grabbed his arm in midair, stopping him abruptly. Though Dellis's heart pounded nervously, she stared him down, daring him to do it. She refused to be intimidated by him or any man—they relished their power too much. Her mother had taught Dellis to be brave and proud. It was time she listened.

"Please stop, James. Alexei will be here any minute, and I'll send him out to look for Stuart. Let Dellis stay and help me." Helena pleaded, looking from Dellis to her uncle.

James pointed at his wife and then at Dellis, a warning to both of them. "Alexei better find him, or else."

A threat? Dellis nodded, a lump in her throat preventing her from speaking.

"Go get changed, Dellis. We have lots of work to do," her aunt said with a tremulous voice. Dellis walked down the hall towards her room, stopping for a moment to listen in on their conversation.

"Stuart better not have gotten into trouble last night—Ruslan promised he would keep him busy. That raving idiot is always causing problems. His father should have dealt with him the minute he realized the boy was a lunatic."

"James, please, he's your nephew," her aunt begged.

"Well, that's what Stephen gets for marrying that native whore—a strumpet for a daughter and a loon for a son."

"Dellis is not a strumpet. She might be reckless, but she keeps to herself."

"I heard talk that she's been seen in town with that Tory merchant," he replied, gruffly. "And he's not the only one I've heard talked about when her name is mentioned. Her mother was the same. Lily kept company with all the Regulars; that's how my brother met her. He disgraced this family the day he impregnated that savage whore and was forced to marry her."

Dellis winced, her uncle's bitter words like a knife in the chest. Her mother wasn't a whore, and neither was Dellis. *How could he say such a thing?* Though in her heart she knew it was just another one of her uncle's insults born out of his hatred for her people, it still hurt. And some of what he said didn't make sense. Her father told her he met her mother when he came to the village during an outbreak of smallpox. Dellis had never heard anything about her parents being forced to marry.

"James, stop, please, Dellis may hear you."

"I hope she does, and maybe she'll think twice before she opens her legs again. Give me the mail. I have work to do."

Dellis moved closer, peeking down the hall so she could get a better look at their exchange. Her aunt handed her husband a pile of letters and kissed his cheek. Dellis watched as her uncle leafed through them, examining each one, taking what he wanted then giving her back the rest. From her vantage point, she couldn't tell what letters he took, but her curiosity was piqued. Why would he be taking her mail?

She could see him carefully opening one, expertly sliding his knife under the wax seal, then reading it. When he finished, he quickly warmed the letter over a candle and resealed it and handed it back to her aunt.

"What was it?" Helena asked, looking up at him.

"Shipping records."

Dellis swallowed, a gnawing pain blossoming in her stomach. *Why would Uncle be reading the Captain's mail?*

When he finally left, she walked back to her room and changed quickly. Not ready to face her aunt again, Dellis grabbed her basket of supplies and took the service staircase to the second floor. The door to the Captain's room was open, and she glanced inside quickly, but it was empty, the bed already set, his desk untouched. Walking to the end of the hall, she knocked on Clark's door.

"It's Miss McKesson. I've come to check on you." She opened the door and peeked around the edge.

"Come in, lass," Clark said with a grin.

"Good morning, Clark." The room was chilly, his fire had almost burned out from lack of tending, just a few embers still emitting a bit of warmth. She walked over and added another log to the pile, stoking it vigorously, taking out her frustration on the wood with the metal poker.

"I think that's plenty good," he said with a laugh.

The fire was blazing now, the heat radiating into the room, starting to warm it. "I just wanted to make sure you stay warm," she said, putting the poker down and walking to the bed. "How are you feeling?"

"I'm well, but the leg isn't so good, my dear." His Scottish brogue reminded her of her father, and the way he stressed his R evoking pleasant memories of their conversations long ago.

"Let me take a look at it." She sat down next to Clark, carefully removing the bandage. The stitches looked good. They were clean and still intact, no weeping from the cut.

"Miss, please, call me Simon, if you don't mind," he said, watching her clean the wound. "But don't tell the Captain; he's all about formality, as you know."

"All right, but you must call me Dellis when he's not around." She looked up and winked, an immediate bond forming between the two of them. "Simon, have you seen the Captain today? His fire burned out, and he isn't in his room."

Clark shook his head, leaning back against the headboard while she re-wrapped his bandage. When finished, Dellis sat back and admired her handiwork—a well-cared for wound—she knew her father would be proud. "Hayes and Smith returned early this morning, but he wasn't with them. Perhaps, he is with Mrs. Allen?"

"I hadn't thought of that." Her stomach knotted up remembering the two of them together in John's room against his desk. "Well, I'm sure the Captain can take care of himself."

"Yes, he can, lass. No need to worry." Clark patted her hand. Surprisingly, she didn't feel the urge to pull away when he touched her. He was innately kind and non-threatening. She couldn't help but trust him.

Chapter Twenty-Five

John awoke with a start, a rush of icy water hitting him in the face like a thousand pins and needles embedding themselves in his flesh. He couldn't remember where he was, and a blindfold over his eyes prevented him from visualizing his surroundings. His arms felt as if they were being torn from their sockets, bound high above his head with his feet barely touching the ground. Shaking his arms vigorously, he tried to free them, metal shackles tearing and gnawing at the flesh on his wrists with each twist and flail.

From his left, he heard footsteps coming towards him. Turning his head towards the sound, he yelled, "Who are you? What do you want?"

Just the act of calling out made his head throb, the pain so acute his stomach heaved violently. He swallowed hard, several times, the sour taste in his mouth making him gag. As the footsteps got closer, he shifted towards them again, trying to face his adversary head-on. "What do you want with me?"

John was met with a sinister laugh and another bucket of cold water, his body trembling on impact. He could feel his assailant circling him, with slow, deliberate steps, as if he was contemplating his next move.

"You know what you've done, Captain."

John tried to identify the voice, but he couldn't, a forbidding pain in his head making it impossible for him to focus on anything but breathing.

"Let me go," he yelled, searching around in spite of the blindfold. "I'm just a merchant."

The man laughed, deep and throaty, then gripped John's chin with fingers like a vice. "No, you're not just a merchant. We both know that."

He could almost feel his assailant's face, only inches from his own, the smell of rum, pungent and spicy on his breath, and something else—tobacco. "Were you ever punished for your crimes, Captain?"

Suddenly, John heard something that sounded like leather slapping against flesh, a short and abrupt snap. *Snap. Snap. Snap.* He knew what it meant, having seen men flogged over his years in the military, but he never anticipated he would experience it firsthand.

"Have you nothing to say on your behalf? If you don't speak up, then I'm going to assume you haven't."

When he heard the loud cracking of a whip, a wave of panic washed over him, bringing with it a rush of uncontrollable shivers. Closing his eyes, he took several deep breaths, trying to calm himself, using all of his training to focus his energy, but with little success.

"Well, then, it would seem I get the pleasure of discharging your punishment." The man cracked the whip again, slowly walking the perimeter, trying to build fear in John—and it worked. His heart thundered in his chest, wondering when and from where the first lash would come. He shifted from the left to the right, following the man's footsteps, waiting... wondering...

Do it, damn it. Do it. The anticipation was like a slow death.

"I know, traditionally, this is done with a Cat, but unfortunately for you, I don't have one. You'll have to settle for my whip instead."

Taking another deep breath, John lifted his head as if looking his enemy in the eyes, refusing to show fear. He was a captain in His Majesty's Infantry; John would meet his fate as a soldier, boldly.

"Look at you... so brave, but it won't last." The assailant hissed in his face. "Scream, so I know you like it."

The man grabbed the neck of John's shirt, and with one tug, ripped the garment in two. Suddenly, with a loud crack, the whip struck the side of his torso so hard it was like a mallet beating a drum. He squeezed his eyes shut, refusing to scream, a searing pain tearing through his body in long, unrelenting waves that built with each passing second.

"Did you like that?" the man whispered. The assailant's lips were so close, John could feel the moisture from the man's breath, the only warmth perceivable in the icy hell. "I've been told that some men find pleasure in pain. Shall I check?"

Crack! This time the whip struck John against the sensitive flesh of his groin, tearing the front of his pants away, splitting the skin cleanly. He cried out, unable to hold back, the muscles clenching in his lower abdomen as a powerful wave of nausea washed over him. Had he been able to, he would have doubled over and clutched himself; ripples of pain rushed down his legs, causing them to spasm.

"Now that's what I wanted to hear. Finally, we're getting somewhere, Captain. Scream louder!"

Crack. Crack. The whip struck him, repeatedly, punishing the flesh on his back and sides, even his buttocks. Unable to bear any more, he tried to curl up and protect himself, but the added torque on his arms was too much; his left shoulder popped out of joint, and suddenly, his hand went numb. He screamed and vomited the contents of his stomach, the pain beyond comprehension.

"Oh, look, you've made a mess of yourself." His tormentor doused John with icy water, rinsing the refuse from his face and chest. He shivered, his wet hair dripping in his face, his body on fire from his injuries yet chilled to the bone from the cold. God help him; if he ever got free, he would kill the man.

"What do you want from me?" John yelled through parched lips, the bitter taste of stomach acid in his mouth. "Why are you doing this?"

"You know why, Captain." The man laughed. "Justice, she's come for you. It's time to pay your debt."

The whip snapped John twice more, once to his left side, then to his breast, but after that, it stopped. He could hear footsteps retreating into the

216

distance and the quiet hum of a merry little tune. John took several deep breaths, his body racked with shivering as the arctic wind whipped around him, irritating each and every one of his injuries. Exhausted and spent, he let his head fall forward, his eyes closing beneath the blindfold.

Let it be over.

Just as he found respite, the sounds of laughing and heavy footsteps broke through his tortured haze along with that same jovial tune. Suddenly, there was the blessed sensation of warmth emanating near his leg. The closer the source got, the more concentrated the heat became, until finally, he could feel his flesh burning.

"No mercy for you, Captain."

John howled as a hot poker made contact with his skin, searing his inner thigh and his groin, then sliding all the way up between his legs, finishing the job. He kicked his feet into the air, flailing, trying to escape the pain.

"I like hearing you scream; do it again," the man yelled, rapt with excitement.

"Go to Hell." John hissed.

"We're already there." With that, the assailant rested the poker on the small of John's back, letting it sizzle and smoke, waiting for him to relent, but he stubbornly refused to scream—a matching of wills.

"I'll kill you for this," John said through clenched teeth, digging deep in his anger to stay strong, the aroma of burning flesh wafting into his nose. His flesh.

"You won't live long enough to try. It's time to meet your maker. But will you confess all of your sins? What say you, spy?"

Spy? Who is this man? How does he know?

With that, the man pulled the poker away, John's flesh already charred and immune to the pain of it. "That's right, I know you're a spy."

John turned his head toward the voice, but bit back a retort. He would not relent. Whatever came next, he could take it, rage making him strong. *What will it to be? More lashes? The ice bucket?* "I am Captain John Carlisle of His Majesty's Eight Regiment, Light Infantry," he said to himself. A mantra to give him strength. He'd served under Roger DeLancie for ten years and managed to survive. John was tougher than anything an assailant could throw his way. *Once more into the breach.*

But he hadn't anticipated what came next, out of nowhere, the man plunged his fist into John's nose, blood gushing out in thick, sticky gobs. He felt the hit all the way into his brain, but thankfully, his nose didn't break. A small triumph. John shook his head several times, his eyes watering profusely under the blindfold, and then he laughed.

"Is this funny? Did you like that?"

"You hit like a woman," John said, spitting the blood from his mouth.

"Let me try that again." And the man did, but this time, he hit John's right cheek, the force of it causing his head to whip to the side. *That hurt.*

Suddenly, the world started to spin around him, his stomach once again gripped by a powerful wave of nausea. He could feel himself falling into a dark abyss, willing himself to endure, he groaned. "I am Captain John Carlisle of the His Majesty's Eighth Regiment, Light Infantry." But it was no use.

"I know who you are."

With one last bone-crushing fist to the cheek, everything went black, the white flag thrown up as John surrendered the fight.

Chapter Twenty-Six

Dellis nervously drummed her fingers on the wooden sill, looking out the window. At least another two inches of snow had fallen since she returned in the morning, and neither the Captain nor Stuart had turned up. Granted, the Captain was capable of taking care of himself, more so than her brother, yet she couldn't ignore the ache in the pit of her stomach.

Patrons had already started to file in for late supper, and soon she would have to help Thomas dish out her venison stew and wait tables. Her evening crowd had started to pick up, for the last two nights there wasn't a seat open in the dining room or at the bar. Dellis looked over her shoulder at her bustling tavern and smiled, perhaps she would find a way to prove her uncle wrong and keep The Thistle open after all.

Suddenly, she felt this strange pain in her chest, like someone had stabbed her with a knife. Something was terribly wrong with the Captain. She just knew it. Rushing through the kitchen, Dellis bumped into Alexei and Ruslan, both of them blocking her way to the door.

"Where are you going in such a hurry?" Alexei grabbed her arm, forcing her to stop.

"I haven't seen Stuart in days. I should try to find him." She lied, hoping he would just believe her so she could be on her way.

"No, you're not, it's worse than you think out there." Alexei stepped in front of the door, preventing her escape. "Besides, you don't need to worry about Stuart, Ruslan saw him last night. He's fine."

Her younger cousin looked up from his bowl of stew and smiled. "He slept in the servants' quarters because he stank so damn bad I wouldn't let him in the house. Last time I saw him he was bailing hay, no need to worry."

She nodded, thankful that at least one of her problems was solved.

"You know I always watch over him, cousin," Ruslan said with a sweet smile. It always amazed her how much her two cousins looked alike. At seventeen, Ruslan was already tall, but not quite Alexei's height, same dark brown hair and blue eyes, and the same chiseled features. Unlike Alexei, who kept to himself, Ruslan already had quite a reputation with the local ladies. He was notorious for his outgoing personality, yet he was still sweet and gentlemanly in demeanor. Both men were so different from their father, like night and day.

"Why are you so worried about Stuart? He's been staying in our servants' quarters for weeks."

"I kicked him out a few days ago," she replied, again realizing the fault in that decision. "Your parents were worried he might be drunk in the street, frozen to death."

Alexei grabbed a biscuit off the counter and stuffed it in his mouth. "Stuart's a big boy. He can take care of himself."

She couldn't agree more with that sentiment. "Can you please relay that message to your parents, Alexei? And while you're at it, tell them he's sleeping in your servants' quarters so they don't worry. Now, if you'll excuse me, I need to check on my guest upstairs, he was injured last night."

Pushing past them, she cursed her bad luck that her nosy cousins would show up when she was trying to escape. There was still the matter of the Captain's whereabouts to be solved and the awful feeling gnawing at her gut. If she couldn't go out and look for him, then perhaps his men could.

Dellis raced up the service staircase to the second floor; as expected, the Captain's room was still empty. At the end of the hall, the door to Clark's room was cracked open, so she entered.

"How are you, lass?"

She noticed how he quickly tied his neckerchief and smoothed his hair back, righting himself. She appreciated his decorum, Clark was a consummate gentleman, always treating her with respect, unlike most men she encountered.

"Ahh, Clark, I mean, Simon." She stammered, remembering to call him by his name. "How are you?"

"I'm feeling better than earlier." He scooted to the edge of his bed, his brow furrowing with concern "Have you seen the Captain?"

"I haven't, and clearly he hasn't returned," she replied, thankful he was the one to bring up the topic. She felt strange butting in on the man's affairs, it was truly none of her business, but she couldn't help herself.

"No, I haven't, lass. I sent Hayes and Smith out to look for him again. Any suggestions?"

She shook her head. "Simon, could he still be with Mrs. Allen? Would he stay with her *this* long?" She didn't want to think about what kept him away for so long, her jealously was the least of their problems.

"It's possible." He looked up, his eyes searching hers. "Why?"

It was ridiculous, she hardly knew the man, but she couldn't fight the feeling that he was in terrible trouble. "Something's wrong."

Clark's eyes lit up. "Why do you think that?"

Dellis let out a deep breath, not sure how to respond. "I don't have an explanation for it, it's just a feeling."

It was getting late in the day; if they didn't do something soon, they would have to wait until morning to search. The thought of him lying injured in the snow brought tears to her eyes.

Clark lifted his bad leg over the edge of the bed and reached for his overcoat and boots. "I'll get up and help you look for him."

"Perhaps I'm worrying for nothing." She put her hand on his shoulder, stopping him. "Don't get up yet. Let me go to The Kettle. Perhaps he is with Mrs. Allen. If your men return before I do, can you have them wait for me?"

"All right, lass, we'll be here."

Dellis rushed down the back stairs and grabbed her cloak and mittens. Looking into the mirror, she scrutinized her appearance, considered changing her dress and fixing her hair, but then stopped. What was the point? She wasn't in competition with Mrs. Allen, nor did Dellis care what the woman thought. All that mattered was that Dellis found the Captain and he was safe, even if he was with Mrs. Allen. Dellis thrusted her hands into her mittens, pulled her hood up, and ran out the back door, hoping not to draw Alexei's or Ruslan's attention.

Chapter Twenty-Seven

Damn. Throwing her ledger down on the desk, Celeste cursed the day she ever met John Carlisle. *How dare he treat me this way!* After all, it was her business, and she was entitled to do whatever she saw fit with the day-to-day running of it. He didn't seem to mind when she told him about the Rebels' movement during the battle of Long Island, a bit of information both he and the army benefited from. Now, because she allowed a few letters to change hands, she was out a business and a lover.

She rubbed her temples. There had to be some way out of the mess she was in. The bottle of scotch he had drunk from the night before was still sitting on the desk. She picked it up and poured herself a glass. Taking a sip, she gagged then choked it down. *How did John tolerate the nasty stuff?* She'd always known he had a weakness for the bottle, but not when they were together; his drinking usually took a back seat to their lovemaking. Something was amiss. She'd never seen him so distant and so damned honorable. No matter, he'd been upset with her before, but he always came back like a faithful lap dog. It was just a matter of time.

A knock on the door drew her attention from her ledger. Celeste waved her arm at Agnes. "Answer it."

She put down her sewing and cracked the door just far enough to look around the edge. "Mrs. Allen, it's Miss McKesson. She says she's the innkeeper at The Thistle Tavern."

"Really?" Celeste smiled, the wheels already turning in her head. What could John's pretty little innkeeper possibly want? "I'm intrigued, let her in."

Agnes opened the door. The young woman hesitated for a moment then walked in, removing her gloves and hood. Her dark hair was parted down the center and pulled up in a tight, chaste chignon, drawing attention to her high cheekbones and defined bone structure. Celeste had to admit, the woman was attractive; her large, dark eyes had a haunting quality about them, and her skin was perfect, frustratingly flawless. The dress she wore was ten years out of style, threadbare, and belonged in the rubbish pile, but it did fit her like second skin, accentuating her lithe frame and exceptionally large breasts.

"What can I do for you, Miss McKesson?" Celeste asked, standing up to greet her guest.

"Good evening, Mrs. Allen, I'm sorry to bother you. I was wondering if you had seen the Captain. He's been missing since last night. Both of his men have been looking for him all day. Clark asked me if I would check with you."

"The Captain?" Celeste smiled, cocking a brow. "You mean John?"

"Yes, Mrs. Allen," Dellis replied, curtly. "That's correct."

Celeste took a slow, steady turn around the room, eyeing her adversary, unable to fathom what John saw in her. She was far from his type: elegant, cultured and sexually experienced. This woman was haughty, simple, and so damned virginal it made Celeste want to heave. "I haven't seen John since he left early yesterday morning. I was under the impression he was with you. He did seem eager to get back."

"As I said, he's not at The Thistle; that's why I'm here. He's been gone all night, and I just assumed he spent it with you again. Obviously, that's not the case. I'm very sorry I bothered you."

So, there was a little fight in the poor provincial thing. Celeste stepped towards Dellis, their eyes locking in challenge. "I assumed the reason he didn't return was because of you. After all, you are one of his business associates. At least, that's how he refers to us."

"I don't follow you, Mrs. Allen," she countered, her eyes narrowing on Celeste. "I'm his innkeeper, he is my lodger. It *is* business between us. I'm just doing a favor for Clark since he's injured and can't get out to look himself."

"Don't worry, it's just us ladies here, you can tell me the truth." Linking her arm through Miss McKesson's, Celeste leaned closer, whispering in Dellis's ear. "We all start out as business partners, investors, whatever he decides to call us, and we all feel the same way about him in the beginning. He promises to help you, he gives you money, and then, well, you know how it goes. Eventually, he finds another business partner, tells you he has to leave, and you're the one left with a broken heart when he never returns."

"I don't know what you are referring to, Mrs. Allen," she replied, pulling her arm away. "There's nothing between the Captain and me except that he and his men are my lodgers."

"Sure there isn't." Celeste rolled her eyes. Oh, the denial. *Damn, John was good.* "I saw the way he was looking at you the other day."

The woman didn't flinch at the comment. "If you see the Captain, can you let him know Clark and his men are very concerned about him?"

"It's only a matter of time, Miss McKesson, no one can resist him, and he knows this. If you haven't given in to him yet, don't worry, you will." Celeste winked, noticing how Dellis blushed, her cheeks and neck turning bright red. Celeste was right—John had already made a play for the woman's favors.

As she opened the door, Celeste added, "Oh, Miss McKesson, eventually he'll leave you, too, when your usefulness wears out."

The woman didn't reply, just slammed the door shut behind her.

Laughing, Celeste shook her head and turned back to Agnes. "Oh, my goodness, I don't know what John sees in her. Truly, he's getting desperate."

"She seemed genuinely concerned, perhaps the Captain is in trouble. Should we send someone to look for him?" Agnes asked, looking up from her sewing.

Celeste shook her head. "You're soft on him, you always have been." Here she was the one who freed Agnes from being a house slave, and all John did was teach her how to read and write. *So much for loyalty.*

"He's probably found someone else to bankroll his little operation and he's busy servicing her for the night."

"You exaggerate. We both know the captain isn't like that. Why did you lie to the woman?" Agnes asked.

Celeste Put her hands on her hips and turned. "You might think you know John, but you don't. The only reason he's never made a conquest of you is because you have nothing he wants, and darkies hold no fascination for him. Remember, the only reason he was kind to you was because of me."

A knock on the door ended their conversation, but instead of opening the door, Agnes went back to her work, ignoring it.

"Who is it?" Celeste asked, grasping the door handle. She really wasn't in the mood for another guest; John's current love interest had provided enough entertainment for the night.

"A friend of John Carlisle's," a deep male voice said through the door.

Opening it, she was pleasantly surprised to find a very tall, handsome man standing in her doorway. He had large, deep-set, brown eyes and long, chocolate-brown hair slicked back tight and tied at the nape. His broad shoulders filled the doorway, and his height allowed him to tower over her, making her feel small and feminine.

"Mrs. Allen?" he said, giving her a devilish smile.

Intrigued, she offered him her hand. "I am. And to whom do I have the pleasure of speaking with?"

He bent down and kissed it, his eyes never leaving hers. The sensation of his lips on her hand made her warm all over, causing a surge of moisture between her thighs. *Damned, he is handsome.*

"Major Roger DeLancie." Slowly, he loosened his grip on her hand, his thumb running over the top of it, caressing her fingers. "I'm sorry to take you away from your business. I was hoping you would have a moment to indulge a former acquaintance of your benefactor."

Looking him over, with his handsome face and his well-tailored navy suit, he didn't seem like the monster John had described in the past. But she knew better. In her line of business, being privy to the secret peccadilloes and fetishes of the socially elite, one could never judge a book by its cover.

"Don't be sorry, Major, I can always make time for a friend of John Carlisle. Though I question whether he would say the same about you?"

He smiled, a solitary dimple forming in his left cheek. "Indeed."

"You don't seem at all like the way you were described." Not in the least.

"John has a penchant for exaggeration. I'm sure he told you I was violent and unpredictable. I'm a military man. There can't be war without violence. Occasionally, one must deal with the enemy harshly. Surely, you don't hold that against me?"

"A military man? I was under the impression you were no longer... Major." She smiled, waiting to see how he would respond, but he didn't, remaining surprisingly unfazed by her quip.

Gesturing to the decanter on her table, she walked over to it and removed the stopper. "Would you care for something to drink? I have some rum. I understand that's what military men prefer. Or is it scotch, like our mutual friend?"

He shook his head. "No, thank you, scotch has a nasty effect on me."

Of that, she had no doubt, John had told her what he had witnessed at the hands of his intoxicated superior, from forcing natives to run the gauntlet through hot coals to raiding villages in search of women for his pleasure.

She poured a drink for herself then sat down behind her desk. "What is it I can do for you?"

Taking a seat, DeLancie crossed his legs, sitting back comfortably in his chair. She couldn't help but notice the fine cut of his breeches and his shiny, black leather boots. Everything he wore was impeccably tailored, from his navy-blue overcoat and waistcoat to the black felt hat he held in his hands. He almost reminded her of John, not just how he dressed, but in the way he carried himself—sophisticated and arrogant with a bit of swagger.

"I have a business proposition for you, Mrs. Allen."

Fascinated, she lifted the drink to her lips and took a sip, her eyes watching him over the rim of the glass. "My curiosity is piqued, do go on."

"John Carlisle *is* your benefactor, am I correct?" He flashed her a wide, roguish grin, proving that he already knew the answer to the question.

Celeste nodded, playing along.

"How is business?"

"Not good, as of late, but that's my affair," she replied, taking another sip. "What do you want?"

He smiled again. "The direct approach, I like that in a woman. What I'm looking for is information, and in exchange, I might be able to help you."

"How is that?" she asked, leaning forward, resting her forearms on the desk. "I've managed just fine with my current business partner. Why would I want to trade up, and to someone with your reputation?"

He clucked his tongue, his eyes tracking over to Agnes then back at Celeste. "The fact that you're here and not in Manhattan, attending to business, leads me to believe things are not as they should be. And I'm in the position to provide much more than John Carlisle ever could. An independent woman such as yourself should always be looking for a wealthier benefactor to help further her business ventures."

"As I'm sure you know, there's more to mine and John's relationship than just business. I understand you have a very particular taste when it comes to women." She paused, purposely, for effect. "Besides, I find his services in that way more than adequate."

"I see that Johnny hasn't hesitated to talk," he said, picking a bit of lint off his breeches then looking up at her, his eyes quickly glancing at her décolletage. "I appreciate all beautiful women, especially when they are as intelligent and enterprising as you are."

She was getting tired of dancing around the subject. It was time for him to show his cards and be done with it. "What do you want to know?"

"What is John Carlisle doing in German Flats?"

"I don't know; he said it was for business, something to do with his family's shipping company." She lied. The man was up to something, and she wasn't willing to give in that easily. Still, she was intrigued, most definitely, and damned if he wasn't incredibly attractive. Considering her present situation, it was worth playing along. "That's as much as I know. But I might be able to find out more."

"That's what I wanted to hear. I'm willing to compensate however you like."

She considered inviting him to stay, having not had a man in days, but refrained. She didn't trust him, especially after all the things she'd heard. Even if John had embellished, some of it had to be true, and once she made a deal with the Devil, there would be no turning back. But her situation was precarious, and without financial assistance, she couldn't even afford to leave town.

"I need some time." She paused, sitting back in her chair. "You understand."

With a nod, he stood up. "Don't take too long."

Walking around the desk, she held out her hand, watching him kiss it again. The tip of his tongue grazed her flesh, sending little tingles down her spine. "How will I contact you?"

"Don't worry, I know where you are." He bowed gallantly, and then put his hat back on. "Until next time, Mrs. Allen." As he neared the door, he stopped for a moment and turned back to her. "By the way, who was the woman I saw leaving here earlier?"

"She owns The Thistle. Her name is Dellis McKesson."

He pondered her reply for a moment then smiled. "Thank you, Mrs. Allen, 'til we meet again."

When the door shut, she leaned her back against it, contemplating their conversation. Before she got in bed with DeLancie, she would give John one last chance to see the error of his ways, and of course, he would.

Chapter Twenty-Eight

Running in the back door, Dellis pulled off her cloak and dusted the snow from her hair. Thankfully, her leaving had gone unnoticed; Alexei and Ruslan were at a table eating while her aunt and Thomas managed the crowd at the bar, plates and dishes already stacked up on the counter waiting for Dellis to clean.

Leaning against the wall, she took a deep breath, glad to be away from that horrible woman. She had some nerve to say such awful things about the Captain. Dellis refused to think the worst of him, especially when he wasn't there to defend himself. *But if he isn't with Mrs. Allen, then where is he?*

Grabbing the keyring, Dellis ran upstairs to his room, saying a silent prayer of apology for invading his privacy as she unlocked the door. Quickly, she leafed through the papers on his desk and rummaged through his drawers, but the only thing she found were the maps she'd seen in his pocket and the key she gave him the day before.

Dellis jumped when she heard a knock on his door.

"Miss McKesson?"

Looking up, she felt a sudden pang of guilt as Hayes and Smith stood in the doorway, curiously watching her rummage through his belongings. Clark hobbled around them and into the room. "Did you find anything?"

Shaking her head, she threw the maps back in the drawer and slammed it shut. "Absolutely nothing, I don't understand how he could just disappear."

"It's unlike the Captain, I agree," Hayes said, sitting down. His face looked worn, lines of worry etched in his forehead and cheeks. "Usually, he tells one of us where he is going."

"What about Mrs. Allen?" Clark asked, taking a seat next to Hayes.

"He wasn't there, and she hasn't seen him since yesterday morning." Dellis shook her head, looking around the room. It used to remind her of her father; now, all she could think about was the Captain and the heady feeling she got when she saw him standing near the window. Putting her forehead in her hands, she mentally ran a list of all the possible places he could be, ticking one after another off until there was none left.

"So, what do we do now?" Smith asked, looking at both of them. "Where do we start? He could be anywhere."

Where indeed? He could be injured, lying in the snow freezing to death. There was also the possibility that a local tribe had taken him as part of a requickening ritual. If that were the case, they would never see him again.

No, she refused to believe that. The only thing they could do now was to go out and search. "I have an idea. Not a good one, but an idea."

Pulling the Captain's maps from the drawer, she laid them on the desk, turning them so his men could follow along. "I think we should split up and search for him. Hayes, take Smith and travel east along the river on the old military road. Understand this is Mohawk territory and they scout it regularly, so you have to be very careful. They've been a bit cagey as of late. Should you encounter any members of their tribe, it might be to your advantage to tell them you're Loyalists on your way to Canada. That is, if they don't shoot first and ask questions later."

Dellis noticed the expression on Hayes's face; he was less than amused by her jest. Clark chuckled, then nodded to his men. "Understand your orders?"

She waited for them to comply then pointed to Clark. "Simon, you go in the opposite direction, west along the river, stay on the old road, then stop when you reach the ruins of old Fort Schuyler. Be discreet. It's Oneida territory, and though they are usually friendly to travelers, you never know what could happen. My cousin is a tracker. I will take her, and we'll go west. There are native villages in that direction and Fort Stanwix. The chief at Oriska doesn't take kindly to strangers. It will be better if I meet with him. He has good relations with Colonel Elmore, and if I need to leverage that, I will."

She drew three rough maps of the territory based on the Captain's original and handed one to each of them. "We'll meet back here tonight. If we don't find him, we set out early tomorrow."

When all three of them left, she continued digging through his desk. The only place she hadn't searched was the top drawer, but it was locked, and she didn't have the key. Dellis pulled at it several times, trying to trick the lock, but it didn't budge. Desperate, she pulled a pin from her hair, and jabbed it into the lock, fidgeting with it a few times until it finally gave way. She searched through the contents but found nothing of significance. Stuffing everything back in the drawer, she picked up one of his gloves lying on the floor and put it back on the desk.

Grabbing her map, she made a mental list of supplies to bring with her: water, some bread cheese, and her supplies for cleaning up wounds. Looking back at the desk, Dellis suddenly realized something—the glove. Picking it up again, she examined it carefully. Running her fingers over the supple brown leather, she put it on, appreciating the fine tailoring and how much larger his hands were.

"Oh, my God." She gasped. It all made sense. Running down the hall, she banged on the door to Clark's room. "I think I know where he is."

Clark opened the door, already wearing his cloak and hat. "What do you mean?"

"This is his glove. I found it on the floor in his room." She handed it to him, her heart pounding with excitement. "This morning, my cousin found a black one just like this at the barn near my village."

"Why would he be there?" Clark asked, handing it back to her and following her down the hall.

"I don't know, maybe he went out looking for the supplies and stopped. I don't have an answer for you, but he must be there somewhere," she yelled over her shoulder.

"Hayes, Smith, we have new plans." He banged on each of their doors; both men came out, already dressed and ready to go.

Pulling out the maps, she drew the route to her village, drawing attention to the area where they should search, specifically around the barn and the little cabin. "We'll ride to the village together. The three of you will check the surrounding area, but keep your distance. I'll see if he is somewhere on the property."

"If he's there, believe me, someone will be answering for it," Smith said, the warning in his voice clear. The three men exchanged looks, something passing between them that she wasn't privy to, nor did they care to share with her. They were hiding something, she could sense it, but she couldn't worry about that now.

"My village was raided two years ago. I promise you, if they see strange white men with guns threatening my people, your scalp will end up on my grandfather's wall, and we'll never find the captain. Besides, he was trading with them; they wouldn't harm him."

"I find fault with your logic, Miss McKesson, I've seen plenty of savages turn on their allies," Smith said.

"Please, we don't have time for disagreements," she said, resisting the urge to give him a tongue lashing, the word savages infuriated her. "It'll be dark soon. If he's injured, he won't make it another night in this weather."

"Smith, enough," Clark ordered. "We leave now. My men and I will search just outside the village perimeter. You see what you can find."

It had stopped snowing earlier, but there were still eight inches on the ground to struggle through on their journey to the village. She rode ahead of them, her nerves on edge, anticipating what they would find.

Could Grandfather and his men have something to do with the Captain's disappearance? No, it wasn't possible. She refused to believe otherwise.

Turning her horse, she noticed Smith was missing. "Where is your other man?"

"He thought he saw something and rode off north towards the hill," Hayes replied, pointing towards the barn. Dellis raced past them—she had to catch Smith before he got too close to the village. Their search would be over in a matter of seconds if Alexei and his men found Smith trespassing.

Lifting up her lantern, she spotted Smith, holding the reins of two horses. "Is that the Captain's horse?" she asked.

"Yes, this is Viceroy." Smith pointed to the beautiful gelding, fussing as he tied it to the tree. "I saw him wandering around in the woods. He's stubborn, but loyal, he wouldn't go far without John."

She couldn't help but smile. It was rather fitting that the handsome, difficult horse belonged to the Captain. "Then we know he's definitely here somewhere. Keep looking. There's a barn just up the hill, and it's watched by the guards. I'll go check it."

The hill shined in the moonlight, a layer of snow and ice had crusted over it, creating a dangerous obstacle for her horse. Dellis slowed her mare, jumping down and carefully leading it up the steep grade. When she got to the top, she tied her horse to a tree and ran towards the barn, the hem of her petticoat wet and heavy as it dragged in the snow. A wintry breeze sent a chill down her spine. Of course, it could've been from fear. She looked up at the barn and said a silent prayer. *Please, let him be here.*

Just as Dellis went to open the door to the barn, something dawned on her—she was unarmed. It was too late to worry now. Reaching into her pocket, she pulled out the knife she'd taken from the Captain days before and held it out defensively. It wasn't ideal, but it was better than nothing.

With all her might, she pushed the heavy, rusted door open, wincing when it squeaked and protested against its hinges. *So much for being quiet.* It was pitch black and eerie quiet inside the barn. Dellis hesitated for a moment, her fear getting the best of her.

"Captain Anderson?" she yelled, her voice echoing off the walls. When there was no response, she took a deep breath and started through the doorway. "Captain?"

Dellis spotted something lying on the ground. Picking it up, she recognized it immediately—his neckerchief. Her hands shook as she examined the fabric, dried blood and dirt had made it stiff and crusty. Her fears were well-founded; he was definitely injured.

Stuffing the fabric in her pocket, she continued inside. "Captain, please, just make a sound."

From behind her, she heard a creaking noise, like chains scratching against the ground. She jumped as a small animal scurried past her feet, billowy cobwebs sticking to her face and hair as she walked towards the noise.

Then suddenly, she heard breathing coming from her right. "Captain, is that you?"

Reaching into the darkness, she gasped when her hands encountered something cold and clammy, like a dead animal carcass hanging from the ceiling. As she felt around, the sounds of the breathing started again. The sick feeling in the pit of her stomach returned as she held up her lantern, but the candle snuffed itself out. Running to the far wall of the barn, she found the latch to the door and threw it open, allowing the moonlight to flood the inside.

Whirling around, she was greeted by a gruesome sight. It wasn't an animal hanging out to dry, it was the Captain. He was unconscious with his arms stretched high above his head and chained to the rafters, his bare torso covered in fresh injuries. The moonlight highlighted his tortured silhouette, permanently imprinting the vision in her memory.

"Oh, God!" She gasped again, covering her mouth with her hands. "Captain."

Composing herself, she ran over to him, a jolt of terror gripping her heart while her eyes took in the enormity of his predicament. His face was covered in black-and-blue bruises, both his nose and lips caked with globules of coagulating blood. Most of his clothing had been torn away, only the legs of his pants still hugged his thighs, the waist hanging down in tatters. She followed the path of his injuries from his chest all the way to his hips, and then averted her gaze when she realized they went all way into his groin.

"Captain Anderson?" she said through tight lips, fighting back tears. When he didn't respond, she touched his face, rubbing his cold, waxy cheek, trying to rouse him. Running her hands over his neck, she could feel him breathing; he was alive, but barely, his pulse weak and thready. His hands were shackled together, both of them black and blue, blood dripped down his arms, the flesh torn away at the wrists.

Dellis untied the wet blindfold from his eyes, gently lifting his chin so she could examine his face. Both of his eyes were swollen shut, with large, black-and-blue rings around them. His hair was frozen in long, curly strands that hung in his face. She pushed a lock of it back behind his ear then cupped his cheeks, trying to warm them. "Captain, it's Dellis; can you hear me?"

His eyes rolled open, focusing on her.

"Captain, don't worry, we'll get you down. I promise."

Dellis ran around the barn searching everywhere for the keys to the shackles, but she couldn't find them. Suddenly, she heard voices from outside the barn. He moaned loudly, his head falling back. Putting her fingers on his lips, she shushed him, the voices getting closer. She was in no position to take on one person, much less two, with only a knife. If something happened to her, Clark and the men might never find either of them. She bit back her fear and accepted her fate. She would have to leave him. "Captain, someone is coming. I have to leave you."

He let out a groan that sounded like her name. "Dellis."

Quickly, she blindfolded him again, watching the door. Tears welled in her eyes as she looked him over, his teeth chattering between his swollen, blue lips. She smoothed his hair out of his face again, her heart aching at the prospect of leaving him with the men approaching.

"Hold on just a little longer," she whispered, running her thumb over his scruffy chin. "I'll be back."

Dellis sprinted to her horse, untied it, and raced off into the woods. As she passed her father's cabin, Skenandoa came out, waving her cousin over. "Dellis, careful, there are strange men lurking in the woods. Anoki spotted them just outside the village."

"It's all right. They're with me. I'll explain later. Please, tell Grandfather I'm with them, and we'll be leaving soon."

She carefully navigated her way down the icy hill, then dug her heels into her mare's flank and took off in the direction she left the Captain's men.

They were running out of time.

Chapter
Twenty-Nine

"Dellis?" John croaked, the pain in his parched throat preventing him from saying more. He swore he heard her voice, her soft hand soothing him, stroking his cheek. She removed the blindfold, and he could see her surrounded by a bright light, like an angel come to save him.

"Dellis?" he called out again.

If he could've reached out and touched her, he would have. She was so beautiful, her fingers like silk against his skin, a reminder of Heaven for a fleeting moment as he rotted in Hell. He could bear it no longer; he wanted to die. If she was the angel that came for him, then he would gladly hand himself over.

"Dellis, please, come back and take me with you." He begged. "Forgive me."

Suddenly, he felt the pins and needles of icy water drenching him again, fresh spasms rocking his body.

"No forgiveness here, Captain, you're beyond that. Even God doesn't want to hear your lies anymore."

"Your retribution is wasted on my flesh," John said between gasps, fighting for every word. "A thousand lashes are nothing compared to what I've done to myself. Revenge is hollow justice, even when it's self-imposed."

"I disagree. I find it very satisfying."

Suddenly he felt a sharp pain in his thigh, followed by the incessant pressure of something moving and twisting, trying to render his flesh in two. The man had stabbed John with a knife, then pulled it out, turning it throughout the motion. He groaned through the pain, a last-ditch effort to stay strong through the agony. She said she would come back. He just had to hold on a little longer.

"We'll feed you to the wolves when we get back if something hasn't already eaten you yet."

He could feel the warmth of his blood running down his leg. It wouldn't be long now. She would never make it in time. "Charon, I'm waiting. Take me to Hell." He begged. John let his head hang forward while he listened to the sound of chanting on the wind as an old woman's curse finally played out.

"Simon! Hayes!" Dellis yelled, frantically, racing towards them. "I found him. I found the Captain. We have to go now. He's in trouble."

"Where is he, lass?" Clark asked.

"The barn… Past the village… Shackled to the rafters." Her words came out in a jumbled mess of blurted phrases and panic-stricken thoughts. She waved them on, turning her horse around. "They're coming! They'll kill him. Oh, God, they'll kill him. Do you have a gun?"

Clark reached into his pocket and handed her his pistol. "Calm down, lass. We'll get to him."

She took a couple of deep breaths, trying to steady her nerves. It would do none of them any good if she continued spouting off like a mad woman. With another deep breath, she was finally able to string a complete sentence together. "We have to be careful; he's on the village property, and the guards have already been alerted to our presence."

"Whatever, woman." Smith sneered, riding up to her.

Dellis grabbed the reins of his horse, forcing him to stop. "Do you want to rescue the Captain, or do you want to face an Oneida fighting force? I promise you, we are drastically outnumbered. They know I'm here with you, but that doesn't mean they won't attack us."

"Like they did the Captain?" he challenged.

"We don't know that they did this, but little good it will do provoking them. Make no mistake, they won't hesitate to kill the three of you, even in my presence. Now do as I say." She demanded, a vision of John, hanging like a dead animal, flashing before her eyes. *Oh, God.* "He won't last long. We need to get him out of here as quickly as possible."

"Smith!" Clark yelled, authoritatively. "Do as she says."

The hot-headed man backed off, deferring to her with a nod of his head and a glance at Clark.

When they reached the top of the hill, she motioned for them to follow. "He's in here," she whispered, pointing towards the barn. "We have to be careful."

Smith went first, his pistol cocked and drawn as he entered the barn. Clark and Hayes walked around the side of the structure, searching the perimeter, while she waited for the okay to enter the barn. The snow started up again with a vengeance, making her even more anxious to get moving. They were running out of time.

"It's clear," Smith yelled, his voice echoing through walls.

Dellis sprinted through the barn to the back door, grabbed the handle, and pulled it open. As the moonlight streamed inside, she heard one of the men gasp.

Pointing to the rafters, she yelled, "He's chained to the beam. I couldn't find the keys."

While the men searched the barn for the keys, she untied his blindfold, touching his cheek, trying to rouse him. "Captain, we're going to get you down. Just hold on for a few more minutes."

She examined him quickly, noticing that his right thigh was oozing blood from a large, ugly looking knife wound.

"Oh, God."

Dellis lifted the hem of her skirts and ripped a section from her shift, using it to tie off the wound at his leg until they could get him down. The men were above her in the rafters, one of them cursed loudly, shaking the chains, and the other was pounding on the shackles with a hammer of some sort. John groaned, his eyes fluttering open, sapphire blue just barely visible through his swollen lids.

"Stay with us, Captain, just a few seconds more and you'll be free."

"All right, here we go, miss," Hayes yelled from above. After several loud pounds and another curse, John fell into her arms. She groaned, taking on his dead weight then sinking to her knees, holding his body against her own. Quickly, Smith came from behind and took over, helping her lower John to the ground. Together, Smith and Hayes worked the shackles with a hammer and a knife, finally freeing the Captain's tortured hands.

Dellis made a mental list of everything that needed to be done, then barked out orders at both men as if she were their commander. "We need to move him now. He'll freeze to death if we don't get him inside fast. Can one of you get a blanket from my horse and my things so I can get him ready to travel? Also, we need to decide the best way to get the Captain back to The Thistle without further injuring him."

Gently she tapped his cheek, trying to revive him. "Captain, do you hear me?"

But he said nothing.

"Call him by his name, lass," Hayes said, covering him with a blanket. "A man always responds to a pretty lady saying his name, especially the Captain."

"John, please, wake up, it's Dellis." She tapped his cheek again, but this time his eyes rolled open.

"Dellis," he whispered, almost inaudibly.

Who would do this to him? She put her hand over her mouth, holding back tears that threatened. He groaned loudly, his face turning towards her. "You're safe now," she said sweetly. "I'll take care of you, but you have to promise me you'll stay with us."

He mumbled something neither of them understood. Hayes leaned over and tapped him on the shoulder. "Say that again, Captain."

John mumbled again, only this time, Hayes snickered. She looked over at him, curiously. "What did he say?"

Hayes cleared his throat, and said very politely, "It wasn't meant for your ears, miss."

Not meant for my ears? Ridiculous. "I'm not such a lady that I haven't heard my share of obscenities. I do have a brother and two male cousins. If it's important, then I need to hear it."

Having been thoroughly scolded, Hayes relented with a dubious answer, "Ahh… he was referring to a specific part of his body that hurts, if that answers your question?"

She rolled her eyes, unable to find humor in the situation. The poor man had been practically maimed, and they were making jokes. *Men.* When Smith returned with blankets and her basket of supplies, she examined the rest of John quickly, her eyes drawn back to the bloody swatch tied around his leg.

"It looks like a stab wound. I'll rebind it quickly then he'll be ready to move. Cover him up as best you can."

Dellis tore another strip of material from her shift and used it to bind the wound tightly closed. Simultaneously trying to warm him and get his attention, she cupped his face in her hands, rubbing his cheeks. "John, we're going to move you now."

He nodded, his body visibly shaking under the blankets.

Looking up at his men, she nodded. "Okay, let's do it."

Just as Smith started to lift the captain's left side, he cried out in protest. Stopping abruptly, Smith looked at her with wide eyes. "What did I do? Is his arm broken?"

Dellis palpated his left shoulder and tried to move it causing him cry out again. "It's out of joint, and I can't fix it here, his muscles are too cold. You'll have to carry him to the horse."

Carefully, the two men lifted him, one at his arms and the other at his feet, carrying him out of the barn towards the horses. John cried out several times, his fist clenching the air, reaching for something. "I am Captain John Car…" he muttered under his breath. Fevered words full of nonsense; she assumed they were meant for his assailant and not for her ears.

"Hayes, you take him, you're a better rider than me, and Simon can't take him with his injured leg," Smith said, inclining his head in the direction of his friend's horse. "Once we get him mounted, you take off and don't stop. We'll follow behind and keep a lookout."

"My God." Clark gasped, watching as Smith and Hayes lifted John onto the horse. "Did you see any of the blaggards that did this to the Captain?"

"No, They were gone." Smith huffed out, while positioning John's limp body in the saddle in front of Hayes. "But I know who did it. Rather obvious, isn't it?"

Dellis refrained from comment—the evidence wasn't in her favor. "Please, we must hurry."

"What about Viceroy?" Hayes asked, looking at Clark. "He's been out all night. John will be angry if anything happens to him."

Smith looked back at the gelding and shook his head. "I refuse to ride that horse. Last time I tried, he bucked and threw me flat on my back."

There was no time to fuss over the horse, her anxiety starting to overtake what good sense she had stored up. "Get going, I'll figure something out," she yelled, frantically. "Just leave now. I'll catch up with you."

Grabbing the reins of her mare, Dellis walked her back to the barn and saw her fed and blanketed and neatly tucked in for the night in one of the stalls. There was no doubt in her mind she could ride the stubborn horse, and Viceroy was likely quicker than her mare. Though she hated the idea of leaving Brynn overnight, she was sure no one would hurt her.

Slowly, Dellis walked over to Viceroy, taking her time, looking into his dark eyes as she got closer to him. "You're a very good boy, and I know you don't like anyone to ride you but the Captain. If you let me, I'll take you home to him."

Putting her hand out, Dellis allowed the horse to smell her, his big, fleshy nostrils running up and down her fingers, breathing welcomed warm air on the tips. After a moment, she patted his neck, and he relented calmly. "Please, let me ride you."

The horse bucked a few times after she mounted then took off, ready to run hard and fast. He was powerful and a bit playful, testing her skill, but she held fast to the reins, exerting her control, adjusting her position in the saddle and gripping with her thighs. The ride was physically exhausting, but it was good to know she could still handle a challenging mount just like her grandfather taught her.

She caught up with the Captain and his men not a mile up the road, and together, the five of them raced back to The Thistle with little issue. It was after hours when they arrived; the dining room would be empty, and thankfully, there would be no need to explain the situation to her aunt. Well, at least, not yet. Dellis directed the men to the stable to board their horses, and then held the door as they carried John up the back steps.

"Put him in this room." She pointed to her room at the end of the hall, and then raced to the kitchen to grab her supplies and some liquor from the bar. Thomas woke up suddenly and looked over his shoulder, his eyes widening at the sight of John's injured body being carried through the back door and going into her room.

"I need two buckets of warm water and all the linen you can find. Make haste, Thomas!" she said tersely, and then hustled down the hall to her room

The two men deposited John face down on her bed, his tortured body visibly trembling underneath the blankets. She put her supplies on the bed and started tearing through her drawers looking for fabric and anything else she could use for bindings.

When Dellis turned around, Smith was standing right behind her, his body much too close for her comfort. As she tried to step around him, he used his hulking form to back her into the dresser and pin her there. "Those natives had something to do with this, and you're protecting them."

Pushing a stray lock of hair behind her ear, she looked up at him, her ire simmering to a boil. The man was obnoxious to bring up such a thing when his employer was lying half-dead in her bed. "What does it matter now? The Captain may die! He needs help, and you're preventing it. Now, please, let me get to tending him."

"If he dies, I'm going to enjoy taking it out on you." He pushed her against the dresser, his hand groping her neck then her breast.

"Don't touch me." Dellis slapped his hand away. Reaching into her pocket, she pulled her knife out just far enough so he could see it. "Don't make me use this on you. Now get out of my way."

"Are you threatening me?" He challenged, his eyes narrowed and focused on her.

"Yes, and believe me, your scalp won't be hard for me to take." She hissed, pulling the knife out the rest of the way then removing the case. "I'm a savage, after all. It only takes a couple of quick cuts and a tug and it's mine. I cook your food; all it would take is a little too much valerian root, and you would sleep through it."

Smith's eyes widened with horror, but before he could respond, Hayes walked over and interrupted, "Is there a problem?"

She shook her head, enjoying the outrage on Smith's face. Clearly, she made her point. "Please, leave, both of you."

"Smith, come with me." Hayes opened the door, gesturing for his comrade to follow. "Let us know if you need anything."

Dellis leaned against the wall, tears welling up in her eyes, choked breaths coming out on the verge of sobs. There was no time to panic, though part of her wanted to shrink down in the corner and weep. The Captain needed her. Taking a deep breath, she wiped her eyes and rallied her strength, giving his tortured form the once over. It was going to be a long night.

"Okay, Captain, I'm going to get you cleaned up," she said with the conviction of one going into battle.

Pulling the blankets to his hips, she reached under and removed what was left of his wet, tattered breeches. His back was covered in whiplashes, one… two… three… seven, all of them jagged and meaty, caked over with dried blood. There was a significant charred patch of flesh at the base of his spine surrounded by several angry looking blisters. Lifting the blanket, she examined his backside. There was a large whip wound on the top of his buttocks, but none on the back of his legs.

When she rolled him over on his back, he cried out suddenly, his body shuddering when his skin touched the bed. "John, I know it hurts, but I need to examine you."

He shivered violently, his teeth chattering as he wrapped his right arm around himself, trying to get warm.

"Thomas, I need that water now!" she yelled to the bartender through the door.

Lifting John's limp torso, Dellis wrapped her arms around him, yelping when his skin touched her own. She expected him to be cold, but it was like hugging a block of ice. Closing her eyes, she held him tightly, willing her warmth into him.

"John, stay with me," she whispered, vigorously rubbing her hands up and down his arms trying to build some friction.

Thomas walked in, depositing two steaming buckets of water on the floor and another one filled with lukewarm water. "Is he going to make it?" he asked, chewing his lip.

"He's going to be fine, Thomas," she said, trying to convince herself more than him. *Of course he would be fine.*

Dousing the linen with water, she wrung it out then gently wrapped both of his feet with it, making sure his toes were covered. He groaned, kicking her several times, soaking the bodice of her dress and the front of her petticoat.

She grabbed his feet, trying to stop him. "I know it hurts now, John, but it will get better, I promise.

It took several moments of fighting before he got accustomed to the wraps. When his hands and feet were pink and warm, she dried them and pulled several layers of blankets over him. Getting a hot brick from the fire, she wrapped it in linen and placed it under the sheets close to his feet.

Gently, she palpated his dislocated shoulder; the muscles were still too cold and stiff to try and relocate it. Putting a couple hot bricks next to his shoulder, she turned her attention to the long, ugly stab wound on his leg. Dellis reached for her needle and thread, her hands shaking as she fought to push the tiny bit of fiber through the eye. With a deep breath, she willed stillness into her hands, fighting against the trepidation and anxiety that loomed under the surface. *You can do this*, she repeated to herself. When she released the binding, the wound gaped open, a fresh flow of blood starting again, oozing down his leg onto the bed sheets. Thankfully, the artery was intact, but still, he needed stitches both inside and out. Luckily, her father had taught her how to do that just before he died.

"John, I have to sew this shut, and some of the stitches will be very deep. Try not to move too much," she said, her lips close to his ear.

He must have heard her because he didn't move a muscle, though he shouted, gut-wrenching cries of unintelligible words. At least he was still holding on, his willful spirit fighting back the only way it could. It took incredible fortitude to live through such torture, but it would take even more to survive the aftermath.

When she finished closing up his leg, Dellis leaned over and gently smoothed his hair back. "John, do you hear me?"

His eyes cracked open for a second, focusing on her, then rolling back. "John?"

He looked at her again, only this time, his lids opened just enough to expose a hint of sapphire blue tinged with scarlet red. She grasped his fingers in hers, squeezing them gently. "You're going to be all right. I promise."

He nodded this time, closing his eyes.

With a piece of linen from one of the extra sheets, Dellis meticulously cleaned the wounds on his chest and arms, trying not to irritate the delicate, damaged skin. But before she went to roll him over, it occurred to her that there was one place left she hadn't checked. Her face and neck grew hot at the thought of seeing John nude. And though she had a quick flash of him in the barn, it was different now that he was lying in her bed, helpless. Granted, she'd seen men partially unclothed before, but never totally.

Goodness. She cringed and blushed again, simultaneously. Good sense won out where fear loomed; there was nothing more to be done, those wounds need tending, too. *You can do it.* Resolute in her decision, though dubious in action, she slid her hand under the blankets and palpated his navel, following the line of hair and a long cut that extended from his lower abdomen into his groin. Much to her horror, it went even farther than she could possibly have imagined, having to stop her descent when her hand encountered his manhood. She knew there was also a large burn on his thigh, having seen it earlier. Turning his leg out so she could get a better look, she noticed that the wound stretched between his legs then continued up to his buttocks. "Oh my." She gasped and then stopped abruptly. That was it. She'd seen enough. Trying to afford the poor man his privacy, she covered him up, exposing only what was necessary to clean his wounds.

The last thing she needed to do was relocate his shoulder. Turning him once more onto his back, she palpated the arm, feeling for the separated ball and socket and groove of the joint. It was dislocated anterior and inferior to the joint, the muscles around it still rock hard with spasm even after several minutes of warmth.

"I'm going to put this back in place. Just bear with me, and it will be over with quickly."

Taking his hand in her own, she lifted his arm up towards his face, then bent it at the elbow, using her body weight to coax the bone up to the joint. He screamed and fought back, but she persisted. It took Dellis several tries, but finally, with a heave and one hard push, the arm popped back into place, the muscles surrounding it drawing the bone into its natural position.

After covering him with blankets and putting more hot bricks under the sheets, she was finally done. "John, that's it for now."

Thank God.

Spent, she sat down on the edge of the bed, her clothing soaked with sweat all the way down to her shift. She had nothing left. How long had she been working? Minutes? Hours? She'd lost track of time. The stress of the day had worn her out, exhaustion rendering her unable to think past the moment. When she looked over her shoulder, he was still shivering, even under several layers of blankets and a fortress of hot bricks stacked up around him. She'd seen plenty of men die from lung infections after being out in the cold. He wouldn't last long if he didn't get warm.

"You're not going to make this easy on me, are you?" She groaned, accepting her fate.

Removing everything but her shift, she stood at his bedside for a moment, watching him, fear getting the better of her. She'd never been this close to a nude man before, except… She swallowed, a pit forming in her stomach. "Dellis, you're being foolish." She chided herself. The man was in no shape to ravish her, but he would surely die if she didn't do something—and quick.

"Just keep your hands to yourself, John," she said, then she climbed into bed and scooted under him, yelping loudly when his icy flesh touched her own. Dellis pulled her shift down around her waist and wrapped her arms and legs around him, her bare skin touching his. He was so cold she shivered on contact, the muscles in her arms and legs cramping against his hard, frozen body.

"Painful," she said through clenched teeth, yet still drawing him in closer.

Carefully, she held his injured face against her neck, her lips pressed against his forehead using every means she had to warm him.

"You… you're going to be fin… fine… John. I'm here with you," she whispered through chattering teeth. Admiring his handsome face, she traced his cheekbones, and then his jawline, feeling the rough stubble under her fingertips. "When I was sick, my father used to sing Greensleeves to me, and it always made me feel better. Do you want me to sing?"

Damn. Looking up, she realized the door wasn't locked, if someone walked in and found them together, she'd be ruined. It was too late now, moving him was nearly impossible. He was so heavy, dead weight against her chest, his head resting on her neck. The feel of his rhythmic breathing calmed her as his uninjured arm wrapped around her, drawing her closer.

He muttered something she couldn't understand. Lightheaded and tired, she closed her eyes, gently stroking his hair.

"*Alas, my love, you do me wrong, to cast me off, discourteously,*" Dellis sang softly to the man in her arms, lulling herself to sleep.

Chapter Thirty

Pain. All he could feel was pain, and the sensation like thousands of pins and needles piercing his skin. John tried to open his eyes, but the light was so bright, he had to close them. *Am I dying?*

He could hear Dellis's sweet voice calling his name, and occasionally he could see glimpses of her brown eyes and white skin, a light in the darkness, proof he was still alive. He tried to answer, but he couldn't form words, his mouth wouldn't move. *Where am I?* It felt like lying on a cloud, a sensation of warmth washing over him, making his bones ache to the point of cracking. Then suddenly, there was a pain in his feet so intense he tried to pull them away, but someone held them to the fire. *Am I in Cocytus, a place so cold it burns? Is it Dellis or a devil woman torturing me?*

"John, I know it hurts, but it will make it better," he heard her say.

Then his other foot started to burn; he wanted to scream, but he couldn't, instead, he just pushed at the demon, trying to stop her. Next, it was his hands, the pressure so intense they felt like they would explode. This was the layer in Hell reserved for traitors, and he was in Judecca for betraying his superior.

"Traitor! Judas! There's a place in Hell for you, I'll see you get there," DeLancie yelled, his voice echoing loudly in John's head.

Did DeLancie win? Am I in Hell?

"John," she said sweetly, her hands like hot coals touching his forehead. "It's Dellis, can you hear me?"

Trying with all his might, he looked into the light, desperately needing to know if it was a devil submerging him in the lake or the angel she claimed to be, come to rescue him.

"John," she said again.

It was Dellis, her long hair hanging in her face, her lovely eyes strained with concern. He wasn't dead, despite how awful he felt. "John, I have to sew this shut, and some of the stitches will be very deep. Try not to move too much."

Damn the pain. He could take it. Squeezing his eyes shut, he embraced the pain, crying out his mantra, "I am Captain John Carlisle of His Majesty's Eighth Regiment, Light Infantry."

When the torment ceased, he could take no more, too tired to fight, but afraid to sleep. What if he never woke? He refused to die in disgrace. But it was no use, he finally surrendered, throwing up the white flag on a well-fought battle.

When he woke again, John found himself lying in his angel's embrace, surrounded by a cocoon of her warmth. Opening his eyes, he smiled, getting a glimpse of delicate, fair skin and dark tresses. Was it Dellis, or an angel protector? Had he died? The feel of her satiny skin against his own and her hand gently stroking his hair was heavenly. Yes, he must have died. Closing his eyes again, he rested, content that he would spend eternity in her arms.

"Dellis," he croaked, wrapping his arm around her, pulling her closer. The sound of her sweet lullaby helped him drift off, and there were no nightmares, no voices chanting in the wind, just peaceful oblivion. Yes, this was Heaven.

Chapter Thirty-One

John Butler was a man of his word, and all the men and supplies DeLancie needed were his for the taking. It was rather convenient. The personality conflicts of the military elite created opportunities for the most exciting alliances. He'd played their game long enough in his former life, and he had no interest in being one of Howe's or Carleton's lapdogs again. DeLancie had his own goals to fulfill. Now that he had his own militia and the weapons he needed, it was finally his time. Time for revenge.

And what a fortunate find he had made in Mrs. Allen. He knew of her from Manhattan, her ladies a favorite of Howe's men, and her presence often spotted at the military social events. There were rumors surrounding Celeste that she had taken up with John, both as her benefactor and her lover. Her reputation preceded her as an intelligent businesswoman whose only allegiance was to her pocketbook, but could she be bought? John had a way of turning the most beautiful of women into simpering fools ready to do his every whim. Only time would tell.

"Sir," Eagle Eyes said from behind.

"What is it?" DeLancie asked, turning around, his trusted friend standing in the door of his new office. Butler had granted DeLancie a house and a place to train his men five miles east of Fort Ontario, on the south side of the Oswego River. The remote location was ideal for what he had planned, and it had access to the port and the river system.

"I have news for you."

"Enlighten me, my friend." He waved his arm for Eagle Eyes to take a seat. "What do you think of my decorating?" DeLancie asked, lifting his arms up in salute to his handiwork. "My trophies."

Looking up at the walls, he smiled, remembering where every one of them came from down to the exact moment he acquired them. It was a gruesome sight of dried scalps, fingers, tongues, and one large map, tacked to the wall, bearing the initials JC in the corner. On his desk, next to his inkwell, were his most precious items. Gently, he ran his fingers over the long, shiny, black braid, stroking it lovingly; next to it was a necklace made of large purple and white beads.

Eagle Eyes glanced around reticently. The Mohawk had no admiration for decorating skills. Not surprising, very little moved his stoic personality to an emotional response. "The Oneidas are thieving again."

"That's no big surprise," DeLancie replied, shrugging. "We already knew that."

Eagle Eyes smiled, something he rarely did, and pulled an object out of his pocket, placing it on the desk. "For your wall; something to add."

"What is that?" DeLancie lifted the prize, taking a better look. It was a finger. The bit of flesh was black and blue, and the nail had been removed, a prelude Eagle Eyes preferred when torturing. "Whose is this?"

"One of the Oneidas I caught stealing. He'll never do that again. He's missing all ten of them now."

"And his life." Nodding in approval, DeLancie placed the finger on the desk. Eagle Eyes snatched the appendage back, putting his trophy in his coat pocket and patting it gently.

"So, what did you learn from your Oneida catch?" DeLancie asked, his curiosity piqued. Eagle Eyes always managed to get the most interesting information out of people, especially with torture.

"It's Joseph and his men that have been stealing."

Wonderful. "From whom?"

Eagle Eyes smiled again. "John Carlisle. They are the ones who took his supplies, initially, and they did it again a few days ago."

"How frustrating that must be for John," DeLancie said with excitement. "Those damn Oneidas best him every time. Tell me more. What else did you learn from your catch?"

"The Oneidas took most of the supplies to the fort, the rest, they hid."

"Why is John Carlisle trying to move supplies down the Mohawk?" He put his hands together, turning his chair so he could face the wall, looking up at the map. "Carlisle Shipping belongs to his brother, and Gavin Carlisle would never turn profiteer. He's notoriously loyal. Besides, Gavin hates John with a vengeance. He would never willingly assist him, not even for the British cause. No, John is up to something, but what could it be?"

Looking over the map, he meditated on it, then closed his eyes, reaching deep into his thoughts for the answer. "Tell me why you're here," he whispered to himself. Suddenly, it came to him. "Ask, and ye shall receive. Oh, Johnny, I know what you're doing. It's all too perfect." Turning to Eagle Eyes, DeLancie asked, "Do we know where this hiding place is?"

"Yes, downriver on the north side, opposite Oriska."

He grinned, the thought of visiting his old friends delighting him. "Even better, we can kill two birds with one stone; first the Oneidas, and then John Carlisle."

Eagle Eyes nodded. "How do you plan on doing that?"

"I'll show you." DeLancie walked to the door and called into the hall for one of his men; seconds later, a soldier walked in.

DeLancie paced for a moment, and then walked over to the soldier, inspecting his uniform. He wore a distinct, forest-green coat with red facing, but instead of traditional breeches and shoes, he wore buckskin leggings and moccasins. Smoothing the wrinkles out of the soldier's jacket, it took everything DeLancie had not to beat the man for insubordination. Taking a deep breath, DeLancie planted his fist in the soldier's face, blood spattering from his nose. "Don't ever come in here looking a mess again. Now get the men together; we travel in an hour."

The soldier nodded, hustling out the door without looking back.

"Where are we going?" Eagle Eyes asked.

"To visit our Oneida friends. Carlisle Shipping is a British company. We're just taking back what's ours and returning it to where it belongs. And if the rest of the Confederacy find out about the Oneida treachery, so be it."

"And what about Carlisle? He'll come after the supplies."

"I certainly hope so." Reaching into the desk, DeLancie pulled out a piece of paper and his quill and started to write. Eagle Eyes watched DeLancie curiously as he penned his letter. "This is for our dear friend; time to see if he remembers all that I taught him."

"What if he doesn't take the bait?"

DeLancie smiled, putting his quill back in the pot. "Of course he will. He can't help himself. But John forgets: the master always knows something the apprentice has yet to learn. Thus, the expert in battle moves the enemy and is not moved by him."

Running his hand over the long, black braid, he smiled, remembering the lovely, fair-skinned brunette he saw at The Silver Kettle. "I think I'll pay a visit to The Thistle Tavern and some of my other friends in German Flats."

Chapter Thirty-Two

"Mary is your name, correct?" he asked, keeping his voice low, praying no one could hear their exchange.

She nodded, her eyes darting around fearfully.

"You must run, Mary. You're safer in the woods than you are here. Take this." John handed her a loaded pistol. She took it, looking up at him with wide, black eyes. "Do you know how to use it?"

She nodded vigorously.

"Good, now go."

When Mary was out of sight, he went the long way back to his tent, trying to forget everything that had happened. The day had turned into one long, unending nightmare that was sure to carry on once word got back to their superiors of what they had done. It was a disgrace.

Suddenly, a sentry appeared at John's tent, throwing the flap open and stepping inside without out being welcomed. "Captain Carlisle, Major DeLancie has requested your presence in his quarters."

He nodded to the Lieutenant, following him. When they reached the Major's tent, John was shocked to see Eagle Eyes holding the woman he'd just released, a knife at her throat, the Mohawk eyeing John suspiciously.

"It would seem you've lost something, John," Major DeLancie said, turning around.

"Let her go. She's mine," John demanded.

"No, John, you disobeyed my orders. Eagle Eyes found her running in the woods after you released her."

Eagle Eyes smiled, pulling the woman by the hair as she struggled and fought, trying to get away.

John cast a sympathetic glance at her, then clenched his fists at his side. How could this be happening? "Major, I brought her here; she is mine to do with as I see fit. Give her back to me."

DeLancie placed a hand on her cheek the let it run down to the front her tunic. "No, John, that's not how it works. You defied me, and now she gets to pay for your insubordination—and you get to watch. I know how you like that."

The Major grabbed the front of her tunic, ripping the material, exposing her bare torso. John's breath caught in his throat. The woman was pregnant; her small, protruding belly the evidence.

"Well, this is a surprise," the Major exclaimed, his eyes feasting on her flesh. "A breeding savage."

"Let her go." John begged, watching his superior grope the woman, his hand caressing her swollen abdomen.

"You are beautiful, even carrying your savage bastard."

She spat at him, boldly meeting his gaze with an imperious one of her own.

DeLancie ran his hand down her cheek, then pulled back and slapped her forcefully, causing her head to whip to the side. "But you will be broken, just like my horse."

"You'll pay for this," she said defiantly, spitting on him again.

The Major grabbed her by the chin, squeezing her face, drawing her in close. "Are you threatening me?"

Slapping her again, he yanked her from Eagle Eyes' grasp and threw her on the ground. Pulling his knife from his pocket, he held it up for all to see. "Your people were stealing from us. We've tried to make deals with them in the past, yet they remain defiant. You're all traitors."

"Let her go," John yelled, frantically. "I'll deal with her."

"*No, John, you've proven yourself weak.*" The Major held his knife in front of her eyes, running the metal down her cheek. "*She's mine now.*"

"*No!*" John yelled, taking a step towards them, but Eagle Eyes grabbed John's arm, holding him back.

"NO!"

"Captain, wake up. It's all right. You're safe."

Opening his eyes, John reached out to save her, but someone held his hands, stopping him. "Let her go!"

"Captain, it's Dellis. Please, don't fight me," she said, her voice cutting through the haze, finally reaching him. "You're having a nightmare."

Looking up, John tried to focus on Dellis, but the light was so bright, he couldn't see her face, only the outline of her exquisite form. With a sigh of relief, he closed his eyes, falling back against the pillows. It was a dream.

"Dellis?" He croaked through parched lips and a sore throat.

"Aye, it's me." The feel of her hand gently stroking his cheek was soothing, like a warm, silky sheet. He turned his head towards her, wanting more. "Captain?"

"Dellis, please, call me John." He croaked again. "I think we passed formality about a mile back."

His whole body felt heavy, like a thousand pounds of wood were on his chest, holding him down. Even his limbs felt thick and immobile, like giant kegs filled to the rim with spiced rum. *Ah, rum, that sounded good, and maybe a cup of tea.* Unable to feel his left arm, he tried several times to move it, but it wouldn't budge. Wincing, he slid his right hand up his chest until he found what he sought. Grabbing her hand, he held it, grateful when she didn't pull away, her touch like an angel's blessing.

"Thank God you've come back to us," she said, gently squeezing his fingers then brushing a lock of his hair from his forehead.

"I thought I was dead," he replied, turning his head a little so he could look up at her. "Where am I? What happened?"

"You're at The Thistle, and this is my room." Again, she brushed his hair back; the gesture, while innocent, was decidedly intimate, too. "Someone captured you, but your men and I found you and brought you back."

She looked beautiful. Her dark eyes were soft, and curly tendrils of her hair had fallen loose, resting on her shoulders. "Do you remember anything?"

He shook his head, unable to focus, the pain in his head so severe he had to close his eyes against the ray of sunlight streaming through the window.

Squeezing his hand again, she said quietly, "Give it a few days. You have a pretty good bump on the back of your head."

"Thank you." He nodded, lifting her fingers, brushing his lips against them. "You saved my life."

She blushed shyly and looked away. "You're welcome, Captain... I mean, John."

He couldn't help but smile. Her inherent modesty was always so refreshing.

"I need to clean your wounds. Do you want something for the pain before I start? It may help." She pulled her hand away quickly, but he reached for it again, causing her pale pink blush to further deepen to scarlet red.

"Do you have that scotch?" The thought of being drunk seemed a rather appealing prospect after all he'd been through, and if it would numb the pain, mores the better.

"Give me a moment."

John released her hand reluctantly. She got up and walked around the bed, rustling through her little basket full of supplies. When she came back to the bedside, there was a glass in one hand and a bottle in the other.

"Can you sit up, or do you want me to help you?"

Putting his right hand on the bed, he tried to boost himself up but couldn't, his body protesting with every movement.

"It's all right. I've got you." She sat down next to him on the bed, wrapped her arm around his waist and carefully helped him up. "Rest your weight against me."

He complied, his body shivered then relaxed as he leaned against her, drinking in her warmth. Grabbing a blanket from the chair next to the bed, she pulled it around him, covering his bare torso.

"I'll have that drink now," he said, the room starting to spin, his vision getting blurrier with each passing second.

He watched her pour the amber liquid into the glass, the aroma of the woodsy, pungent liquor reaching him across the short distance, making his mouth water. Heaven in a glass. When she handed it to him, he squeezed his fingers around the circumference of the little tumbler, but for the life of him, he couldn't lift it. His arm was too heavy, and his fingers were swollen like large, fat sausages, making dexterous movement impossible. Taking it from him, she held it to his lips and tipped it, helping him throw it back. He swallowed it slowly, coughing, as the liquid warmed him all the way to his stomach.

"Do you want another?"

He could drink the whole bottle at this point, and still, it wouldn't be enough. When he nodded, she poured another, helping him again.

"I can't move my left arm," he said through coughs. "It feels so heavy, like dead weight."

"While you're seated, I'll look at it. Is that okay?"

He nodded, watching her as she gently palpated the joint. She touched him carefully, her fingertips a light as butterfly wings, tenderly feeling under his arm, then tracking back over his collarbone.

"Okay, let me see you try to move it."

Pulling the blanket down, she sat and waited as he tried to lift his arm, her eyes following every step of his failed attempt. With each effort, stabbing pain shot through his arm, followed by a burning sensation radiating to his hand.

"Let me try to move it," she said, grasping his hand. "We'll just take it slow."

He nodded, taking a deep breath in preparation.

As she gradually lifted it, he winced, trying to focus on her and not the pain building in his shoulder. Suddenly, the joint clunked, and pain, like lightning, shot down his arm, causing his stomach to pitch.

"Dellis, get me the basin, now," he said, knowing what was coming.

She managed to hand it to him, just in time, before he vomited repeatedly.

"I'm so sorry. I didn't mean to make you sick." She held the basin under him, wrapping her other arm around his waist, supporting him while he retched several more times.

When he was finished, he leaned against her, grateful for the support, his hair coming loose again, hanging in his face. She smoothed it back behind his ear and adjusted his tie-back. He'd never felt this awful in his life. *Never.* Dying seemed a more pleasant alternative to the torture he was enduring.

"Are you going to be sick again?" she asked, taking the basin from him.

He shook his head, looking up at her. "I don't know what hurt worse, pissing through my teeth or you trying to move my arm. Please, don't do that again."

When she didn't respond, he was suddenly embarrassed. "Forgive my vulgarity, Dellis. I didn't mean to offend you." Rarely did he use such language in the presence of a lady, and certainly not when she'd just saved his life.

Instead of a stern rebuke for his ungentlemanly behavior, she laughed loudly. "No need, I'm not offended. After everything you've been through, a curse here and there is justified. Trust me, I say my share."

John sat still long enough for her to make a sling for his arm, tying it behind his neck then adjusting it in place. The feel of his dead-weight arm resting against his body was comforting, and at least now, he'd be able to sleep on his side. When he looked up at her, there was a strange look on her face, as if she was contemplating something dire but was afraid to ask.

"What is it? Please don't tell me you need to move my arm again." He'd need more scotch for that.

She chewed her nail, her face turning red as she looked up at him. "Ah... John, do you need to relieve yourself? I'm sorry to ask something so personal, but while you're up..."

He laughed, in spite of how bad he hurt. "Honestly, I can't tell."

Blushing, Dellis grabbed the chamber pot and handed it to him, then turned around. He looked down at the basin, intent on using it, then back at her, suddenly finding himself distracted by the view. She had beautiful, wide shoulders that tapered into a tiny waist then dipped and curved perfectly into her rounded hips like an hourglass. And much to his delight, he could even see the outline of her heart-shaped bottom through her layers of skirt. The thought of putting his hands on her hips and pulling her backside against him sent a fresh jolt of desire through his loins, despite his sorry state of affairs.

"Are you okay?" she asked over her shoulder but didn't look back.

"Yes," he replied, the sound of her voice reminding him what he should be doing. As he tried to move the basin, it fell on the floor, hitting the wood with a loud clank. She leaned down and picked it up, handing it back to him.

"Do you need me to help you?" she asked, sheepishly.

"Just give me a minute." He couldn't help but chuckle at their predicament. Under different circumstances, the thought of her hands on him was an absolutely delectable prospect, and he would have taken her up on the offer, but now wasn't the time.

When he finished, she took the basin from him and helped him back on his side, pulling the blankets to his hips. He watched her as she intently cleaned his wounds, her hands gently grazing his tortured flesh, always careful not to cause him more pain. The look on her face was so serious as she inspected each wound, taking the greatest of care with him. She was the angel come to save him, but not in Heaven... she was real.

"John," she said, interrupting his thoughts. "There's a burn on your upper leg, and it looks like it went into your groin; I checked it, but..." He couldn't help but notice how she blushed, her voice trailing off.

As a gentleman, he should leave the conversation to rest, but he just couldn't help himself; she looked so lovely when she turned red. "Frankly, it's hard to tell from this vantage point, and moving around is rather challenging. Perhaps you could..."

When her eyes widened, he bit back a laugh, unable to keep a straight face when her cheeks turned from pale pink to deep crimson. "Why don't we assume everything is functioning appropriately unless I tell you otherwise?"

She nodded, her lips gently turned up in a knowing grin. "You're making fun, aren't you?"

"Yes, I was having a bit of fun with you. But I'm rather singed, and it hurts like the devil to sit." He confessed. Grabbing her hand, he slowly brought it to his lips, kissing it again. "Here you're trying to be serious, and I'm playing games. Forgive me. I'm truly grateful for your help."

She nodded, tears brimming her eyes. "You're welcome."

When she finished tending his wounds, she touched his forehead and neck, her nose scrunching up curiously. "You feel a bit feverish, are you chilled?"

He was so tired, and the room suddenly felt terribly cold, his body aching something fierce. Closing his eyes, he replied. "Yes, all the way to my bones."

She pulled the rest of the blankets over him, the warmth so enveloping he felt like he was in a nice, tight cocoon. He heard her walk to the door then stop. "Captain, I'll come in and check on you as often as I can. If you need me, call."

Unable to turn back and look at her, he said over his shoulder, "Please, call me John. That is… I would like you to call me John."

"Call me if you need me… John," she replied, and his heart leapt with the sound of his name rolling off her lips.

Chapter Thirty-Three

Leaning her back against the door, Dellis took several deep breaths, trying to slow her racing heart. She closed her eyes, remembering the sensation of his lips against her hand and the look of sadness in his sapphire-blue eyes when she tried to pull it away. Her stomach took a nosedive, and her body flushed from head to toe. Of course, he noticed, but like a gentleman, he pretended not to. *God, I must look like a chaste virgin with a crush.* Thankfully, he didn't seem to remember the night before. What would he think of her then? It was scandalous of her to do such a thing, lying naked in a bed with a man who wasn't your husband. With a groan, she put her head in her hands, trying to block out the vision of his head resting against her breast.

When she woke to the sounds of John's slow, even breathing, she panicked, forgetting how she got into that position. It was the closest she had been to a man, save the blaggards that ruined her. By all rights, she should be terrified—but she wasn't, he wouldn't hurt her, there was something innately gentle about him. Even when he was sick and fighting, he was still careful, never using the full force of his powerful frame to harm her. Too long she had prevented herself from indulging in a man's touch, and now, she could think of nothing else but the feel of his skin next to hers, wanting it again.

With a shake of her head, she willed thoughts of him away. There was work to be done and breakfast to serve. When she walked into the kitchen, her aunt was kneading dough for bread, her body rhythmically moving as she worked it back and forth on the counter. Thank God Dellis had woken up when she did, or she'd be trying to explain her way out of an awkward situation, and frankly, she wasn't quite sure how she would have accomplished that.

"How is your patient?" her aunt asked, looking over her shoulder.

Dellis put the bottle of scotch back on the counter and deposited her basket of soiled linen in the hall. "He's a little better."

"Is there something you want to tell me, Dellis?"

Sensing suggestion in her aunt's tone, Dellis opted to play innocent. After all, this was her house, she could do what she liked in it. "No, why do you ask?"

Throwing her ball of dough on the counter, Helena turned around, staring her niece down. "One of the lodgers came down inquiring about the health of the Captain. Apparently, he was injured last night? That's who you are taking care of in your room, isn't it?"

She nodded. "Yes. We found him beaten to within an inch of his life yesterday. I didn't think he was going to make it through the night."

Her aunt shook her head and opened her mouth, but Dellis turned her back. She knew what was coming: something about being a lady, and it isn't fitting, and she's not a doctor. Oh, she'd heard it all. "Dellis, this isn't behavior befitting a lady. Traveling with three men alone, and now you have a man in your private quarters."

Dellis snorted. *Predictable.* But she had no intention of having this conversation with her aunt. It was none of her business what Dellis did after hours. "Do I need to make more stew, or can I start prepping supper?" she asked, changing the subject to something more relevant.

Her aunt grabbed Dellis by the upper arm, forcing her to turn around. "Dellis, what are you doing? You have to be careful. You don't know anything about this man. Yes, he may seem like a gentleman, but what if he isn't? Think of your reputation. After all you have been through, my dear, I worry about you. You may not believe it, but I have your best interest at heart."

Taking a deep breath, Dellis prayed for patience. *God, have mercy.* "Please, stop pretending you care about my reputation. I get a regular reminder of my social status every time Uncle James comes for a visit." She noticed how her aunt winced at the mention of her husband. "Besides, the man would have died if I didn't care for him."

"You're not a doctor, my dear. Your father would have done better teaching you to be a lady in society and not how to run around taking care of sick people," Helena said, with wide eyes, her brows drawn together with strain. "Now, your uncle and I have little to work with in the way of finding you a husband. I don't want to see you end up a spinster. I want you to have a home of your own and a family."

"I may have a house and not a home, but I'm happier living out my days alone than being with a man who marries me out of pity. Now, if you will excuse me, I have to wait tables, and I need to finish the bread and make some butter before I have to go back and check on my patient again."

Dellis hated walking away from her aunt but was much too tired to argue, and there was no point to it, they would never see eye-to-eye. But Dellis refused to apologize for speaking her mind. This was her house, and it was within her rights to take care of whom she pleased.

After she finished her work, Dellis went into the dining room, putting some distance between herself and her aunt. Surprisingly, again the dining area was full of patrons drinking and eating as they chatted with each other. One of the guests had even brought a fiddle with him and was sitting by the fire plucking out a merry tune.

Dellis noticed Clark near the window, eating a plate of her ham and potato stew. Grabbing a pitcher of cider, she walked over to him and set it down on the table. "Would you care for something to drink?"

He nodded. "Yes, thank you. How is the Captain?"

"He's resting." She sat down, too tired to stand any longer, and poured him a cup. "I was worried about him bleeding out and frostbite, but we're past that now."

"Does he remember anything?"

"No, he has a large bump on the back of his head. Someone hit him pretty hard," she replied, remembering the large bloody gash on the base of John's skull. How he survived that and kept his wits was nothing short of a miracle.

"Can I speak with him?" Clark asked, dark circles under his eyes, lines etched deep in his forehead. She could read worry in his countenance, and curiosity. He wanted to get to the bottom of what happened to the Captain, and so did she, but the poor man was in no shape to offer up any information.

"Simon, perhaps tomorrow he'll be more up to conversation. Can it wait until then?"

Again, Clark nodded. "Thank you for taking care of him. I hope he isn't too much for you. He can be quite difficult when he wants to be."

"He's just fine." She blushed, remembering the joke he played on her earlier. Even as a patient, he was still charming.

"By the way, I'm very sorry about Smith. I understand he was inappropriate with you last evening," Clark said as she stood up and went for his empty plates. "I promise you, it'll never happen again, and I'll make sure the Captain is aware of it."

With everything that had happened, she'd completely forgotten about the odious man that threatened her. "Yes, well, thank you, Simon."

"John is libel to horsewhip Smith for his behavior. No pun intended, lass."

Simon must have noticed how she flinched at the word horsewhip. The irony lost on neither of them. "I would rather you not tell him. Let's just keep this between the two of us; besides, I'm sure he learned his lesson from your rebuke."

Yes, Smith had learned his lesson—but from her. He'd probably have nightmares about being scalped in his sleep for the remainder of his stay.

But at least he'd keep his distance, and that was all that mattered. She chuckled to herself as she made her way back to the kitchen. Looking at the clock, she saw it had been a couple of hours since she last checked on the Captain. Washing her hands, she dried them in her apron and put a pot of water over the fire to boil.

"Are you going back to check on him?" her aunt asked, cocking a brow

The look on her face made Dellis's temper flare. "Yes, and if you so desire, you may tell every person in this tavern what I'm doing."

She walked back to her room and slammed the door behind her, glad to be away from her aunt. Quietly, Dellis walked over to the bed, putting a hand on his forehead. "John?"

When he didn't respond, she noticed his eyes were moving rapidly under his swollen lids while he muttered inaudible words. His breathing pattern was different, more rapid and shallow than usual. Putting her basket down, she leaned over, touching his neck and chest. He was burning up with fever.

"John? Can you hear me? John?" She repeated his name several times, but he didn't respond.

Dellis tapped his cheek lightly, trying to get him to open his eyes, but he wouldn't. Panicking, she grabbed a bucket from the kitchen, ran out the back door, quickly filled the container with water and snow, and then raced back inside. Sitting down next to him on the bed, she dabbed his forehead with the cool, damp cloth. His eyes opened reflexively, then rolled back.

"John, talk to me."

Again, he opened his eyes to his name, but that was it.

"Stay with me."

Remembering her father's teachings, she took several of the linen swabs, dunked them in the cold water, rung them out, and placed them under each of his arms, near his groin, and on his forehead. His skin was blazing hot, and the sheets were soaking wet underneath him. The more she tried to cool him with the damp cloths, the more agitated he got. Muttering loudly, he thrashed around, his good arm batting back and forth, nearly hitting her. When he rolled onto his back, he cried out in pain, grabbing at the air.

"Not the gallows," he yelled. "I'll tell you everything I know. Please, don't send me there."

She grabbed his hand, holding it against her chest. "John, it's the fever. You're all right."

He looked at her with a strange, empty gaze, as if he didn't recognize her. "Sir, there was nothing there. Everything was gone. Let them go," he said, his voice sounding hoarse and breathy. He jumped suddenly, his eyes darting around the room, searching for something. "You'll all die."

"John, it's okay, you're safe."

Dellis tried to roll him back on his side, but he fought her, sitting up abruptly and looking her straight in the eyes. "I didn't know. I swear, I didn't know."

She wasn't sure if he was actually talking to her or still in the midst of a fevered nightmare. His eyes were open and wide, but it was if he was looking through her at apparitions just beyond. "Please. Please." He begged, grabbing her lower arm with a vice-like grip.

"John, you need to rest." She kept trying to get him to lie back and rest, but he wouldn't, frantically muttering to the ghosts in his mind.

"Let them go. Let them go…"

"Shh…" she said sweetly, pressing him back into the bed. Finally, he relented, lying back, his head finding the sweat-soaked pillows. "John, it's just me. It's Dellis. You're going to be okay, I promise. It's the fever that's making you confused."

"Dellis?" he said, suddenly recognizing her.

"Yes, I'm here," she whispered, smoothing back his hair. "I won't leave you."

His fevered cries ceased, though his eyes were still darting around in whatever nightmare he was reliving. She could only imagine what horrors must have been witnessed to render such a strong man helpless and petrified.

He coughed, a loud, heavy hack causing his body to spasm with each additional one. His lungs were infected—she could hear the wheezing as he labored to breathe, occasionally interrupted by another wet, barking cough.

Dellis tried to think of all the ways her father treated pneumonia, percussion on the torso, steam, liniments, none of which was an option in his current state. And she didn't believe in bleeding a patient; the idea of taking one's life essence to treat an infection was utter nonsense. Besides, the poor man had already lost his share of blood in this battle; bleeding had proven useless—as she anticipated.

"Oh, John." Her heart ached for him; he'd been through so much already, but this battle he would have to fight on his own. "I won't leave you, I promise."

He curled into the fetal position and started hacking again, his body shaking violently. He was getting worse, the muscles in his torso visibly retracting as he fought for air.

She fought back tears. There was nothing more she could do but stay with him through the worst of it and try to manage the fever.

Grabbing one of her father's journals, she leafed through the pages and started to read aloud while she swabbed John over and over, trying to break the fever. He grabbed on to her several times, anchoring himself, while he worked through spasms of painful coughs. She kept her vigil deep into the night, reciting anything that came to her mind, like how to place sutures and how to treat burns, even how to make bread. She just wanted him to know she was there, hoping the sound of her voice would keep him fighting.

When he finally rested, she let out a sigh of relief, her body exhausted beyond comprehension. Leaning down, she touched his forehead, gently brushing a lock of his hair back. He was still hot to the touch, but at least he was sleeping, finally. He looked peaceful, his eyes still underneath his lids, his long, dark lashes resting against his high cheekbones. His lips were no longer moving but gently parted, an even little wheezing noise escaping between puffs. Her heart leaped in her chest when he slid his hand up the bed and sought hers, their fingers entwining for a moment. There was something sweet about the gesture; he was so vulnerable, the walls she built around her heart started to crack under his tender, unwitting assault.

Gently placing his hand back on his chest, Dellis took a seat in the chair next to the bed and closed her eyes. She could see her father smiling, his blond hair messy from the wind, her mother's purple and white wampum necklace tied around his neck.

"Dellis, some things are in God's hands, alone. Yes, I'm a doctor, and though He gave me the knowledge and the gift to save, I have to be respectful of His greatness and wisdom." He reached down and caressed her cheek, a smile lighting up his face.

"Why would he give us the gifts, Father, if they don't work?" she asked, her young mind unable to comprehend the greater meaning of his words.

"You must always respect His wisdom, for He knows better than us what is meant to be. God gave me the gift to heal, and so He has you, and one day, you will use it to help those in need. But you must remember this: You will save and lose many lives, but always do it with a pure heart, my Dellis, and God will see you through."

"Father, please protect John." She fell asleep in the chair, holding her father's book against her heart, feeling his warmth all around her.

Chapter Thirty-Four

After several days of her gentle tending, John's fever finally broke, though he was barely able to move around, his injuries still too fresh. At least now he could breathe, the pneumonia slowly resolving, leaving him weak and plagued with a deep, painful cough that rattled in his chest.

"Good God, John, you look bloody awful. How are you feeling?" Clark asked, walking into the room.

"How do you think I feel?" John rolled his eyes, mildly annoyed with the question. "What happened to you?" he asked, noticing Clark's limp.

"I was hit in the leg; don't you remember?"

John racked his brain, trying to recall the last time he saw Clark, but came up empty. "No."

"You really don't remember, do you?" Clark sat down, removed his boot, then put his injured leg up on the bed.

"No, and it's unnerving." *To put it mildly.*

"We were ambushed on the Carry, near the fort. I was hit with a tomahawk, and the supplies were stolen. Hayes and I came back here and told you what happened, and then you disappeared. We found you a day later hanging from the rafters in a barn, beaten and half frozen to death." Clark shook his head. "I'm damn grateful we found you when we did. You wouldn't have lasted much longer."

John was fully aware of how close he had come to death, having lived it firsthand; he opted to change the subject. "How much was lost?"

"All of it."

It took everything he had to keep his temper from boiling over. Apparently, all of his plans had gone completely to hell in a matter of days, and he couldn't remember a damned thing. "Do you have any idea who did this, or where they went?"

"The weather was bad that day; we tracked them as far as we could, but they disappeared. We assume they used the river to move the supplies."

"How did it happen?" John asked, closing his eyes, trying to keep everything Clark was saying straight. John's memory was in a perpetual state of forgetfulness. Nothing would stick for more than a few moments. A knock on the door got both of their attention. "Come in," he said, his throat still sore and dry.

Smith walked in, shutting the door behind him, leaning against it.

John glanced at his friend and nodded. "Go on with your story, Simon."

"It was a total whiteout. The next thing we knew, they were coming at us from all sides, most of them on horses."

John rested his head in his hand, trying to focus through the throbbing pain behind his eyes. His chest ached as he coughed a couple of times. "They couldn't have counted on the whiteout for concealment. It was pure luck. They must have been tracking you. Can you describe any of them?" He looked up, unable to focus, actually seeing two each of Smith and Clark.

"John, I did recognize one of them," Smith said. "He was unusually tall with very long, dark hair."

He did not just say that. John clenched his fists, fighting back a tirade. "Smith, I hate to generalize, but most natives have long, dark hair. Pray, tell me you noticed something else. Perhaps moccasins? Or snowshoes? Tell me, did they have tomahawks?" The sheer stupidity of his man's comments left John in awe. "I didn't ask for the obvious. What else can you tell me?"

Smith let out a breath, taking John's rebuke with reticence. "Captain, it's not what you think. He was very, *very* tall with long, dark hair. Think about it."

"I'm not following you." John covered his mouth, another coughing fit coming on.

Smith turned and locked the door, then walked over to the bed, lowering his voice. "It was Alexei McKesson, sir."

"Are you sure?" John asked, eyeing the door.

Smith sat down on the edge of the bed, waving Clark over so they could speak quietly. "I saw him with Miss McKesson the other day. I'm sure it was him."

"Go on." John nodded.

"She could easily have told him when we left and where we were going. The Rebels are dangerously low on supplies, and that's the same village of Oneidas that was stealing from us two years ago. It's too much of a coincidence. The only place those supplies could've disappeared that quickly, on a night like that, was Fort Stanwix. It was the closest, and safest, location."

John rubbed his cheek, feeling the growth of hair against his palm as he considered the situation. There was no doubt in his mind that the Oneida were working with the Rebels—he knew that from the meeting he'd witnessed at Oriska. And it was obvious they were the ones that stole the supplies from his storage. It all made sense. But whether Dellis would betray him to her cousin—that, John couldn't answer.

"John, this is the same group of Oneidas, doing the same damn thing they were doing two years ago. Only this time, we can catch them and prove we were right."

He didn't want to think about it, his head hurt too much to concentrate, the incessant throbbing making him close his eyes. "How did you find me?"

Clark pointed to the door. "She found you, and none too soon."

"What do you mean?" John's memory was so fuzzy nothing was making sense. "I don't understand."

"When we got back the next morning, you were missing. Miss McKesson was also gone all night."

"Where was she?" John asked, looking at both of them.

"Apparently, she got caught in the snowstorm and took shelter. She claimed she never saw you, but she's the one who found you in the barn at the village." Clark added.

"The barn?" John asked, looking up at Clark. "Why was I there?"

"I don't know."

"How did she know to find me there?"

Clark shook his head. "Another good question."

Could she have something to do with his kidnapping? He could feel her gentle hands on his cheek, her soft voice in his ear comforting him. No, it couldn't be true. She had to be innocent. No one could fake such caring and concern.

"Thank God she's rather good at mending. You were in a bad way," Clark said.

"Rather convenient, isn't it?" Smith quipped, exchanging looks with Clark.

"What are you implying? Do you think Miss McKesson did this to me?" John countered, feeling suddenly protective of her. What they were suggesting was preposterous. Whatever Dellis's involvement, she would never be a party to torture. He refused to believe it. He couldn't.

"No, sir, I don't, but it's an awful coincidence you were captured the same night the supplies disappeared."

"Simon, I agree, but that doesn't mean she has anything to do with this." John shook his head. There had to more to it. "Smith, I want to you find Alexei McKesson, and I want you to keep your eyes on him. I want to know everywhere he goes, and everyone he talks to, do you understand?"

Smith nodded. "Yes, sir."

John inclined his head towards the door. "Go, now."

Once Smith left, Clark closed the door behind him and walked towards the bed, speaking in low tones. "John, I need to say something to you. It's personal, and it can't wait."

"Go ahead." Simon was one of the few good friends John had left in the world, and the only one who knew all his secrets, down to the most sordid detail. When he had faced the court-martial, Clark had staunchly defended John's character, and the man's support was one of the factors that kept John from being decommissioned.

"I'm going to give you a bit of advice; do with it what you will," Simon said quietly, his expression grave. "Miss McKesson is a lovely, kind woman, and I know you have a way with the ladies, even when you aren't trying."

John shook his head, knowing where the conversation was going. The last thing he needed was advice on how to handle women, even from his closest friend.

"No, John, listen to me. The lass is fond of you, and I sense interest on your end, despite your denials, but I think it might be clouding your judgment. It's entirely possible that she could be helping her cousin and her tribe steal from us. The woman disappeared that night, right after Hayes and I returned, and then you disappeared. She could easily have gone to warn her people that we were on to them, and they, in turn, went after you. It's too much of a coincidence."

John shook his head. It wasn't true; he refused to believe it. He'd stake his life on her innocence. "Both you and Smith are out of line. That woman saved my life, and no matter what you think, there's no way she would steal from us. All she's ever done is help us."

Clark raised his voice against the denials. "John, you're losing your objectivity where she's concerned. Trust me, you need to separate yourself from her…"

"Clark, you're bordering on impertinence—" A knock on the door prevented John from further dealing Clark a stern reprimand.

"I have some dinner for you, Captain. Sorry it's late; the tavern has been rather busy tonight," Dellis said, peeking her head around the door.

He smiled, glad to see her in spite of the conversation that preceded her interruption. "Please, come in. Clark was just leaving."

He watched her carefully, noticing her every movement as if seeing her for the first time. She was beautiful and innocent, but was she also playing him for a fool?

John waited for Clark to leave before speaking.

She looked lovely, a lock of her dark hair falling into her face as she put the tray down on the bed and sat down next to John. "How are you feeling?"

"Like I have a horse on my chest," he answered, adjusting himself so he was sitting up.

"Oh, speaking of horses, we found Viceroy. I rode him back. He's safe and sound in my stable."

"You rode him?" He shook his head, finding that incredibly hard to believe. "I think now you're teasing me."

"Really?" she said, clearly taken aback. "You don't think I could handle him?"

"You're an exceptional horsewoman, Dellis. I'll credit you with that. But..." He still didn't believe a word she said. It took him months to get Viceroy to do his bidding; the horse was notoriously stubborn, and he hated new riders. "I'm having a rather hard time with this. At times, even I struggle with him. He obstinate and requires a skilled hand to coerce him."

"Just like his master?" She cocked a brow, a grin tugging the corner of her lips. "Actually, I mounted him easily. All he needed was a well-placed stroke to his ego and a few gentle words, and he was eating out of my hands."

"Are you referring to the horse, or me?" he asked, enjoying this new-found playful side of her character. Yes, she liked to banter, but never had she been remotely suggestive.

"A lady wouldn't comment." She handed him a plate full of eggs and toast, a mischievous smile on her lips. "But does it matter?"

Yes, it did. But he certainly couldn't say that, so he opted for the more diplomatic route. "Well, it would have worked on me." He grinned and took the plate from her, his stomach growling from the delicious aroma.

"And apparently, it did for Viceroy, too. He's smarter than I gave him credit for."

As she got up and started to walk away, he grasped her hand. "Stay with me for a while. I'm tired of being alone."

She hesitated for a moment then nodded. "Let me get some tea."

Dellis walked out of the room then reappeared a couple of minutes later with a pot and two cups on her tray. She poured some tea for both of them, and then sat down in the chair next to the bed, sipping it quietly. There was a faraway look in her eyes as she stared into the fire; he wondered what she was thinking.

"May I ask you a question?" he asked, his voice sounding raw. "It's personal."

"Only if I get to ask you one after." She sipped her tea, winking at him over the rim of her cup.

"All right, fair is fair." He nodded, appreciating her sense of opportunism. "Why don't you have a husband?"

She closed her eyes for a second, her face looking serene in the firelight, as if she was considering his question carefully. Putting her cup down on the saucer, she turned to him. "I'll answer your question, but are you sure you want to know the answer? I'm afraid it might change your opinion of me."

"Yes, very much," he replied, wanting to hear the truth from her lips, not the convoluted story he heard whispered around town. "Dellis, nothing will change what I think of you. Nothing."

She visibly swallowed, preparing herself, her brown eyes searching his as if she were questioning the truth in his words. When she finally began, there was a tremor in her voice. "I was betrothed to my cousin's best friend, Patrick Armstrong-Jones. I introduced you to him at The Kettle."

She stopped for a moment, taking a deep breath and audibly letting it out. "He was a good match for me, and his father was quite wealthy and well respected, mine, not so much. My father was the town doctor. He was married to a native woman, which isn't that uncommon in this area, but some people still find it inappropriate. Regardless, Patrick convinced his father to let us marry. At the time, he was a soldier in His Majesty's army, and that made my father happy." She paused, looking towards the fire. He noticed how proudly she sat, her back ramrod straight, head held high, but her hands were trembling, betraying her austere calm.

"Two years ago, the Regulars came to our village looking for stolen weapons. My grandfather and the rest of the men were away at a Confederacy meeting in Onondaga. We were alone, unprotected, save a few guards and my poor, sweet brother. My mother told Stuart and me to hide and not to come out, no matter what. I heard someone call for her and my father, so she went out and tried to reason with them." Her voice cracked as she stood up and walked over to the fireplace.

"I hid under one of the cots. When my mother returned, someone was with her, I could hear him talking, but I couldn't see him. She told him she knew he was coming after our tribe to get even with her for marrying my father. He accused my father of lying about him to win her hand. Next thing I knew, they were fighting; I could see them rolling around on the ground, and the man stabbed her. Stuart came running through the door, but when he saw my mother on the floor fighting, he stood there, stunned, unable to move. I was so afraid, and I didn't know what to do. When I heard Stuart screaming, I crawled out from under the cot, and one of the men grabbed me and threw me against the table. I knew what he wanted; I fought back, but he threatened to kill my brother if I didn't stop. He ripped my dress, and then he…"

She didn't need to say more; it was obvious what came next.

After collecting herself for a moment, she started to speak again, "They used me, two of them. When it was over, the last thing I remember was my head hitting the table and everything going black, I woke two days later and learned my mother was dead. I was sick with fever for weeks after. Apparently, they made Stuart watch as they did that to me. The poor dear, he didn't speak for months after that. Stuart always had problems, but it made them so much worse." She stood with her back to him, her hands braced on the mantle over the fireplace, supporting herself.

"Most of the women had been raped, and more than half of them were dead. Kateri was the only one that got away unscathed. As you're aware, she claims one of the soldiers took pity on her and let her go. They took three of our women hostage, and their bodies turned up several days later near the village. One of them had been pregnant; her name was Mary. They murdered a pregnant woman. What kind of fiends would do such a thing?" she asked, looking back at him, shaking her head.

"My father had many contacts still in the military. He questioned Guy Johnson and then the colonel at Fort Niagara, but both turned him away. They refused to acknowledge what happened. My father knew the Major who led the regiment and challenged him to a duel. When I found out about it, I went after him, but by the time I got there, my father was dead, shot in the back. His second died a couple of days later from a bullet wound in his chest."

John closed his eyes, the whole story coming together for him at that moment.

"I *will* find the man that did this someday, and I'll make him pay, I swear it. I don't care about myself; it's for them," she said, her voice cracking.

He could tell she was crying, though her back was still to him.

"For now, all I have are the cryptic words my mother said and a random name. But someday, it will make sense. I know it."

"What name?" he asked. Could it be DeLancie?

Turning around, she wiped the tears from her eyes, composing herself. "When word got out, as you can imagine, no details were spared. Patrick broke our betrothal. My Uncle James paid his father for the embarrassment and inconvenience of the situation. When my father's youngest brother, Dane, found out what happened, he came here and offered to take Stuart and me back to Scotland with him. But I couldn't leave, this is my home."

She walked back to his bedside slowly, and then sat down on the edge, her hip close to his thigh. They sat quietly for several moments save the crackle of the fire. "My grandmother passed away five days after my mother, devastated by her loss. But before she died, she told me she cursed the man that did this to us."

He remembered seeing the ancient woman, chanting and pointing to him, the bloody rag held to her breast. He could never forget her. They'd met every night thereafter in his dreams. "What was the curse?" he asked.

"That his fate would forever be tied to our village until justice was served," she replied, her eyes full of hatred.

Justice.

He didn't know how to respond. *What did it mean, until justice was served?* There was no justice, not for any of them. *And who will pay the price? Me? DeLancie?*

"This house is all I have left of my father. He loved it. My Uncle Dane is very wealthy; actually, he's a duke, though I don't know how the youngest brother inherits such a title. Anyway, he built and furnished this house as a wedding gift for my parents. I moved down here so I could let the rooms upstairs, but little good that has done me. I've sold all of the more valuable furniture save what is in your room. Eventually, I'll have to sell the house. My Uncle James is determined to see it done, and I fear I can't fight it any longer."

"Where will you go?" John asked, an ache developing in his heart at the thought of her selling her beloved house.

"My uncle and aunt's farm. Either they will find someone who will marry me, or I'll live out my days helping them maintain their house. I've written to my Uncle Dane several times asking for help, but he's never responded." Her eyes teared up again, one solitary drop rolling down her porcelain cheek.

He fisted the blanket beneath him, resisting the urge to wipe it away.

"If I could have one wish, it would be to know the truth. I've never understood why the Regulars came, and my father would never explain to me what the conversation between the man and my mother was about."

John looked away, guilt getting the better of him. Because of his actions, her life had gone to ruin. Part of him wanted to confess his sins and beg for her forgiveness, and part of him wanted to take her in his arms and comfort her. She deserved to know the truth, but no matter how much he wanted to give it to her, he couldn't. There was so much he didn't know, and there were parts of her story he didn't understand, either. Reaching over, he took her hand, squeezing it, giving all the comfort he could offer her at that moment.

She worked to maintain her composure, her back straight, her head held high. Wiping her eyes with the heel of her hand, she looked at him and smiled. What a strange dichotomy of character, to smile when one was confessing the ruin of their whole world. What a strong woman. She put him to shame; his guilt was nothing compared to her loss.

"So, now I'm permanently ruined because of this, by no fault of my own. Everyone in town talks about Dellis, the whore who sleeps with Regulars. That's what Jussie was referring to the other day. And poor Stuart, the horrors he was forced to witness. I blame myself for how he behaves, that's why I keep letting him come back. His mind was addled before it even happened, and he didn't have the strength or ability to cope."

"What do you mean?" John asked, confused.

"Stuart was always a quiet, precocious child, a lot like my father, then around age fourteen, he started to see and hear things that weren't there. My mother's people thought it was the spirits talking to him, but my father said it was an affliction of the blood that ran in generations of our family. After that, Stuart was distraught and difficult to control, so he stayed with my people in the village where they looked on his disease as a gift from the spirits as opposed to believing he was a lunatic. After this all happened, he was unable to deal with the loss of our family, and I think part of him blames himself for what happened to me."

"Dellis, how did you find me?" he asked, desperate to know the truth.

"I wanted some fresh air, so I went out for a ride. It was foolish, I know. The weather was bad, and I had to stay in the village overnight. When I was leaving, my cousin found a glove where I was stabling my horse. When I got back, I went into your room looking for clues and found another glove of the same kind lying on the floor. It dawned on me then where you were." She shrugged. "It was a pure coincidence, though a lucky one. You wouldn't have made it another day."

There was no wavering in her answer, just her usual frankness. Knowing her impulsive nature, the idea that she would ride out in a winter storm without thinking it through was indeed plausible. He couldn't help but believe her—the story was too imperfect to be a lie. Slowly, he brought her hand to his lips, brushing them lightly against her fingers. To his surprise, she didn't pull away; instead, she stretched her fingers out and rested the palm of her hand on his cheek. He closed his eyes, her touch like salve to his aching, exhausted body.

"I owe you my life."

She smiled, pushing a stray lock of hair behind his ear. "That might be true, but you also owe me a chance to ask you a question."

He laughed, rolling his eyes. "Ask your question."

"When you were feverish, you cried out several times that you were sorry, that it was your fault."

He looked away, unable to face her as she repeated his fevered confessions.

"You were a soldier, weren't you?" she asked in a quiet voice. "Did something happen to you?"

How am I supposed to answer that question? With more lies? There were so many building on top of each other, he was suffocating under the weight.

"There are things about me I'm not proud of"—he paused, taking a deep breath, choosing his words carefully—"particularly in my past. I know you understand that."

She nodded.

"I wish I could tell you about them now, but I can't. Not until I find a way to make it right."

She reached over and took his hand in her own, gently squeezing his fingers. "You will find a way. I know it. You're a good man, Captain John Anderson."

The irony of her comforting him, the sound of his nom-de-guerre, almost made him sick. He had never met a more unselfish person in his life. "I promise, someday, I'll tell you everything."

"I believe you." She smiled, nodding her head. "Since you won't answer that question, I believe I get to ask you another one."

285

"Fair enough." He laughed. She was relentless.

"Where are you from? I know you grew up in England, but where is your home?"

"I don't have one," he replied, bitterness in his voice he'd long suppressed. *Home.* He'd forgotten what it felt like to have one. "The place you're referring to is near Bristol. I left when I was seventeen, and I've never gone back. I can't go back. I'm no longer welcome."

"Then you're alone, too?" she stated more than asked, sadness in the depths of her lovely, dark eyes.

He nodded, her astute observation surprisingly painful when vocalized. They were both very much alone in the world.

"Well, you're welcome here, John, as long as it is still The Thistle. Now, neither of us is alone."

"Thank you." Unable to resist, he lifted her hand to his lips again.

Instead of pulling away, her fingers slowly glided down his cheek to the base of his neck, fingering the little cross Kateri gave him. Dellis's touch was so innocent, yet utterly intoxicating, his body reacted, the pressure between his legs making him ache to reach out and take her.

"You should get some rest," she said, breaking the spell, her face and throat flushed.

It took him a moment to recover, every inch of his body focused on what he wanted with an intensity bordering on need.

As she opened the door, it dawned on him, something he meant to ask her earlier. "Dellis, you never said what his name was."

"Whose name?" she asked, her face still flushed.

"The man who killed your father."

The firelight cast a shadow on her face, but he could see her usually warm brown eyes turn cold. "His name was John Carlisle, and someday he'll pay for what he did to my family."

286

Chapter
Thirty-Five

Dellis woke to sun streaming through the window, a ray directed right at her eyes. She'd barely slept, wondering what he must think of her now that he knew the truth. He said nothing, no judgment, just stoic silence while his hand reached for hers. It was a simple gesture, yet she found the solace in it that had eluded her for the past two years. It was as if he understood her pain, shared it with her, even if only for a moment. *Why did you tell him?* Groaning, she buried her head in her pillow, trying to forget the entirety of their conversation, wishing she could take it back.

Getting up quickly, she washed and dressed in a light-gray wool dress, pinning her hair out of her face, covering the back of it with a white cotton cap. Just as she went for the door, Stuart came barreling in, a fetid odor following him as he pushed her out of the way and started tearing through the dresser. He was filthy, as usual, his clothes caked in layers of dirt, his shoes soaked, leaving muddy footprints wherever he stepped.

"Stuart, what are you doing here? Where have you been?" she asked, watching as her brother searched his drawers. She'd slept in his room, figuring he wouldn't be back now that she'd thrown him out, but apparently, she was wrong.

"I need clothes," he replied, slamming the drawer shut so hard the chest shook.

He was lying. The only time he changed clothes or took a bath was when she or Alexei forced one. No, Stuart wanted something. Suddenly, he turned to her, his eyes darting around the room, then he got down on his hands and knees and looked under the bed.

"There's nothing under there." She shook her head. *God give her strength to deal with him.*

Stuart stood up quickly and looked over her shoulder into the parlor. Following his gaze to the silver candlesticks on the mantle, she realized what he came for—money. Walking past her, he bumped into the door frame, leaving a bloody print on the wood as he stomped into the sitting room.

"Stuart, where have you been?" her aunt asked, suddenly appearing in the doorway. He ignored her, walking into the kitchen, grabbing a biscuit from the counter and stuffing it in his mouth, crumbs sticking in his scraggly beard.

"Dellis, there's a gentleman in the dining room who'd like to speak with the Captain."

"Do you recognize him?" Dellis asked, watching as Stuart drank directly from one of the pitchers of cider, the liquid dripping down his chin and staining his shirt. Grabbing it from him, she pulled out a tankard, slamming it down on the table in front of him.

"No, but he's quite handsome."

Dellis noticed how her aunt's voice perked up—the last thing Dellis was in the mood for was her aunt's matchmaking. Besides, being flirtatious with one of the Captain's associates seemed in poor taste. "The Captain isn't up to visitors. Did he give his name? Perhaps Clark can assist with whatever he needs."

"No, he didn't say; he just asked to meet with the Captain."

"Watch after Stuart, please." She deserved to have a taste of Stuart's reckless behavior; perhaps next time, she might stand up for Dellis when Uncle James raved about her brother disappearing.

"I'll be back." She removed her apron and walked into the dining room. The mysterious visitor was standing with his back to her. Hearing her approach, he turned around and removed his hat. "Hello, Miss."

He was handsome, devastatingly so, not with blond hair or boyish looks like John, but dark and strikingly masculine. She blushed when he smiled; his full lips were sensuous, a day's worth of dark hair already showing on his jawline.

Her hands trembled as she tucked a stray lock of hair behind her ear, her heart fluttering like a bird in a cage. "I understand you're here to see Captain Anderson?"

He nodded, his eyes searching her face as if he recognized her. "That's correct."

There was something strangely familiar about his voice, but she couldn't quite place it. He had a bit of accent, but not Scottish, though it was similar. "The Captain isn't here at the moment. Would you like to speak with one of his men?"

"No, I need to speak with the Captain, personally. It's about business," he said with a pleasant smile that lit up his face.

She had to force herself not to stare at him. He had the most captivating dark eyes, with something deep and mysterious hiding in their depths, adding to his allure. "If you are staying nearby I can give him a message."

He rubbed his chin, looking over her shoulder towards the bar. "May I at least get something to drink before you send me on my way?"

"Oh, where are my manners? Please, take a seat." She stammered, gesturing to the nearest table.

He pulled out the chair and sat down.

She couldn't help but notice how slow and methodical his movement was, as if his every step was done with purpose. He was elegantly dressed in a forest-green jacket and breeches, the cut so precise it fit him like a second skin, accentuating his broad shoulders and muscular arms. His black leather boots shined, perfectly polished.

"Can you bring me something hot? It's quite cold out, Miss..." he asked, purposely trailing off. "I'm sorry I didn't get your name."

"McKesson, Dellis McKesson. Please, forgive me, and you are?"

289

"Miss McKesson." He said her name several times, as if he had heard it before. "Dellis, that's rather unique."

The way her name rolled off his tongue made her heart skip a beat. And he pronounced it Day-lis, the correct Scottish way. "Thank you. It's Scottish. My father was from Scotland."

"It's as lovely as the lady it belongs to."

She blushed instantly, from head to toe. He really was quite charming. "If you'll excuse me for a moment, I'll bring you some tea."

Dellis hurried to the kitchen, her heart still fluttering from his hypnotic gaze. Putting the kettle on the fire, she turned to her aunt, smiling. "You're right. He *is* handsome."

"Did he say what he wanted?"

"Just to talk to the Captain," Dellis replied, reaching for a cup and saucer from the cupboard. As she prepared tea, she could hear Stuart yelling in the hall, his fists pounding on her door. Putting the kettle on, she walked into the hall to investigate.

"Why is this locked?" He yanked at the door handle, trying to pull the door open. Turning around, he came at her, his eyes full of rage. "Open the door."

Pushing her brother away, she put her back against it. "This is my room. There's nothing of yours in here."

"Why is it locked?" he yelled, his face inches from hers.

When he tried to push her out of the way, she stretched out her arms, grabbing the wood frame, protecting her door and, ultimately, what was inside. "Since the lodgers moved in, I've been locking my room."

Stuart grabbed her, his fingernails digging into her arms, as he tried to pry her away from the door, but she held fast, determined to keep him out. The last thing she needed was him disturbing John while he was still recovering.

"Open it." Stuart demanded, slamming her against the door, her head hitting the wood with a loud thud.

No longer frightened by his violent behavior, she stood her ground, meeting him eye-to-eye. "Stuart, you aren't welcome here. Now, please, leave, before I get one of the Captain's men to escort you out."

She grabbed his wrist in mid-air, stopping his hand before it connected with her cheek. There was no way she was going to allow her brother to hit her again.

Her aunt appeared behind him, a look of horror on her face. "Stuart, what are you doing?"

Dellis didn't give him a chance to tell any more of his lies. It was time her aunt faced up to the truth. "He needs money, and that's why he wants in my room," she answered. "He thinks I've hidden Father's silver in there."

"Stuart, is this true?" she asked, looking at him.

Ignoring them both, he raced into the kitchen, grabbed some bread off the counter, and ran out the front door, nearly hitting their guest on the way out.

Dellis dusted herself off, walked past her aunt, and finished preparing the tea. There was nothing left to be said, and now it was time she and her husband accepted the reality of Stuart. He was beyond help.

The handsome stranger was still sitting at the table, looking out the window. Putting the tray down, she poured him a cup of tea. "I'm sorry it took so long."

"Please, no need to apologize. Is everything all right? I heard some commotion, and then a lad came tearing through here."

"I'm sorry, that was my brother. I hope he didn't disturb you," she replied. "He can be a bit of a handful."

"Not in the least; you seem to handle him well." He smiled, giving her a look of approval. "Great results can be achieved with small forces."

"Thank you." Dellis knew there was a compliment buried in his cryptic statement, but she was too jarred from her fight with Stuart to make sense of it.

"Now, I'll have my tea and then be on my way." He sipped it, lifting the cup to his lips with the delicate precision of a socialite. "This is quite good."

She nodded. "We are fortunate with the Captain staying here; he does keep us stocked with some excellent tea."

"Yes, he's always been known for his taste in the finer things." His eyebrow cocked slightly, as his gaze boldly dipped to her bodice, making blush and her tingle all over. He finished his tea then reached into his pocket, pulling out a letter. "Could you please see that he gets this?"

She took it from him, his fingers grazing hers intentionally. Pulling away quickly, she stuffed the letter into her pocket, hiding her shaking hand. "I will."

The man stood up, put his hat on, and bowed to her; when he looked up, his lips twisted into a smirk. "It's been my pleasure, Miss McKesson."

She nodded, watching him leave, suddenly realizing she never got his name.

Chapter Thirty-Six

"Gentlemen, you will each take ten paces then you'll turn and fire," John said, watching both men remove their coats then take one last look at each other before they turned back to back.

"Are you sure you want to do this? You're a doctor, not a soldier, McKesson. Does the Navy actually teach you how to use one of these?" DeLancie asked, holding up his pistol, shaking it, purposely antagonizing his opponent.

"You murdered my wife… your men raped my daughter; of course I want to do this." Stephen looked at DeLancie then at John. "You're both a disgrace to the uniform, raping and murdering innocent women, leaving bodies defiled in the woods—it's barbarous."

John felt every bit a disgrace, the actions of him and his men were not worthy of soldiers in His Majesty's army… but of savages. The doctor was justified in wanting revenge after what happened to his family, but dueling DeLancie was a mistake; he was an impeccable shot—this would only end one way.

"Gentlemen, are you ready?" he yelled, the two men taking their places, back-to-back. It was ominously quiet, the only sound that could be heard was the bubbling and rushing of the river nearby. The sun peeked through the clouds, reflecting off the morning fog that carried over the river banks, swirling around the two men like a ghostly mist. Suddenly, a flock of ravens flew overhead, their loud, shrill cries carrying over the dueling field, an omen of what was soon to come.

293

John took a deep breath, trying to calm his racing heart. This was so wrong. Finally, with a heavy heart, he yelled, "One."

The two men took their first step. John and the doctor's second exchanged quick glances, as gentlemen, both men understood their roles in the test of honor. They would see to it that this was a fair fight, though the word fair was not in DeLancie's vocabulary, nor was honor.

"Two." Both men advanced another step. John took a deep breath—ten more to go. How could it have come to this? Why was this happening? He tried to talk the Major out of the duel, but he was enraged and boastful, as if he wanted this, and it was all part of his plan.

"Three."

Suddenly, DeLancie whipped around, aimed his gun, and fired, hitting the doctor in the back, right between the shoulder blades. A fatal shot. Blood spattered from the wound as the doctor crumpled to the ground. Out of the corner one eye, John spotted the doctor's second aiming his pistol at DeLancie. With lightning speed, John pulled out his pistol and fired, dropping the man where he stood, the body rolling down the hill.

"Good eyes, Johnny," DeLancie said, looking back with a smile. "That's why you're my second in command; you never miss. I've trained you well."

Oh, God. John put the gun down, his hands shaking violently. He looked up at his superior, their gazes meeting over the distance, the horror of what DeLancie had done leaving John speechless. DeLancie had broken the rules of the duel.

"Let's get out of here, Johnny, we have work to do."

John composed himself, ran to the doctor, and rolled him over; his blue eyes were fixed, staring lifelessly into the heavens. Gently, John ran his fingers over the man's eyelids, closing them forever. The doctor's second was lying on his side, making a painful gasping noise as his hand clutched the wound in his chest. When John leaned down to help the man, he spat, a look of disgust on his face.

"Don't touch me, fiend." The man scooted away, averting his gaze. He wouldn't look at John, not even a sidelong glance, and when he tried to cover the wound with a handkerchief, the man pushed John's hand away.

Wiping the spit off his cheek, John looked around in horror, the gravity of the situation finally manifesting.

"I didn't do this," he yelled, waking suddenly. "No!"

Opening his eyes, John sat up abruptly, his gaze darting around the room. There was no field and no bodies lying in the grass, just two old chests of drawers, and pale-blue walls surrounding him. It was morning, the first rays of the day peeking through the faded linen curtains that were drawn over the window. Lying back on the bed, he looked up at the canopy, wiping the sweat from his forehead, trying to slow his racing heart. It was just a dream. *Thank God.* But it felt so real. He could still smell the morning dew in his nose and feel the brisk morning air, sending a chill down his spine. What he wouldn't do to take that moment back.

From the hall, he could hear yelling, the door rumbling back and forth on its hinges, bending and flexing as if it would burst open any second— something was amiss. Carefully sitting up, he threw his legs over the side of the bed, determined to help no matter how his body protested. When the door opened suddenly behind him, he glanced over his shoulder; it was Dellis with a tray of food in her arms. There was a scowl on her lips and furrow on her brow when she noticed he was sitting up.

"You should be resting," she said tersely, putting the tray down on the edge of the bed and rushing over to help him. She wrapped her arm around his waist and gently helped him back into bed, a whiff of lavender and vanilla perfume filling his nose. Grabbing a couple of pillows from next to him, she leaned over again and stuffed them behind his back, propping him up. "You've been through so much, and you're still as weak as a newborn colt. Have patience, John."

"Fine." He nodded, watching her back away, noticing every little curve of her long, graceful neck as it sculpted into her exquisite décolletage. And what an unintentional tease she was, affording just the slightest glimpse of her breasts beneath her well-tucked kerchief. His eyes drank up every dip and crevasse they could take in, yet still longing for more.

She slid the tray over to him and sat down in the chair next to the bed.

"Dellis, is everything all right? I heard noises, and I thought you might need help."

She shook her head. "Stuart showed up earlier raving like a lunatic. He was looking for money. When he realized the door to this room was locked, he got flustered and started banging on it." Pausing for a moment, she poured some milk into his teacup, and then filled it with the dark, aromatic brew, finishing it off with a bit of sugar.

When she handed it to him, he looked up at her in wonder. Just how he liked it.

"He's gone now, at least until the next time he needs something."

"Thank you." He sipped it, the warmth soothing his sore throat. "How did you know that I like my tea this way?"

With a shrug, she said, "I'm a waitress and sometimes a bartender. It's my job to be observant."

But it was more than that. He'd drank tea with many ladies, most of them his paramours, and they never even noticed how he prepared it. She was very observant. Almost too observant. This would not do. Things were happening too fast. He liked having *this* woman make his tea for him, and he liked eating her food and having her care for him. Every time she walked into the room, he wanted her to stay longer. Her smell. Her eyes. And, by God, the way her body moved with unwitting sensuality. She was drawing him into her thrall, and he was going willingly, like a besotted fool with his first infatuation. It was time to put a stop to it. He didn't want to hurt her, and inevitably that was going to happen, especially when she learned the truth about him.

Taking a deep breath, he took one step towards the unavoidable. "Dellis, now that I'm on the mend, I should probably move up to my room."

Apparently, it was a more significant step than he had anticipated; her eyes cast down, and she nodded, looking almost disappointed. "I understand," she whispered, chewing her bottom lip.

"I'm grateful for everything you've done for me. But I don't want to risk further tarnishing your reputation by being found in your private quarters.

I know you understand that. It's for the best." After she'd left the night before, he'd spent the remainder of the evening dreaming of holding her naked and warm in his arms. He wanted her. And though she was guarded, he could see it in her eyes; she wanted him, too. He had to do this, for both their sakes. He needed to stay focused on his mission.

After a moment of sullen, awkward silence, she finally spoke. "Perhaps you're right, it would be for the best to move you back to your room. But just because you go back upstairs doesn't mean you're ready to be up and about. Your wounds aren't healed yet, and you're still very weak."

"Understood." He nodded, appreciating her genuine concern in spite of her obviously hurt feelings. "I'll eat, get dressed, and then make my way upstairs."

"I'll get help." Getting up quickly, she scurried to the door, avoiding his gaze.

It was evident that she was very upset. Just as he started to dig into a plate of sausage and eggs and a side of fried potatoes, she showed up at the door with Clark and Hayes, ready to move John upstairs.

"No breakfast?" he asked, looking up at her with pleading eyes, his fork still in mid-air, a thick piece of sausage impaled on it just waiting to be eaten. "Can this not wait a few minutes until I finish?"

"No, it can't wait," she said, taking the plate from his hands and then his fork, depositing both on her tray. "We need to get you upstairs before more of the patrons start coming in for breakfast."

His stomach growled loudly, watching his half-eaten tray of food get boosted up on her shoulders and taken away to be discarded. He felt like a hungry dog begging for scraps. Perhaps he should have waited to tell her he needed to move until after he ate? He didn't think she would take it this badly.

"Okay, Captain, we'll walk together." Clark took up position under John's right arm while Hayes came around the other side and did the same. Together, the two men helped John up, using their arms and body weight to support him. "Just lean into us if you need to."

When they passed through the kitchen, Dellis was already dumping his leftover food into the trash and wiping down his tray. John resisted the urge to call her out on her behavior, biting back his frustration instead. She was hurt, her ego was bruised, and his stomach was on the receiving end of her anger. *Women.* Their methods of revenge were just effective as men's and twice as crafty.

When the trio passed through the bar into the dining room, John could feel the curious glances from the tavern patrons sitting at the bar. Thomas, the bartender, even winced when he looked up and saw the three men ambulating from the kitchen. John hadn't seen his reflection in days, but from the expressions on the patrons' faces, things couldn't be good.

Just as they passed the front door it flew open, bringing with it a gust of wintry wind and Celeste in a swirl of royal-blue satin.

"Oh, Johnny, what happened?" she said with a sad, lady-like gasp. She made a show of running over to him and taking his face in her hands, kissing both of his cheeks and then his sore, swollen eyelids. "Only you can look so handsome and so God awful at the same time."

"Celeste, can we do this upstairs before I fall over from exhaustion?" Even with his men's assistance, he wasn't sure how much longer he would be able to stand up. The room was starting to spin with each passing moment; his eyes were full of black, hazy stars.

"Oh Johnny!" she cried, her eyes brightening with beautiful, premeditated tears. She was purposely creating a scene and doing an effective job of it. All eyes were on the four of them while forks full of food were being shoveled into mouths. The guests probably thought this was practice for dinner theater with the scandalous way it all looked, or that Dellis was, in fact, running a questionable establishment.

John let out a groan. If he could've buried his head in the sand, he would have. *So much for covert operations.*

"You poor darling," Celeste said, following them up the stairs. "I've never seen you look this bad. No wonder you haven't come to see me. And here I thought it was because you didn't want to be with me anymore."

He rolled his eyes, trying to ignore the incessant banter that was coming from behind him. It was hard enough, physically, getting up the stairs, the three men working together, but listening to her prattle on was finishing off his nerves nicely. He hated drama, and Celeste had more than a Shakespearean flare for it, The Globe would have been honored with such a performance.

Grateful when they finally made it to the room, he pointed to the chair behind the desk, unable to go any further. Leaning forward, he closed his eyes and took several deep breaths, trying to stop the room from spinning and his temper from boiling over.

When he opened them again, Dellis was on her knees in front of him, her eyes wide with concern. "John, are you all right? You should have eaten more; now look at you, you're white as a sheet. Well, when I have a free moment, I'll have something brought up for you."

Oh, now she's concerned about my stomach? Is she not the one who took my breakfast away five minutes ago? What sort of game is she playing? Women. Damned infuriating. He should give up on them entirely. "I'm fine. Please, if you don't mind, I'd like to speak with Mrs. Allen." He paused, looking up at Celeste, and then said, "In private. You can bring me something up later after she leaves."

Dellis stood up, her dark eyes casting a look of reproach at Celeste then at him. "By the way, Captain, a gentleman stopped by earlier and left this for you." Dellis reached into her pocket and pulled out a letter, handing it to him.

"Who is it from?" There was no address on it, only his name written in an unfamiliar script.

She shook her head. "I don't know. The man left before I could get his name. He said he was a business acquaintance of yours. I assumed you could figure it out."

"Thank you," he replied, snatching the letter from her and placing it on the desk. Taking several deep breaths, he waited until Dellis and everyone else had left the room before he addressed Celeste. "What can I do for you? As you can see, I'm a bit under the weather."

As expected, she was dressed to impress, her hair perfectly coiffed on top of her head, her ample bosom on display over the neckline of her blue dress and a tinge of rouge on both cheeks. He used to find her strikingly beautiful in her fashionable attire and makeup, now she just looked gaudy, like she was trying hard for attention but overdoing it. When she walked around the desk and planted her bottom on top of it, he knew what was coming next, and he was in no mood for it. *Women.*

"I haven't seen you in over a week. I figured it was long enough for you to cool down so that we could discuss business. Now I find someone has been using you for their amusement."

"I don't know that I would call this amusement." He snorted. Being flogged, burned, and beaten was not his idea of amusement; he didn't need to remember the explicit details to feel strongly about that.

She shook her head, running her fingers under his collar, massaging his neck. "I know exactly what will make you feel better." He groaned in pain when she grabbed his hand and put it on her thigh, the wounds around his wrist smarting.

"Celeste, while I appreciate the gesture, I haven't the energy to get from this chair to the door, much less get my cock to stand long enough to please you. Sorry to disappoint," he said, pushing her hand away. "And I think I made myself very clear at our last meeting. We no longer have any business to discuss, except perhaps the money you owe me."

Angrily, she pulled away, stomped around to the other side of the desk, and planted her fists on her hips like a petulant child. "John, you're acting like a brute, and I don't like it."

"I'm sorry I displease you so much. Perhaps you should leave now and spare yourself my company," he retorted, too tired and sore to further play games.

She turned up her pert nose as if she smelled something foul, and then said, "I wonder if it's not the recent company you've been keeping that's brought about this sudden change in you."

"What are you talking about?"

"I see the way she looks at you, like an innocent at a society ball, and you're her first dance. For God's sake, she was just on her knees in front of you, practically begging you to take her. But to be honest, I never pictured you preferring that type of woman. Perhaps you have a bit of your former superior's predilection."

"Celeste, you go too far," he said, dangerously close to losing his temper. Being compared to DeLancie was far from a compliment, and something John didn't take lightly. And her vitriolic words about Dellis were uncalled for, albeit correct, she did wear her emotions on her shoulder for everyone to see. "Miss McKesson is my innkeeper. It *is* a business arrangement."

"From my experience, most of your business arrangements involve your personal services as part of the deal. You're no better than one of my ladies, getting paid for services rendered. The irony is they're called whores, and you're called a scoundrel. How it's shameful for a woman to sell herself and a badge of honor for a man is rather vexing. I fail to see the difference between the two."

"Enough." Unwilling to let her bait him a moment longer, he stood up, putting his hand on the table to support himself. "Celeste, it's time to go."

She shrugged her pretty, silk-clad shoulders as if what he said had no bearing on her. "Fine, I have others interested in investing in my little venture. One I can think of in particular has a lot of money and access to the right social circles."

Walking over to the mirror, she smoothed a loose curl back into place, admiring her reflection for a moment. Turning to him, she smiled, her finely arched brow raising suggestively. He knew that look: she was about to deal her *coup de grâce*. "I'll be traveling to Niagara, in case you change your mind, and I know you will. It's the chase you love, and the variety, of course, and I can provide it. You'll grow tired of your provincial innocent once she's smitten and wanting a proposal. You can't help yourself, John, your appetite demands more than any one woman can offer, especially one like her. This was your last chance. Next time you come back, it will be on my terms."

That was the last straw. He pounded his fist on the desk, ignoring how it smarted from the effort. "Celeste, you go too far." He refused to be threatened by a deceitful, malevolent woman he'd been bankrolling for the past two years. "You forget, I have the arrest warrant."

"And what will you do with it, John, in your current state? You can barely get out of that chair," she said with a voice full of humor and eyes shooting daggers.

"Leave now." He hissed, dangerously close to throttling her. "And make no mistake, I'll get my money from you, one way or the other."

Celeste picked up her skirts and practically skipped to the door, turning back to him just before she opened it. "When you're well enough, I dare you to try. I relish the thought. Making-up was always my favorite part of fighting with you. You're rather inspired when you're penitent. Until then, Captain Carlisle."

With that, she threw back her shoulders, picked up her skirts, and started down the hall as if she'd just turned down a dance with an unworthy suitor.

"Well, she's none too happy with you," Clark said from the doorway, watching Celeste stomp down the hall, her long, brown curls bouncing with each step. "There's nothing good that can come from that woman, John."

"I'll deal with her later," John replied, looking back at his friend. But Clark was right; Celeste was trouble, John had known that since the very beginning but ignored his intuition. The first time he saw her at her place in the Holy Ground, she was as enticing as Eve, in her hands the apple that he craved, money to purchase his commission back and all the women and drink he could consume. Now Celeste was drunk with power—addicted to it. She was a loose cannon, vacillating in whatever direction suited her fancy, and allowing the Rebels to trade secrets in her house was only a glimpse of what she could accomplish if crossed. From now on, he would tread lightly with her.

Trying to forget their exchange, John grabbed the letter off the desk and opened it.

Dear Sir,

Unfortunately, it would seem that I have missed you. I would like to have had the chance, in person, to show something very unique to you. As a merchant that is well traveled, you often covet what belongs to another. I would gladly show it to you if only I had met with you. Upon return to Tryon County, I will come and seek you out, if only to get your approval and see if you want it.

Difficulties be damned...

"Who's that from?" Clark asked, stuffing a piece of bread that suddenly appeared in his hand into his mouth.

John looked up, eyeing the bread, and then replied, "It's not signed, but it's closed with the Eighth Regiment motto." He reread the letter, trying to make sense of it. "It's written as a cryptic message, a cipher of some sort."

It wasn't started with an A for acid, so it wasn't written in invisible ink and needed a reagent, and didn't start in H for heat, but what was most unusual about it was the use of the Eight Regiment motto.

"What did Miss McKesson say about the man who delivered it?"

"Not much." John shook his head, reading it over again, looking for patterns.

Clark sat down across the way, putting his injured leg up on the chair and leaning back comfortably.

"Hayes," John yelled loudly, his man showing up at the door presently. "Can you please ask Miss McKesson if she would join us for a moment?"

John mulled over the letter, considering all the possible ciphers he knew off the top of his head. Perhaps it was masked, but that would require a specific decoder, and he didn't have it. Whoever sent the letter meant for him to be able to decipher it, so the answer had to be in the motto.

When Dellis entered the room several minutes later, she looked at both of them, her eyes wide with concern. "Is something amiss, Captain?"

Before he could say anything, Clark said, "No, lass, we're just wondering if you can give us a better description of the gentleman who brought this letter."

She rolled her eyes skyward and closed them as if she were replaying the event in her mind down to the minutest detail. "He was tall, dark hair, expensively dressed, very pleasant looking. He had a bit of an accent, not Scottish, but similar." She repeated the specifics of her conversation with the man, then looked at the other two with a blank expression on her face. "I'm sorry, my brother interrupted me in the middle of our discussion. Stuart was misbehaving again. I never got the man's name, nor did my aunt."

"Are you sure he didn't make any reference to where he worked or what he did?" John asked, his tone purposely gruff. He was tired and hungry, part of which was her fault, and he was eager to get some rest. "Miss McKesson, the man left a letter for me, and you didn't ask him any questions? Did he say anything unusual, something that stands out to you?"

"No, nothing, it was all rather quick," she replied, nonchalantly, and then stopped in mid-thought, flashing him a grin. "Oh, wait, he did say something interesting. How could I have forgotten this?" She narrowed her eyes at him, then smirked. "He said you're known for having a taste for fine things."

"And what is the significance of that?" John asked, meeting her gaze.

"I don't think I need to explain that to you, or have you really lost that much of your memory, Captain?" she asked tartly.

"No, please, do." If she was going to be difficult, then he would match her in kind. The woman was being downright unreasonable.

She shook her head in exasperation. "You don't really mean that, do you?"

John noticed how she blushed suddenly, though the expression on her face was one of pure accusation. *Celeste*. Dellis was jealous and still angry with him from earlier, but there was also more to this interaction than she was confessing. He needed to know what she was hiding, and he couldn't care less about her modesty or her tart disposition at the moment. "Miss McKesson, you blushed head to toe just now. In what context did he say that to you?"

"I did not," she said, blushing even more. "Captain, how ungentlemanly of you to comment on such a thing!"

Frustrated with her to the point of amusement, he snorted. "Please, tell us what he said."

She looked at Clark for support, but he shook his head. "Fine, it wasn't what he said, it's what he did."

"What did he do?" They both asked simultaneously.

"He looked at my… attributes." She gestured to her chest, too shy to say it. "I'm not completely daft. I know when a man is observing my form. I believe you've been guilty of this once or twice, *Captain*."

John noticed how she stressed the word Captain, her chin jutting out in defiance when she met his gaze. Clark smirked, and then covered his mouth with his hand, pretending to cough.

"What I deduced from his comment was that you have a taste for fine beverages and fine women. I believe the man assumed there was an association between the two of us. Apparently, he's not familiar with Mrs. Allen." She threw him another accusing look, her dark brow arching. "Now, if you have no more questions for me, I'll excuse myself, my dining room is full of people, and Thomas is alone tonight."

As she walked to the door, Clark grabbed her hand, stopping her. "Lass, he didn't mean to be cross with you, it's imperative that we know who sent this. Are you sure there was nothing else he said to you?"

She chewed her lower lip while her eyes cast down at the floor. "Let me think again," she said, quietly.

John's mother once told him sugar got much further than salt with women. He should have listened to her. But something about sparring with Dellis provoked him to the point of frustration and forgotten sense. Somehow, their conversation had spun into an argument right in front of Clark; a talking to was sure to follow once she left the room.

"Yes, there was something else. At the time I found his phrasing rather strange…"

"What did he say?" John asked.

"Something like, 'Great results can be achieved with small forces.' It was after I fought with my brother, so it's hard to remember anything more." Keeping her back to him, she asked, "Are you finished with me? Am I excused?"

"Yes, thank you," he replied tersely.

She walked out quickly, slamming the door behind her.

John watched her leave, trying to ignore her outburst, though deep down, he found the whole situation upsetting.

Clark looked at the door then back at John. "That didn't go well either."

"No," he replied, focusing his attention on the letter. John read it again, but still, there was no specific pattern, no hidden message. Nothing.

"If she's angry with you, it serves you right. I told you to keep your distance." Clark blurted out as anticipated, though it took him five minutes longer than John expected.

Huffing out a breath, he looked up at his friend. "Truly, nothing has happened between Miss McKesson and myself. I swear."

"That may be so, but she has an attachment to you," Clark added. "It doesn't help that she just saw Celeste leave here, and it appears our mysterious visitor went out of his way to make her aware of your reputation. The woman is jealous and confused, John. She's an innocent; leave her alone."

"I know that," John said, angrier with himself than his friend. "I'll deal with Miss McKesson, and the topic is no longer up for discussion. I didn't ask you for your counsel. You forget yourself, Lieutenant."

"John, you do realize the woman will hate you when she finds out the truth." Clark persisted. "And she will find out."

"You're bordering on impertinence, Simon," John muttered under his breath, his attention focused on the letter. "Great results can be achieved with small forces. Where have I heard that before?"

Clark pushed the letter out of the way and looked John in the eyes. "To hell with impertinence, you don't get to pull rank on me when we're talking about personal affairs. That's just your way of avoiding the topic."

Damn, right it was. But he had no intention of discussing the subject of Dellis McKesson any further. His lack of restraint where she was concerned had been on his mind all day. He didn't need to be reminded of it.

"Difficulties be damned," he whispered to himself. Then it hit him, it *was* a ciphered message, and the clue was in the motto. Counting every eighth word, he wrote them out on another piece of paper, the answer revealing itself.

I have something that belongs to you. Come and get it.

"I've got it. Look at this." He handed the decoded message to Clark, waiting for him to read it.

"But what does this mean? Are they referring to the supplies? Smith swears he saw Alexei McKesson the night of the storm. How would he know the Eighth Regiment motto? Besides, I don't picture him as the type to use a cipher."

Nothing made sense. Who would send him such a letter? It was an easy cipher, purposely done so that he could decode it in a matter of minutes. The fact that the man didn't leave his name was also a clue. And as far as John knew, no one knew of his whereabouts save General Howe and...

"The letter isn't from McKesson," John replied, the whole picture becoming disturbingly clear. "It's Roger DeLancie. It has to be."

"I don't understand, John," Clark said in disbelief. "Why would you think that?"

"Great results can be achieved with small forces." John provided. "It's from the *Art of War*."

Clark's dark eyes widened with curiosity and a bit of fear. "How is that even possible? The man went to court-martial and was sent to the gallows. He's dead, John."

As far as John knew, that was DeLancie's fate, but he was well connected and incredibly resilient, so it wasn't a stretch that he could've found a way to persevere. "When Dellis and I were in town, I saw Eagle Eyes, and he definitely saw me. DeLancie fits her description, and the little tidbit of information he told Dellis was for my benefit, not hers. He left all the pieces, and I just had to put them together. This is from Roger DeLancie. I would stake my life on it."

A tall man with dark hair, expensively dressed, and an Irish accent who quoted the *Art of War;* yes, it had to be DeLancie. It was all too much to be a coincidence.

"My God, John," Clark exclaimed, in a low, breathy voice. "The man is bloody crazy. If this is really from him, what do you think it all means? Do you think he's helping the natives?"

Roger DeLancie was fanatically loyal to the British cause; everything he did he justified for the good of King and country. This was just his style; he loved plotting and toying with his victims, like a cat with a mouse, until he was ready to deal a deathblow.

"He's not working with Alexei," John said with conviction. "But I have no doubt he knows everything that's happened. Eagle Eyes is well connected; that's what he was doing in town, scouting for DeLancie."

"So why come here and bring this letter if they don't have the supplies?"

"He had no intention of actually seeing me. He came to deliver the letter. He's baiting me. It's part of the game"—he paused, a sense of foreboding coming over him, causing an ache behind his eyes—"to see if I remember my *Art of War.*"

"Do you think he did this to you?"

Clark's question was valid, but it lacked merit for one particular reason. "If Roger DeLancie tortured me, I would never have gotten out alive. He would have finished me off right then, his ego leaving nothing to chance. Not to mention, he would have boasted about being able to catch me, his student, the lesser stag. No, whoever did this was an amateur compared to the likes of him."

"He wants revenge, John." Clark looked at the letter again, then discarded it on the desk, its association to their former superior tainting it worse than any poison.

"Yes," John replied, the words coming out easily, undermining how he really felt. "Time to settle old scores."

"John, he's been here, he met the lass already. You need to warn her to stay away from him. You and I both know how he is with women, specifically native ones."

Closing his eyes, John tried to shut out the image of DeLancie and Eagle Eyes the night they captured the Oneida women. Eagle Eyes held John back, forcing him to watch as his superior raped and beat them, and then passed them off to his men to use before they killed them. John could still hear them screaming. And poor Mary, DeLancie scalped her right before John's eyes, showing no mercy for her delicate condition. Clark was right; Dellis was in danger by association.

"I'll deal with Miss McKesson."

"Aye, but what will you do?"

He couldn't very well tell her to stay away from DeLancie, knowing Dellis's headstrong nature that would only encourage her to do the opposite.

"I'll come up with something." He paused, imagining the look on her face when he told her not to talk to the man. She would narrow her eyes in challenge then tell him to mind his own business. No, he would have to find a way to finesse her into doing what he wanted. Dellis required a more skillful hand.

"We need to find out what he is planning, anticipate his next move. I have no doubt it involves the Oneidas and that village in particular."

"John, we can't go down this path again. It won't end well." Clark warned. "We have a mission."

He was right, but what choice did John have? "DeLancie has made his first move, and he won't stop until he has me in checkmate."

"What do we do?"

Considering all the possibilities, he knew of only one that would protect Dellis and possibly flush DeLancie out. "We need to get the job done and get out of here as soon as possible. That includes finding my supplies and the bastard that did this to me. When we've finished, we'll travel to Oswego. Knowing DeLancie, he'll follow me, and that will keep him away from Dellis and the Oneidas. He wants me more than them."

It was the most viable option. He had the maps that he required, the war was at a standstill, and it would put some much-needed distance between himself and Miss McKesson. Problem solved.

Clark shook his head. "You're making this sound much easier than it is, John. First of all, we have no idea who took you or why, that alone is going to take time to figure out, and our stolen goods have all but disappeared." Simon pointed out the window, drawing John's attention to the wintry storm, giant flakes coming down like feathers from a newly torn pillow. "If we manage to accomplish all that, and in good time, it will still be impossible to get to Oswego. The river is frozen by now, and the roads are impassible."

"I understand all that," John replied, trepidation making his gut ache—or was it hunger—either way, he felt sick. "No matter, we collect the information we need, and then we leave. You and the men need to step up your efforts, and I'll do my best to get moving. The quicker we go, the better.

Chapter
Thirty-Seven

DeLancie looked at the old wooden clock hanging over the bar, wondering if John had received the letter yet. But would he figure it out? He was always slow on the uptake. Oh, yes, DeLancie relished the thought of John discovering who wrote the letter.

Patience, DeLancie reminded himself. *Patience.* He wanted to prolong his pleasure and John's pain for as long as possible. Revenge, much like sex, was so much better with protracted anticipation; it heightened the experience.

Looking across the bar, DeLancie eyed a familiar dark-haired, dirty fellow sparring with the bartender, spewing venom that would make even the most seasoned sailor blush. It was Miss McKesson's brother, there was no mistaking his resemblance to her with his high cheekbones, dark hair, and striking dark eyes. They both reminded DeLancie of his beautiful Lily, so like her, tall and graceful with her fathomless gaze.

Getting up, he walked over and sat down next to the younger man, listening in on the argument. "What is the problem, sir?" DeLancie asked the bartender.

The light-haired man snatched the tankard from in front of Stuart and placed it under the bar top, out of his reach. "He has no money, but he wants more to drink." The bartender pointed to Stuart and then the door.

"You need to go, McKesson, before I throw you out. I don't need you scaring away what little customers I have left. Let your sister take care of you."

Stuart leaned up on the bar top and reached under the counter, trying to get at his tankard just as the bartender slapped his hand away. "That's it, Stuart, you have to leave."

Taking advantage of the unique opportunity, DeLancie put some money on the counter and slid it over to the bartender. "Let him stay for a few more minutes. I'll buy him a drink."

"Fine, but you're responsible for him when he's acting like a raving idiot," the bartender said, refilling Stuart's tankard then pointing at him. "You behave."

"I'll take care of our friend here," DeLancie replied, patting Stuart on the back.

The young man was a mess with his long, black hair tangled around his face and a short, scraggly beard catching beads of ale as he tipped his tankard and guzzled it down. DeLancie sat quietly, watching as Stuart finished his drink then slammed his mug on the bar top several times demanding another. How did this miscreant, this abomination, come from DeLancie's beautiful Lily? Clearly, the McKesson blood was in play here, for when he pondered Stuart's angelic sister, DeLancie saw all the lovely attributes of Lily and her native lineage. No, he wouldn't associate this freak of nature, this disgusting little gutter rat, with his Lily. It was McKesson who was responsible for this blight on society.

Stuart watched DeLancie suspiciously as the bartender refilled the drink. "I saw you earlier today, talking to my sister."

"Miss McKesson is your sister?" DeLancie played along, interested in what little tidbits of information would seep out of Stuart McKesson's drunken mouth. There might be a use for him; drunkards had ears where other men heard only silence.

"Yeah, why, you want her?" Stuart asked, slurring his words. His eyes darted around the room as if he was looking for someone. "He wants her, too. She whores for him."

DeLancie found that hard to believe, remembering the way she blushed shyly when he smiled at her. She was a demure, proper lady, much like her mother. He'd never forget the first time he saw Lily; she was breathtaking in her native clothing, her long, silky, black hair blowing in the gentle breeze while the water in the lake sparkled like diamonds in the sun. It gave him chills just thinking about her.

"What do you mean? Who wants your sister?" He sipped his ale then put it down, the taste too bitter and hoppy for his liking. He slid the tankard over to Stuart and motioned to the bartender, pointing to the bottle of whiskey on the counter and lifting up two fingers.

"The Redcoat who lives in my house; he wants her." Stuart smiled, guzzling down what was left of his drink, the liquid dripping down his chin. "She likes Redcoats."

The thought of John groping that beautiful flower made DeLancie want to put his fist through a wall. No, she was much too lovely and sweet to be tainted by the likes of him. He refused to believe Lily's daughter could be so easily seduced by a scoundrel just as her mother had.

"What is your name, boy?"

"Stuart," the young man replied, looking DeLancie up and down. "Who are you?"

He removed his hat, putting it on the bar top. "Just call me Major." He held out his hand, the boy shaking it heartily. "It's a pleasure to meet you, Stuart."

After their introduction, DeLancie took a linen rag off the counter and wiped his hand, scouring the dirt and grime left behind by the filthy rat. Stuart definitely took after the vile, drunken, Scottish side of his family.

"Are you one of them Regulars, Major?" Stuart blurted out. "Cuz we don't like Tories or Redcoats in these parts."

"No, my friend, I'm not."

"Neither am I." Stuart sipped his drink, the liquid running down his chin and neck, staining his shirt. "Neither is my cousin. We've been making trouble for that Redcoat since he showed his dirty lobsterback face in town."

"Who is your cousin?" DeLancie motioned to the bartender to bring another round, turning attention back to Stuart. "Perhaps we could help each other deal with your Redcoat."

"His name is Alexei."

"You mean James McKesson's son?"

"Yeah, that's my uncle," Stuart replied with a nod. "They've been giving him a lot of trouble lately. He'll never find the supplies they stole from him. But I got him really good."

"What did you do?" DeLancie asked, intrigued by his newfound friend.

Stuart smiled, showing black, rotted teeth. "I was the one who told Alexei about him. I saw him and his men when they came."

Drunk or not, Stuart was intelligent and privy to many secrets. DeLancie underestimated that, and if he did, so did everyone else; that could work to his advantage. The perfect spy is the one that nobody suspects and has access to all the players. "Where did the supplies go, Stuart?"

Stuart shook his head innocently though a huge grin lit up his face. "Don't know. But he'll never find them."

Brilliant. So, history was repeating itself; the Oneidas were stealing again, and rather conveniently, he and John were once again locked in this fight to the death. Only this time, DeLancie would win. Karma, or perhaps the wheel of fate, finally tipping in his direction. "Well, that deserves another round of drinks to celebrate." DeLancie clinked tankards with Stuart then waved to the bartender for another round. "Why don't you come work for me? I'm in charge of a local militia, and we could use a tough young buck like you, especially one that has an aversion to Tories and is willing to act on it."

DeLancie finished his drink, pushing the one the bartender just brought towards Stuart.

"My cousin Ruslan and I are already in the Tryon County militia," Stuart said, resting his arm on the bar. "But I'll work for you if you help me get him out of my house."

DeLancie smiled. *All too easy.* "For now, just keep your eyes on our Redcoat friend then report back to me. I'll come up with a plan."

"That's easy. He's usually following my sister around trying to get under her skirts."

Before DeLancie could comment on Stuart's observation about his sister, a charming female voice interrupted their conversation. "Well, well, if it isn't Major DeLancie."

As he turned around in his chair, Mrs. Allen sat down next to him, setting her little black velvet purse on the bar top. She looked tantalizing, her large breasts threatening to spill over the top of her bright blue dress, her hair all done up like a society whore. She flashed him a look of utter amusement when Stuart blew his nose into his shirt then wiped it clean. "Unless you prefer your present company?"

"Don't mind Stuart here." Taking her hand, DeLancie kissed it lightly. "Mrs. Allen, what an incredible pleasure it is seeing you here."

"Likewise," she cooed, her eyes never leaving his. "When you've finished with your friend, meet me in my room, first door on the right at the top of the stairs." Picking up her purse, she walked past him, her lovely hips swaying back and forth with a promise of delights to come.

"He fucks her," Stuart said, his eyes following Celeste up the stairs. "She's one of his women."

"Yes, well, Mrs. Allen doesn't share our revulsion for King George's men, Stuart." Roger slapped his new minion on the back causing some of Stuart's ale to bubble over the rim, dousing his sleeve and the front of his shirt. "I'll get you a room here for the night; tomorrow, you'll follow him, and we'll see if we can't come up with some way to deal with our mutual friend."

Stuart lifted his tankard in salute, wobbling a bit on his feet, more ale spilling over the top.

"When was the last time you had a woman, Stuart?"

"Don't know," he muttered, looking into his tankard. "They don't much fancy me."

DeLancie called the bartender over, looking at Stuart, then back up. "Do me a favor. Get this young buck here a bath and some clean clothes. And while you're at it, get him a room, and see to it that a woman visits him tonight. I'll cover the expenses." Patting Stuart on the shoulder, DeLancie smiled. "You do as I ask, and I'll see to all your needs. Do we have a deal?"

Stuart nodded, his eyes wide as he watched DeLancie pull a bag of coins from his pocket and drop them on the counter with a heavy clunk. "Yes, Major."

"Good, now enjoy your evening. I have business to attend to, but I'll see you soon."

What a fortunate find he had made in Stuart McKesson; he could prove to be very useful. At least one good thing would come from McKesson's mongrel seed, well, and his lovely daughter.

Walking up the back stairs, DeLancie knocked on the door to Celeste's room. This was a meeting he had long been anticipating. Mrs. Allen was in the unique position to help him, the honey to attract his bear, and when it came to sweets, John was notoriously weak for overindulgence.

When Celeste opened the door, she was wearing only a long maroon robe, the front of it tied closed exposing a delectable sliver of her décolletage and just a peek of her breasts. Her glossy, chestnut mane hung in large curls at her shoulders, adding to her state of en déshabillé. She had premeditated this whole moment, orchestrated it for her benefit but disguised it as his. She wanted something.

With a suggestive cock of her brow, she welcomed him inside. "You said you would find me, and here you are."

He nodded, taking a step inside, his eyes scanning the room for potential threats. One had to be careful, even in a woman's room; they made the most efficient assassins, striking when a man was at his weakest and most diverted.

Her room was small and plain, just a bed, a desk and a chest of drawers with a mirror over top of it, but she had managed to turn it into her own private palace. Royal blue fabric was draped above both window valances and around the canopy of the bed, creating make-shift curtains that could be drawn closed, forming a decadent web for a proficient female spider to trap her flies. Everywhere he looked, beeswax tapers were burning, the sweet smell of honey and spice permeating the air, dulling his senses, drawing him in against his will. The bed was covered with a large fur blanket and a plethora of fat, overstuffed, intricately embroidered pillows. On the desk was a crystal decanter full of dark liquor and two tumblers; sitting next to it was a tray of cheese and bread and a little jar of strawberry preserves. All the pleasures a man could want in one room, but when one looked closer, they could see Lilith's hand.

"Have you considered our business arrangement?" he asked, looking into Celeste's eyes, seeking the truth, though his loins ached to succumb to her trap. That's what she wanted, another weak male with an overactive cock that she could seduce with her body and her charms while sinking her fangs in deeply. But he was not John, nor was DeLancie a fool. He made the rules, and if she wanted to play, she would have to learn that.

"I have." She crossed her arms over her chest, the front of her robe opening a bit more, giving him a view of crevasse between her breasts. "Fortunately for you, I'm now in the position to negotiate."

"So, John turned you down, did he?"

She shrugged her shoulders and grinned in response.

"How unsporting of him." *Thank you, John.*

He reached up and touched one of the curls that rested on her shoulder, feeling the silky stuff between his fingers, then lifting it to his nose for a whiff of perfume. Vanilla and sandalwood, his favorite; it reminded him of a brothel in India and the beautiful, exotic, dark-skinned women that so fascinated him there. Slowly, he ran his fingertips down the front of her robe, opening it just enough to tease himself. She was nude underneath, her large, full breasts emerging as he untied it. A powerful jolt of lust coursed through his veins, his cock hardening at the sight of those twin peaks.

"Lovely, Mrs. Allen," he murmured, his eyes feasting on her long legs, her tiny waist, the dark thatch of expertly groomed hair at the apex of her thighs. Johnny always did have excellent taste in women, and she was no exception.

"Are you sure you wouldn't prefer one of your native whores?" she asked, the corner of her mouth turning up.

DeLancie pulled her against him, taking her hand and putting it between his legs so she could feel his desire. "What do you think?"

Laughing, she closed her robe and pulled away from him. "First business, then pleasure, Major."

"Fine. What are your terms, Mrs. Allen?" he asked, his body hungry for release. He desperately wanted to throw her down and slap her mouth for talking back to him. The haughty bitch, he would make her beg for him to fuck her when he bent her over the desk.

"You give me the money I need to open my establishment, and I'll collect whatever information you require."

"Why is John Carlisle here?"

"He's undercover for General Howe, but I don't know what for. He's also had a bit of trouble with his shipments—a naughty group of thieves has been stealing from him. That's all I know." She stepped closer to him, unbuttoning the front fall of his breeches, her fingers wrapping themselves around his shaft, stroking it gently. "Well, at least, for now."

He gasped, his cock quivering as she traced the sensitive vein on the underside with her fingernail. He was fast succumbing to her expertly laid trap. With a shake of his head, he tried to clear the amorous fog, at least until he got what he wanted. He grabbed her wrist forcefully, stopping her from going her any further. "What else can you tell me?"

She yelped, trying to free her hand from his grasp. "Give me time. Eventually, he will come to me, and I'll find out all you need to know."

DeLancie gave her a look of warning then released her hand. Instead of appearing outraged by his show of force, as most women would, she smiled, the wheels of thought turning behind those hazel-green eyes.

Dropping down to her knees, she put the tip of her finger in her mouth, then looked up at him suggestively. She was absolutely tantalizing in her submissive position—and she knew it. "I'll handle John, I always do. Now, do we have a deal?" With that, she started to suck on her finger, her tongue drawing out over the tip, driving him over the edge.

"Yes, we have a deal." He groaned in anticipation. "Just do it. Now."

She leaned forward, her lips as light as a feather, grazing the front of his leg. "What's your next move?" Slowly, she made hot circles with her mouth up his inner thigh, kissing and nipping at him, driving him crazy as she neared his cock. He wanted to put it in her mouth and shut her up for the rest of the night, but she persisted. "What are you going to do to John?"

"Let's just say I've left the bait. I'm just waiting for him to take it."

When she nuzzled her face into his lower abdomen, his eyes rolled back; he was on the verge of coming already. "John loves when I do this to him," she whispered.

Finally, he felt her silky lips on the end of his cock, her tongue swirling over the tip, lapping up some of his seed. He looked into her eyes, watching as she toyed with him, her hand reaching between his legs, cupping him firmly.

"What else did he like?" DeLancie asked, his hips starting to move instinctively.

"All in good time."

She looked up and smiled, her painted lips opening, taking him deep into her mouth. He couldn't take it any longer; he grabbed her by the hair, thrusting himself deeper, his hips pumping against her mouth. He closed his eyes, imagining dark eyes and black hair as Celeste's skillful lips worked him, making him come within seconds.

Chapter Thirty-Eight

John hobbled to the fireplace and threw another log on the fire, watching it pop and smolder before it finally ignited. After three weeks of nearly constant bed rest, he was finally able to move about, though his body protested anything excessive. Two weeks was a long time to just sit and wait, and still, there was no word from DeLancie. It was quiet. Too quiet. As sure as the day was long, he would strike again, but when? At least John's memory had finally started to come back, though the more he learned of his torture, the more he wished it would stay forgotten. The sensation of pins and needles from being doused with icy water, hot pokers branding his side, combined with the woman's incessant song waking him in the night, stole away any chance at respite. He remembered the cold, his bones aching, and the feel of Dellis's warm body wrapped around his, saving him from certain death. *But is it real or something I created during my nights of fevered torment?* He was in no position to ask her about it; she'd been avoiding him since the day he questioned her about DeLancie's visit, obviously still smarting from the argument. Even when she came to bring meals, the conversation was quick and curt, refusing John's attempts at engaging her in a discussion.

Looking over at the fireplace, he remembered a sliver of something important. The letters. Reaching under the mantle, he felt around for the hidden compartment, prying the wood loose with his fingers. The papers fell out on the floor, along with the two miniatures, the metal frames making a clanking noise as they hit the wood. He picked them up and carried them to his desk.

He held the miniature likeness of Dellis to the candlelight, admiring its accuracy. Turning it over, he rubbed his fingers over the smooth metal frame, feeling the sharp edges where it was engraved. He held it closer the candle, examining the fine script, SMM—her father's initials, John assumed. Putting the miniature down, he opened the letter on the top of the pile, the yellow paper crackling in protest as he unfolded it.

Dearest Brother,

We are desperately in need of supplies. The children have been sick with the pox, and several of the village children have died. The soldiers came, but they have nothing to trade with us, and I have little money to procure what we need.

Please send: Linen, spirits, tea, and whatever money you can spare, so that I might purchase food and clothing for our people. Use the rest of my inheritance, that you so generously returned to me after redeeming our family from the disgrace of our dear older brother, to cover the expense. I miss you terribly and long to sit and talk with you again. Please tell the Duchess I love her.

Your loving servant,

Stephen

John leafed through the rest of the stack. Some of the letters were just brotherly correspondences, and the others were supply lists from London to Montreal and Oswego, traveling by way of the Royal Navy. All of the ledgers were signed and dated by His Grace Admiral Dane McKesson, as would be expected. Nothing significant. John was missing something. It was right in front of his nose, yet he couldn't see it. He opened another letter, reading it carefully.

Dear Brother,

I have the shipping notices you sent us, and they were quite extensive, I am in awe of your generosity, brother. However, I have only received the linen and the spirits. I have gone myself to question authorities, yet none of them know the whereabouts of our supplies, and the money you sent is also missing.

Surely if the ship had been stopped by pirates, I would know about it. I understand that this captain is a friend of yours. Please advise.

Your loving brother,

Stephen

Again, nothing of importance. John opened the last letter, this one severely damaged, stains marking the paper in several places.

Dearest Brother,

How I long to see you and your lovely family. Dellis must be as beautiful as Lily by now, almost eighteen, and Stuart practically a man. I promise to come to you as soon as I can. The Duchess has lost another child, and I fear we will not be blessed with one to fill her arms and broken heart. She misses you terribly, longing for your wit and humor in her times of sorrow. I wish you were here, my dearest brother, to help us through these dark days.

Of course, I have sent the supplies I promised and the money from your trust and then some. Please take heart. When I return, I will see that an account is opened in Manhattan so that you may have the money you require to continue your work with your native family.

Give my love to Lily and the children.

Your loving servant,

Dane

John's arm ached as he sat back in his chair and adjusted his sling. *Why would her father have copies of letters he sent to his brother?* Again, there was nothing unique or inherently secretive about them. Looking back at the stack of papers on his desk, John could think of nothing unusual about those either. He folded the letters carefully and put them back in the mantle.

Unexpectedly, he heard music coming from the hall, the loud high-pitched toots of a fife in a merry rhythm. Slowly, he made his way down the hall, his injured leg cramping with each step. To his surprise, he found Clark playing his fife with Hayes sitting next to him singing "Wee Cooper O'Fife," stomping his foot to the beat. Standing in the doorway, John watched as Dellis danced, her hair hanging loosely down to her back, as she jumped about, lifting her skirts, exposing her shapely, stocking-covered calves.

Noticing him, Hayes stopped abruptly. "You know the words, Captain. You're welcome to join us."

Dellis looked up, her face flushed from the exercise, her eyes bright and wide. "Do you sing?"

"He's rather good," Hayes said. "But he prefers bawdy English tunes to our rousing Scottish ones. Don't you, Captain?"

John shook his head, ignoring the jest. He did sing, but only when drunk. "If Miss McKesson knew what that song was about, she wouldn't be dancing, she'd be horsewhipping the two of you drunken Scots."

"What is it about?" She looked at him, her eyes getting wider, then she turned her attention to Hayes and Clark. "What don't I know?"

Clark stopped playing his fife and burst into laughter. "It's about a naughty wife who gets reprimanded by her husband for not cooking and cleaning."

"Oh, for goodness sake." Dellis grabbed a pillow off the bed and hit Clark with it while he laughed loudly, holding his sides. "How could you?" she said with a laugh.

Turning around, John walked back to his room, a green-eyed monster nipping at his ego on the way. She could talk to his men, and dance with them, but she'd all but ignored him for the past two weeks. Granted, putting distance between the two of them was his plan when he moved upstairs, and it was the right thing to do, but still...

He could hear her heels clicking on the wood floor. She was following him.

"Captain, how are you feeling?" Dellis called from behind.

Now she was concerned. "Better, thank you," he replied, turning his attention to her.

She was peeking around the door, tendrils of her silky black hair hung down to her shoulders, her face still flushed from dancing. As she walked into the room, the light from the fireplace cast shadows on her face, accentuating her high cheekbones and deep-set eyes. The muted blue dress she always wore, clung to every curve and crevasse of her breasts and torso like a second skin. She needed no expensive clothing or adornments to look enchanting, her natural grace and untarnished beauty were enough to capture even the most experience reprobate—himself. She was seducing him, yet she did it unwittingly. Many women had made his blood boil, but never had one made his heart flutter in his chest. It was disconcerting and utterly intoxicating. He yearned for her with a ferocity that matched a starving man's at a banquet.

"Dellis, we've sidestepped the rules of society for far too long. It's not a good idea for you to be alone in my room with me. What if someone came looking for you? They would think inappropriate things about us."

"We're no longer under false pretenses, Captain, you are well aware of my reputation." She paused for a moment, pushing a curly lock of her hair out of her face and smoothing it behind her ear. "I don't think it matters anymore."

"No, Dellis, it does. As you have already assumed, I'm a man with a reputation, and being alone with me will only further tarnish yours. My concern is for you and your future prospects."

"Yes, well, I don't have any of those either," she said, an edge to her voice. "Why is it suddenly everyone is so concerned about my well-being? First my aunt, and now you. I've been on my own for a while and done just fine. I don't need your concern, nor do I want it."

She was angry with him, her eyes smoldering like hot coals in the hearth. He liked when she was provoked because she let her guard down;

it was her austere façade that frustrated him. It was virtually impenetrable. "Why have you been avoiding me?"

She didn't answer, a wide-eyed, astonished look on her face as if he were speaking in a foreign tongue.

"Dellis, tell me why?" She wasn't going to play innocent this time, he wouldn't let her.

"Why would you think I was avoiding you?" she murmured, looking down at her hands, fidgeting with them.

"Dellis?" When she tried to retreat towards the door, he followed her, bridging the distance between them. "I think it because it's true. The evidence is straightforward; you refuse to look me in the eyes, and you've reverted to calling me Captain."

"I'm not avoiding you... John," she replied, looking up at him through her eyelashes coyly.

He marveled at how she went from being so strong and defiant to shy and evasive in a matter of seconds. She was an intriguing combination of contradictions, likely built up from years of fighting her fears and a strong sense of self-preservation. No matter, he still wanted an answer—his ego demanded it.

"You're avoiding me, Dellis. Why?" He stepped closer to her, their bodies so close they were almost touching. Whatever force existed between them, spiritual or chemical, he couldn't fight it any longer. And from the way she was behaving, it was clear she was fighting a losing battle, too.

"It's because of how I spoke to you, isn't it?" Pushing a little more, he added, "And because I asked to move upstairs?"

"Yes," she replied softly.

"I'm sorry if I upset you. My intention wasn't to hurt you." Gently touching her chin, he tipped her face up so he could look into her eyes. Those incredible, dark pools looked enchanting in the firelight; once again, he found himself hopelessly lost in them. "And today, I was rather tired and frustrated."

"I understand. You've been through a lot." She swallowed, her eyes trailing down to his lips. "You don't need to apologize."

"But you were upset with me before that, weren't you?"

She nodded, hypnotized by him.

John knew he should pull his hand away, but instead, he cupped her cheek and ran his thumb over her lips, feeling their softness. She closed her eyes, turning her face into his hand, her lips parting, allowing him to trace the seam. "Why were you angry with me?"

Blushing on cue, she parted her lips even more, the tip of her tongue grazing the pad of his thumb, sending sparks straight to that atrophied muscle in his chest—the one that he'd neglected for so long. "I…"

His heart throbbed, engorged with blood and passion, and something else, an unknown feeling, an ache. "It couldn't be because of Mrs. Allen?"

Immediately, the spell was broken, the coals that smoldered in her eyes blazed red hot as she slapped his hand away. "Your affairs are none of my concern, Captain."

"Celeste and I are business partners, nothing more."

She snorted. "You don't need to explain yourself to me, but don't insult my intelligence. I might be provincial, but I'm not naïve. I know that's what you call your paramours. I know that's your game; you travel around collecting patrons for your goods and business partners for your bed. After all, you have a taste for fine women. Do you deny it?"

Instead of letting her bait him, he chuckled, enjoying the show. Again, she was blowing hot and cold within a matter of seconds—now the Dellis tempest had turned her fury on him. It was mystifying and rather entertaining. "Are you jealous of her?"

"You're an arrogant bastard and a scoundrel," she said, looking him up and down as if he were a piece of discarded rubbish.

He shrugged his shoulders, watching her angrily stomp towards the door. "A scoundrel, perhaps, but I think my mother might take offense with your other endearment. Granted, I'm the only blond in my family; perhaps I should question her?"

She stopped dead in her tracks but didn't turn around, her attention directed at the door, releasing another round of outrage at it. "I'm not jealous. There is nothing between us, and there never will be," she yelled, reaching for the door handle. "I know what you're doing. You're making sport of me, and I'll no longer play a part in your amusement. I'm done with you... Captain."

John knew he should let her go, an argument the perfect way to put an end this intrigue, but he couldn't; he was beyond restraint. With a yank on her wrist, she was in his arms, like magnets drawn together by mystical forces, opposites attracting, sun and moon, man and woman. He looked into her eyes, demanding more than asking, "Nothing between us? Nothing? Do you feel that?" Yes, he certainly could. It was mystical, primordial.

"Unhand me, brute, I won't let you force me." Her whole body tensed in his arms, her pupils wide with panic as she pummeled her fists into his chest. She was genuinely fighting him. These weren't feminine little punches designed to play at defense when really she wanted more. No, she was frantically trying to get away. Only one-handed, he could do little to subdue her, but he managed to catch her wrist in mid-air when she took a swing at him.

"Let me go!" she yelled.

She was overreacting, but it was real fear that drove her to behave so dramatically. Releasing her, he held up his hand and backed away, the last thing he meant to do was frighten her. An innocent in the ways of seduction, she had no concept of foreplay between a man and a woman. She functioned in extremes, misunderstanding his advances for only one result, but what he wanted to show her were all the lovely things that existed in-between.

"I didn't mean to upset you, Dellis. I've never touched a woman who didn't want me to."

"Because you're so used to women throwing themselves at you?" she asked. "I imagine you've never had a woman turn you down? Well, now you know how it feels, Captain." With that, she turned her back on him and, once again, went for the door.

Grabbing the edges of the sling, he ripped the damned thing from around his neck and threw it on the floor. It was driving him crazy. He needed both of his hands to… to what? *What am I doing?*

Let her go, Carlisle. Let. Her. Go. But he couldn't.

"Whether you believe it or not, I don't make a habit of seducing every woman I meet, and that's the truth. And I know you're upset about Mrs. Allen; yes, we were once lovers, but I assure you, there's nothing between us now. I told her to leave."

"Why?" She looked back at him, his honesty reaching her more than any of his bravado.

"Because I didn't want her," he replied, his confession on the tip of his tongue. "I want you." The truth rolled off with more ease than he expected, unlike the lies he was forced to tell her.

She turned around slowly but hesitated to look up at him. He stepped to her, unable to avoid her magnetic pull on his heart. Lifting her chin, looking into her eyes, he waited, giving her the chance to back away, but she didn't. He'd wanted to kiss her for so long but resisted the urge. Nothing would stop him this time: his mission, her past, the truth, to hell with it all. For now, she was a woman, he was a man, and nothing else mattered. The scoundrel, a beast he kept locked deep inside, wanted a taste. Slowly, he bent down, lightly brushing his lips against her softness, his thumb caressing her cheek, gently coaxing her to respond. She was trembling like a leaf on the breeze, but she didn't push him away; instead, she ran her hands up his chest, making his heart quicken in that unique way only she could evoke. Encouraged by his progress, he deepened the kiss, gently urging her lips apart with his tongue until she finally complied, giving him his first taste of her sweetness. She was honey mixed with smoky tea, the last thing she drank, but with a deeper plunge, he finally tasted her, an excellent highland scotch, peaty and earthy yet so very smooth. The finest single malt, and one he could drink all day. Her tongue shyly touched his, with a gentle, experimental stroke, and then again, but this time toying with his own in long, flavor-filled pulls. He groaned, pulling her into his arms, the feel of her lithe body against his own better than any dream or fantasy he could conjure.

"John," she whispered, his name like a benediction, rolling off her lips. Suddenly, he was rock hard, straining for her against his breeches, the timbre of her voice as she said his name like oil to fire. She reached up and pulled the tieback from his hair, freeing it, her fingers entwining in the wavy locks, tugging at it, spurring him on.

A kernel of reality seeped into his brain, casting doubt on his impulsive decision. *What am I doing?* "Dellis, we have to stop, this was all wrong of me." He groaned, trying to pull away, but she held fast, her fingers buried in his hair, her dewy lips parted and ready for him like a tantalizing treat.

"No, John, don't stop." She pulled his hair, trying to draw him back to her. "Please."

He was helpless to resist. Now she was the aggressor, and he was the one fighting back. Resting his forehead against hers, John took several deep breaths, a war waging within him, the scoundrel and the gentleman—a duel for his soul.

"Don't stop." She commanded, her lips making a little trail of kisses from his cheek to his ear. And with fevered adore, she spoke the words that drove him over the edge. "Touch me, John, everywhere, all over. I want to feel your hands on my skin." There was no room for misinterpretation, she was in command now, and he was the subordinate. And he liked it. God, he liked it.

With one swift tug, he pulled her kerchief loose, exposing all that lovely flesh to his gaze. Curves and crevasses and a wonderland of milky white flesh, it was just as he'd imagined night after night in torrid fantasies that ended with him sweaty and spent. He looked up, wanting to see her desire in those black beauties, and she didn't disappoint, smoldering coals, and parted, swollen lips—passion's expression. He'd seduced many women in his days, always conscientious of their pleasure, but never had he felt more selfless, more determined to give more than receive. He wanted this for her. To drive the fear away and show her, with no uncertainty, how a man touches a woman.

The first graze was Heaven, her skin like smooth porcelain as he ran his hand down her long, graceful neck, indulging in every dip and curve. She bit her lower lip, her eyes never leaving his, allowing him to explore and touch what no man had ever touched before. His mouth watered with jealousy, anxiously wanting to taste and suck on every inch that his fortunate hand touched, to feel the silky texture against his tongue. Boldly, he leaned down, pressing his lips to her shoulder, his eyes watching hers for any sign of hesitation, but there was none to be found, only innocent longing. He savored and suckled that lavender skin, his tongue trailing over the sharp curves of her collarbone to the base of her neck where he nuzzled and kissed, submerging himself in her until he was drowning. He was beyond thought and reason. He wanted to consume her, feed the beast that craved her touch like it did sustenance.

When his hand grazed her breast, she let out a heady little gasp, but instead of pulling away, her breast thrust forward, offering itself up to the altar of his hand. The sacrificial lamb. He pulled the front of her bodice and stays down, cupping her breast, filling his palm and then some, with pillowy, soft perfection. He explored the supple mound, feeling it swell, his thumb worrying the taut rosy peak until it was hard and pebbled to a point, and she was moaning in his ear. He wanted to suckle and worship, bury his face in the beautiful valley, fall on his knees and declare she was his mistress, his goddess.

"John," she said breathlessly, sending shivers down his spine. Nuzzling her neck, he breathed in that incredible scent of lavender and vanilla, heady and fragrant and uniquely her.

Reality breached the amorous fog, but he fought back, not ready to let her go, not yet. Claiming her lips again, they fell back against the door, his body pinning hers. His hips moved against hers while his tongue plunged in and out of her mouth, teaching her their rhythm, and like an adept pupil, she learned his trade, using it against him with the skill of a proficient. Oh, the feel of her skirts pressing into his aching loins; he wanted to rip away every shred of fabric that separated them and bury himself deep. It took no magic spell or crystal ball to know she was ready for him, wet and hot and so very inviting. She would wrap her powerful thighs around his waist, and he would press himself, inch by glorious inch, inside till he was buried to the hilt. And she would moan out his name, loud and husky—yes—with her willful, fighting spirit, she would moan to the gods his name.

But no matter how badly he wanted it, he just couldn't do it. The gentleman had won, the scoundrel taken down with a bullet of reality. Groaning against her lips, he pulled away, bracing his hands on the door next to her head while he fought to regain control of himself.

Damn.

She emerged from their passion first, looking up at him with eyes full of wonder. "Captain." She tugged at his hair, wrapping a lock around her fingers, toying with it, just like she'd done to his heart. "I wasn't jealous."

She was never one to give up the fight, but he was determined to get a confession out of her if only to say he was right. "Yes, you were," he said, kissing the tip of her nose, keeping things chaste. "Admit it."

But instead of giving in, she wrapped her arms around his waist, pulling their bodies closer again. For an ingénue she was turning out to be a rather adept seductress.

Feeling devilish, he brushed his lips against her earlobe, gently flicking it with his tongue. "Does this mean we're business partners, Miss McKesson?"

Dellis grabbed the front of his waistcoat, using it to turn him around and force his back to the door.

"I'll take that as a—" Before he could finish, she kissed him again, her scotch-flavored tongue sliding against his with such devastating precision he could barely form a thought.

Suddenly, out of the corner of his eye, he saw her hand and a flash of metal, moving with lightning speed. With a loud thud, she planted her knife into the door, only a hair's breadth from his head. Stunned, he looked up at it, realizing just how accurate her aim was.

"You forget yourself, Captain. I'm no man's whore or business partner, or whatever you call your women. My fortunes haven't fallen that far." She hissed, her face inches from his, their eyes locked. "Make no mistake about that."

The virago had returned, her passion quelled by anger, but he was still shoulders deep from that kiss she just gave him.

"Do you hear me?" she asked, forcing him back to reality.

"I've learned my lesson; always be ready for a direct assault," he said, though he found the whole incident unsettling. "Once again, I find myself in awe of your skills in self-defense. Thank God you didn't aim lower." *Thank you, God.*

Pulling the blade from the door, he handed it back to her. She took it and put it in her pocket, refusing to look at him. "Was that really necessary, Dellis? I was only teasing."

"How could you say such a thing, knowing what you do about me?" Her eyes were glassy, brimming with tears. She was just as shaken as he was.

He'd only meant to have a bit of fun with her, but his jest had the opposite effect. For some reason, his usual finesse with women was completely useless when it came to her. "I'm sorry, forgive me. I didn't mean to provoke you," he said, feeling incredibly foolish. "It was wrong of me."

Dellis adjusted her clothing, the candlelight allowing her to hide in the shadows and shyly redress. When she turned around, her lips were still red and swollen from his kisses, her neck and shoulders marked by his passion, yet she wasn't his. She couldn't be. Turning away, it took every ounce of restraint not to take her in his arms and finish what he'd started, his body starved for hers.

"I'll be leaving as soon as I can ride. I imagine it won't take longer than a couple more weeks to be fit to travel," he said, turning his back to her, trying to shut her out.

"Why are you leaving?"

There was sadness in her voice. He looked over his shoulder at her, selfishly wanting to see it on her face. She'd manipulated him so brilliantly only minutes before—now, it was his turn. "I have business that can no longer wait. I owe shipments to several people, and I intend to keep my promise to your grandfather."

"John, it's not safe for you to travel, especially after how ill you've been. The weather hasn't let up in days, and the roads are barely passable."

"That might be so, but I still have to go." He nodded, her genuine concern for his well-being unwavering in spite of what he was doing to her. "I can obtain replacements for what I've lost in Oswego or Montreal."

"When will you come back?" she said so quietly he barely heard her.

"I don't know." He turned away, unable to look at her and lie again. "Perhaps it's better this way."

It was his fault. Clark had warned John to stay away from her, but he didn't listen. Now there was no way not to hurt her; the die was cast.

"Maybe you're right, John. Perhaps it's better that you go." She hesitated for a moment then left, shutting the door behind her.

Closing his eyes, he cursed himself. He should never have let it go this far.

Chapter
Thirty-Nine

Dellis raced down the stairs to her room, wanting desperately to bury her head in her pillow and forget what just happened. She could feel John's lips on her neck, the sensation of his hands all over her body, making her ache for more. The dining room was surprisingly full again. She avoided making eye contact with any of the patrons, wanting only the sanctuary of her room.

Just as she passed through the archway from the bar into the kitchen, Alexei stepped in front of her, halting any further retreat. "Where are you going?"

"Damn." She cursed, and then followed it with more expletives in her head. He had a knack for showing up at the worst possible times; she just wanted to be alone. "I need to get something from my room," she mumbled, looking down at the floor, praying he would just accept what she said and let her go. But of course, he didn't, Alexei was too damned perceptive and nosy for his own good.

"Something's wrong," he said flatly, lifting her chin and looking her in the eyes.

"Please, don't do that." Pushing his hand away, she tried to inch her way towards her room, but he followed her. "You're flushed. You look a mess. Is everything all right?" he yelled from behind her, his heavy footsteps echoing off the wood floor. They passed by her aunt on the way through the kitchen, Dellis waved, and said, "Give me a moment, and then I'll come help," then continued down the hall.

Alexei followed Dellis into her bedroom and shut the door behind them. She could feel him eyeing her neck and her sleeve, which she hadn't noticed until just then was hanging down her arm, leaving her bare shoulder exposed. Quickly she pulled it up and righted herself. "Did one of the Captain's men put his hands on you?"

Alexei looked like a handsome, angry giant with his impressive height and fists on his hips, daring her to lie. She didn't bother. Alexei could always read her like a book, there was no point in trying. But when she said nothing, it only further provoked him. "Fine, I'll ask the Captain what happened if you won't tell me." When he started to walk back towards the dining room, she panicked, stopping him in mid-stride. "Alexei, please, nothing untoward happened."

"Be honest with me; did your Tory captain try something?" His voice was deadly serious.

She knew he would go after John if she didn't come up with an excuse, and fast. "Alexei, the captain didn't do anything wrong. He's in his room, recovering from his wounds."

"Wounds? What are you talking about?" The look of confusion on Alexei's face confirmed what she suspected all along—he had nothing to do with John's torture.

Dellis breathed a sigh of relief, grateful for that kernel of knowledge. "He was attacked more than a fortnight ago. We found him in the old barn near the village."

"What was he doing there?"

"I don't know. He doesn't remember. Whoever attacked him hit him over the head and tortured him. We found him hanging from the barn rafters, whipped and beaten. He just barely survived."

Alexei's expression changed, his dark brows furrowed, a fierce look in his eyes. He knew something, more than he was willing to admit to her.

"Alexei, did our people have something to do with this?" she asked, afraid of the answer. "Be honest."

"No." He shook his head, but she wasn't sure she believed him. "When did it happen?"

"The night of the first big snowstorm."

Before she could ask him any more questions, he changed the subject. "You never told me why you look so disheveled."

She let out a sigh. Alexei was like a dog with a bone when he wanted something. "I was listening to one of the Captain's men play music, and I started dancing. You caught me on my way to put myself back together." That wasn't entirely a lie.

"Dellis, you need to be more careful." She could feel him eyeing her neck and chest, her skin still smoldering from John's touch. Alexei wasn't buying her excuse, but at least he was no longer prying. "I'm sorry. I promise, I'll be more careful."

"Don't apologize to me. It's you I'm concerned for." He took her hand, walking her across the hall to the parlor.

She sat down on the couch, waiting as he shut the door. "Alexei, you don't need to worry about me. It's Stuart who needs you. He showed up drunk, looking for money."

"I can handle Stuart." He sat down next to her, and then gently brushed a stray lock of hair behind her ear, his hand cupping her cheek. "Dellis, someone has to worry about you. If you had a husband, then—"

"Stop!" She pushed his hand away. First her aunt, then John—not Alexei, too. "I don't need a husband. I can take care of myself. You taught me well. I know how to use a knife and a pistol. I can protect myself." Dellis was pretty sure John could attest to her skill if need be.

"I owe it to your father to look after you until you're settled. He would want me to." She smiled when he grasped her hand, squeezing it gently. Alexei and her father were always close, their shared love for the Oneidas bonding them despite the anger between the two brothers. "I had hoped things might change between you and Patrick. I know you still care for him."

"Alexei, you know that's over," she replied, looking away. Even if Patrick wanted her, there was too much history, too many hurt feelings, to ever go back. And though she wanted to, she could never forgive him. At the worst moment in her life, when she needed his love most, he discarded her. No, she wanted a man who would love her in spite of everything that happened. *If that man even existed.*

"Besides, Alexei, when are you going to settle down and start having a family of your own?" she asked, turning the tables. "You don't seem too eager yourself."

She noticed Alexei wince, a hint of sadness in his blue eyes she'd never seen before, but he shook it off quickly. "Dellis, give Patrick a chance."

"I don't want to talk about this anymore," she replied, finishing the conversation. She loved that he was concerned for her, but she refused to let him, or anyone else, meddle in her affairs. "How is Grandfather? Has there been any news about the war?"

"Since the battle on Lake Champlain, the British have taken York City completely. They chased Washington all the way to New Jersey, and now they control all of the southern Hudson."

"What now?"

Alexei shook his head then stood up, pulling her to her feet. "Now get yourself cleaned up and help my mother in the kitchen. And do me a favor: be careful."

She nodded, standing on her tiptoes and placing a kiss on his cheek. "I will. Please, find Stuart."

"By the way, I brought your horse back from the village. Brynn is in the stable," he said.

"Thank you," she replied.

He reached down and gave her a hug, lifting her off the ground, her feet dangling in the air. When he set her down, she looked up at him, his handsome face and quirky grin making her smile. In many ways, he was just like John, strong and caring yet so reticent. There was something deep and troubled about both of them; she couldn't help but wonder what secrets they both kept locked away from her.

Once Alexei was finally gone, she ran to her room, shutting the door behind her. Looking into the mirror, she touched her red, swollen lips, remembering the feel of John's mouth against hers, the fevered way he said her name into his kiss. Her hair had fallen out of her bun in a mass of tangles, her kerchief was hanging loose on one side, and there were red splotches on her neck where John's lips branded her. There was no way she fooled Alexei. Thank goodness, for once, he respected her privacy and backed off. The last thing she wanted was for him to get into a fight. He was always so cantankerous whenever they met, and John was in no shape to do battle with Alexei.

Dellis sat down on the edge of the bed, her mind absorbing what had happened in John's room. She didn't mean to overreact, but he made her so angry. If he hadn't behaved like such an arrogant scoundrel, she wouldn't have lashed out at him. When he told her he was leaving, there was something in his eyes akin to sadness. He was hiding something, and whatever that was, he was fighting it. One minute he wanted to be close to her, the next he was pushing her away. Hot and cold, just like the autumn wind. It was so confusing.

She knew what John meant when he said he wanted her. She would never forget the way the soldiers brutally used her body and the pain and shame that resulted. John was so gentle when he touched her; she innately came alive in his arms. It couldn't possibly be the same. She wasn't in the business of deceiving herself; she was far from marriage material, and certainly not for a man like John. He was worldly and from a family of means, and she was the disgraced half-breed daughter of a poor country doctor. *Is that why he hesitated? Because he knew the truth about her past? Of course.* If she were lucky enough to find a man who would marry her, surly he would never touch her with such tenderness. *Damaged goods, forever her cross to bear.*

Part of her wanted to go back to his room and give in to him. She wanted to know what it was like to be with a man that truly wanted her.

It didn't matter if they would never marry; she just wanted to be touched tenderly, maybe even loved a little. If only for a moment, just to know Heaven in a man's arms. Yes, she confessed to herself, even if it meant being his mistress, his "business partner." But he was leaving soon, and she had a gut feeling he was never coming back.

She could still hear his husky voice in her ear, making her blush again, her breasts aching against her tight stays. She closed her eyes, trying not to think about how lonely she would be once he left.

Chapter Forty

It was unearthly quiet as DeLancie and his men approached the little cabin. From his vantage point, he could see two guards flanking the doors and two more at the back of the structure, all four Oneida braves. The log cabin sat on high ground within the swamp, the only access to it from a strip of land on the west side. A perfect hiding place unless, a stronger, more adept foe, found it—which he was.

"Half of you go to the right, half of you to the left, Eagle Eyes behind me. Don't come out until you hear my signal," he whispered, adrenaline coursing through his veins, evoking a heady feeling that always preceded a battle. It was the anticipation of the act he loved most, holding back until the right moment, and then striking with full force.

"Save one for me," DeLancie said with delight, looking at Eagle Eyes.

The reticent native nodded.

The full winter moon reflected off the snowy blanket of the forest, illuminating it with a heavenly glow. The wind was quiet and still, the chilly night air their only adversary sent by Mother Nature. It was the perfect night for an ambush. Taking a deep breath, DeLancie readied himself. It was time to make an entrance, his favorite part of the show. Slowly, he cantered his horse towards the cabin, both Oneida braves simultaneously aiming their muskets at him.

"*Shekoli*, friends, I believe you have something that doesn't belong to you," he yelled. "We've come to take it back."

From behind, his men came out from the trees, descending on the small wooden cabin, the sounds of whooping and howling slicing through the tranquility of the night. The two guards closest to him went down before he even had a chance to blink, both of them with bullets to the forehead.

Dismounting his horse, DeLancie motioned for one of his men to follow and approached the cabin with both shoulders thrown back and head high like Caesar the conqueror come to see his plunder. Throwing the doors open, DeLancie grinned with excitement. Inside were hundreds of barrels of gunpowder and shot, all marked with back-to-back C's topped with a crown, the symbol of Carlisle Shipping.

"Thank you, Johnny," he said, running his hands over the branded symbol on one of the powder kegs. "I'll find plenty of use for this."

Turning around, surveying the area, DeLancie spotted a figure running towards the river, the bare trees providing no cover for his retreat. With a blast and a puff of smoke, a musket when off right next to him, the retreating figure taking a bullet to the calf but continuing to run.

"Got him," the soldier nearby said, grinning. "I'll run after him, Major, he won't get far."

"You idiot, one spark and this whole barn will go up in flames." DeLancie grabbed the soldier's musket by the barrel and pushed back, bashing his nose in with the stock. "Don't make that mistake again."

The soldier nodded, blood running down his lips and chin.

"Eagle Eyes, one of our Oneida friends has run towards the river. Please, bring him back to me."

There would be no one escaping to tell tales, DeLancie would see to it. It was time the Oneida learned their lesson once and for all.

Slowly, DeLancie walked towards the back of the barn to investigate. Two of the guards were lying dead in the snow, blood seeping from their wounds, turning the snowy white blanket crimson—the color of war.

Suddenly, he heard a crack coming from behind him and then a footstep; he stopped, waiting for whomever it was to make a move. When they didn't, he pulled out his pistol and advanced slowly, anticipating a strike. "I know you're there. If you try to take me, I'll gut you and eat your heart. If you run, I'll hunt you down, flay your skin off, and feed you to the wolves."

From above came a crushing weight, as a brave landed on top of the man, both of them falling to the ground in a large in a heap, DeLancie's pistol flying out of his hand. Disoriented, he tried to get up while the warrior on his back pounded his fists into DeLancie's flank. Once, twice, three times, until finally, he felt a crack, one of his ribs breaking from the direct hits. He took several deep gasps, fighting against the pain for air, the world fading to black. When DeLancie looked up for one of his men, another Oneida warrior jumped down from the roof, running past them towards the river.

"Eagle Eyes!" DeLancie yelled, the pain in his side making it near impossible to shout. "Another has gone for the river, stop him!"

"*Ohná:ka' nukwa:* Behind you," the brave on DeLancie's back yelled to the retreating Oneida.

Drawing in a deep breath, DeLancie willed himself strong. This was the fight he'd wanted for so long. Nothing would stop him. He focused on the anger and ignored the pain, and with Herculean strength, he elbowed the brave in the stomach, trying to free one pinned arm. But the warrior was a worthy adversary; he threw both legs over DeLancie's back, straddling him, then grabbed his queue and bashed his forehead into the ground several times. Blood ran into his eyes, obstructing his vision, the pain in his head spurring him on, sending another shot of adrenaline to his heart. Freeing his arm, he grabbed the knife from his hip and buried it in the man's thigh, causing him to draw back in pain. Seizing the opportunity, DeLancie rolled out from underneath the man, stood up, and pulled the tomahawk out.

"*Hányo*, come on," the Oneida taunted, standing up.

They walked in a circle, stalking each other like feral cats, waiting for the other to strike. It was exciting and primal—DeLancie's heart pounding in his ears as he eyed his foe, searching for his weakness. The brave lashed out with his knife, cutting into DeLancie's chest, blood seeping through the linen fabric. He smiled. More pain, more blood, it only heightened his senses, making him feel alive, aroused.

He noticed the brave was limping, favoring his injured leg, blood oozing from the knife wound. DeLancie lunged at the injured leg, using all his weight to take the warrior down. When they landed on the ground, DeLancie rolled the man onto his back, and with one quick stroke, embedded the tomahawk in his scalp, blood spattering like a crimson waterfall. Taking a deep breath, DeLancie pulled back, watching as the warrior screamed and flailed, the tomahawk still in his scalp.

"You're mine," DeLancie yelled, pulling the tomahawk out then burying it between the brave's eyes, splitting his face open, exposing a mass of bone and brain underneath. Blood sprayed back at DeLancie; he savored the metallic taste of it on his tongue as the body fell limp between his legs. His foe vanquished. DeLancie grabbed the dead warrior's hair, made several cuts in his scalp, then with one quick tug, tore the flesh away, claiming the prize.

When DeLancie stood erect, the stabbing pain in his side resumed, forcing him to take short, shallow breaths. His fractured ribs crunched and protested with each attempted to fill his lungs. A good battle always involved an injury, an intimate reminder of dominance over your foe. He smiled, remembering the look in the brave's eyes when the tomahawk was planted in his skull.

Walking back to the men, DeLancie held up the scalp in salute to their victory, causing them to whoop and holler in his honor. Eagle Eyes walked over, his face grave in spite of their celebration.

"Did you catch the two who ran?" DeLancie asked, grabbing his side, the pain getting worse with each second.

"No, they both got away."

"Why didn't you go after them? John would have picked him off before they even got close to the river." He purposely taunted the native, knowing how much he hated the former second-in-command. Eagle Eyes was notoriously brutal when provoked. *All the better, for him.* "You're slipping, my friend."

"If we even get close to Oriska, Han Yerry and his men will be on us. We're in no position to take on a whole village of Oneidas."

DeLancie grabbed his side again, watching while his men started to empty the cabin and load the weapons onto a cart. "They won't come after us, no need to worry. It's obvious they don't want the rest of the Confederacy to know what they're up to. No matter, we will see that their brothers find out. If forces are united, then separate them. Now get the men together; we move the supplies tonight."

Eagle Eyes directed the men as they loaded the barrels on the carts, the oxen fussing and huffing out steaming breaths as they waited in the cold night air. "Major, this can't be everything, there were two shipments that went missing."

"No, it isn't. The rest of it is in the fort; I'm sure of it." DeLancie paused, looking down at his bloody prize, stroking the silky black hair. "But I know Major Butler will find all of this very intriguing."

Mounting his horse, DeLancie rode ahead of his men, keeping his eyes on the forest. He owed his old friend a debt of gratitude, and now, because of John, DeLancie had the means to pay the Oneidas back for turning against him. *Time to settle old scores.*

"Thank you, Johnny," he said quietly to himself. "Thank you."

Chapter Forty-One

After what happened the night before, Dellis didn't know what to say to John, her mind revisiting the details of their intrigue over and over. She behaved like a wanton, like the shameless whore Jussie accused Dellis of being and not the proper lady she was. Goodness, she practically begged for him to touch her. She *did* beg him. With a groan, she buried her face in her hands. *Why did I just walk away?* Part of it was his fault; once again, he'd provoked her with his heated glances and his velvety smooth voice, and then when she succumbed, he pushed her away as if he was appalled at her behavior. *If he doesn't want me, why won't he just leave me alone? Damn.*

She could ponder the moment no longer, driving herself mad with unanswerable questions. She needed to get out and clear her head. Thankfully, the weather had finally let up, the sun peeking in through the frosty windows.

Walking back to the kitchen, she put her tray down and removed her apron. "Auntie, I'll be back in a few hours. I need some things from town."

Up to the elbows in soapy dishwater, Helena looked over her shoulder and smiled. "We could use more flour and cheese. I know we have more at my house. Ask Alexei, he'll see that you get it."

"All right." Dellis tied her white cotton bonnet in place then pulled her gray cloak over her dress, drawing the hood up. Once outside, she took a deep breath of cool winter air, letting it fill her lungs with relaxation. She made her way to the barn, saddled her mare, and then took off for her uncle's house. The ride felt good, the contrast of the cold wind and warm afternoon sun refreshing against her skin.

Her uncle's two-floor Georgian-style farmhouse was the biggest in town, with large windows and bright blue shutters that were visible through the evergreen trees that surrounded it. She'd heard it said that her uncle built his house to rival Johnson Hall, the palatial residence of Sir William Johnson, the deceased superintendent of Indian Affairs. It was beautiful and spacious, no expense spared, a stark contrast to the condition of The Thistle.

Dellis walked up to the front steps, kicked the snow off her boots on the mat, and knocked. When no one responded, she picked up her skirts and walked around the side of the house, looking through the windows to see if anyone was home. As she neared the rear, she spotted her uncle in his study talking to two men, their backs to her. One of them was Alexei, his height and long hair making him easily recognizable, the other man was surely her cousin Ruslan. Her uncle pointed to the table, bellowing so loud she could hear everything he was saying.

"Why didn't you pursue them down the trail? They would have been in the middle of Oneida territory. What good are all those natives to us if they won't fight?" His piercing blue eyes focused on his sons, staring them down with icy anger.

"We can't draw any more attention to ourselves, not yet," Alexei yelled back. "There's too much going on. It wasn't safe."

"You just blew hundreds of pounds, letting that shipment go." Her uncle crossed his arms over his chest, shaking his head. "What are you planning on doing now?"

"We'll get it back. My men are already tracking their movement. They won't get very far in this weather," Alexei responded.

"I knew you would cock this up eventually, Alexei. Now, what do we do about Stuart? He and his militia friends could very well have ruined this for all of us. Ruslan, where the hell were you?"

"Father, he's injured, there's no need to worry about him right now." She heard her younger cousin's voice chime in on cue.

What was he talking about? Stuart wasn't injured. She'd seen him fighting fit, not a couple days ago, in town. None of their conversation was making sense.

"At least we got the maps from him, father," Ruslan paused, his voice sounding strained. "Why fight to get the cargo back? Our contact in Niagara will tell us when the next shipment is due to come."

"If Major Butler discovers our man this could all be over," her uncle said, his tone getting more severe.

"What about the letters?" Alexei asked, walking around the table.

Dellis scooted closer to the window, her ears tuned in, remembering the letters her uncle put in his pocket.

"Did you find anything?"

"Nothing, only your cousin writing to your Uncle Dane. The rest of the letters were just shipping records."

"Just give me some time. I'll handle this." When Alexei glanced towards the window, she crouched down to hide from view. Her mind raced as she waited for the right moment to run. What did all of it mean?

Dellis's teeth started to chatter, the front of her dress now soaked all the way through to her shift from kneeling in the snow. When she looked up, Alexei was again peering at the window. There was no doubt in her mind that he saw her. Quickly, she bolted for the front door where a servant girl opened it before Dellis got a chance to knock.

Dusting the snow from her skirts, she said through chattering teeth, "Mariah, I'm here to see Alexei. Is he here?"

The pretty red-haired servant girl smiled, giving a nod. "Yes, Miss Dellis, follow me."

Wiping her boots off again, she stepped into the foyer, waiting for the servant girl to shut the door. The opulence of James's home always amazed Dellis, the foyer and main hall were dominated by a large, ornately-carved, wooden staircase, with a giant glass candelabra suspended from the ceiling above, casting glittering shadows from the flickering tapers. She followed Mariah into the parlor, Dellis's favorite room in the house. It was painted in the subtlest blue that reminded her of her mother's sitting room, and the original Chippendale furnishings that once graced The Thistle now made up the entirety of the parlor, along with Dellis's parents' blue and gold oriental rugs. When she'd fallen on hard times, two years before, her uncle had bought all the precious furniture from her home, helping her keep The Thistle open. It was heartbreaking, selling her father's belongings, but at least this way, she could still visit them and remember. As they walked into the dining area, she couldn't help but admire the china, beautiful blue and white porcelain with intricate designs from the Far East, all on display in her mother's mahogany china cabinet.

Mariah propped open the door to James's study and said quietly, "Miss Dellis is here to see you."

"What does she want?" Dellis heard her uncle yell. She pushed past the girl, undaunted by his temper and unwilling to let him use it to frighten his servant.

"Hello, Uncle." Dellis walked into the study, facing him head-on, then nodded to Alexei and Ruslan, who were both eyeing her suspiciously.

"Were you listening outside, Dellis?" her uncle asked forcefully. "Tell the truth, girl."

"I was not." She looked him in the eyes like a practiced liar. When it came to her uncle, she felt no remorse for lying, had he not been stealing letters from her house and calling her names behind her back?

When he didn't respond, Dellis looked around the room, taking in her surroundings. She'd never been in her uncle's study before. It was a large room, the walls covered in expensive, intricately carved oak paneling, the alcoves stacked full of ledgers and leather-bound books. Knowing her shoes were covered in mud, she avoided standing on the beautiful red and white oriental rug that covered most of the floor.

"Actually, I came to see Alexei." She glanced at the map on his desk; it was of the county with a large black X marking her grandfather's village

348

and a small swamp north of the river. When her uncle flipped the map over, she saw one of John's maps lying underneath it. "If this is a bad time, Alexei, I can come back."

Alexei looked at the map, and then at her, an understanding passing between them. He knew what she saw, his eyes narrowing in silent warning to keep her mouth shut. Putting his fists on his hips, he replied, "No, it's fine. I was coming to get you next."

The tension in the room was palpable. Her uncle was suspicious of her intrusion, and whatever they were talking about was not meant for her ears. What had she stumbled in on? "Is there something wrong, Alexei?" she asked, playing the innocent bystander, though it was obvious she wasn't.

"Dellis, you know your place. This is none of your concern," her uncle said.

She hated how her uncle talked to her, as if she was an insignificant woman. When she was with her grandfather, it was just the opposite; a woman's advice in her tribe was invaluable. It was a strange dichotomy she was forced to exist in, never free to be herself, always vacillating between the traditions of her native family and the rules of the white man's world. Thankfully, Alexei learned his habits from her father and the village, always treating women with respect.

"I'm sorry for the intrusion, Uncle," she replied, biting a tart comment. "What did you need from me, Alexei?"

"Some of Joseph's men were injured last night. Anoki was shot in the leg."

So that was what they were talking about. Suddenly, it all made sense. John's men were right, Alexei and his men had stolen the supplies from the Captain, and now, someone had done the same to Alexei.

Holding back a gasp, she put on her most reticent face and said, "Where are they?"

"They're at your father's cabin. Skenandoa's looking after them, but I would prefer it if you would come."

"Of course, we should go right now." She nodded, glad for the opportunity to escape her uncle's looming presence and have a much-needed word with Alexei. "Goodbye, Uncle."

Picking up her skirts, Dellis walked to the front door, Alexei following a few paces behind. When they reached the barn, she whirled around and attacked. "What is going on, Alexei? Don't lie to me."

He brushed her off, walking to his horse and saddling it. "Dellis, you need to stop."

She moved to stand between him and his horse. "I heard you and your whole conversation—they're my people, too. Tell me the truth. What have you done?"

"Six of our men were attacked last night, not far from Oriska. Four of them were killed, and Anoki and Samuel were both shot. We think they were militiamen."

"Then it's the same group that went after the Mohawks?" she asked.

He nodded. "Most likely."

"So, these men stole from you what you stole from John."

A smirk started at the corner of his mouth and spread all the way across his lips. She was right, but there was no way he would admit it. No, she would have to wring it out of him. "You're wasting precious time, Dellis. Anoki and Samuel are not well."

"Fine, let's go. But you *will* answer my questions later." She mounted up, gave her mare a gentle kick, and they took off, Alexei following close behind.

The two of them rode hard the whole way to the village. It had warmed up a little, allowing the trail to thaw and become more passable, though occasional patches of ice still made it treacherous. Neither of them spoke over the long journey, a cloud of anger looming between the two of them, threatening to ignite with the slightest spark. She kept her frustration in check, focusing on the issue at hand; someone needed her help, and arguing with Alexei could wait. Besides, it would do him some good to anticipate when she would reprimand him, and that was exactly what it would be, a reprimand. This was all his fault. He was always blustering on about the Rebel cause, and now he'd dragged her village into this mess. *Damn him.*

When they reached her village they found it deserted, as expected, her grandfather and the rest of the people had finally moved on to Oriska for the remainder of the winter. The little houses were all closed up and the fires extinguished; even the pens where they kept their livestock were empty. From her vantage point, she could see smoke coming from her father's cabin. Together, they rode up the hill quickly, and she dismounted, handing her mare's reins off to Alexei.

With a knock, she opened the door to the little cabin; inside Anoki and Samuel were both lying on the cots, and Skenandoa was sitting by the fire, sewing.

"Thank goodness, Dellis." Skenandoa got up and hugged her cousin, lines of concerning forming at the corners of tired eyes. "I don't know what to do. The bullet is lodged deep in Anoki's leg, and Samuel won't stop bleeding."

"All right." She patted her cousin's hand, then quickly removed the cloak and bonnet. Dellis got down on her knees next to the cot and carefully removed the blanket from Samuel's abdomen. She gasped at the bloody sight—he'd been disemboweled. The bullet had torn a hole through his belly, blowing it completely open, exposing pink, moist organs and meaty flesh. When she touched his forehead, he opened his eyes for a second, glancing at her, before they rolled back again. He was feverish, the wound already starting to fester.

Walking outside, she motioned for Alexei to follow. "He's not going to make it much longer. The wound is deep and penetrated his organs; even if I take the ball out, I can't save him."

"What do we do, Dellis?" he asked between tortured breaths. She put her hand on her cousin's shoulder, trying to comfort him. Samuel was one of Alexei's best friends.

"We need to get Kateri, she deserves to say goodbye to her brother."

"Dellis, I can't leave him," Alexei said, walking back inside and kneeling down next to his friend.

She ached for her cousin and the loss of his dear friend, but it was in God's hands now, just as her father taught her. Touching Alexei's arm, she said quietly, "Alexei, Samuel is the only family Kateri has. The woman watched as her mother was raped and murdered by Redcoats. She never got a chance to say goodbye. We owe her a chance to send her brother on his way and release him from his duties to the tribe. Please, get her. Skenandoa and I will look after him until you return."

Alexei nodded, taking one last look at his dying friend. Grabbing her cousin's hand, she squeezed it lightly. "He knows you're here."

"What will you do to help him along?"

"If I can get him to drink, I'll give him opium. It'll help him rest and go peacefully." She wrapped her arms around her cousin, wanting desperately to comfort him. He buried his face in her neck, hiding his tears, though she could feel the little drops of sadness and wet eyelashes flickering against the sensitive skin. With a pat on his back, she whispered in his ear, "I'll stay with him, now go."

"Thank you," he said, hugging her again before he left. "I'll be back."

Once Alexei was gone, Dellis turned her attention to Anoki's leg. She smiled, addressing him in Oneida. "*Shekoli*, Anoki, I'm going to take the ball out. You won't be able to walk or ride for a few days, but it will get better, I promise."

He nodded, his black eyes watching her curiously. His long, straight, black hair hung to his shoulders, his face smeared with red and black paint, making him look every bit the fierce warrior he was reputed to be. The metal ball had embedded itself snugly against the bone in the fleshy part of his calf. As an Oneida brave, there was no need to warn him about the pain. He was up to the challenge; his life full of battle and injuries since the very beginning.

"I'm going to start," she said, waiting for him to be ready.

He nodded, stoically, as if what she was about to do was beneath his concern.

Reaching for a bottle of spirits, she doused the wound and went at it, digging the ball out with her knife. Anoki curiously watched as she

352

worked, never wincing or looking away. When she finally retrieved the bullet, a fresh flow of blood started again; she daubed it with a linen swatch then cleaned the wound and wrapped it tightly.

"Thank you, Dellis," he said, looking into her eyes. He was handsome with high, razor-sharp cheekbones and wide-set, black eyes that were regarding her intently. His skin was the color of tea with too much milk in it, and so smooth it looked like the most skilled woodsman carved it.

To her surprise, he touched her face, gently running the backs of his long, sinewy fingers down her cheek, then grazing her lips. She didn't feel the urge to pull away, his touch warm and soft, and the sensation surprisingly pleasant. "You are beautiful, just like your mother. I have often wanted to tell you, but like her, you have the fire for the white man."

She blushed, never realizing his attraction to her until now. "You are right, Anoki, I have the fire," she said, thinking of John.

"Be careful it doesn't burn you like it did Lily," he replied.

Chapter
Forty-Two

J ohn made several trips up and down the stairs, his lungs winded, but the rest of his body was on the mend, finally able to take the steps at a normal pace. Granted, he still looked like hell, with black and blue bruises around his eyes and healing cuts on his lips, but he could breathe out of his nose, which was thankfully not broken. The rest of his injuries were gradually getting better; only his left arm was still weak, clicking and protesting when he overexerted himself.

As he retook the stairs, he spotted Stuart walking through the front door, suspiciously clean and dressed in new clothing. John wasn't quite sure what to make of that. Last he'd heard, Dellis had thrown her brother out for good. But to that point, she wasn't speaking to John either; she disappeared most of the day, and when she was around, she avoided conversation with him when they came in contact.

He walked to his room and sat down at the desk, resting his head against the back of his chair and closing his eyes. Several times he had a vision of Dellis holding his tortured body against her own, her sweet voice whispering in his ear while she wrapped her arms and legs around him, keeping him warm. He could see her silky hair resting against her cheek, her eyes closed serenely, as she pressed her lips to his forehead and stroked his hair. The dream was so vivid he was beginning to believe it was real.

Clark and Smith walked into the room, their yammering and loud footsteps disturbing John's quiet reflection.

"Captain, we know where the supplies went," Smith said, removing his hat and scratching his head.

John lifted his head, looking at his men. They were both wind-blown and tired, with red cheeks and dark circles under their eyes, occasional pieces of straw sticking out of it Smith's hair. Apparently, they had fallen asleep in a barn somewhere while on surveillance. "Where are they?"

Smith pulled a map out of his breast pocket and put it on the desk. "Yesterday, I followed Alexei McKesson to a cabin not far from the fort, south of the river." He pointed to a location between Fort Stanwix and Oriska. "I wasn't able to get away without being seen, so I waited until it was late. Before I got very far, DeLancie showed up with his men and Eagle Eyes. They killed the guards and took everything, and then headed west, towards Wood Creek. The cabin was full of powder, and more than what we had in our shipments. The Oneidas have been stockpiling for a while."

"So, we were right, McKesson and the Oneidas are the thieves." John's ire rose as he remembered all the women who died, his ruined career, all because of the whim of some fool who fancied himself a Rebel.

"But if they're stockpiling weapons, why would Joseph arrange a trade? To keep up the guise of innocence? Could Alexei be a profiteer?" John asked, thinking out loud, trying to put the pieces together. "McKesson doesn't seem like the type; he's too much of a martyr to his cause, and I don't give him that much credit. The Oneidas are definitely not selling the supplies, they could easily be tracked. There has to be more to it."

"What about Miss McKesson?" Clark added. "She's the one who took you to the village to trade with the Oneidas, then a few days later our supplies go missing. She was their front, their cover to keep you distracted while they learned as much as they could about us." With each statement, Clark's excitement rose, and so did the volume of his voice, until it bordered on a yell. "She was probably giving them the information all the time. Hell, there's no way she isn't part of it. It's time to face facts, John."

He shook his head, his own power of deductions showing him a different version of the story, a more practical one. "It actually makes no sense for her to help them. Did they use her as a front? Of that, I have no doubt, but there's no way she actively took part in their plan. She's naïve and, like her cousin, a martyr to her cause. She wants more than anything to keep her people out of this fight, British side or American, and she would do anything to make that happen. You've seen how headstrong she can be. That's why she wanted me to trade with them so badly, to keep her tribe out of the war."

John breathed a sigh of relief. He hadn't realized how much her potential involvement was weighing on his mind. His revelation proved she was as innocent as she seemed, though it also revealed the depths of her family's treachery. It was one of many devastating betrayals she would eventually have to face—including his own.

"Then how does DeLancie fit in?" Smith asked, looking at both of them.

"He doesn't. He has his own agenda."

Smith shook his head, slow on the uptake. "I don't understand; DeLancie just stole the supplies from Alexei and his men."

"He wants me. The Oneidas are collateral damage." Gathering the papers up from his desk, John carried them over to the fireplace and stuffed them in the mantle with the secret letters. Grabbing his cloak from the back of his chair, he pulled it on, reaching into his pockets for his gloves.

"Where are you going?" Clark asked, standing up.

Suddenly the whole picture was clear to John: the theft, the Oneidas, Alexei, all of it, and there was no time to lose. It could be his last chance to prove he was right. "We're going to see if there's anything still in that barn at the village."

Smith shook his head. "There's nothing there. When we found you, it was completely empty."

"No, someone tried to kill me over whatever was in that barn. It's the perfect place to hide excess. They can't keep it at Oriska or they'll be discovered, and whatever they kept at the cabin is gone."

"This is a fool's errand, John," Clark said, accentuating his R's with his rich, Scottish brogue. "They caught you there once; don't you think they're on to us?"

John turned to Clark and smiled. "When the second shipment disappeared, you were ambushed on the Carry, close to Stanwix. They could easily move the load to that storage cabin or the fort—neither were that far away. But my first shipment they took was here, in town, at our storage shed. They would've had to travel an additional fifteen miles, cross the river, and row against the current in bad weather to move the supplies to that cabin. It was too much work not to be discovered, especially if DeLancie has been watching them all along. Even if they're stockpiling to sell to the Rebels, they still have to be keeping some for themselves. And we know the Oneidas wouldn't leave that village unprotected, not after what happened to them two years ago.

"You know what this means, don't you?" Smith asked, exchanging looks with Clark.

John turned to both of them and nodded. "What's left of my supplies are hidden in that barn, and Alexei McKesson is the son of a bitch we were looking for two years ago."

"It's too easy, John, and it doesn't explain DeLancie."

"No Simon, it doesn't, but let's solve one problem first, and then we can deal with the other." Pulling his gloves on, he pointed to the door. "Get your stuff and get Hayes. We need to hurry in case they get an itch to move everything now that DeLancie is on to them."

Chapter
Forty-Three

When they arrived at the village, it appeared to be deserted, though John knew things were never what they seemed. The moon was shining brilliantly through the trees, no canopy of leaves to temper its light. As he walked towards the barn, the past came back to him, the screams echoing in his head, and all around him a heavenly, haunting glow—the specters of the forest. Suddenly, right in front of him, the woman appeared, a bloody rag at her breast as she pointed her finger and chanted her breathy refrains, "*...until justice is done. Your fortunes will forever be tied to ours until justice is done.*" He looked into her eyes, as he wished he had done that day, and said with no uncertainty, "I'll get justice for you. I swear it."

"John?" Clark called John's name from behind. "Who are you talking to?"

He ignored it, his friend would never understand. No one could. The ghosts were John's burden to carry. He looked into her eyes one last time, and then stepped through apparition with enough determination for himself and every lost woman of their tribe. He could almost feel their spirits around him, spurring him on towards the truth. Were they really a curse, or in fact, just wronged souls reaching out to him, their only witness to the crime. It was a strange turn of fate that brought him back to this place after two years, that he would be the one to take up their worthy cause.

"Cover me," John said over his shoulder, and with his finger, he pointed out his orders: Clark to the right, Smith to the left, Hayes to follow. John opened the door to the barn, the sweet smell of hay hitting him upon first entry, then the sensation of bone-chilling wind whipping through the cracks and crevices between the wood boards. He pointed for Hayes to investigate the hayloft while John searched the perimeter. Walking towards the far wall, he looked up and saw grooves on the wooden rafters from where the chains that held him once hung, and on the ground, his shackles lay unlocked. He shuddered, remembering the pain he suffered at the hands of his unknown tormentor, his body yet to fully recover. So many secrets hidden in that barn; if those walls could only talk, the questions he would ask.

As expected, all of the horses' stalls were empty, the ground covered in hay with random traces of food and excrement. He'd searched them that night and found nothing, no hidden cubby, nothing buried under the hay. Then he remembered something; the night he was captured, Dellis's horse had been in one of the stalls, he'd never searched that one.

Opening the gate to the last stall, he got down on his knees and shuffled the hay around, feeling the ground with his hands. When he got to the corner, he moved a haybale out of the way, only to find a small stack of wooden boxes, and on the ground underneath, a large piece of wood placed flush with the ground. Carefully, he lifted one the boxes. It was heavy, the sound of metal rolling around inside confirming his suspicions. They were all full of musket balls. He picked the box up and carried it to the door; in the moonlight, he could see the imprint of his family's shipping insignia burned into the wooden surface.

His heart racing with excitement, he ran back to the stall and pulled the heavy piece of wood back revealing a small hidden space in the ground. He leaned over to look inside, but it was too dark to see anything.

"Clark, Hayes, in here!" he yelled over his shoulder.

Yes. Finally. After two years, and the ruin of his career, he was justified. They had hidden the supplies in the barn; it was just as he said.

His two men showed up, both of them looking on, slack-jawed. "John? Did you find a hidden storage place?"

"Yeah, I sure did," he said, breathless with excitement. "Help me get these boxes out of here, and then we'll take a look." He waved them on, pointing at the wooden boxes stacked neatly in the corner. "Did Hayes find anything?"

"He's in the hayloft looking around," Clark replied.

John picked up two of the heavy boxes, his shoulder smarting in protest, but he barely felt the pain, he was too elated at his revelation. As he neared the door, he heard footsteps and the crack of a tree branch. John adjusted the boxes in his arms, pointing to Clark and Hayes to investigate. Someone was out there, but there was no way John was leaving without his supplies, not this time. If they wanted a fight, then he was more than ready for it.

Quickly, he rushed down the hill, carrying the boxes to their horses, then made his way back up again. There were at least ten boxes in the stall, and who knew what was hidden in that storage cubby under the ground. They would have to find a cart or something to help them haul everything back to their storage shed in town, but that was just a technicality; one way or the other, it was all going.

Just when neared the bottom the hill again, he heard movement and the crunching of snow underfoot coming from the woods. Slowly, he walked towards it, the crunching noise getting louder with each step, picking up pace. He scanned the trees, their bare, spindly fingers offering no camouflage, nor did the moon, like a giant lantern in the night sky, yet still he saw nothing. But his spy was there, somewhere, John could feel it, his soldier's instincts well honed. Suddenly, he heard a noise again, on his left, the cracking of tree branches and quick feet darting off into the brush. The noise that followed sent a chill down his spine. *Hiss!* It was incessant and persistent as only that sound could be, for he knew it all too well.

John threw the boxes down and ran up the hill, his feet slipping and sliding on the slick, icy ground beneath him. "Get out of the barn!" he yelled, landing on his knees in the snow. Clark and Smith came rushing through the door, just as the barn burst into flames.

With an earth-shattering boom and an intense gust of wind, the blast lifted him off his knees, throwing him several feet into the air. He landed on the ground with the hard thud of gravity and thirteen stones worth of weight, forcing the air from his chest. He gasped and fought for breath against his paralyzed lungs, debris flying at him in all directions, like little pins and needles piercing his skin through his shirt. Burying his face in his arms, he coughed several times, drawing in what little air he could. The snow was wet and cold beneath him, a stark contrast to the intense heat that blew in powerful gusts around him like a tempest. When he could finally breathe again, John lifted his head, his eyes watering from the smoke and heat as he surveyed the area. The forest and everything around it were engulfed in flames, the debris from the barn spread out over several yards.

Slowly sitting up, he spotted a figure running towards the cabin, her familiar form and dark hair identifying who it was.

My God. "Dellis!" he yelled, getting up as fast as he could and running after her. As he got closer to her, another explosion erupted from the barn, the force blowing him back to his hands and knees, more debris flying into his face. He put his head down, self-preservation forcing him to take his eyes off her.

When he finally looked up again, she was several feet ahead of him, lying face down in the snow. "No," he murmured, his heart racing in terror. He got up and ran to her, adrenaline and fear making him quick on his feet though the ground was slick beneath him. "Dellis! Dellis." He got down on his knees, wrapped one of her arms around his shoulder, and lifted her up. She was limp and light in his arms, small cuts littered her forehead, and both her cheeks were blackened from soot, but she was all right. As he carried her back to their horses, another explosion erupted from the barn, blowing wood fragments and pellets in all directions. He wrapped himself around her, creating a protective barrier with his back, while more wood and debris embedded itself in his flesh.

Gently, he brought her down to the ground, still cradling her body in his arms. "Dellis, wake up." He shook her a little, trying to rouse her. She started to cough, her eyes rolling open as she looked up at him. "John?" She groaned, shaking her head. "What happened?"

"Thank God," he whispered, burying his face in her neck, breathing in her lavender scent. He kissed her cheek, holding her close for a couple of seconds, grateful she was unharmed. When he looked up again, the whole forest was an inferno, the flames like hands greedily reaching for the trees towards the heavens.

"Oh, my God, Anoki, Skenandoa," She pulled away from him suddenly and started to run back towards the remnants of the barn. He let out a groan. *Damned headstrong woman.* John got up quickly and chased her down before she could get very far. Wrapping his arms around her waist, he pulled her back, while she kicked in screamed in protest. "John, let me go. I have to save them."

"Save who?" What was she talking about? He tried to subdue her, but she thrashed about, her arms and legs flailing around, trying to break free from his grasp. "Stop, Dellis, stop," he yelled, but she continued fighting as if her life depended on it. "Would you just tell me what's going on? Save who? Dellis, what are you doing here?"

"They're in the cabin!" She pointed to it frantically, her eyes wide with terror, tears streaming down her cheeks. "We have to help them."

He looked back at the wreckage and shook his head, the truth like a knife to the gut. "Dellis, there's no way anyone could've survived that explosion. The roof is caved in."

But instead of seeing reason, she rebelled, much to his chagrin. "If you won't save them I will. I'm going, and don't try to stop me," she yelled, breaking free and taking off towards the cabin.

"Damn," he yelled, and then let out a string of expletives that would've made a sailor blush. He admired her fighting spirit and sense of loyalty, but this was beyond reason. John ran after her; only this time, he didn't have to subdue her, she stopped just a yard from the cabin, her eyes wide as she looked up at the fire.

"John, please, please," she begged, turning those wide, tearful doe eyes on him, and he was lost.

There was little chance any of them were still alive, with the cabin completely engulfed in flames and half collapsed. But he had to try if only to save her from herself. "If you stop fighting me, I will go."

She nodded. Quickly, he removed his cloak and overcoat, handing them to her. She wrapped her arms around his coats, hugging them to her chest. "Stay here," he told her, looking into her eyes. "Do *not* come after me, no matter what happens. Do you hear me?"

"Yes," she replied, though there was a haughty protest in her compliance. He'd better find them, or he would soon be rescuing her, too. Of this, he had no doubt.

Taking a deep breath, John looked at the cabin, made another long run of expletives, and went for it. When he got to the door, he kicked it in, the trapped smoke gusting in his face with a loud whoosh, singeing his eyelashes. He winced and pulled back for a second, closing his eyes against the pain. When he could see again, he covered his nose and mouth with his sleeve and crossed the threshold. The first thing he spotted was a pair of legs and a torso trapped under one of the fallen ceiling beams. After kicking it several times, the smoldering wood cracked and popped as it rolled out of the way, allowing him access to the unmoving form. It was Skenandoa. With a grunt, he lifted her up and carried her outside, laying her down in the snow.

"Anoki and Samuel are still in there," Dellis yelled from behind, following him back to the cabin.

"Dellis, get out of here." He waved her off, motioning for her to stay back; the last thing he needed was to worry about her, too. Coughing several times, he undid his neckerchief, wiped the sweat from his forehead with it, then tied it around his nose and mouth. When he entered again, in the corner, he could see two pairs of legs, both of them were stuck under one of the cots, another smoldering ceiling beam lying on top of them. Pushing the wood out of the way, he rolled the cot over and found

Anoki unconscious with Samuel in his arms. John leaned down, grabbing Samuel's hands, and dragged him through the door.

Rushing back inside, John went back to the corner and got down on his knees next to the injured brave. "Anoki, can you walk?" John yelled over the rumbling of the fire.

Anoki pointed to his calf, a large bloody bandage tied around it, then shook his head. John looked up and gasped. The building was starting to rock with the wind, white-hot flames licking the walls of the cabin, threatening to bring it down on top of them in any second.

"I'll help you walk." Leaning down, John grabbed Anoki's arm, got under it, and lifted him to his feet. "Okay, here we go."

John gripped Anoki's waist, helping him limp to the door. As they passed through the door frame, the lintel broke in half with a loud pop, both pieces landing on his back, forcing him to the ground. Stunned, John lay immobile for a moment, the weight of the wooden beam crushing his chest. Anoki lay next to him, pinned to the ground.

"Crawl out of here." John gasped, trying to catch his breath, a sharp pain shooting down his back into his leg with each attempted movement. With a loud grunt, he fought the pain, pushing his chest up, giving Anoki just enough room to crawl out from underneath.

"You're on fire," Anoki yelled, his eyes wide.

Gasping for air, John fell back on the ground, too tired to fight anymore. His shirt smoldered beneath the burning wood while smoke filled his lungs with poisonous gas. Everything faded to black; his senses dulled to the point of nihility. Suddenly, he heard voices and a sweet song that penetrated the fog. *Justice, John.* He looked up towards it, expecting to see the ghost coming to get him, but instead, it was Dellis and Anoki. They were trying to free John. "Help." He gasped, barely able to push out a word under the weight of the wood.

"Hold on, John," she yelled, and a second later he felt the weight lifted off his back. Blessed relief and a surge of air filled his lungs, bringing him back to life. Warm hands grabbed his own and started to pull him through the doorway. His injured shoulder screamed in protest, pain shooting through his arm causing his hand to go completely numb. He let out a howl, using it push through the pain, while Dellis and Anoki dragged John the rest of the way out and deposited him in the snow.

He barely had a second to catch his breath; a pair of strong hands grabbed his shoulders, pushed him onto his back, and forced him to roll back and forth. "You're on fire, roll around," Anoki yelled, tossing John about on the wet, cold ground.

John rolled around several times, the raw wounds underneath his clothes protesting the cold, while he worked to smother the flames. When his clothes were finally snuffed out, he lay still for a moment and closed his eyes. Though he was sure God wanted none of John's praise, he said a silent thank you for sparing his heathen-scoundrel life one more time.

Before he even started to get up, Dellis was on her knees next to him, her hands already on his face, examining it. "John, thank God, I saw the door cave in on you, and I thought..." She started to cry, wrapping her arms around him.

He buried his face in her neck, indulging in the comfort of her soft, womanly embrace, and her sweet words in his ear.

"Oh, John, I thought I was going to lose you."

"I'm all right," he replied, holding on to her for a moment, catching his breath. "I don't know about Samuel. You should check on him. How is everyone else?"

When she backed away, he could see tears in her dark eyes. "Skenandoa is fine, but Samuel didn't make it... and before his sister could say goodbye."

He nodded, grateful at least, that she was safe; everything else would have to wait. "I have to find out what happened to my men." Slowly, he eased his way onto his feet, every muscle in his body fighting back in protest. He pulled his pistol out of the holster and handed it to her. "You know what to do with this. Stay here."

The fire raged on, now spreading into the woods, consuming the trees with the might and hunger of Cronus. John walked the perimeter quickly, staying as far away from the blaze as he could. Everywhere he looked there was debris, the barn and the cabin reduced to unrecognizable ash—but there was no sign of his men. He had seen Clark and Smith run from the barn, right before the blast, but there was no hope for Hayes or his evidence. All of John's supplies had blown up, his proof once again cruelly snatched away from him by Karma's sleight of hand.

"Damn!" He cursed, loudly, kicking a smoldering piece of wood with his foot.

As he continued to search the wreckage, John spotted two riders approaching; one of them was a woman, and the other was Alexei, his tall stature and arrogant carriage unmistakable even across the distance.

"What the hell happened here? What did you do?" Alexei yelled, riding up and dismounting quickly. Kateri got down from her horse and ran past them, falling on her knees next to her brother and bursting into tears.

Just as John was about to deliver Alexei an earful, Dellis ran over, strategically placing herself between the two of them. "The barn blew up out of nowhere, Alexei. Thank God Captain Anderson was here and rescued us."

He looked down at Dellis, dwarfed between the two of them and ignorant of their silent feud, yet she fearlessly held them back. Had she known the true origin of their hate, and the depths of both of their treachery, she might have pulled out her gun and shot them both.

Alexei's nostrils flared, his eyes narrowing. "How in God's name did it blow up?"

John crossed his arms over his chest, relishing the opportunity to watch his adversary's frustration. "That's an excellent question, McKesson. I'd like to know the same thing. Perhaps it was full of gunpowder and bullets?" He pointed to one of the metal balls lying on the ground.

"You had something to do with this," Alexei yelled, stepping closer to Dellis, posturing for a fight.

"Alexei, no! Stop, now." Dellis grabbed her cousin's arms, preventing him from advancing further. The men's eyes locked above her head.

"I was trying to figure out why someone would torture me in this barn. I have a pretty good idea now. It was full of my supplies." John said, cocking a brow. "I guess I was getting a little too close for comfort."

"Too bad they didn't finish you off," Alexei said, grinning.

That was it. John grabbed Dellis's shoulders, trying to move her out from between them, but she wouldn't budge. Turning around, she stopped him with pleading eyes and outstretched hands. "John, please, go find your men. Arguing will do neither of you any good."

Two years of pent-up frustration was ready to come out in the form of his fist, but she stood between them begging, silently, for him to relent. No, he wouldn't fight her cousin in front of her, no matter how badly John wanted it. But perhaps he would later, when she wasn't around.

"I'll be back. Wait for me." He kissed Dellis's palm, grateful for her safety. When he looked up, Alexei was watching, rage in his eyes.

Leaving the wreckage, John mounted his horse and rode off towards the river, glad to get away and let his temper cool off. The longer he was around Alexei, the more likely it was they would come to blows.

John found Clark on his horse a mile outside the village, looking disheveled. "John, what the hell just happened?"

John turned his horse around, watching the skyline light up with flames, a blanket of black smoke floating over the forest. "I can't believe someone just blew the barn to kingdom come." Rubbing his forehead, John willed himself calm, though a tirade was slow brewing under the surface. "Hayes was in the hayloft. He didn't make it."

"Good God!" Clark exclaimed, crossing himself.

"What about Smith? Where did he go?"

"He rode off like the Devil on a hellhound after something. I think he saw the blaggard that lit the blaze. John, why in the bloody hell did they blow the barn? They just lost everything now that DeLancie took the magazine."

John shook his head. "The goal wasn't to blow the powder; it was to kill us."

"Do you think it was McKesson?" Clark asked his eyes focused horizon.

"No. As a matter of fact, he showed up seconds later, blustering like an idiot."

"I bet McKesson was bloody well lit up over seeing his powder blown to shit." Clark snorted.

John rolled his eyes. Actually, it was his powder that was blown up, but there was some humor to be found in witnessing his tormentor's misfortune. Whoever was responsible for the explosion would pay for what happened to Hayes. John would see to it. "Go find Smith. If he catches someone, I want him brought back alive. No one touches him but me."

Once Clark was out of sight, John gave Viceroy a kick and rode back to the wreckage site. As he neared, Dellis ran up to him, her eyes full of concern. "Did you find your men?"

"Yes, they went in the opposite direction of the blaze. Clark and Smith are all right, but Hayes didn't make it."

"John, I'm so sorry. Did he have a family?" she asked, offering him a hand to help him dismount, but he waved her off.

It did take more than a soldier's effort to get down from the saddle, and when he put his feet on the ground, there was a moment where he questioned whether he would ever be able to ride again. Viceroy whinnied behind him, a laugh at his sorry state of affairs.

John gave his horse a look of warning. "Keep it up; you can be replaced," he said, then turned his attention to Dellis. "Why don't we get out of here? We can talk on the way."

"Oh goodness, Brynn! I forgot all about her." She ran ahead of him towards the blaze, then stopped and turned around, a look of confusion on her face. "She was next to the cabin. John, my horse, did you see her? Did she get away?"

Shaking his head, he walked over to her and pulled her into his arms just before she started to weep. "No, she didn't run, Dellis. Nothing could've lived through a blast that close to the source."

"What am I going to do now? She was a gift from my father. I can't afford to get another." Her eyes brimmed with tears, still searching around for her precious mount. "Oh, God, she's really gone? How could this have happened?"

His heart ached for her—one more thing she loved was gone. She held on to him, crying softly into his shirt, her body trembling with grief. He kissed her forehead, gently stroking her hair, a surprisingly loving gesture that oddly felt good and right. She pulled back, wiping her eyes with the heel of her hands, then looked around at the wreckage. He reached out and took her hand, giving it a little squeeze. "Dellis, we need to go; it's not safe here. I'll take you home."

Like a storm rolling in, Alexei slapped John's hand away and blustered like thunder. "Take your hands off her. Dellis will ride with me."

"Really? Don't you trust me with her?" He smirked, sizing Alexei up. John had taken down more formidable foes in a round of fisticuffs before.

"Of course not, rogue." Alexei spat back. "Don't you have a woman already?"

Before John could throw out a bit of provocation, Dellis again stepped between the two of them, putting her hands on her cousin's chest. "Alexei, please, I'll be fine, no need to worry. I'll ride with the Captain, and Skenandoa can ride with Anoki on Hayes's horse. Please, go with Kateri and take Samuel's body back. She'll need you."

John mentally threw up his hands with frustration; once again, she'd put herself in the middle of his argument. The woman was headstrong to the point of impertinence. His temper was already threatening a tirade, and she'd just redirected the focus. He clenched his fists, resisting the urge to throttle her.

"Fine." Alexei backed off and turned to his horse, leaving John just enough time to see a sly grin.

How John would like to wipe it off. This whole debacle was of Alexie's making.

"I'll see you later Dellis, and you too, Captain," he said, with a taunt and a wink.

John grit his teeth. *You just can't leave it alone.*

Dellis gave him a look that said, "Please, let it go," her feminine intuition picking up on their inevitable cockfight and their mental posturing. For her sake, he would.

Once again, she circumvented a fight, and though he hated to admit it, she was right; now was not the time to deal with Alexei McKesson, no matter how much John's ego demanded it. There would be opportunities later for payback, and he relished the prospect of doing so.

"Dellis, we should go."

He clasped her hand and led her back to his horse, looking one last time as the inferno claimed what was left of his supplies and his only chance of completing his mission. *Damn! What now?*

Chapter
Forty-Four

Opening her eyes, Dellis rubbed the sleep from them, her body protesting as she looked at the canopy above her bed, unsure how she got there. The last thing she remembered was riding through the woods on Viceroy, the cool night air causing her to snuggle into John's warmth. She could still feel his body pressed against her own, the intimacy of his thighs touching hers, tensing and relaxing as he controlled the movement of his horse. Resting against him, she'd closed her eyes, indulging in the incredible sensation of his arms around her as he gripped the reins, his warm breath on her neck sending a chill down her spine that rivaled the night air. At one point, Dellis felt his lips touching her ear, his caress so light and heady she ached, her thighs instinctively gripping the horse. She reached up and touched his cheek, feeling his smooth skin against her fingertips as he whispered inaudible words into her hair. It was heavenly to be so close to him, her body feeling light and buoyant just from the memory.

Dellis sat up and threw the blankets off, her mind still groggy from sleep. It wasn't even morning yet, the moon still high in the sky, shining through her window, reflecting off her white coverlet. It occurred to her that she was undressed, wearing only her stays and under petticoat. Her dress was neatly draped across the chair next to her bed, and her stockings were hanging near the fire drying. She must have fallen asleep on the ride home, and he'd brought her inside and put her to bed. She blushed from neck to cheeks, imagining him undressing her and removing her stockings, which went well above her knees.

Throwing her legs over the side of the bed, she grabbed her long, wool robe and tied it around herself, taking a moment to perform simple ablutions. The fire had left traces of soot on her cheeks, and her hair was littered with pieces of wood and rubbish. Quickly, she washed up then retied her hair at the nape. Looking into the mirror, she remembered the feeling of terror as she watched the cabin collapse around him. She could see him rolling around in the snow, his clothes smoldering. Closing her eyes, she thanked God for sparing John. The thought of another person she cared for being taken from her was like a knife through her heart.

Without thinking twice, she grabbed her basket of supplies and ran up the servants' staircase. She needed to know he was all right. When she closed her eyes again, she saw the beam fall on his back, and John crumpling to his knees. *Oh, God.* A panic set in, her heart racing as she stepped into the hall.

It was dark, a hint of light coming from his cracked door like a beacon in the night. When she pushed it open, he was standing with his back to her looking out the window. His shirt was charred black, and she could see the wounds on his back where the linen burned, the skin underneath red and blistered.

She waited for him to turn around before she entered, resisting the urge to run and throw her arms around him. He looked tired, the bruises on his face still prominent, his dark blond hair loosely tied back, some of it hanging to his shoulders. She couldn't help but notice how it waved and curled, almost shining in the firelight. He was beautiful—and dangerous. The more she got to know him, the more evident it became.

"John, are you all right? You're barely recovered from before." Her voice was oddly calm, betraying none of the trepidation that loomed.

"I'm fine, don't worry yourself," he replied in his usually mellifluous baritone, sounding raspy from the smoke.

"Why did someone blow up the barn?" Noticing the stained linen binding his hand, she rushed across the room and started to unwrap it slowly.

"Dellis, it's fine; it's just a burn." He pulled his hand away from her, rewrapping it.

"Let me see it." She grabbed it back again, frantically removing the binding, her emotions taking over where practicality failed. "I saw the building cave in on you, and then your clothes were on fire. I'm not an imbecile, John; I know what's going on. You're tortured within an inch of your life, and now a barn blows up while you and your men are inside. Tell me the truth. Is someone trying to kill you?"

When she saw his burned, blistered hand and the raw, ugly scars on his wrists still healing from being shackled, she choked up. Tears welled up in her eyes, spilling over, as she considered all she'd learned. *Why does someone want him dead?*

He tipped her chin up, forcing her to look him in the eyes, those sparkling sapphires drawing her in like magic. "I can take care of myself."

Gently, his thumb grazed her cheek, wiping the tears away. Little wrinkles appeared at the corners of his eyes and bracketed his grinning lips, lighting up his face. She could barely breathe, unable to think tangibly when he looked at her that way.

"Why does someone want to hurt you?" she barely whispered, the words lodged in her throat next to her heart.

He closed his eyes as if trying to shut her out.

Undeterred by his silence, she pushed for an answer. "John, tell me why someone wants you dead."

"Dellis, please."

No, he wasn't going to get away from her again, there were too many secrets. She was tired of always being on the outside looking in. "I want to know. Why is someone trying to kill you? What did you do?"

"It's better that you don't know. Trust me." He pleaded, looking away— as if that would stop her.

"That's why you're leaving, isn't it?" Taking his face in her hands, she forced him to look at her, their eyes meeting, blue against black. "You're going away to deal with whoever this is. I'm right, aren't I?"

Reticence. Silence. *Damn him.*

She implored him with her eyes, trying to link herself to him in some way, but he looked away. "John, look me in the eyes and tell me what's going on. I deserve to know."

"Dellis, I told you I would explain everything when I was able to, and now isn't that time. Please, I'm a selfish man, I always have been. For once, I'm trying to put what's right ahead of my wants. Please, let me do that. Don't fight me." The rawness in his voice was a mere glimpse into his inner turmoil—she sensed that. He was like a locked door she could never seem to open.

"You're still planning on leaving, aren't you?" she asked, knowing the answer.

"Yes, as soon as possible. I'm waiting for my men to return."

"I don't want you to go." Reaching out, she touched his chest, feeling his warmth through his linen shirt. "You belong here with me."

His heart quickened with her confession, his body stiffening.

"Please, don't leave me." She looked up at him with longing, desperate to change his mind.

Taking her hand in his own, he kissed her fingers then lightly brushed his lips against her palm. She cupped his cheek in her hand, tracing his jaw, feeling the day's worth of stubble under her fingertips. When his lips grazed the pad of her thumb, her body came alive like a tinder suddenly lit, allowing passion to smolder.

"John, touch me, please." The words rolling off her tongue before she had a chance to think twice. "I want you."

Pulling her hand away, he shook his head. "No, Dellis, I can't do that."

"Why? I know you want me. I've seen it in your eyes." She held his hand, keeping him from pulling away. "Please."

"Don't do this." He groaned, trying to back away from her, but she wouldn't let him. "Dellis, you're not thinking straight. I know you're only saying this because you want me to stay. But I can't."

"No, it's true, I want you." She'd never meant anything more in her life, every fiber of her being cried out to be with him. She was dead before he came into her life, and then he appeared and brought color and laughter; she could feel again. Somehow, she had to find a way to make him understand.

"Dellis, I don't want to hurt you. It would be wrong of me to make love to you then leave the next day. You deserve better than that."

He'd come back at her with a valid excuse, one she couldn't refute with good sense. But she wasn't thinking with her head; this was about heart—and it was breaking.

"I don't care. I'm not afraid. You said you would come back." She grabbed on to his waistcoat as if it were a lifeline to him and held fast. "I know you have to go, I accept that, but doesn't what I want count?"

"Dellis, stop." He grabbed her hands, trying to pull away.

"I don't understand you. One minute you tell me you want me, and the next you're pushing me away. I want to be with you."

"Believe me, you don't know what you're asking." John countered, freeing himself and walking away. He turned his back to her, facing the window. "You don't know anything about me."

"Yes, I do," she said, their eyes meeting in his reflection in the glass.

"No, Dellis, you don't. When you called me a scoundrel, you weren't wrong. I've done terrible things. You wouldn't want me to touch you if you knew the truth about me." His voice was so full of loathing, she almost believed him. But there was no way this kind gentleman would do her harm. It didn't matter what he had done.

"John, you're not that man anymore. I know it. I only said those things to you because I was angry. You were right. I was jealous of Mrs. Allen, so damned jealous that you would be with her and not me."

"It's not like that." He shot back, facing her.

"No?" she asked. "Then how is it?"

He smoothed his hair out of his face, interlacing his fingers behind his neck. She could see the strain on his face; he was fighting her, but she refused to let him get away.

"John, you kissed me the other day. You said you wanted me, but now you're pushing me away. I don't understand."

"I shouldn't have done that." He bowed his head, his voice so low she could barely hear him. "I led you on, and it was wrong of me."

"No, it wasn't, I know you want to be with me. Let me comfort you. It doesn't matter that you have to leave." Her body ached for him to touch her, but he wouldn't, the distance between them mere inches, yet wider than an ocean and just as impassable.

"If something happens to you while you're gone, if you don't come back, I'll never know…" She paused, the truth too difficult to fathom, but she persisted. "I'll be alone again."

"Dellis, stop." He pleaded, trying to walk away, but she grabbed his arm. "I'm not spurning you. I'm trying to do right by you."

His words brought on a rush of emotions, her tears bursting forth like a waterfall, flowing fast and turbulent, bringing with them all the pain and sadness of two years spent alone, unwanted. "You say you're not rejecting me, but it sure feels that way. So suddenly, you're no longer in need of a business associate? I'm too damaged to be a wife, not enough to be a mistress? Mrs. Allen must have an unfortunate story, indeed."

"Dellis, don't turn my words against me. You know I don't feel that way," he said, the muscles in his jaw working—clearly she'd struck a chord with him.

She wanted him to be angry, to push him into reacting, just like he so often did to her. Two could play at his games.

"Really, you don't feel that way? How do I know that? You said it yourself, I know nothing about you except that you have a penchant for dark-haired women with scandalous reputations. Is that why she followed you here? You told her you had to leave and never came back? Is that your game?"

"I know you're trying to bait me," he said, his blue eyes turning icy. "It won't work."

"There must be some truth to it. Or is it because there's no thrill in chasing a woman who throws herself at your feet and begs you to take her? Where's the sport in that?" She looked at him, waiting for an answer, but he didn't give her one. *Typical.*

Throwing her arms in the air with defeat, she said, "No answer? You have nothing to say? I'm going to assume that I'm right. Thank you, Captain, for helping me understand that. You're more than welcome to leave, right now if you like. Just leave the key in the room. I'll get it once you're gone."

"Dellis, stop!" He grabbed her wrists, wrenching her body into his arms.

Breathless with anticipation, she looked into his eyes, waiting for him to react, wanting it badly. They were silent, eyes locked, both of them panting breathlessly on the precipice. But he backed away, lifting his hands so she could see them.

"My men and I will be leaving for Oswego tomorrow. I think it's better for both of us that I leave sooner than later."

As she calmed down, her anger dissipated, leaving behind a dull, throbbing ache in her chest, like a wound that could never heal. He was beyond her reach, the door was locked, and she didn't have the key.

"I agree, it's better that you go. I wish you and your men a safe journey," she muttered, turning away, closing the door behind her.

Chapter Forty-Five

John downed what was left of his drink, wincing as the sweet, pungent liquor burned a trail from his mouth to his stomach. *Rotgut, local whiskey.* Not his favorite. He would've drunk till he passed out, but after finishing what little spirits were left in the decanter, he wasn't even close, a rather inconvenient side effect from years of being a career drunk. Apparently, nothing was going according to plan—not even getting sauced. Now, his supplies were blown to kingdom come, and he was no closer to completing his mission. Complicating the matter was his elusive former superior, DeLancie, and Dellis's amateur Robin Hood cousin.

Unable to sleep, John watched as the sun rose, remembering Dellis, half-dressed in his room, begging him to make love to her. She was gorgeous and so damned tempting. It took a herculean effort to walk away from her, his body asking for what his head couldn't reconcile. But he just couldn't do it, no matter how much he wanted to, the gentleman winning over the scoundrel. In the past, he would have thought nothing of making love to a maid and disappearing into the night, but not anymore, and not with her. Dellis was different. She was special.

Keep lying to yourself, Carlisle. How he wished it was true, and he really was Captain John Anderson, the war profiteer. There were times he almost fooled himself into believing the lie, and that he could find a way for them to be together. But now, looking out the window, playing out every possible scenario to fruition, he knew it was impossible. And she deserved better than a one-night tumble in the hay with a lying rogue.

From behind, he heard the clicking of Clark's boots against the wood floor when he entered the room. Finally, something else for John to focus on—anything to help him forget the delectable proposition he just walked away from.

"Are you pissed, John?"

"Unfortunately, no." He glanced over his shoulder. His friend looked about as bad as John felt. "Not enough whiskey to do the job properly, and I'm too tired and sore to go downstairs and get more. What did you find out?"

"You're not going to believe it when I tell you."

"Out with it," John said impatiently. At this point, nothing could surprise him.

"It was Stuart McKesson who blew up the barn."

"You're right, I don't believe you, Clark." He snorted—the idea was preposterous. Yes, the boy was crazy, and a bit overzealous, but dangerous—no.

Clark shook his head. "I'm dead serious. We have him in our storage shed."

John got up from his desk, grabbing his hat and overcoat. "Let's go, now. Get Smith. I need to see this for myself before I'm willing to give it any credence."

He ran out the front door quickly, Clark in tow, hoping to avoid another confrontation with Dellis. John wasn't sure he would be able to face her again and keep up the lie. And how her lunatic brother could possibly have caused the explosion was beyond comprehension. Stuart could barely dress himself, much less set a charge. No, someone was apparently using him to cover their tracks.

They saddled up quickly and rode off to the opposite side of town, avoiding the main street. When they arrived at the storage barn, Stuart was sitting on the ground with his back against the wall, his head resting on his forearms. He looked up and smirked when he saw them approaching. Again, just like last time John saw Stuart, he was surprisingly clean, his clothes new and fresh.

"We're going to get to the bottom of this nonsense quickly," John said, closing the door to the shed and locking it. The younger man looked John up and down, as if sizing him up for a fight.

"Stuart, what were you doing in the woods last evening?"

"I live there now that my sister has taken up with the likes of you." Stuart laughed, the corner of his mouth turning up in sly, wry grin. "What were you doing there? Were you following my sister again, or were you coming back to the scene of the crime?"

John shook his head, ignoring Stuart's taunts. That was his modus operandi, to pick at you until you exploded, rather like a little gnat caught in your collar. "I don't have time for your games, Stuart. Did you blow up the barn?"

"Will you beat me if I don't tell you? I know your type gets off on that." John knew what Stuart was referring to; there were no illusions about each other's identities any longer. To him, John was a Redcoat, just like the ones that raped Dellis and murdered her mother, and there was no room for technicalities. In Stuart's addled mind, things only existed in black and white; there was no such thing as gray.

"What say you, Redcoat?" he hissed.

John paced for a moment then stopped abruptly, remembering something Stuart said. "What did you mean when you asked me if I was following your sister again?"

Stuart smiled, showing his brown, rotted teeth, one of them missing in the front since he was last seen. "You followed her, didn't you?"

"You said *again*, Stuart. What did you mean by following her again?" John asked, crouching down, meeting Stuart eye-to-eye.

"What will you do if I don't tell you? Will you make me marry the adjutant's daughter? But will you get to ride the doctor's daughter, Tory?"

Stuart licked his lips suggestively, then gyrated his hips, stoking John's ire to a blaze.

"Don't speak about your sister that way." John fisted Stuart's hair, forcing him to look up. "Do not."

"How many women have you used your fists on, or your cock for that matter?" Stuart asked, his expression quizzical. "Do you get off on it? Will you like it if she screams? I heard her scream like a mare in heat when the Redcoats had their way with her. I even got to watch." John noticed how Stuart winced, the memory still plaguing him, even after two years. "Will you do the same to her? But with you, I think she might enjoy it."

Grabbing Stuart by his shirt, John hauled the boy to his feet, their faces only inches apart. "Don't speak ill of your sister. It's because of her that I don't kill you now. I owe your sister my life, you drunken scum, and so do you. She let them do that to her to protect you."

Stuart hacked loudly, spitting in John's face. "Don't tell me about my sister. I know you burn for her, even though you don't like fire."

Wiping his face with his sleeve, John replied with a cold, authoritative voice, "Don't try my patience, McKesson. I can give you what you've been asking for. I can beat the truth out of you."

"Ah, but will you like it, Tory?" Stuart smiled, his eyes wide and mercurial. "I don't think so, at least, not as much as I did."

"Then I'll do my best to prove you wrong." John lifted Stuart off his feet and slammed his back against the wall, watching him crumple to the ground in a dirty heap. "I think I'll show you a bit of the King's justice you so fervently crave."

"Clark," John called, looking over his shoulder. He grabbed Stuart by the back of the shirt, pulling him to his feet. "Please, take the prisoner out front and tie him to a tree."

"So, I'm right. You're going to beat me."

John looked Stuart in the eyes, ready to deliver him the treatment he asked for. Mad or not, the young man could use a bit of discipline. "I'm a man who does his best to keep his company amused. I see this as simply giving you what you've asked for. Now, you have one last chance, did you blow up the barn?"

"No forgiveness here, God doesn't want to hear your lies," Stuart muttered, with a huge grin on his lips, shaking his head.

"What did you say?" The sound of his voice jogged John's memory, the cryptic nonsense making sense in an instant.

"Justice, my friend…" Stuart put his finger to his lips, his voice almost inaudible. "Shh… She's come for payback."

It all came back to John: the barn, the voice, the smell of liquor on his captor's breath, and even his words, *"Scream, so I know you like it."*

"Tie him to the tree." John motioned to Clark. "Now!" John's mind reeled, remembering the timbre of Stuart's voice and the disjointed, cryptic words of the captor.

Clark dragged Stuart outside towards the woods, the younger man flailing as he was thrown face-first against a tree, his arms tied around it.

John fumed, the scars on his back aching as he remembered the whip striking him, each lash deeper and more devastating than the one before. Clark handed over a crop. John held it for a moment, rage taking over reason while he contemplated his next move. He whipped the leather against the tree several times, snapping it, allowing Stuart to feel the fear of anticipation. How well John knew that fear, the waiting, the heart palpitations and cold sweats, while the seconds ticked by like hours, awaiting the first lash. Stuart deserved this. Had he not earned it? John snapped the crop against the tree again. Time to make his own justice.

With one hand, John tore the back of Stuart's shirt open, remembering the first slice of the wintry wind as it ripped across his own flesh. Stuart shrieked, looking around, his body shivering, goosebumps visibly bubbling up on his arms and legs

"You're much braver when you're the one delivering the punishment." John hissed, his mouth close to Stuart's ear. "But as a favor to you, I will only use a crop, and not the whip. Not all Englishmen find pleasure in preying on the weak, and you are not my equal as an adversary. Call it mercy, or perhaps a kind heart. I call it British justice."

Slapping the stock against one palm, John gave Stuart one last chance. "Now, tell me, why did you blow the powder last night?"

Stuart turned his head, hacked and spat at John, the gooey mess landing on his sleeve.

"Fine." Stepping back, he took a deep breath, preparing himself. A little fear would do Stuart good, curb his rebellious streak. John struck the tree above the younger man, purposely missing him, as the crop sliced through the air with one swift motion.

Stuart yelped and buried his face into the bark, anticipating the strike.

"Oh, this is nothing compared to what you did to me, coward." John raged. "You tortured me, and then you killed one of my men when you blew that barn. By law, the punishment is your life. Tell me why you did it, Stuart, and I may spare yours."

"I hate you and the rest of your Redcoat bastards. Burn in Hell!" Stuart yelled, his eyes blazing.

Using very little force, John struck Stuart with the crop, the leather leaving a small red mark across his back. He cried out loudly and squeezed his eyes shut, his body trembling violently against the tree.

In the grips of fulminant rage, John raised the crop again and yelled, "Stuart, answer my question. I can hit you harder!"

Stuart let out a demented howl, his coal black eyes full of terror, tears spilling down his cheeks. As John went to strike again, he stopped, the sight of the younger man twisting and flailing against the tree suddenly a mortifying sight. *Am I mad? How has it come to this?* Suddenly, he felt sick, his stomach pitching furiously with self-loathing and a side of disgust. There was no justice in beating a weaker adversary. He swallowed, looking down at the crop, his hand shaking.

"They told me to do it. They told me to do it. Justice, they want justice," Stuart muttered between sobs, looking around at the trees. "Don't you hear them screaming? They're innocent!"

John threw down the crop, his rage suddenly quelled. "Clark, bring me some water."

"Please," Stuart cried out loudly, tears streaming down his cheeks. "Don't do it again. I did what they told me to do."

John leaned over, looking Stuart in the eyes. "I don't remember you being particularly merciful to me."

"Dellis will never forgive you for this" He spat back in rage. "I've seen the way you look at her. I know you want her for your own."

"It's because of your sister I don't hand you over to the garrison. The price for murdering one of the King's men is death by hanging. Believe me, I'm being very merciful to you."

Clark returned with the bucket of water and set it on the ground, ice floating on the top, sloshing over the rim. Stuart started to scream when he saw it, his body trembling like a leaf on the breeze.

"Stuart, I'll let you go, just tell me who ordered you to blow up the barn." John said, their faces only inches apart.

"I did it on my own." Stuart's voice cracked as he looked at the bucket of water.

John shook his head. "I don't believe you."

"Why, because I'm not the only one that wants you dead?"

"What are you talking about? Who wants me dead?" John demanded, their eyes locking.

"Everyone." Stuart cackled loudly. "We don't take kindly to Redcoats in these parts."

Knowing a lie when it was told, John released Stuart, grabbed the bucket of water, and held it close to his face. "Tell me who you're working with."

"The spirits want you dead, don't you hear them?" he yelled. "They're screaming for your soul."

"Stuart, answer me." John threatened. When there was no response, he tossed the cold water at Stuart, forcing an agonizing scream from his lips. "Answer me!"

Suddenly, he started banging his forehead against the tree, quietly mumbling nonsense to himself with each hit. When he looked up, there was blood oozing down his forehead into his eyes. John had seen Stuart behave this way before, two years earlier, when John had stopped one of his men from killing the boy.

There was no point in any of this; John would get nothing from Stuart, the man was demented beyond reason. Untying his arms, John released the boy. "I owe your sister my life; for that, I'll spare yours. It's the least I can do to repay her kindness."

"Mounting her wasn't enough?" Stuart broke into a loud, sinister laugh. "She's not the type to ask for money."

John's rage resurfaced, a beast unleashed from within. He punched Stuart so hard he fell back on the ground, blood spattering from his nose. "That's for hitting your sister and speaking ill of her. What happened to her was not her fault."

"No, it was yours, spy." Stuart countered, wiping the blood from his lips with his sleeve. "That's right, I know you're a Tory spy."

John grabbed Stuart by the collar, pulling him to his feet. "I'll show you the mercy you didn't show me. See how much of a Redcoat bastard I really am, by all rights I should kill you. Tell me, who's the savage now?" John slammed Stuart's back against the tree. "Who's the savage now?"

Clark grabbed John by the sleeves, stopping him before he permanently embedded Stuart into the tree trunk. "John, don't do this. You'll only regret it."

Clark was right. John released Stuart, the younger man smirking as he adjusted his shirt and collar.

"What do we do with him? He knows who we are."

"You're right, Clark, we can't have him talking, and I have no intention of letting him roam around, hell-bent on killing me. He's gotten close twice. I don't know that he won't succeed the third time." John's thoughts went to Dellis. She would never forgive him if something happened to Stuart.

"Take him back to the town gaol; tell them we caught him drunk, attempting to steal from me. I want them to hold him until we return. Also, see that he is cleaned up and the wound on his back is cared for. I didn't hit him hard."

Pausing for a moment, John turned back to Clark and said, "I need eyes on Alexei McKesson. My guess is he will go for the supplies. I'm sure some of his Oneidas already know where DeLancie took them."

"We leave tomorrow then, John?" Clark asked, grabbing the collar of Stuart's shirt when he started to walk away.

"Yes." John nodded, watching Stuart chew his nails to the quick. The poor, pitiful wretch; had none of this happened, what might have become of him? "Do me a favor. I want both you and Smith to visit The Kettle tonight. See that you come down with sickness from the food, and make sure the patrons know about it." John handed over a bag of coins from his pocket. "Be discreet; you know what to do with this."

Clark shook his head with incredulity. "John, that's all the money we have left. We shouldn't waste it bribing local drunks."

"I know, but Miss McKesson will need the money after we leave." It was small consolation for all that had passed between them, but if John could help her save her precious house by greasing a few palms, it was worth it. "Just do as I ask. Meet me tomorrow at first light."

Stuart looked up at John and smiled, spitting a torn fingernail on his boot.

"I'm no longer a vengeful man, Stuart, lucky for you."

"But he is." Stuart smiled then winked, spitting another nail. "Not so lucky for you, spy."

Chapter
Forty-Six

Leaning her forehead against Alexei's back, Dellis indulged in his warmth, grateful for his presence. Thank goodness Alexei took her to the village to check on Anoki, or she would have been stuck in the house all day waiting for John to leave. After the way their meeting ended the night before, she was at a loss for words, her heart still smarting from his refusal. And now, he was gone, and suddenly, she wished she could take back the day, if only to see him one last time.

As they rode quietly, her mind wandered to everything that had happened over the past couple of months: the explosion, John being kidnapped, his supplies disappearing. She could no longer lie to herself. It was all related, and Alexei and her uncle had something to do with it. She refused to believe her grandfather would willingly hurt John, but clearly, the man was in a desperate situation with the mysterious militia trying to frame his village. While she was tending to Anoki, she'd overheard her grandfather mention something about a treaty with General Washington. Apparently, the natives were helping the Rebels now, forced to take sides in a fight not of their making. There was no point in trying to question Alexei; he would tell her nothing.

How she wished her father was still alive so she could ask him for advice. Closing her eyes, she prayed for one last chance to see John, not only because she wanted to be with him, but she desperately needed to talk to someone she trusted.

When they arrived at The Thistle, Alexei helped her dismount, walking her to the door. "I'll bring you one of Father's mares. You can keep it until we can get you a new one."

"Thank you." She nodded, smiling at him. "I appreciate it."

He hugged her, giving her a tight squeeze before he released her.

Dellis walked down the hall, past her room, and to the kitchen. It was late, but her aunt was still cleaning, several stacks of dishes left to be washed.

"Dellis, you're finally back?" she asked, looking over her shoulder.

"You must have had a busy night." From the looks of the kitchen, it was very busy indeed.

"Yes, it was. We've had so much business the past couple of weeks, and with you being away so often, we're going to need to hire more help."

Although it was excellent news, it didn't do much to improve Dellis's spirits. She just wanted to be alone with her thoughts. "Why don't you go. I'll take care of this. It's the least I can do for leaving you all day to fend for yourself."

Her aunt didn't hesitate, removing her apron and grabbing her cloak. "Oh, by the way, the Captain's here for one more night. He was unable to make arrangements elsewhere. I knew you wouldn't have an issue with it since we have no other lodgers."

"That's fine," Dellis replied nonchalantly, trying to hide her excitement.

"Well, have a good night. I'll come early, and we'll get whatever you don't finish taken care of them."

Dellis hugged her aunt, bidding her good night, then walked back to the bedroom, shutting the door.

He hadn't left. Dellis's heart leaped at the thought of seeing him again. Looking into the mirror, she unpinned her hair, smoothing it out over her shoulders, using her fingers to separate the curls. Carefully, she removed her dress, putting it on the bed, and then washed her face and hands in the basin. When she looked into the mirror again, she knew what she wanted. She wanted to be with him, even if it was only for the one night.

Dellis refused to believe the only reason he stayed was because of lodging issues. No, this was her chance, and he was giving it to her. She had to believe it. Reaching into her drawer, she dug around, looking for the trinkets she wanted to give to him, and then stuffed them into her pocket. She opened the door to the servant's staircase and slowly walked up to the second floor.

Standing at the end of the hall, Dellis wrung her hands, her heart racing when she noticed a sliver of light emanating from his room. She couldn't allow herself to think; if she did, her conscience was bound to talk her out of what she was about to do. Taking a deep breath, she started to walk, her body drawn to his room like a moth to a flame.

When she opened the door, he stood where he was the night before, his back to the door, looking out the window, the only light coming from the fireplace. The sight of him made her breath catch in her throat, his long blond queue stretching between his shoulder blades; his navy waistcoat fitted perfectly, accentuating his muscular torso and tapering to his waist. She blushed, remembering how he looked with his clothes off, the feel of his bare skin against her own.

Reaching behind, she loosed her stays, her hands shaking as she pulled at the strings. Her heart threatened to leap out of her chest as she waited for him to turn around, but he didn't. She knew he'd heard her enter, his head tipping to the side when she opened the door, but he made no move to acknowledge her. Was he ignoring her or just giving her a chance to walk away?

Dellis took a couple of steps then stopped, paralyzed with fear. She could go no farther, both of her feet rooted to the floorboards like a tree to the ground. She closed her eyes, mentally willing him to turn around and cross the threshold between them. When he finally did, she felt her heart skip a beat, those twin sapphire jewels regarding her intently. Unable to meet his gaze, she turned around and lifted her hair, exposing her loosened stays. Her hands shook as she held her hair, the anticipation like a slow death. Would he turn her away again? The seconds stretched on forever, her body aching for the answer, every fiber of her being waiting for him. And then she felt it, his hands on her shoulders, his lips on the nape of her neck.

"Dellis," he whispered, his lips touching her ear, and she was lost.

Chapter
Forty-Seven

John heard her come in, not yet ready to turn around and face her. He knew why she came and what she wanted. Only a scoundrel would take an innocent, damaged maid to his bed and find pleasure in her embrace. He must turn her away like he did the night before—better her anger now, before she knew the truth, than after.

Taking a deep breath, he turned around, knowing when he saw her that he was a damned fool doomed to perdition's flames. She was intoxicating, her hair falling about her shoulders, her creamy skin glowing in the firelight. Her stays were loosened, allowing her shift to fall off her shoulders, baring her exquisite décolletage. When she turned around, showing him the back of her stays, he walked towards her but resisted the urge to touch her. It was his last chance to do the right thing... But he couldn't, the scoundrel in him winning at last.

Gently, he placed his hands on her shoulders and brushed his lips against the nape of her neck

"Dellis," he whispered, his lips touching her ear. He buried his face in the back of her hair, indulging in its silkiness, the smell of lavender filling the air. "Tell me to stop."

"I don't want you to," she replied breathlessly, her hands reaching for him.

She was afraid, her body trembling. Pulling away, he bent his head forward, his lips grazing her ear. "Are you afraid of me?"

"Only because I know what is coming." She confessed. "I'm sorry you're not my first and that you'll have to bear the burden of what happened to me."

His chest ached for her, knowing what horror she must've faced. The thought of someone beating and defiling this gorgeous creature drove him to the brink. She was a woman to be worshiped—loved. He wrapped his arms around her, holding her close, trying to soothe his own raging emotions. "Dellis, don't apologize; they took from you what was yours to give. But I would gladly pay their penance to be with you."

He could feel her body relaxing against his, her voice barely above a whisper when she finally spoke. "You're so gentle. If you hurt me, I can't believe you would do it intentionally."

It took no small amount of courage for her to hand herself over to his care, knowing the depths of her fear. He was humbled by her trust in him... and so unworthy.

"Is this what you want?" he whispered, brushing his lips over her earlobe, his conscience needing to hear her admission one last time.

"Yes." The most perfect word.

"Then I'm yours to command."

"I like the sound of that." She groaned, her hand reaching for him, pulling at his neckerchief. "Kiss me, Captain."

"As you wish," he said, laughing, loving the haughtiness in her voice. With that, he gave in to the lie, making it true in his mind. He was John Anderson, the profiteer, the gentleman, the man who would make love to her and protect her from John Carlisle, the spy, the scoundrel who was trying to turn her people—the man whose failure ruined her existence.

Gently, he kissed her ear, his hands nimbly untying her stays the rest of the way and depositing them on the floor. She reached behind, her hands encountering his as she helped him untie her petticoat, letting it drop. Looking up, he could see their reflection in the mirror, the firelight highlighting her silhouette through her gauzy linen shift, her nipples pink and prominent under the diaphanous fabric. He tipped her chin up so she could see her reflection.

Kissing her neck, he noticed how she blushed and looked away. "Don't you want to see how beautiful you are?"

She shook her head, shyly, her eyes meeting his for a second in the mirror.

Making a trail of kisses down to her shoulders, he gently pulled her shift down, letting it fall in a pool of fabric at her feet. Holding his breath in anticipation, he looked into the mirror, finally seeing her body in the flesh. Letting it out, he whispered, "My God, you *are* beautiful."

Her large, rosy-tipped breasts stood out, almost begging for him to touch them, and her long, lean abdomen tapered into narrow hips, the dark hair at the junction of her thighs just barely visible at the edge of the mirror. He stopped for a moment, waiting for her to look up. When she finally did, there was fear in her eyes, those dark pools glassy and wide; he ached to take all that pain away, fill it with pleasure.

He desperately wanted to tell her it would be all right, but she wouldn't believe him. The only way to convince her was to awaken her passion, draw her out, make her want it so badly she could surrender to it.

So many times, he had imagined feeling her supple breasts in his hands. Greedily, he cupped them, squeezing them together, his fingers gently massaging and learning what they liked.

She gasped, her hands reaching up and grabbing his hair, her chest thrusting forward and filling his palms. Gently, he thumbed her nipples, worrying them until she cried out his name, her eyes meeting his in the mirror again.

"You're mine, Dellis," he whispered into her ear, their gazes still locked. "No matter where I go, you'll always be mine." *God, he meant those words.* He'd kill any man that tried to harm her again. She was his now.

"John." She whimpered, biting her lip, her dark eyes pleading as she pressed her hips against his. His need for her was bordering on madness. He ached to bury himself deep and lose himself completely within her, but he had to take it slow, this wasn't about what he wanted, it was about her. For once in his life, someone else's needs meant more to him than his own. That was the kind of man he wanted to be, the one he saw in her eyes. A gentleman. A lover.

"Let me touch you." Her hands reached for him, pulling his mouth to hers. Expertly, her tongue slid against his, caressing and stroking it, sending fire roaring through his veins. "Please." She groaned against his lips until he could no longer deny her.

Turning around in his arms, she buried her face in his shirt, holding him close, seeking comfort from the thing she feared most: him. She trembled, though her body was rigid in his arms, her breaths quick and shallow. Taking her hand in his own, he placed it over his heart, letting her feel it race. "You do this to me," he said. "Only you…"

After a moment, she looked up, her questing fingers starting on the buttons of his waistcoat, fumbling with them. With an inquisitive look on her face, she removed his neckerchief, and then pulled his shirt over his head, dropping them both on the floor. Gently, she ran her fingertips over the healing scars on his chest, her touch as light as a feather, sending shivers down his spine. When she touched her lips to the scar on his breast, he closed his eyes, submitting to the sweet torture.

"I've wanted to touch you for so long." She looked up at him, her fingers stroking a scar on his collarbone, then fingering Kateri's cross at the base of his neck. "After everything I told you, I was afraid you could never want me."

"You have no idea." He groaned. If it was possible, her confession made him want her even more. Lifting her off the ground, he carried her to the bed, gently lying down with her against the downy mattress. Leaning back, he drank in the sight of her unclothed in his bed. She looked like a sculpture of a Greek goddess, resting against the white sheets with her dark hair lying on her plump, perfect breasts, her hands next to her face, and her long legs stretched out. Blushing under his gaze, she looked away, wrapping her arms around herself.

He leaned forward, turning her face towards him. "Are you still afraid?"

"Only that I'll disappoint you." She reached up and touched his lips with her finger, tracing them, sending little jolts of pleasure racing through him.

"It's not possible."

John backed away, removing only his boots and socks, and then climbed back into bed next to her. Carefully, he rested against her torso, putting one of his legs between hers, giving her a moment to get accustomed to his weight. He noticed how she stiffened when they touched, her eyes widening and darting back and forth like a frightened doe's.

Trying to be gentle, he kissed her, coaxing her lips open, tasting her sweetness with his tongue. He whispered into her mouth, "Kiss me, Dellis, like you did earlier."

Instead of shying away, she responded, her tongue finding his in a heady dance while her hands pulled at his tie-back, loosening his hair. When he touched her breast, she let out a moan, her chest thrusting up for more, her thighs clenching together. Her breasts were incredibly sensitive; he'd noticed that earlier. This time, he thumbed the taut peak, listening to the symphony of moans that played over and over with each pass of his thumb over her nipple. Her hips bucked instinctively, searching for him, ready to find release.

"Oh God, John," she gasped, on the verge of finding her first orgasm. How fortunate for him, he'd found a direct line to that lovely valley between her legs, a way to stoke her passion whenever he wanted, on demand, at his whim. What a wonderful secret only he was privy to. Far be it for him not to indulge, he took one of the taut peaks in his mouth, lavishing it with his tongue until it was swollen and hard, and she was panting with fevered breaths.

"John." She gasped, holding his head to her breast, her fingers entwined in his hair. "John!" she said again, her voice going up an octave, her hips reaching for him. But he backed away, forcing her to wait just on the edge.

"Not yet," he whispered, his hand trailing down her abdomen to her inner thigh, lightly caressing at the junction. He desperately wanted to see the first taste of pleasure in her eyes when he touched the slick little bud with his fingers and later when he pushed his way inside. But as he got closer, she clasped her legs together, pulling away from him. Undeterred, he used his tongue and lips on her breast, distracting her, as he gently tried to coax her legs apart, but again she fought him.

Trying another approach, he wrapped his arms around her and rolled onto his back, bringing her with him. Holding her for a moment, he stroked her back while she trembled in his arms, her eyes wide when she finally looked up at him.

"Dellis, touch me, please," he said. "I want you."

Slowly, she sat up, straddling his hips. She looked incredible, the dark waves of her hair falling down her shoulders in luxurious cascades, her creamy breasts, full and proud, the dark curls at the junction of her thighs pressed against his breeches. She wriggled a bit, trying to get away, but he held fast, the sensation of her moving against his manhood driving him to the brink of insanity.

"Touch me," he half said, half groaned.

Taking both of her hands in his own, he placed them on the front fall of his breeches, showing her what he wanted, and she complied, slowly unbuttoning them. When he sprang forth, she hesitated, pulling back, her hands shaking, too afraid to touch him. Instead, she ran her fingertips over the long, deep scar that went from his navel to his groin. Her hands so close to his swollen cock he could no longer form words, the suspense rendering him speechless.

"John, why did they do this to you?"

Answering her question was the furthest thing from his mind; instead, he took her hand in his own and wrapped it around his length, holding it there. She was still for a moment, her eyes wide as she held him, hot and throbbing, in her palm. He waited on the verge of pain and pleasure, the seconds ticking by until a groan escaped him. Slowly, she started to move, her fingers tracing his length up and down, exploring every inch of him with a touch so light he almost spilled his seed right then.

"Did I hurt you?" she asked fearfully.

"No," he replied. "Don't stop."

She continued her gentle investigation, her eyes curiously looking into his while her hand moved up and down his length, gently stroking him. Leaning down, she placed a soft kiss on his chest, resting her head there. "You are the beautiful one, John. So beautiful."

Her words left him shattered, his chest aching, his body ready to devour hers. With that, he rolled her on her back and nudged her thighs apart, resting himself between them. He loved the little sound she made when their skin touched, a light, breathy gasp of surprise with a hint of wanton. When she did it again, he claimed her lovely sound with his lips, his tongue sliding inside, touching hers, and then darting out, teaching her their rhythm as his hips moved against hers. When she responded ardently, he pulled away, resting his forehead against her breastbone.

"John, why did you stop?"

He was panting, holding back. "I want you so badly. I don't want to hurt you."

"You won't."

There was so much conviction in her voice he ached from it. If only she knew what kind of man she was placing her trust in; he could still end it right here. It wasn't too late.

"John?"

His conscience pleaded with him, a pain forming in his chest when he considered how the truth would devastate her.

"I will hurt you, Dellis," he said, ready to confess his sins, but when she lifted his chin, forcing him to look into her beautiful black eyes, he couldn't do it. It didn't matter what his conscience wanted; no, he just couldn't deny her. Swallowing, he gave in to the lie once more, the scoundrel. "It will hurt, but only long enough for you to grow accustomed to me. You're not used to lovemaking."

"But I'm not a maid anymore," she replied, looking away from him, almost shamefully.

He tipped her chin up so she could see he was in earnest. "You are to me, Dellis."

She stiffened, her eyes widening, and with a smile, she asked, "What comes after, John?"

"You'll want more." He teased, avoiding the deeper question.

"So sure of your skills, Captain?" There was a hint of sarcasm in her voice, and challenge.

He grinned. "I have no doubt."

"If it makes you happy, neither do I."

"Dellis." He groaned, her selfless concern for him striking at his very core.

Pulling away, he got out of bed and discarded his breeches. After he undressed, he stood at the side of the bed, letting her see him. He'd never held himself up to a woman for close inspection, the sensation was heady and arousing while she looked him up and down. He noticed how she chewed her lower lip as her gaze leveled on his cock. He couldn't help but imagine those lips around him, her tongue gently toying with the tip. Their eyes met for a moment, then she nodded, accepting all of him, even the parts she feared most.

She was still wearing her stockings. Lifting her leg over his shoulder, John slid the cotton fabric down, marveling at how soft the skin of her inner thigh was. He repeated the same thing with the other leg; only this time, his lips followed the trail of his hands. When he reached the top of her thigh, he gently parted her swollen flesh with his fingers, breathing in her scent as he placed a single kiss at the junction of her thighs. She was already slick and swollen for him.

"John, no, you shouldn't." She panicked, trying to wriggle away, her hands tugging at his hair.

"Dellis, don't fight me; you'll like this." John pulled her hands away, resting them on the bed. "Trust me." He looked into her dark eyes until she relented.

Bending his head, he deftly touched his tongue to the slick, sensitive nub, drawing a deep, lusty moan from her. He looked up, their eyes meeting through a valley of lush white skin and two perfect mounds, and then shook his head. "Don't fight it."

His first taste of her was like Heaven, his highland scotch, intoxicating and sweet, and like the insatiable drunk he was, he wanted more. Gently, pulling her hips down towards him, her legs fanned open further, giving him better access to the lovely little jewel hiding beneath the thatch of dark hair. Pulling her flush to his mouth, he swirled and suckled the taut flesh with his tongue, worshiping it relentlessly until she was moaning out his name in a frenzy. He loved the sound of her husky shouts and the way she melted against his mouth with unfettered passion, spurring him on. He'd spend the rest of his life dreaming of this moment, remembering her silky legs spread out in front of him, and the taste of her, warm and wet on his lips, was better than any drink or comfits he'd ever tried.

"John?" She groaned out almost painfully.

"Do you want me to stop?" He paused, watching her fist the sheets, her hips thrusting up, seeking him.

"No." She threw her head back against the pillows, squeezing her eyes shut, his name rolling off her tongue in desperation. "John, please, don't."

Bowing his head, he touched his teeth to the sensitive nub again, nipping and pulling at it, his fingers gently plunging inside her, matching the rhythm of her hips. She grabbed the back of his head, tugging his hair, demanding more. This time, instead of pushing her hands away, he obliged, following her lead until she was screaming his name, her hips riding his mouth.

Unable to wait any longer, he wrapped both of her legs around his waist, his erection poised at her entry so she could see it, waiting for her permission. When she nodded, he gently spread her with his fingers, slowly guiding the tip between her silky, slick folds. Her body opened up, soft and wet, inviting him to immerse himself with one swift stroke— and he did, with a glorious surge of his hips. He could hear nothing, see nothing, consumed with being inside her, the earthy taste of her still on his lips. Retreating and plunging into her again, he groaned as she screamed, burying himself deep, filling her completely.

Suddenly, the amorous fog lifted from over his senses, and he could hear her high-pitched cries. When he looked down, her eyes were squeezed shut, on her face a look of pure, utter terror—and pain.

"Dellis, it's all right. The pain will stop."

But she didn't hear him. Her fingernails dug into his arms, clawing at his flesh; she thrashed about, frantically trying to push him away. He knew he was hurting her, but she was so incredibly tight he could barely concentrate. When she started to claw him again, he grabbed both of her wrists, pinning them to the bed.

"Dellis." He tried to reach her, but she was fighting with her memories, an unearthly fear possessing her like a demon. He tried again; only this time, he nuzzled her ear, gently kissing her lobe. "Dellis, it's John. Look at me."

At the sound of his name, she looked up, a quiver in her lip. "It won't hurt for long, I promise." Trying again, he gently slid out of her, then eased his way back in, the sensation making his body jerk from sheer pleasure. She yelped, trying to free her hands from his grip, her thighs clamping down on to him again. He could see tears welling in the corners of her eyes.

"My love, trust me." He released her hands, turning her face so she would look at him. "I'll stop if that's what you want."

He wasn't exactly sure he could keep that promise, but he'd die trying if that's what she wanted. She looked away for a moment, considering his proposition, then shook her head.

John turned her face towards him then kissed her, whispering into her lips, "You are brave."

She shook her head in disagreement.

He bit back a laugh at her conviction. "Yes, you are, my love. Very brave."

With a slow, gentle stroke, he pushed back inside her, giving her his full length, then wrapping her legs around his waist. When she thrust her hips up towards him, he repeated the motion, easing her into the rhythm of their lovemaking.

"Let me show you, Dellis. Follow me."

Taking her nipple into his mouth, suckling, he teased the sensitive flesh, trying to distract her while he pushed a little harder, and then pulled out. This time, she let out a loud, lusty moan, squeezing him with her thighs. Encouraged, he flicked the pearl of flesh where they were joined until it was hard and swollen, watching pleasure sweep across her face as her hips surged up, instinctively taking him deeper.

"John," she said his name like it was her dying breath, her head thrown back on the pillow, her body now rising to meet his with each stroke. *Yes.* This was the way he'd imagined her; not the fearful ingénue from earlier, but spirited, willful Dellis, the one that ordered him about and drove him to distraction. She grabbed onto his buttocks, her nails like needles as she dragged them across his flesh, showing him what she wanted. He moaned, following her lead, his hips pumping harder and faster, slamming into hers, almost punishing her with his desire.

"Please." She whimpered, the desperation in her voice causing an ache to form in his chest. He wanted it for her so badly. She deserved to know pleasure in a man's arms; his ego swelled, knowing he was the one who would give it to her.

"Soon, my love."

He used every last bit of skill he'd learned over his years of debauchery to take her to the edge of pleasure, pushing her towards it. When she called out his name, her eyes widening with wonder, he knew she was finally there. Suddenly, he felt the rhythmic spasms of her release, a lush warmth enveloping him, her legs squeezing him so tight he could barely draw breath.

"Dellis, don't fight it."

She surrendered, a lovely flush running down her cheeks to her neck. Her hooded eyes focused on him, and then fluttered closed as she moaned his name one last time. Slowly, she relaxed underneath him, her legs trembling as they eased down to his sides. When her eyes opened again, the corner of her mouth turned up in an impish grin of pure, unabashed satisfaction. She brought him down to her for a deep, luscious kiss, her tongue ravaging his mouth as she wrapped her legs around him, squeezing him tight.

"My God, John," she whispered into his mouth.

Finally, it was his turn.

"Yes, my love." He groaned, burying himself deep. She was so warm and slick from her release, he went at her with the ferocity pent up from months of wanting her yet pushing her away. Hiking her legs up higher, he leaned back, using his knees and hips to help him keep with the furious pace. Just when he thought he might die from need, she reached up and put her hand over his heart, the simple but stirring gesture giving him pause. Looking into her eyes, the emotion he saw in those dark pools stripped him bare, shattering his well-honed defenses. It was as if she could see into his soul—see the truth behind the lie.

"Don't fight it," she whispered, the deeper meaning of her words not lost on him. She was in love with him, it was there, shining in those dark, beautiful eyes and expertly delivered in sweet, torturous caresses that rendered him speechless. Taking her hand in his own, he gently kissed her palm, his body shaking from her tender yet skillful assault on his heart. Who was the proficient and who was the novice now?

Burying his face in her neck, trying to hide from her omniscient eyes, he plunged into her again, surrendering to her will. At that moment, he would have given her anything she wanted—anything—to make the incredible ache that was building go on forever.

"Dellis." He groaned out her name in homage to her supernatural power over his body. And then he yelled it. And suddenly it was there, he could feel it, right on the edge; he knew he should pull out, but he just couldn't, selfishly wanting every last moment inside her.

He was beyond control, beyond reason, unable to continue but unwilling to stop. She was like the most incredible opium, making him high, euphoric to the point where he could feel nothing but her tight walls around his cock and her silky thighs grasping his hips. He indulged even more, like an addict, punishing her with powerful thrusts until she whispered his name, her sweet voice taking the last ounce of control from him. He looked into her eyes and lost himself, falling breathlessly over the cliff into her oblivion.

Rocked with spasms, he exploded over and over, submerging in the ecstasy that belonged to her alone, giving himself, body and soul, the gentleman and the scoundrel, the spy and the profiteer.

She wrapped her arms and legs around him, holding him as she did the night he lay sick, his body still twitching from his release. Never had he made love to a woman so unselfishly nor allowed himself to surrender so thoroughly. Part of him wanted to fall at her feet and worship her, but part of him desperately wanted to get away and regain control of himself. But it was no use, he lacked the strength and the fortitude to resist her thrall.

"I'm once again rendered helpless in your arms," he confessed, his body too heavy to move.

After several moments, he leaned up on his elbows, looking at her. She was thoroughly ravished with her hair a mess against the pillows, and her lips red and swollen from his kisses. He smiled, unable to hide his pleasure at knowing he'd rendered her in this beautiful state of disarray.

"You remember, don't you?" she whispered through labored breaths. "How long have you known?"

"Only a few days."

He rested his head between her breasts, enjoying the feel of her fingers combing through his hair.

"You would have frozen to death if I hadn't done that."

"And I'm most grateful for the use of your body." He teased, tickling her ribs. When she didn't respond to his jest, he looked up, adjusting himself so that he lay on his side. "What is it?"

She fingered the metal cross at the base of his throat, while her eyes cast down regarding it intently. "You almost died that night. Then the explosion, when the cabin caved in on you and Anoki, I was sure you were dead."

He took her fingers from his neck, brushing his lips over her knuckles. "I'm rather good at surviving. Though, I have to admit, I'm still not quite myself. Now you've worn me out. I'll be no good to anyone." He grinned devilishly. "But at least it would seem everything is working properly."

She slapped his chest, her face turning bright red. "You were awful teasing me like that, John Anderson."

The sound of his nom de guerre made him wince, but he wouldn't be deterred from his pleasurable pursuits by something as trivial as a name.

He laughed it off, rubbing his scruff against the soft skin on her neck, making her giggle. "But you should have seen the lovely shade of red you turned."

Dellis turned away, looking out the window. He followed her gaze, the moon shining through the window just barely lighting the room. Then suddenly, without a word, she rolled away from him, getting out of bed, picking up her clothes from the floor.

He grabbed her hand, stopping her. "Where are you going?"

"You have to leave early tomorrow. You should get some rest. Besides, I need to go back to my room," she muttered, her voice quivering with emotion.

The thought of her leaving his bed after they just made love was like a knife in the chest. He reached out his hand, pulling her back. "Stay with me, please. I'll wake you before anyone returns."

"You need to rest, John."

"I want you beside me when I wake." He refused to release her hand until she came back to bed. He needed her next to him; a war of emotions was raging within him, and she was his only defense.

Dellis hesitated for a moment, and then crawled into bed next to him, resting her head on his chest. Her body felt heavenly in his arms, brushing her hair away from her face, he watched her fall asleep. She looked lovely, her sooty lashes resting against her cheeks, her lips gently parted. She was perfect; demure yet instinctively passionate at the same time, the dichotomy of her character leaving him curious to find out what another night in her arms would be like now that her fear had subsided. But he couldn't let that happen—he'd already gone too far.

Chapter Forty-Eight

"No, please, don't do this!"

Dellis woke to the sounds of John muttering in his sleep, a look of pain etched on his face, sweat dampening his brow and his hairline.

"Stop, what are you doing? Let them go!" he shouted, his fingers biting into her arms.

She'd seen him do this when he was sick, thinking it was fevered nightmares from his lung infection. Now, watching him flail about restlessly, she realized the depth of his inner turmoil, his dreams plagued with memories. What had they done to put such fear in this man? "John."

He didn't wake, only yelled again, "Stop, please!"

Trying to soothe him, she leaned over him and smoothed his hair out of his face, then caressed his cheek. "John, I'm here. You're safe."

He woke suddenly, his eyes darting around the room and then leveling on her.

Gently she nuzzled his ear, and with a kiss on the cheek, she whispered, "You were having a nightmare. What was it about?"

Ignoring her question, he turned on his side, burying his face between her breasts, his voice muffled against her rib cage. "I dreamed I was in the mists of this lovely valley, indulging in its sweetness, and then a nagging woman woke me." He kissed both of her breasts, rubbing the stubble on his chin against her sensitive skin. "Can't you just be my warming pan?"

"Stop it." She laughed, trying to get away as he scoured her flesh. "I won't be able to hide that with a kerchief. My cousin already suspects something."

John laughed, doing it again. "I'm just marking my property. These beauties were made for my hands alone. They love my touch. They crave it." He nipped at her breast, his thumb taunting and teasing her nipple, while he watched her with curious eyes. "Even now they are longing for me. Am I right, love?"

"Yes, John." She gasped, sparks shooting through her breast all the way to her core, causing a lush warmth and slick result.

Suddenly, he stopped his gentle ministrations, leaving her on the edge of beautiful, breathtaking release. When he looked up, a lock of hair fell into his eyes, making him look like an awful, naughty boy.

"You're incorrigible."

"So it would seem, but I find myself completely content to spend my days between all your lovely peaks and valleys."

She lifted his chin, trying to get him to look into her eyes, but he wouldn't comply. "You're trying to change the subject. Won't you tell me what your nightmare was about?"

"No, because I find you a more decadent indulgence than my dreams." He rolled on his back, his hands making their way down her sides then gently caressing her bottom. She melted like butter in his arms, unable to resist his touch.

"I want you again," he said, his voice husky in her ear. "Touch me."

She could feel how much he wanted her, his hands holding her hips against his own, his shaft thick and ridged, pressed between them. She ran her fingers down his neck, nuzzling his ear, taking his lobe between her teeth. He was beautiful with his long, lean, corded muscles, so different from the soft curves of her body. Gently, she bent her head, kissing his neck, then his collarbone and chest, her hand sliding down the flat planes of his abdomen, feeling the light dusting of hair on his belly.

When she grazed his manhood, he gasped, his eyes following her hand. Curiously, she traced it from the tip to the base, rubbing her thumb over the top when it wept some of his seed. Then gently she wrapped her fingers around him, feeling the silky skin grow swollen and taut when she started to stroke.

"Dellis." He reached for her, his head lifting, his lips seeking hers. Bringing her lips an inch from his, she pulled away, boldly teasing him. She stroked him harder this time, watching the pleasure in his eyes, his hips rising in response. When he reached for her again, she gave him a taste of what he wanted, their tongues just barely touching, following the rhythmic thrusting of his hips. Enjoying their game, she released him abruptly, her hand hovering over him, letting him pant and beg with his eyes. She leaned in for another kiss, loving how he groaned into her mouth.

"I can't wait anymore. I want you to ride me like you did my horse."

Grabbing her hips, he set her down on his manhood. She cried out loudly, her body still tender as he filled her to the brim.

"Show me?" she asked, unsure in her new position.

"You know how to ride, my love. I've obsessed over it every night." John grabbed her bottom, gently moving, teaching her how to ride him, then releasing her, giving her back control. Slowly, she rose up, completely unsheathing him, and then took him back in, watching as his eyes rolled back. Excited by her newfound power, she repeated the motion, only slower, the sensation so amazing she moaned, all the way up and down.

"Dellis." He gasped, his jaw dropping open. She leaned forward, burying her hands in his silky hair, her breasts rubbing against his chest, making them tingle and ache, sending a surge of pleasure right to her core. He was like a beautiful stallion between her legs, strong and powerful, following her body's every command. Wrapping his arms around her waist, he sat up, bringing her with him, his lips and hands seemingly everywhere at once. When he took one of her nipples in his mouth, sparks shot through her, making her cry out, her rhythm speeding up. *Oh, my.* That mouth of his, the things he did with his tongue. It was a wonder. He swirled and sucked her nipple, drawing on it as if he wanted to suck the very essence from her.

"John, please, take me there." She begged, her hips bucking wildly, trying to move fast enough for her need.

Lying back against the pillows, he held onto her hips, helping her, lifting her up and down, her body riding his as fast as she could. When he touched her little nub of flesh at the junction of their bodies, she sped up instinctively, but he held back, pulling out, then plunging into her again, with such painstaking slowness she thought she might come undone.

"John, I'm so close, don't stop."

She tried to move faster again, but he held her steady, continuing their slow lovemaking with the skill of a practiced lover.

"Patience, love," he whispered, repeating the motion until she was screaming his name. When he finally released her, she was in a frenzy, riding him to the edge but desperately unable to reach it.

"John, I can't." She confessed. Her body refused to give in, no matter how she tried, her need bordering on pain. He reached up, taking her breasts in his hands, squeezing them together, stroking her nipples as his hips met hers with quick, deep strokes.

"Yes, you can." The deep timbre of his voice and the conviction of his words pushed her over the edge. The ache started again, building with such intensity, and like a fabric tearing in two, it suddenly released. She screamed his name again, her body surrendering to the pleasure. She fell forward, melting like hot lava around him, her thighs gripping his while she rode out each wave of her release.

When she looked up, he was in the depths of pleasure, his eyes squeezed shut, his hands gripping her thighs as his hips pumped against hers. With a groan, and her name, he thrust up one last time, burying himself so deep inside she felt it in her heart. When he finished, John wrapped his arms around her, holding her close, their bodies still joined intimately. She never imagined it would be like this, the thought of him leaving her brought tears to her eyes. Wiping them away, she reminded herself that her pain was self-inflicted. This was her choice and one she would make again if given a chance.

Resting her chin on his chest, she smiled, her body felt tired yet heavenly. "I'll never look at riding a horse the same way again."

He laughed, closing his eyes, a dimple forming in his cheek. "I told you a gentle hand and stroke to the ego would work on me."

"Though it seems Viceroy is better at following my commands than his master, perhaps I'll take a crop to you next time you disobey me."

"Promises, promises." He grinned, cocking a brow. "I'd like that, especially if you order me about, and ride me hard after."

"You're shameless," she said, slapping his chest as he laughed.

Rolling over, she pulled him into her arms, and he went willingly, resting his head against her breast. Time passed unknowingly, but she lay there watching him, memorizing every curve and contour of his face for when she was alone again. Would she ever sleep again without him next to her? When he was blissfully asleep, she carefully reached over the bed, grabbing her petticoat, searching her pocket for the trinkets she brought with her. Taking the lock of hair that always fell on his face, she braided the silky strands, weaving a piece of leather around it. She repeated it again with another lock of his hair.

She felt the gentle caress of his hands running up her sides. When she looked down, he was watching her, his head tipped up, his blue eyes sparkling like sapphires in the candlelight. "What are you doing?" he asked.

"I'm braiding your hair," she replied nonchalantly, continuing with her work.

When he reached up and grabbed her hand, she pushed it away, determined to finish what she started.

"Why in the world would you do that?" His voice was full of humor, yet she was trying to give him something important.

When she finished, she showed him a long, thin braid of his hair, intertwined with the leather and a horn-shaped bone at the end of it. "This is a lucky charm. It was my father's."

He crossed his eyes, looking up at her handiwork. She giggled, shaking her head. "I'm trying to be serious."

"Fine, fine." He relented, an over-dramatic furrow forming in his brow. He was giving her serious face now.

Stifling another giggle, she showed him the other braid, holding up the end so he could see the blue and white beads she'd tied into it. "These are wampum. They're valuable. My mother gave them to my father, long ago; he also wore them in his hair. When they were married, she gave him a necklace of these beads, too, but they disappeared when he died."

Giving her an awkward look, he asked, "Are you saying I'm unlucky?"

"Well, you've been tortured and blown up in only a matter of weeks. Thankfully, you had me to take care of you."

His sudden, wide-eyed expression brought on laughter.

"Well, it's true. And now that you're leaving, I thought you could use the extra luck."

He nodded, seemingly content with her answer. "Why braid it into my hair? I can just wear it."

"This way you won't lose them, and no one can use them against you." She pulled at the cross at his neck, showing him what she meant. "See?"

Carefully, she tucked the braids behind his ears, content to know part of her was with him now, wherever he went. "There, you look like a proper brave."

"I'm English, Dellis, if you haven't noticed," he said, leaning up on his elbows. His weight on top of her was decadent, so many contrasting sensations, from lean, hard muscles to the light hairs on his legs and the warmth of his core pressed into her own. She never imagined there could be so much pleasure where once there was fear.

And God, John was handsome, the lines that bracketed his cheeky grin spread up to his eyes, forming at the corners. She reached up and took his face in her hands, planting a soft kiss on his lips. "Then you look like a proper English brave, just like my father did. When you tie your hair back, they'll be barely noticeable."

He cocked a brow suggestively. "Don't get any ideas about me running around bare-assed in buckskin leggings."

Dellis groaned, grabbing the thick, muscular globes of his buttocks, squeezing them hard. The thought of seeing him dressed in buckskin made her want him again.

They lay together quietly, languid lovers passing the time, all the things that had happened over the past couple of months running through her mind. Now that the walls had been broken down between them, there was so much she wanted to tell him before he left. *But where to start?*

He kissed her fingers, his beautiful, blue eyes searching hers. "What are you thinking?"

"John, I haven't been completely honest with you." She looked away, trying to collect her thoughts. "I don't know how to say this and not upset you."

"You can tell me anything, love."

"It's... It's," she stuttered, the sincerity in his voice rendering her speechless. *Did he just call me love?* Taking a deep breath, she started again. "It's about your supplies. I think I know who took them."

She gave him a moment to say something, but he didn't. He was quiet as he pushed a stray lock of hair behind her ear.

"John, before I tell you, I want you to know I only learned this a couple of days ago. I promise I would have told you sooner if I had known."

"Go on," he replied, his brow furrowing.

"A few days ago, I went to my uncle's house, looking for Alexei. When no one answered the door, I walked around the side of the house, and I overheard my uncle yelling. I peeked through the window, and I saw Alexei and Ruslan standing around his desk, looking at something. It was a map with X's on it, marking our village, Oriska, the fort, and two other locations, one in town and one near the Carry. The night you disappeared, I went to the village, and none of the guards were at their posts. I was sure the village was deserted, and then the next morning my grandfather was there with the rest of them. John, I think my cousin Alexei was the one who stole the supplies from you, and I think my grandfather and his men helped. When I told Alexei you were injured, he seemed surprised, but not that surprised. I questioned him, and he denied it, but clearly, he wasn't telling me everything."

She swallowed, looking up at him. "But there's more. Several weeks ago, I saw my uncle with a stack of letters. I overheard him talking with my aunt, and it was clear he'd been intercepting and reading your mail. He mentioned it to Ruslan and Alexei in his study, and when I eventually went inside, I saw your maps on his desk. He must have stolen them from your room or had someone do it for him. Alexei said he knew who took the supplies and where they were. My uncle was angry. He said they lost several hundred pounds when they were taken. I think they were selling what they stole, and they have a contact in Oswego or Niagara; that's how they know about the shipments."

"How do you know they have a contact?" John asked, his eyes searching her face.

"Ruslan mentioned it, then my uncle said something about Major Butler, and if he found out who their contact was, they'd be finished."

John nodded but didn't say anything.

Dellis leaned back on her elbows, her hands shaking as she considered the gravity of the situation. "If this is the case, then my uncle and my cousin have been stealing all along, and my grandfather is working with them. The man who killed my mother accused my grandfather of stealing. John, their actions are what got my father and mother killed, not to mention what happened to the rest of the village. Whoever is trying to frame my people for murdering those women knows this, and they're coming after us. I don't believe my grandfather would do this for money, but I do believe my uncle would. This would explain where all his money is coming from and why he and my father were fighting. What if my father discovered the truth: that my Uncle James was using Alexei and my village to raise money? He could be buying their loyalty by letting them take what they need, then selling the rest. If my Uncle James has a spy or some major on his side, who knows what he could do? I think that's why they were coming after you, because you were onto them. You have to help me stop this."

He was quiet, too quiet, and grave. His reticence almost scared her more than his anger. "John, say something, please. Say you're not angry with me for not telling you sooner. I didn't want to believe it was true, but all the signs are telling me something different."

"No, Dellis, I'm not angry," he replied, his eyes softening as his hand gently stroked her cheek. "I understand why you didn't say anything."

"You have to help them, please. I know Alexei is the one who got my grandfather into this mess with the Rebels. That's why my grandfather has been so guarded when I try to talk to him. He's in over his head, and now there's someone who knows they've gone against the neutrality treaty. If you get them the supplies, if we confront Alexei, maybe we can make this stop before anyone else gets hurt."

He nodded, still deep in thought. She wished she could read his mind; he was always so tight-lipped about everything. When he looked up at her, his blue eyes were serious. "I have to go to Oswego today, and I will find a way to get more supplies for your grandfather. But if he and Alexei have made their decision about siding with the Rebels, there's nothing I can do about that. And whoever is trying to frame your people is doing his damnedest to provoke an argument between the tribes."

"I overheard my grandfather today, he told Alexei that General Schuyler got word from General Washington about forming a treaty with our tribe. Oh, John, what do we do? If you stay, we could…"

Before she could finish, he put his fingers on her lips, stopping her. "You aren't going to do anything, Dellis. You can't stop Alexei or your grandfather; this plan has long since been set in motion. And I don't want anything to happen to you. These people are dangerous."

"But, John, they may come after you again."

"Dellis, I can protect myself." He paused, an impish grin slowly forming. "Even from you."

She laughed in spite of the tears that had started to fall. She wanted to beg him to stay, and make him agree they would face this together, but he had to go, if only to get more supplies for her village. Her people desperately needed what he could offer, and for that, she could give him up.

"I'll come back, and we'll find a way to deal with this," he murmured, running his fingers over her lips, tracing them. "You do believe me?"

There was such intensity in his eyes, how could she not? Unable to speak, she nodded, a lump forming in her throat from already missing him. The tears started again, freeing her throat to tortured words. "John, I won't be able to say goodbye to you properly, my aunt will be here when you leave."

"Then do it now," he replied, his lips taking possession of hers, a bittersweet reminder of what she was going to have to do without.

"I love you, John," she whispered against his lips, needing to say it just once before he left. "I love you."

He didn't respond, his lips devouring hers again for a long, devastating kiss. When she tried to repeat her words of love, he claimed them with his mouth and his tongue, stopping her before she could say more. Bracing his hands on the bed, he spread her thighs with his own and buried himself deep, taking her breath away one last time.

Chapter Forty-Nine

"There's no need to announce us, my dear. I promise, Mr. McKesson will be eager to see me," DeLancie said, pushing past a slip of a girl who was trying to play gatekeeper. As he walked through the spacious house, he realized just how much money James McKesson had made off his recent business ventures. Apparently, his son and the Oneidas had gotten better at their thievery, or McKesson had found himself another means of acquiring his assets.

"This is rather lovely," Celeste said, following close behind him, occasionally slowing to take in the surroundings "I find it hard to believe that someone with such a grand home could have such ragamuffin relatives."

DeLancie ignored her quip about the lovely Miss McKesson and her brother; it was irrelevant for the moment, but he would chide Celeste later. Excitement bubbled up inside him at the prospect of meeting his old adversary. *Finally.* When DeLancie entered the study, James McKesson looked up, his blue eyes widening, and then evolving into an icy stare; the papers in his hands shook, contradicting his notorious reticence and steely grip. *Fear. Priceless.* DeLancie smiled, relishing the moment of surprise. It was almost as good as when one takes an opponent's queen.

"I'm no ghost, McKesson, no need to think you've developed sickness in the mind, though it does run in your mongrel family." He noticed how

James flared his nostrils at the quip—a well-placed jab to his ego. "I bet you never thought you would see the likes of me again."

"You're correct, DeLancie, but the dead have been known to walk." James stepped out from behind his desk and made his way over to Celeste, taking her hand in his. "Mrs. Allen, am I correct?"

"I don't believe we've had the pleasure," she replied, a twinkle in her eye as James kissed the top of her hand. DeLancie could already see she had attracted McKesson. She was utterly perfect, a master at manipulating men. DeLancie admired her skill, calculating and devious, and what incredible opportunities it would offer him in the future.

"We haven't officially met, but I understand your former business partner was a guest at my niece's tavern."

She nodded, feigning a look of surprise. "You mean John Anderson?"

James smirked. "I think you mean John Carlisle, Major DeLancie's former second-in-command."

"How do you know this?" she asked, looking over at DeLancie.

"I have eyes all over this town, my dear. Just as our friend here does." James released her hand, gesturing for them to sit. "Now, tell me what I can do for you, Major?

"Oh, I think you know why I'm here." DeLancie smiled, crossing his arms and sitting back in his char. He knew McKesson's game. Always let someone else do the dirty work for you while you sit back and reap the fruits of their labors. But not anymore.

James sat quietly for a moment, choosing his words carefully. "So, you've taken my supplies, that's nothing, I have plenty more where they came from. Was that move meant for me or for your traitorous second-in-command?"

"Two birds with one stone, McKesson. You didn't think I would leave you up here on your throne like a provincial king while I faced the court-martial and lost everything."

"Oh, I think this one is on you and your obsession with my younger brother's whore of a wife."

DeLancie pounded his fist on the desk, papers flying into the air from the force. "Do *not* speak of Lily that way."

"Instead of going after my brother, Stephen, when he discovered our alliance, you went to the village to kidnap her, knowing full well he wasn't there. Only it didn't work out so well did it? You killed her, and Stephen had enough time to get word to my brother before you finally dealt with him."

James laughed, sitting back in his chair. "The one wild card you didn't count on was John Carlisle. When confronted with the court-martial, he told everything instead of covering for you. But the question is, how did you manage to avoid the noose?" McKesson paused for a second, their eyes locking. "It's obvious who covered for you, John Butler, your partner in this crime. And my brother, Dane, threw his weight around and freed Carlisle for telling the truth about what happened to Stephen."

"You loathe your younger brother because he has what you lost. And now you've made yourself a duke here with enough power and money to manipulate both sides of this war." DeLancie paused, mentally moving his rook towards McKesson's king. "But your hands aren't clean either, McKesson, you're a traitor to your King and disgrace to your family. I'm sure your brother, the real Duke, would find it interesting to know about your involvement in your dearly departed brother's death. You have just as much to lose as I do."

Celeste looked at DeLancie and smiled, like a spectator at an exciting match, and he and McKesson were waiting in the lists. Clearly, she understood what was going on, having been privy to John's limited knowledge of the story. The question was, who would she tie her favor on to in the end?

"That son of yours is a self-proclaimed Rebel, and so are the Oneida. It's only a matter of time before the rest of the Confederacy finds out about it, and then they'll rain hell on those traitors. The Rebels will have nothing to fight back with, no savage army to help, and your little enterprise will be finished. I've already set the stage; the Mohawk no longer trust them," DeLancie said, moving his queen into position.

"You're next for the noose, DeLancie. It's only a matter of time before you're found out."

"Yes, and pretty soon, you will be, too." Leaning over the desk, he caught McKesson's icy glare and whispered, "Checkmate, Your Grace."

"You have nothing on me." James hissed, slamming his fists down on his desk as he rose to his feet.

How DeLancie relished this moment; all the pieces on the board had finally moved into place. *Now to deal with my white knight.*

Standing up, he offered his hand to Celeste. "If you know thy enemy as you know thyself, you need not fear the result of a hundred battles. Now, if you will excuse us, we have business to attend to."

"You have nothing on me, DeLancie, do you hear me! You have nothing!" he heard McKesson yell as they walked out the door.

Chapter Fifty

Looking out the window, Dellis restlessly watched as the snow came down, imagining John and his men traveling the perilous miles to Oswego. It seemed like a year since she'd last seen him, and yet it had been only a fortnight, her body already starved for him with a hunger that was insatiable. And every night, she went up to his room, hoping she would find him looking out the window, only to be faced with the painful reality of his absence. The sheets on his bed were neatly set, no sign of the decadent night spent in each other's arms. Everything was back to the way it was before he came into her life—except her; she was different now. She was loved. And though he never said the words, she knew John felt it. It was in his eyes and the way that he touched her with such tenderness. He would find his way back; he promised, and she refused to believe otherwise. They needed each other. "Oh, John," she whispered, touching the window, remembering his reflection in it.

As she did every day since he'd left, she closed her eyes and remembered their last moments together.

"Thank you for keeping my gift." Gliding her fingers over the woven fabric of his overcoat, she adjusted his collar and smoothed down the front facings.

He smiled, running his hand over his hair. She noticed the braids were barely visible with his hair pulled back, the trinkets tied up neatly in his queue. "I will wear them until you require them back."

"They're yours now." She lifted his hand to her cheek, her eyes brimming with tears, imagining days without him.

"Dellis, don't cry. I'll come back, my love."

She nodded, wiping the tears away with the back of her hand. He gave her his promise, and she believed him, but with forces out there hell-bent on killing him, she couldn't help but be afraid for him.

"By the way, I found this in the desk." He reached into his pocket and pulled out two small frames.

When she realized what they were, her heart fluttered with excitement. "You found this in the desk?"

"Yes, they were in your father's locked drawer... in the back."

She turned them over, the sight of her beautiful mother making Dellis's heart ache to the point of breathlessness. God, how she missed her mother.

"I thought they went with my father." Handing them back to him, Dellis wrapped his fingers around the little frames. "So you have something to remember me by."

"Dellis, I don't need a picture to remember you."

"Will you miss this?" she asked, looking around the room, unable to meet his gaze without bursting into tears.

"I'll miss you." John gently tipped her chin up, looking into her eyes. "And I confess... this, too." He kissed her long and lingeringly, his tongue gently caressing hers.

She nodded, tears rolling down her cheeks. "I love you, John," she whispered, needing to say it, wishing he would, too.

He gently rubbed her tears away with his thumbs, taking her face in his hands, he kissed her tenderly. When he pulled away, he was smiling, his eyes searching hers. "Will you miss this, or will you miss me?"

"I have to think about that." She teased, though her heart was breaking.

Later that morning, before he left, she prepared enough food for his travels and slipped a little note into his haversack. Her aunt was already in the kitchen making breakfast when he came in to say his goodbyes.

"My men and I thank you," he'd said, removing his hat and bowing to Dellis.

She could see the braids neatly arranged in his hair, her hands aching to touch them.

He took her hand in his own, his lips brushing over the top of it as he looked into her eyes. He gave her one of his devilish grins, an ache building between her thighs, evoking the sensation of him steely and deep inside her.

"I'm grateful for your hospitality," he reiterated to her aunt, bowing and kissing her hand.

When Dellis handed him the provisions for his travel, he took them from her and walked to the door, stopping for a moment, before giving her one last look.

"Goodbye, Miss McKesson," he said, running his hands over his hair before he put his hat on, turning the front point to the right and cocking it down towards his eye.

She'd curtsied, bowing her head, trying to hide her moist eyes. "Goodbye, Captain."

"Dellis, we have lots to do." From behind, she heard her aunt walk into the kitchen, her shoes clicking on the wood floor. "It looks like we are going to be very busy this Christmas. That's a very good thing."

Dellis turned around, watching her aunt remove her cloak and dust the snowflakes from her chestnut brown hair. Part of Dellis wanted to confront her aunt about everything that had been learned, right then, but Dellis could help John and her village more by being quiet and playing ignorant for a little while longer. Not to mention, she had no idea how much her aunt had to do with her husband and son's deception. For the first time, Dellis looked at her aunt with a bit of sympathy. Perhaps she, too, was being manipulated by the men.

"Auntie, I've made a few decisions about the future of The Thistle."

She looked up, her eyes widening in surprise. "And what are they?"

421

Dellis smiled, walking over to her aunt and taking the basket of supplies she was carrying. "The Thistle is mine, and you and I both know Stuart is never going to help me maintain it. That being said, it's time I take full responsibility for this house. Now that we are making enough money and have more customers, I'm going to hire more help. I think a dish boy and another waitress will suffice for the moment. Also, I'll be taking over the ledger and handling the finances. For too long, you and Uncle James have had to care for me, and I'm truly grateful for all you've done, but it's time I stand on my own."

Shocked, Helena asked, "Dellis, are you telling me you don't need my help any longer? Because I think you're underestimating what I do to help you run this tavern."

"Not at all." Dellis shook her head, hugging her aunt, and then pulling back just quick enough to see her eyes widen. "You've done so much for me, and now it's time I repay you. I have Thomas, and we managed just the two of us before, we can do it again. And now that we are busier and bringing in more money, I can hire more help. You and Uncle James will no longer need to be concerned with the finances of his brother's children. My father would want this, too, I know it."

"But…" Helena stuttered. Before she could get the words out, there was a knock on the door.

"Excuse me, Aunt." Dellis walked to the door and took the posts from the courier, leafing through them. Her heart sank; there was no message from John, but much to her surprise, there was one for her Uncle James. She'd read it later when she had time. After all, it was her house, and the mail that came to it was hers as well. Dellis smiled to herself then stuffed the letters into her pocket and walked back into the kitchen.

"What came in the mail?" her aunt asked, crossing her arms over her chest.

"Nothing that concerns you. Now, where was I?" Dellis continued. "From now on, the discussion of my getting married is off the table. You're welcome to continue working here, and I want you to, but no more trying to find me a husband."

She waited for her aunt's reply, but there was none. There was no doubt in Dellis's mind that her Uncle James would insist her aunt continue working there. How else would he continue receiving his secret correspondences? "That's all I had to say, and I think I just saw Alexei walk in the front door. Excuse me for a moment."

She gave Dellis the most slack-jawed, dumbfounded look, she had to stifle a giggle as she walked past towards the dining room. When Alexei noticed Dellis, he smiled, removing his hat. "Good morning."

"Good morning, Alexei," she replied, an edge to her voice. This was a meeting she'd long anticipated. He'd conveniently stayed away for the last two weeks, which happened to coincide with how long John had been gone. There was no question that Alexei and her uncle had been out looking for John and his men.

"Is Stuart here?" Alexei asked, removing his gloves, his nose and cheeks red from the cold.

"No, as usual, he's been missing for days," she said, anger blooming in her gut from all she'd learned about him. How could he do this to her and their village? He was like a brother to her and Stuart. Her father and mother had raised him as their son and cared for him when his own father shunned him.

"I'll go find him." Alexei put his gloves back on then stopped, turning back to her. "By the way, where is your merchant friend? I'd like to speak with him."

Of course, he did.

"He's in Oswego getting our supplies, but he'll be back soon." Dellis gave him the most innocent look she could muster, her fists clenching at her sides. She fought back the urge to spit in his face, her heart aching from his betrayal.

Dellis watched as Alexei rushed out the door, slamming it so hard a section of the glass shattered in the window and landed on the floor. She knew exactly where he was headed—he was going after John. And as sure as she knew the sun would come up each day, she knew John would be ready for Alexei. But could she handle seeing two men that she loved fight this out? She'd given up so much already, the thought of parting with either of them, in spite of Alexei's treachery, was heart-wrenching. But someone had to stop her cousin and her uncle from taking her people down the road to Hell. She couldn't bear to lose another person she loved. John promised he would find a way to protect them, and he would see it done.

Dellis leaned down and picked up the pieces of broken glass off the floor. Running her fingers over them, she watched as the light glittered and danced off the shards, making them sparkle in the sunlight.

"Bring John back to me, Father," she whispered, closing her hand around the shards. "And I vow I will find the man that murdered you and mother, and I will make him pay." Squeezing her hand tight, she could feel the sharp pricks of glass cutting into her palm and drops of crimson blood oozing down her arm.

Chapter Fifty-One

John raced up the hill as fast as he could, the sounds of screaming echoing in the forest. The whole village was on fire, smoke billowing up into the trees. As he passed through the stockade, he stopped dead in his tracks, horrified at the sight that greeted him. At his feet lay the slaughtered bodies of several Oneida squaws, all of them stripped bare. Kneeling down, he closed the eyes of one of the women, her vacant stare unnerving. Suddenly, he heard a loud, high-pitched wailing, like a banshee warning the village that death had arrived. When he looked over his shoulder, he saw one of his lieutenants dragging a young man from a log cabin, kicking and screaming.

"Shut up, boy, or I'll give you something to scream about!" Grabbing the boy by his hair, the soldier brought his blade down inches from the boy's scalp, holding it there, tormenting him. Sickened, John pushed his man away, sending him sprawling in the dirt. "Have we reduced ourselves to scalping children? Stand down, Lieutenant."

Suddenly, the boy shoved John and went for the dagger at his hip. He caught the kid's hand in midair, twisting it behind his back, pinning him against the little house. "I wouldn't do that if I were you."

"Innocent, we are innocent."

The boy banged his forehead against the logs several times, repeating the same phrase, the timbre of his voice sending a chill down John's spine. When the

425

boy stopped, there was blood running down his face, a look of pain in his eyes as he glanced at the cabin behind them.

Following his line of site, John pulled the boy over to the cabin and pushed him inside. It was small and deathly quiet. John carefully dodged the pots and plates littering the floor, almost stepping on a young woman lying motionless on her side. Next to her was the body of an older woman, lying on her back, a knife embedded in her chest.

The boy began to wail again, his high-pitched cries sounding eerie, otherworldly. Crouching down, John rolled the younger woman onto her back, checking for signs of life. She was alive but unconscious, her chest rising and falling with slow, rhythmic breaths.

The young man fell on his knees next to the older woman, wrapping his arms around her lifeless frame.

"Save her," he cried loudly. "Save her."

John looked down at the large knife lodged in her breast, the bodice of her dress stained with blood. "I can't save her."

"You did this," the boy shrieked with rage, pulling her body closer. "You'll pay, Redcoat."

"I didn't kill her," John replied, shaking his head. "But you are right to want justice, and you're welcome to come for it. I'll be ready."

He scooted over to the other woman, picking her up and carrying her to a small cot in the corner of the room, placing her carefully on the bed. What remained of her dress lay open, exposing hand-shaped bruises all over her breasts and torso, a smattering of blood on her inner thighs. Unable to find a blanket, he removed his great cloak and covered her with it. Her long, silky, black hair was in tangles around her face; gently, he smoothed it back, noticing how soft it was. Even with the large wound on her forehead and her face swollen and bruised beyond recognition, she looked like an angel, her skin unusually translucent for a native, with razor-sharp cheekbones and large, deep-set eyes that were closed serenely.

John stroked her cheek for a moment, captivated by how peacefully she slept, even after the hell she'd lived through. But a devil didn't deserve to look upon an angel. Not after what he'd done. Backing away, he looked down at the boy, his arms still holding the dead woman, rocking her, and his angry gaze still fixed on the intruder. "Justice."

"There's no such thing, boy..."

John had relived that moment over and over; it was the day that changed both of their lives forever. It wasn't irony that brought him and Dellis together again—it was fate. How fitting after so much had gone wrong that he should find himself in the position to set it right. But to do that, he risked losing everything he held dear. He'd only just gained the trust of General Howe, and the chance of redeeming John's reputation was on the line, but it also meant having to betray Dellis and her village. Looking down at his whiskey, he swirled the glass, watching the brown liquor sparkle in the candlelight before throwing the drink back.

It had been two weeks since he left her, the journey from Oswego to Montreal arduous at best, even when traveling with the current. Parts of the river had frozen over, and the snow-covered ground was nearly impossible to traverse when they were carrying their boats. Still, every night, in the arctic cold, he lay under the stars, reminiscing about his last moments with Dellis, finding warmth in his memories and a moment's respite in black eyes and silky tresses.

It was only a matter of time before she found out the truth about him—and what defense did he have? He was guilty on all counts: a spy, a Redcoat, and a liar. But it wasn't that simple. Yes, he'd made mistakes, and yes, he'd lied to her, but some of it was beyond his control. He'd tried to push her away, he'd tried to do the right thing, but in the end, he'd just made matters worse. It was as if they were trapped in a vise, pushed together by the forces around them, and all they had was each other for comfort.

"What's got you so downcast, Captain?" Simon asked, slurring his words, making his already strong Scottish brogue less understandable. He was clearly inebriated, already partaking in the Christmas celebration

General Carleton arranged for his men. Simon put his glass on the table and poured them both a drink, some of the liquor spilling from his drunken aim. "I see you over here brooding with your sullen face. You're thinking about the Lady McKesson, aren't you?"

John gave the best "mind your own business" look he could muster. He wasn't in the mood to share, and the last thing he needed was for Clark to say, "I told you so."

Catching on to the nonverbal communication, Clark changed the subject. "What about Carleton? What will you tell him tomorrow? We didn't exactly complete our mission, and now that the war is at a standstill, he's likely to send us back."

The thought of returning to the purgatory in Manhattan made John's stomach turn. *Not a chance, Carlisle.* He refused to go back to being the groveling drunk he'd been three months ago, too much had happened since then. He knew now that he'd been right about the supplies, and Alexei and his father were responsible. There was no way John would go to Hell without bringing McKesson or DeLancie along—there was room for four on that carriage ride if need be. Better to go down swinging than fall on one's sword.

"I'll come up with something," John said, and he meant it. But what he was going to do was the question.

"Well, don't think too hard, John. It's Christmas, and the drinks and ladies are aplenty." Standing up, Simon gave John a mock salute. "Now, if you will excuse me, I have a redhead waiting for me and lots of mistletoe on hand."

"Simon, never keep a lady waiting," John said, his stomach lurching at his own hypocrisy. Hadn't he left Dellis waiting for him, believing he was going to come back when he had no intention to?

"I know you're trying to get rid of me so that you can brood some more." Clark grabbed his bottle from the table and winked. Just as he started to stumble away, he turned back, almost running into a pretty brunette waitress carrying a tray of drinks. "Oh, by the way, I found one of your blades and a letter addressed to you in my haversack. I put it on your desk."

"Go, enjoy your evening." John preferred to be alone with his thoughts, and he only had about twelve hours to come up with something to report to General Carleton.

Can I do it? Can I betray her? John reached into his pocket and pulled out the little miniature of Dellis. Running his fingers over the picture, he could almost feel her smooth skin and soft lips. He just couldn't imagine how she would ever forgive him when she learned the truth. And all the lies he told, and then making love to her under false pretenses. No, it was too much. *Scoundrel. Reprobate. Devil.* Turning the picture over, he placed it on the table, unable to look at her a moment longer.

"Is this seat taken, Captain?" When he looked up, there was an exquisite blonde sitting across from him, a bottle of scotch in one hand and a tray with a tea service in the other. Not so very long ago, that was his favorite combination—but not anymore.

"I'm afraid I'm not good company tonight," he said, his eyes unable to avoid her breasts brimming over the bodice of her low-cut dress. His hands ached for a touch, but not of her.

"What is this?" She snatched the picture off the table before he could stop her and turned it over. "So, this is why you look so downcast? Your wife?"

"No, my elusive mistress." And forever beyond his reach; a truth he'd long since faced up to. Taking the picture from her, he stuffed it in his breast pocket. "Now, please, excuse me, I would prefer my own company and the bottle this evening. You can take the tea with you."

The woman smiled, her dark, deep-set, brown eyes lighting up, almost reminding him of Dellis's. "I've been told that the cure for one woman can be found in the arms of another."

"It's not possible," he replied, the truth going down like a bitter pill. There was no cure for Dellis; he'd tried for months to find one and failed miserably. She was in his blood. His favorite, rare, single malt.

"Perhaps." The waitress smiled, cocking a brow as she reached over and placed her hand atop his. "Then why not use me to indulge your fantasy? I can be any woman you want me to be."

He considered her proposition, the exceptional amount of alcohol he'd consumed lowering his inhibitions; a fire, long raging in his loins wanting to be snuffed out. Taking her hand and the bottle of scotch, he led her upstairs to his room, shutting the door behind them. Before he could unscrew the cork, she pushed him against the door, unbuttoned his front flap, and used her warm fingers to stroke him to a turgid erection. Closing his eyes, he took a swig, the feel of her soft lips on his neck and the smell of her perfume conjuring images of dark silken tresses and porcelain skin lying on his bed.

"Dellis." He groaned, opening his eyes, but the pair he looked into weren't the ones he sought. The haze broke suddenly like a bucket of cold water to the face, his lust curbed in an instant.

"Is there something wrong?" she asked, obviously noticing the change in his body.

Pulling away, he buttoned his breeches, leaving her standing, dumbfounded. Suddenly, he noticed the moonlight shining through the window, reflecting off something lying on his desk.

It was the knife Dellis had taken from him, atop it a letter addressed to him in handwriting he didn't recognize. Picking up the letter, he cracked the crimson wax seal and unfolded the crisp pieces of paper. His heart hammered in anticipation as he looked at the signature. It was from her. Holding it close to the candle, he skimmed it, noticing her handwriting, feminine yet bold, with thicker strokes accentuating the words she wanted to stress.

"Captain, I'm waiting."

His company's playful tone interrupted his focus, bringing him back to reality. When he turned back to her, she was lying in the middle of his bed, her shift dangling over her left shoulder, exposing one lovely breast. Lifting her hand, she crooked her index finger at him, her lips curling up into a smile. "Come join me."

John shook his head. "Forgive me, this letter is urgent. I must attend to it immediately. Please, leave now."

He waited for her to climb out of bed and get dressed, the letter folded in his hand, as if he dared not read it in the presence of another woman. The sound of the door slamming so hard the frame undoubtedly cracked was his cue that she'd left. Unfolding the letter, he read it again, only slowly this time, taking in every word.

My Dearest Captain,

I am returning your dagger to you. I thought you might need it more than I, as any good Oneida squaw, upon observation, can see you neglect your right side.

He chuckled at her jest, even in prose, her determined wit shined through. Lifting the dagger, he held it in his hand, remembering the night she took it from him and the look of pure satisfaction on her face when she challenged him. Putting it down, he continued reading.

As I sit here looking out your window, I wish you were here with me, speaking the words I know you carry in your heart but are afraid to say. The only consolation I can give my own aching heart is the knowledge that I leave you with this written word to remind you of my love, and press it to my lips, and pray to God you are safe and will find your way back to me...

Yours,

Dellis McKesson

He read it several times, her short but eloquent words reverberating in his head as if she were there, speaking directly to him. She knew him so well, better than he knew himself. He *was* in love with her, since the moment he first saw her. Yes, he had awakened her passion, but she'd taught him how to love, something he'd never done before.

Holding the letter to his face, he could almost smell lavender on the pages as he imagined her sitting behind a desk, putting pen to paper.

And even now, she was waiting for him, trusting that he would keep his promise and return to help protect her people. Yes, it was John Anderson the profiteer who made the promise, and not John Carlisle the spy. But he wanted to be that man, the one he saw when he'd looked into those dark, lovely eyes—the gentleman, not the scoundrel. *But how?*

Sitting down at his desk, he leafed through a pile of letters until he found the copies of the maps he made of Oswego and the trade routes. He closed his eyes, trying to come up with a solution, racking his brain for the answer, then suddenly he heard them calling… and it came to him.

Looking out the window, he could almost see the ghost of Dellis's grandmother as the wind whistled through the window, bringing with it her sad lament.

"I hear you calling. There will be justice… I promise. I *will* find a way."

Chapter
Fifty-Two

John got out of bed and dressed quickly, putting on his uniform for the first time in months. Looking himself over in the mirror, he fastened his stock in place and adjusted his collar over it, then tied his gleaming silver gorget around his neck. His madder red waistcoat, signifying his commission in the light infantry, fit snugly around his torso, the skirts cutting off just above his hips. He adjusted his hair, using tallow to slick it back tight then folding it over, clubbing it in place. He'd left Dellis's trinkets in his hair, arranging it so they were somewhat hidden. Pulling on his tunic, he gave himself the once-over. His one gold epaulet on his right shoulder sparkled in the candlelight, the royal blue facings of the Eighth Regiment contrasted against the red of his coat. Lastly, he put on his shoulder belt with his sword, fastening it in place.

When he arrived at General Carleton's headquarters, John was escorted in immediately, his arrival already anticipated, per their correspondences. The fifty-two-year-old General and governor of Quebec was a well-seasoned soldier with a sterling reputation that had only recently been tarnished by his failure to catch Benedict Arnold and his men on Lake Champlain. John had never met the man but was aware of his notoriously prickly demeanor and reputation for being a strict disciplinarian. John adjusted his tunic and righted himself, following the sentry into Carleton's office, ready to put the plan into action.

"General Carleton, sir," John said, removing his hat.

The General turned around upon hearing the voice, his stony expression unreadable as his dark eyes examined every inch of John's uniform, trying to find fault with him somewhere. But Carleton didn't because John was no longer that slovenly drunk that showed up in Howe's office three months before, desperate for a crumb to be thrown. John was a different man now. Satisfied that everything was as it should be, the General finally spoke. "So, you're the infamous Captain Carlisle?"

"Yes, sir," John said confidently, holding his head high, meeting the steely gaze. No longer was he embarrassed by his illustrious past; the truth would define him in the end; of this, he was confident.

"You may sit, Captain." John did as he was asked, taking a seat in the large, wingback chair behind him. Perched on the edge of his seat, he watched as the General removed the lid from a crystal decanter on his desk and poured himself a drink.

"Do you care for some?"

"Yes, thank you." Whatever it was, John could use three, his nerves more and more on edge with each passing minute.

Carleton poured another glass and handed it to over. It was an excellent Spanish sherry, strong and sweet with a nice finish; a drink only a wealthy and influential man could afford. Even the glass was expensive, a delicate little thing more suited for a woman with its thin stem and curled-over lip. As one of the senior officers in His Majesty's army and the King's representative in Canada, John would expect nothing less than elegance and class. Carleton was a notoriously rich man and a powerful one too, and John needed him on his side. If ever there was a moment he had to be convincing, this was it.

"Captain Carlisle, as you know, the war is at a standstill. Since we chased Washington out of New York, he and his men are hiding out for the winter, and General Burgoyne has returned to England. I know initially

General Howe was eager for the information you could provide, but now it's of little use. I see no reason not to send you and your men back to your posts."

John's heart hammered in his chest; it was now or never if he was going to make his plan work. "On the contrary, sir, I think some of the information I've obtained is very useful."

"What do you have for me, Captain?"

Taking a deep breath, John could hear the sound of Dellis's voice as she spoke her words of vengeance. *"His name was John Carlisle, and someday he will pay for what he did to my family."*

This was the only way he would ever be able to go back to her and plead his case. Resolute in his decision, John reached into his coat pocket, pulled out the maps he created, and handed them to the General. John had to give up something to prove his value, and he only hoped it was enough. "Those are maps of the perimeter of Fort Stanwix and the two forts being rebuilt just twenty miles east in German Flats. Also, on those maps, you will find all the local trails and supply routes, even the ones the natives use. All three of these forts are anticipating our strike; Stanwix, specifically, is being refortified. It's under the command of Colonel Samuel Elmore, but it's minimally garrisoned."

Hesitating for a moment, he put his hand in his pocket, feeling the little metal frame resting against his hip. He was doing this for her, he reminded himself. "The Oneidas of Oriska and some of the villages closer to Fort Stanwix have been intercepting supply chains from Montreal, Niagara, and Oswego and trading them with the fort and the local militias. Samuel Kirkland has persuaded some of the Oneidas to side with the colonists, and they follow his lead. The rest of the Confederacy doesn't know this; the Oneida are still believed to be following the neutrality treaty."

The General sipped his sherry, his face as expressionless as a marble statue. John tried not to look at the clock behind the desk as he waited for the General to say something; the seconds ticked away like hours. Finally, Carleton clucked his tongue against his teeth and looked up. "Do you think the Oneida would still be willing to negotiate?"

This was a good sign. Treading lightly, John responded, "Possibly, but it will require someone who they trust implicitly."

"We have Major Butler, our deputy agent; it's his job to deal with the savages while the superintendent position is in dispute. No one knows more about the Six Nations than him."

"Yes, but I understand he hasn't been successful when it comes to dealing with the Oneida. But I have."

John held his breath, waiting for the General's response. *Would he take the bait?*

Carleton's dark eyes leveled, his brow cocking slightly. "How so?"

Trying not to smile, John continued. "While undercover for General Howe, I gained the confidences of an Oneida woman and her village. I might be able to negotiate with them, if you allow me to."

"So, what do you suggest, Captain?"

John couldn't believe it—his plan might actually be working. "I request permission for myself and my men to join Major Butler at Fort Niagara and assist him with uniting the local tribes to His Majesty's cause. If I can't get the Oneida to join us, then I'll find a way to get them to stay neutral."

Much to his surprise, Carleton nodded. "All right then, if General Howe is willing to give you another chance, then so will I."

"Thank you, sir." John mentally sighed with relief.

"I've given the Major orders to negotiate with all the boarding tribes, including the Six Nations. He will be planning a meeting with them in the early spring. I suggest you be there. The savages are not to fight or terrorize the colonists. They are to wait for orders. Until then, we'll hold our present position. Report to Major Butler at Fort Niagara. You're dismissed, Captain."

"Yes, sir," John replied, already anticipating the next part of his plan.

With Butler's resources, he would have the power to pursue McKesson and negotiate with the Oneida. If he could catch Alexei, then it might be possible to use him to force the Joseph and his village into a deal; perhaps he could even use McKesson to draw DeLancie out.

"You're dismissed, Captain."

John stood and nodded. "Thank you, sir." He put his hat back on and went for the door.

Finally, he was in the position to get justice. After it was all said and done, he could go back to Dellis, confess everything, and beg her forgiveness. He knew it was a gamble, but one he was willing to risk his life and his love on.

In Loving Memory
Edwin F. Lasak
July 4,1940-January 12, 2018.

Acknowledgements

I hope you found enjoyment in you moments with John and Dellis, and know there is much more to come from this story (two books). I owe thank yous to so many people I am at a loss for where to start. Perhaps the best place is with the history of this book, to allow you a glimpse into where this story comes from. The Tory was never meant to be a book, nor did I intend on being an author. Four years ago, my life was turned upside down by two of the most devastating events that occurred simultaneously. In my grief, I did something brilliant; I reached out for help, and started seeing a counselor. With the usual candor and directness that a hard-headed girl like me needs, she suggested I get a hobby, painting or writing, something to help me deal with the well of anxiety that I was drowning in. I loved history, and I loved the American Revolutionary War, specifically, so I started to write. Unable to put words to my pain, as my counselor and I met weekly, I would go home and build this story scene by scene, and John would take my hand and lead the way. Little did I know that under layers of action, and adventure, I was writing my own story. The Tory and the whole Rebels and Redcoats Saga is truly a story about seeking truth and justice, and learning that sometimes in this world we will never get it, so we must find a way to make our own. It is a story of betrayal, love, redemption and forgiveness, things I had to learn to deal with along this journey, and John and Dellis, together, taught me the way.

After this book was completed I allowed two of my very good friends to read it, and they both fell in love with the story and pushed me towards the idea of publication. I fought it for a while, but as you can see, my friends got their way. And here I am, now, four years later, and The Tory and the entire Rebel and Redcoats Saga is proof that even in the worst moments of our life, something wonderful can come from it, if we only believe. I've often said, if life gives you lemons, make lemonade with vodka, so here's mine!

Along the way I have had many struggles, but I picked up some true believers that have kept me going, so now I must thank them for traveling the journey with me. Again to my entourage, Katy and Janine, you are the first fans of The Tory, and I thank you for that. Teres, thanks for being my cheerleader, friend, mother, and wine partner, I love you. Lorrie, my counselor, only you and I know where this all comes from, thank you for helping me make my own path to justice. Kathe, the world's greatest editor, thanks for believing in John and this story, for pushing me hard, and liking the fact that I have a gritty, raw side to how I write. David, my copy editor, damn you make me look good, where would I be without you. Truly, where would I be? My dearest Layla, my cheerleader, my critique partner and go-to-girl, you're brilliant and I love you. Kelly Ann Scott, you came in late in the game, but you made an impression, seeing things in John even I didn't see. Thanks for your words of wisdom and amazing spirit.

With every hard fought battle there are war wounds to follow; mine was chronic, debilitating migraines that often robbed me of my writer's voice that I so aptly call John. Here is where I give a shout out to my doctor for never giving up, and always having a plan. Dr. Rob, you're the best, thank you for always listening to me and fighting with me. Without a doubt, I know I made you crazy. But I am behind my computer, pounding away (probably at this moment), because of your efforts. My forever gratitude.

I would also like to thank Loretta Metoxen, the Oneida Tribal Historian of the Oneida National Museum in Wisconsin, for allowing me to pick your brain and for making reference recommendations so I could try to be as accurate as possible with the rich, incredible history of our first allies. It was an honor to speak with you.

To the Oneida Nation, our first allies in the Revolution. They joined the American cause when there wasn't much of one, even before the

French, and they paid dearly for turning against the Iroquois Confederacy to support our new nation's birth. I know it comes late, far too late, but thank you for your sacrifices, they do not go forgotten. If through this story, I can provoke one reader into investigating and learning more about the rich history of our brave, proud allies, then I will be truly elated.

Thank you to the staff and historians of Fort Stanwix National Park, Fort Niagara National Park, Fort Ticonderoga, Colonial Williamsburg and The American Revolution Museum at Yorktown-Jamestown. You were all so very giving with your knowledge. I am forever grateful.

Last but not least, my husband Fred, for being there for me... for everything.

Finally to John and Dellis, my muses, my inspiration who taught me so much about life; as an author, it is strange to be at a loss for words, but I am...

Dear Reader

Thank you so much for spending your evenings with John and Dellis and for allowing me to take you into the world of eighteenth century Colonial America. I hope you fell in love, had an adventure, and learned a little about the wild Northern Frontier that is now Upstate New York.

As an author I love feedback, I learn so much from hearing what my readers have to say about my stories and what little kernels of themselves they can relate to in my characters. It is because of my readers The Tory exists today, so I owe a great deal to your wisdom.

If you love my books please leave a review on Goodreads or Amazon. I encourage all of your feedback, good or bad, it's what continues to fill the well of love I have for writing and recreating those unique areas of forgotten history.

Subscribe to my newsletter at revolutionaryauthor.com to keep up on all that is happening with T.J. London. I am also on Facebook at TJLondonauthor and twitter @TJLondonauthor. You can also follow me on Good Reads.

John and Dellis's story continues Fall 2018 in, The Traitor, Book #2 in the Rebels and Redcoats Saga.

About the Author

T.J. London is a rebel, liberal, lover, fighter, diehard punk, and pharmacist-turned-author who loves history. As an author her goal is to fill in the gaps, writing stories about missing history, those little places that are so interesting yet sadly forgotten. Her favorite time periods to write in are first and foremost the American Revolutionary War, the French Revolution, the French and Indian War, the Russian Revolution and the Victorian Era. Her passions are traveling, writing, reading, barre, and sharing a glass of wine with her friends, while she collects experiences in this drama called life. She is a native of Metropolitan Detroit (but secretly dreams of being a Londoner) and resides there with her husband Fred and her beloved cat and writing partner Mickey.

CPSIA information can be obtained
at www.ICGtesting.com
Printed in the USA
BVHW04s0100120518
515920BV00009B/1/P